A *New York Times*, *USA Today* and *Wall Street Journal* bestselling author, Elle Kennedy grew up in the suburbs of Toronto, Ontario, and holds a BA in English from York University. From an early age, she knew she wanted to be a writer and actively began pursuing that dream when she was a teenager. She loves strong heroines and sexy alpha heroes, and just enough heat and danger to keep things interesting!

Elle loves to hear from her readers. Visit her website www.ellekennedy.com or sign up for her newsletter to receive updates about upcoming books and exclusive excerpts. You can also find her on Facebook (ElleKennedyAuthor), Twitter (@ElleKennedy), Instagram (@ElleKennedy33), or TikTok (@ElleKennedyAuthor).

Also by Elle Kennedy

The Play

BRIAR U

ELLE KENNEDY

PIATKUS

PIATKUS

Originally self-published in 2019 by Elle Kennedy, Inc.
This updated version published in the US in 2022 by Bloom Books,
An imprint of Sourcebooks
Published in Great Britain in 2023 by Piatkus

3 5 7 9 10 8 6 4

A CIP catalogue record for this book
is available from the British Library.

ISBN 978-0-349-44106-1

Printed and bound in Great Britain by Clays Ltd, Elcograf S.p.A.

Papers used by Piatkus are from well-managed forests
and other responsible sources.

MIX
Paper | Supporting
responsible forestry
FSC® C104740

Piatkus
An imprint of
Little, Brown Book Group
Carmelite House
50 Victoria Embankment
London EC4Y 0DZ

An Hachette UK Company
www.hachette.co.uk

www.littlebrown.co.uk

To Sarah J. Maas, for your support and enthusiasm.
And for reminding me why I write.

1
HUNTER

THIS PARTY BLOWS.

I probably should have stayed at home, but these days "home" is like living on the set of a Kardashian reality show. Thanks to my three female roommates, it's estrogen overload over there.

Granted, there's a helluva lot of estrogen here at the Theta Beta Nu house, but it's the kind I'm allowed to be attracted to. My roommates are all in relationships, so I'm not allowed to touch them.

You're not allowed to touch any of these women either…

True. Because of my self-imposed abstinence, I'm not allowed to touch anyone, period.

Which raises the question—if a tree falls in the forest and you can't fuck anyone at the sorority-house party, is it still considered a party?

I curl my fingers around the red Solo cup that my friend and teammate Matt Anderson just planted in my hand. "Thanks," I mutter.

I take a sip and make a face. The beer tastes like water,

---

although maybe that's a good thing. A nice incentive to not consume more than one. Morning skate isn't until ten a.m. tomorrow, but I was planning on showing up at the arena a couple hours early to work on my slapshot.

After last season's disastrous end, I vowed to make hockey my top priority. The new semester starts Monday, our first game is next week, and I'm feeling motivated. Briar didn't make it to the national championship last year and that's on me. This season will be different.

"What do you think about her?" Matt discreetly nods toward a cute girl in tiny boxer shorts and a pale pink camisole. She's not wearing a bra, and the outlines of her beaded nipples are visible beneath the silky material.

My mouth actually waters.

Did I mention this is a PJ party? Yup yup, I haven't had sex in nearly five months and I'm kicking off junior year at a party where every single woman in attendance is wearing next to nothing. I never claimed to be smart.

"She's smokin'," I tell Matt. "Go make a move."

"I would, but…" He lets out a grumbling sound. "She's checking *you* out."

"Well, I'm closed for business," I answer with a shrug. "Feel free to go over there and tell her that." I poke him good-naturedly on the arm. "I'm sure she'll view you as an adequate consolation prize."

"Ha! Fuck off. I'm nobody's second choice. If she's not dying to hook up with me, I'd way rather find someone who is. I don't need to compete for a woman's attention."

This is why I like Matt—he's competitive on the ice, but off of it he's really decent. I've been playing hockey my entire life, and I've had teammates who wouldn't even blink at stealing another guy's girl, or even worse, hooking up with her behind his back. I've played with guys who treat our hockey groupies as disposable, who've shared girls like Tic Tacs. Guys with zero respect and terrible judgment.

But at Briar, I'm fortunate to play with some stand-up dudes. Sure, no roster is without a douchebag or two, but for the most part my teammates are good guys.

"Yeah, I don't think it'll be too hard," I agree. "The brunette at two o'clock is already boning down with you in her head."

His brown eyes widen in appreciation as they land on the curvy girl in the short white nightie. Her cheeks flush when their gazes meet and then she smiles shyly and raises her cup in a silent toast.

Matt abandons me without a backward glance. I don't blame him.

The living room is packed with girls in lingerie and guys in Hugh Hefner pajamas. I hadn't known this was a theme event, so I'm in cargo shorts and a white wife-beater, and I'm good with that. Most of the dudes around me look ridiculous in their get-ups.

"Having a good time?" The music is blaring, but it's not loud enough that I don't hear the girl. The one Matt had originally been checking out.

"Yeah. Nice turnout." I shrug. "DJ is pretty good."

She sidles up closer. "I'm Gina."

"Hunter."

"I know who you are." Sympathy creeps into her voice. "I was there for the conference championship against Harvard, when that jerk broke your wrist. I can't believe he did that."

I can. I fucked his girlfriend.

But I keep that to myself. It's not like I did it intentionally, anyway. I had no clue who that girl was when I slept with her. Apparently she knew who *I* was, though. She wanted to get back at her boyfriend, but I didn't know that until he launched himself at me in the middle of the second-most important game of the season, the one that determines who goes to the Frozen Four, the *first*-most important game of a college season. The broken wrist was the result of a tackle to the ice. The Harvard asshole didn't intend to break it, but it happened, and just like that I was out of the game. And so was our team captain, Nate Rhodes, who was ejected for fighting while trying to defend me.

I snap myself out of the past. "It was a shitty way to end the season," I say.

Her hand finds its way onto my right bicep. My arms are looking huge these days, if I do say so myself. When you're not having sex, working out is imperative for your sanity.

"I'm sorry," Gina purrs. Her fingers gently glide over my bare skin, sending pinpricks of heat through my arm.

I almost groan out loud. Sweet fuck, I'm so horny that a woman caressing my *arm* is giving me a semi.

I know I should brush her hand off me, but it's been so long since I've been touched in a non-platonic way. At home my roommates are constantly pawing at me, but there's nothing sexual about it. Brenna likes to mockingly smack or pinch my ass whenever we pass each other in the hall, but that's not because she wants me. She's just an asshole.

"Want to go somewhere quiet and talk or something?" Gina suggests.

I've lived on this planet long enough to be able to decode what "talk or something" means in girl speak.

1) There won't be much talking.

2) There'll be a lot of "or something."

Gina couldn't have made this clearer if she were holding up a sign saying DO ME! She even licks her lips as she voices the question.

I know I should say no, but the idea of going home right now and jacking off in my bedroom while my roommates marathon old seasons of *The Hills* isn't too appealing. So I say, "Sure," and follow Gina out of the room.

———

We end up in a small den that contains a couch, a couple of bookshelves, and a desk against the far wall under a window. It's surprisingly empty. The party gods have taken pity on my celibate ass and provided us with the kind of dangerous privacy I should actively be avoiding. Instead, I'm on the couch and letting Gina kiss my neck.

Her satin camisole rubs my arm and it's almost pornographic how good the barely there friction feels. Everything is turning me on these days. I got a stiffy watching a YouTube ad for Tupperware the other day because the MILF in the ad was peeling a banana. Then she chopped it up into bits and placed the banana pieces in a plastic container and not even that horrific symbolism could dissuade me from jerking off to Banana Woman. Give me a few more months and I'll be fucking the apple pies my roommate Rupi bakes every Sunday.

"You smell so good." Gina inhales deeply, then exhales, her warm breath tickling my neck. Her lips latch on once more, a hot, wet brand against my neck.

She feels good in my lap. Her shapely thighs straddle mine, her satin-clad body warm and curvy. And I have to stop this.

I made a promise to myself, and to my team, although none of them asked me to do it and they all think I'm insane for even attempting abstinence. Matt flat-out stated he doesn't believe that me setting aside my sexual urges is going to impact our hockey games in the slightest. But I think it will, and for me it's a matter of principle. The guys voted me captain. I take that responsibility seriously, and I know from personal experience that I have the tendency to let women mess with my head. Screwing around got me a broken wrist last year. I'm not looking to repeat that.

"Gina, I—"

She cuts me off by pressing her lips to mine, and then we're kissing and my mind begins to spin. She tastes like beer and bubble gum. And her hair, which falls over one shoulder in a thick curtain of red curls, smells like apples. Mmmm, I want to eat her up.

Our tongues dance and the kiss grows deeper, hotter. My head keeps spinning as lust and unhappiness war inside me. I've lost all capability to think clearly. I'm so hard it hurts and Gina makes it worse by rubbing herself all over my crotch.

Thirty more seconds, I tell myself. Thirty more seconds and then I'll stop this from going any further.

"I want you so bad." Her lips are fused to my neck again, and then, *fuck*, her hand slides between us. She cups my cock over my shorts and I almost weep with pleasure. It's been so long since a hand that didn't belong to myself touched my dick. It feels criminally good.

"Gina, no," I groan, and it takes all my willpower to remove her hand. My cock protests by leaking precome all over the inside of my boxers.

Her cheeks are flushed red. Eyes glazed. "Why not?"

"I'm…taking a break from all that."

"From what?"

"Sex."

"What about it?"

"I'm going without."

"Without what?" She looks as confused as I am miserable.

"Without sex," I clarify glumly. "As in, I'm not having it for a while."

Her brows crash together. "But…why not?"

"It's a long story." I pause. "Actually, it's not a long story at all. I want to concentrate on hockey this year, and sex is too big of a distraction. That's pretty much it."

She pauses for a long beat. Then she touches my cheek and sweeps her thumb over the stubble on my jaw. She licks her lips, and I almost come in my pants.

"If you're worried that I'm going to want anything more, don't. I'm only looking for a one-night thing. My course load is insane this semester and I don't have time for relationships either."

"It's not a relationship issue," I try to explain. "It's sex in general. Once I have it, I want to keep having it. I get distracted and—"

She cuts me off again. "Fine, no sex. I'll just suck you off."

I nearly choke on my tongue. "Gina—"

"Don't worry, I'll get myself off while I'm doing it. Blowjobs turn me on so much."

This is torture.

Pure torture.

I swear, if the military needs any ideas on how to break someone? Give them a hard-up college guy, throw a hot chick on his lap, have her tell him how she wants nothing but no-strings sex and offer him blowjobs because it turns her on *so much*.

"I'm sorry," I manage to croak. Then I accomplish the even more difficult feat of easing her off my lap and getting to my feet. "I'm not in a good headspace for…any of this."

She stays seated, her head tipped back to stare at me. Her eyes are wide with incredulity and a touch of…I think it might be *sympathy*. For chrissake. Now I'm being pitied for my celibacy.

"I'm sorry," I say again. "And just so you know, you're the hottest girl at this party and my decision has nothing to do with you. I made myself a promise back in April and I want to keep it."

Gina chews on her bottom lip. Then, to my surprise, her expression takes on a glimmer of admiration. "I'm not going to lie," she says, "I'm kind of impressed. Not many guys could stand by that conviction in the face of my hotness."

"Not many guys are as stupid as I am."

Grinning, she hops to her feet. "Well, I guess I'll see you around, Hunter. I'd like to say I'll wait for you, but a girl has needs. And obviously they don't align with yours."

With a laugh, she saunters out of the den, and I watch her sexy ass sway with each step.

I rake both hands through my hair and then release a silent groan into my palms. I don't know if I should be proud of myself or kick my own ass for this ridiculous path I've chosen.

For the most part, it *has* helped keep me focused on hockey. I take out all my sexual frustration on the ice. I'm faster and stronger than I was last season, and there's almost a desperation in each shot that I snap at the net. The bullets hit their mark, almost as if in tribute to my suffering dick. An acknowledgment that his sacrifice must be honored.

It's only until the end of the season, I reassure myself. Seven more months, which will put me at one full year of celibacy once I cross the finish line. And then I'll reward myself with an entire summer of sex. A sex summer.

A dirty, decadent, endless sex summer...

Oh Christ. I'm so tired of fucking my own hand. Granted, I'm not helping my cause when I do idiotic things like opening myself up to temptation with gorgeous sorority girls.

For the first time in a long time, I'm dying for classes to start. Hopefully I'll have so much work this semester I'll be drowning in it. Homework, extra ice time, practice, and games—that's all I'm allowed to focus on. And definitely no more sorority parties.

Avoiding temptation is the only way to keep my head in the game and my dick in my pants.

2
DEMI

"Lock it," I order as my boyfriend Nico shuts the
bedroom door behind us. Just because my sorority is hosting
tonight's party doesn't mean my room is open to the public.
The last time we threw a party and I forgot to lock up, I
went upstairs to grab a sweater and walked in on a three-
some in progress. One of the two guys had even committed
the atrocity of using my one-eyed stuffed panda Fernando
as a pillow to shove under the girl's bottom. You know, to
create easier access for the double penetration that was about
to commence.

Never again, Fernando, I silently assure my childhood
friend as I move him onto the nightstand to make room for
my boyfriend.

Nico falls backward onto the bed, covers his face with
his arm, and releases a weary breath. He missed the party
because he had to work, but I appreciate that he made the
effort to come over after his shift instead of going home to
the studio apartment he rents in Hastings. The little town is
a ten-minute drive from the Briar campus, so it's not super

far. But I know it would've been easier for him to go straight home and crash.

"Tired?" I cluck in sympathy.

"Dead," is his muffled reply. His forearm shields his eyes from my view, which gives me the opportunity to admire his body without getting teased for it.

Nico has the long, lean build of a basketball player. Although he played point guard in high school, he didn't land any college basketball scholarships, and he was never good enough to go to the NBA. I don't think he cares much. Playing ball was something fun to do with his high school buddies; his real passion is cars. But though he doesn't play sports these days, he's still in great shape. He gets a good workout hauling boxes and furniture at the moving company where he works.

"Poor baby," I murmur. "Let me take care of it."

Smiling, I start at the bottom of his body and work my way up. Pull his sneakers off, slide his belt from its loops, peel his pants down his legs. He sits up to help me with his hoodie, then collapses back down. Now he's bare chested, wearing boxers and socks, with his arm over his face again to protect his eyes from the light.

Taking pity on him, I turn off the main light and flick on the lamp on the bed table, which emits a pale glow.

Then I settle beside him, clad in the black silk nightie I wore for the party.

"Demi," he mumbles as I start kissing his neck.

"Mmmm?"

"I'm way too tired for this."

My mouth travels along the angular line of his jaw, rough stubble abrading my lips. I reach his mouth and kiss him softly. He kisses me back but it's a fleeting caress. Then he gives another tired moan.

"Baby, seriously, I don't have any energy. I've been working fourteen hours straight."

"I'll do all the work," I whisper, but when my hand slides down to his crotch, there are no signs of life down there. His junk is a limp noodle.

"Another night, *mami*," he says sleepily. "Why don't you put on your creepy show or something?"

I swallow my disappointment. We haven't had sex in more than a week. Nico works on the weekends and several nights during the week, but he has tomorrow off so this is one of the rare Saturdays when we could actually stay up late fooling around if we want.

But he hasn't moved a muscle since he lay down.

"All right," I relent, rolling over to grab my laptop. "The latest episode is *Children Who Kill*, but I don't remember if I made you watch the one before that—*Clowns Who Kill*…?"

Nico is snoring softly.

Wonderful. It's Saturday night, there's a party raging downstairs, and it's not even ten o'clock. My hot boyfriend is sound asleep in my bed and I'm about to watch a show about murderers. By myself.

Living the college dream. Woo-hoo.

To make matters worse, this is the last stress-free weekend we're going to have in a long time. The fall semester starts on Monday, and my schedule is intense this year. I'm pre-med, so I need to excel and then some during my last two years at Briar if I want to get into a good med school. I won't have nearly as much time to spend with Nico as I'll want.

I shoot a quick glance at the snoring lump beside me. He doesn't seem bothered by our impending lack of quality time. But maybe he's right not to be. We've been dating since the eighth grade. Our relationship has had its ups and downs over the years, with some breaks along the way, but we survived every single hurdle, and we'll survive this, too.

I crawl under the covers, a feat of skill because Nico's heavy body is weighing down the other side of the blanket. I position the computer on my lap and load the next episode of my favorite show. I want to say I watch this series solely for the psychology component, but…who am I kidding? It's fucked up and I love it.

Ominous music fills the bedroom, followed by the host's familiar British monotone informing me that I'm in store for sixty delightful minutes of children who kill.

———

The rest of the weekend flies by. Monday morning brings with it the first class of my junior year, and the one I'm most excited about—Abnormal Psychology. Even better, two of my good friends are also taking this course. They're waiting for me on the stone steps of the massive ivy-covered building.

"Gawd, you look hot!" Pax Ling throws his arms around me, pulls back to smack a loud kiss on my cheek, and then reaches around to pinch my butt. I'm wearing denim shorts and a striped tank top, because it's a million degrees out today. Not that I'm complaining about the summer spilling over into September. Bring on the heat, baby.

"The *things* those shorts do to your *legs*, babe," Pax gushes in approval.

Beside him, TJ Bukowski rolls his eyes. When I first introduced them, TJ wasn't a fan of Pax's outrageous personality. But he eventually warmed up to Pax, and now they have a love-hate friendship that makes me laugh.

"You look pretty hot yourself," I inform Pax. "I love the shirt."

He flips up the collar of his pea-green polo. "It's Gucci, bitches. My sister and I were in Boston this weekend and spent a little too much money. But hey, worth it, right?" He does a quick spin to show off his new shirt.

"Worth it," I agree.

TJ adjusts the straps of his backpack. "Come on, let's go in. We don't want to be late for the first class. I hear Andrews is a strict prof."

I laugh. "We're fifteen minutes early. Don't worry."

"Did you seriously just tell *Thomas Joseph* not to worry?" Pax demands. "That's his default mode."

He's not wrong. TJ is a walking, talking ball of anxiety.

TJ glowers at us. He doesn't like being made fun of, especially about his anxiety, so I reach out and take his hand, giving it a warm squeeze. "Don't sulk, hon. I like that you're a worry-wart. Means I'm never late for anything."

With a slight smile, he squeezes my hand back. TJ and I met in freshman year when we lived in the same dorm. My roommate had been absolutely unbearable, so TJ's room became sort of a sanctuary for me. He's not always the easiest person to get along with, but he's been a good friend to me from day one.

"Waaaaaiittt!"

The female shriek pierces the breezy morning air. I turn my head to see a petite girl sprinting down the tree-lined path. She's clad in a knee-length black dress with big white buttons running down the middle. One arm is thrust skyward, waving what looks like a plastic food container.

A dark-haired guy pauses near the steps. He's tall and noticeably fit, even while wearing a bulky gray hoodie with the Briar U logo on it. A frown creases his handsome face when he realizes he's being chased.

The girl skids to a stop in front of him. I can't hear what he says to her, but her response is loud and clear. I think she might be one of the loudest people I've ever encountered.

"I made you lunch!" Smiling broadly, she presents the container as if she's handing him the Holy Grail.

Meanwhile, his body language conveys annoyance, as if what she's actually handing him is a bag of dog poop.

Seriously? His girlfriend made him lunch and he's not throwing his arms around her in gratitude? Jerk.

"I hate that guy," mutters TJ.

"You know him?" I can't hide my dubious expression. TJ doesn't hang out with many jocks, and the guy we're looking at is one hundred percent a jock. Those broad shoulders are a dead giveaway.

"That's Hunter Davenport." Pax is the one who speaks, and I instantly recognize that tone of voice. Translation: *oh-em-gee I want to lick that boy up.*

Sure enough, he's got a dreamy look in his eyes. "Who's Hunter Davenport?" I ask.

"He's on the hockey team."

Nailed it. I knew he was an athlete. Those shoulders, man. "Never heard of him," I say with a shrug.

"You're not missing out. He's just some rich prick jock," TJ says.

I arch a brow. "What do you have against him?" TJ doesn't normally bash student athletes. Or anyone, for that matter, aside from the occasional jab at Pax.

"Nothing. I just think he's gross. I caught him banging some slut in the library last year. Fully clothed, but with his pants pulled down revealing half his ass. He had her right up against the wall in one of the study rooms." TJ shakes his head in disgust.

I'm disgusted too, but more so with my friend's rude representation of Davenport's companion. "Please don't use that word," I chide. "You know I'm not into slut-shaming."

TJ is instantly contrite. "Sorry, you're right, that wasn't cool. If anything, Davenport was the slut in that scenario."

"Why does anyone have to be a slut?"

"I want to be his slut," Pax says absently. His gaze remains glued to the dark-haired hockey player, who's still bickering with his girlfriend.

The girl keeps pushing the Tupperware into his hand and he keep pushing it back into hers. I think he's saying he won't have time to eat, because her answering screech is, "There's always time to eat, Hunter! But you know what, fine. Go hungry. Forgive me for trying to offer you nourishment!"

Grinning, I cup my hands around my mouth and holler, "Just take the fucking lunch already!"

Davenport's head swivels my way. He gives me a deep frown.

The girl, on the other hand, beams at me. "*Thank* you!" She shoves the container in his hand one last time and flounces off. Her kitten heels snap like tap shoes against the cobblestones that comprise most of the historical campus.

Hockey Boy is glowering as he stalks toward us. "You have no idea what you just did," he growls at me. His voice is deeper than I expect, with a cute rasp to it. He lifts the container. "Now we set a precedent. She'll be making my fucking lunch all semester."

I roll my eyes. "Wow, forgive her for trying to offer you *nourishment*."

Sighing, he starts to move away. Then halts. "Oh hey, how's it going, man?" he says to Pax.

My friend's jaw drops to his white tennis shoes. They look new too, so I guess the shirt wasn't the only thing he picked up in Boston.

"Hi," Pax blurts out, clearly stunned to be singled out.

"You were in my Alternative Media class last term. Jax, right?"

To my disbelief, *Pax* nods stupidly.

"You in this Abnormal Psych class, too?"

"Yes," Pax breathes.

"Cool. Well, see you in there." Davenport claps Pax on the shoulder before sauntering up the stairs toward the building's entrance.

I stare pointedly at my friend, but he's too busy gawking at Davenport's ass.

"Hey Jax," I mock. "Earth to Jax."

TJ snickers.

Pax snaps out of his trance. He gives me a sheepish look.

"He fucking remembered me, Demi. I wasn't going to correct him after he *remembered* me."

"He remembered Jax!"

"That's me! I'm Jax. I now live life as Jax. Hunter Davenport said so."

I smother a sigh and glance at TJ. "Why are we friends with him again?"

"I have no idea," he replies with a grin. "Come on, Jax, let's escort our lady to class."

I enter the lecture hall sandwiched between the two boys, my arms linked through theirs. The bulk of my friends are male, a fact that my boyfriend has come to accept. In high school he wasn't too thrilled about it, but Nico's never been a controlling boyfriend, and I think he secretly likes how well I get along with his friends.

Don't get me wrong, I've got girlfriends too. My sorority sisters. Pippa and Corinne, who I'm meeting for dinner tonight. But my guy friends do outnumber the girls, for whatever reason.

Inside the cavernous room, the boys and I find three seats together in a row near the middle of the room. I notice Hunter Davenport one row ahead of us at the end of the aisle, hunched over his phone.

"Gawd, he is perfection," Pax groans. "You have no idea how often I've fantasized about luring him over to the D-side."

I pat my friend on the arm. "Maybe one day. I have faith in you."

The room fills up, but all chatter dies when our professor enters at nine o'clock sharp. She's a tall, slender woman with short hair and shrewd brown eyes behind a pair of square black frames. She greets us warmly, and goes on to introduce herself, her credentials, and what we can expect to learn this year.

I'm pumped. My father is a surgeon and my mother used to be a pediatrics nurse, so it was inevitable that I'd wind up in a medicine-related field. It's probably programmed into my DNA. But surgery and nursing never interested me. Since I was a kid, I've been drawn to the *mind*. I'm especially fascinated by personality disorders. By destructive patterns of thinking and how they impact an individual when they interact with the world.

Professor Andrews discusses the specific topics we'll be covering. "We're going to see how abnormal psych was dealt with in the past and how modern approaches to it have evolved over the years. Clinical assessments and diagnosis will play a large role in our studies. Also, I believe in a hands-on approach to teaching. Which means I'm not simply going to stand here at this podium and spew facts about stress disorders, mood disorders, sexual disorders, and the like."

I lean forward. I'm already enthralled. I like her no-nonsense tone, and the way she sweeps her gaze over the room and tries to look everyone in the eye. I've had a lot of classes where the prof reads off a laptop in a monotone and doesn't seem to notice there're other people in the room.

She says we'll be expected to write summaries of the case studies she talks about in class, that there'll be a few multiple-choice tests. "All test dates are in the syllabus that was emailed to you. As for your major research project, it requires a partner, and it will be an ongoing partnership, with the final research paper and in-depth case study due before the holiday break. Now this is the fun part…"

I notice several uneasy glances being exchanged throughout the lecture hall. I guess it's a red flag when a prof uses the word "fun." But I'm not concerned. Everything she's described so far sounds interesting.

"You know that old childhood game—playing doctor?" Professor Andrews grins at the room. "That's the gist of this research project. One partner will play the role of the psychologist; the other will be the patient. The former will be provided with diagnostic tools in order to make an assessment and write a detailed case study. The latter will be assigned a psychological disorder that they'll be required to research and, for lack of a better word, play-act for the doctor."

"I love it," Pax says to me. "Please, *please* let me play the patient."

"Why do you assume you're partnering with Demi?" TJ objects.

"Boys, there's plenty of me to go around."

But Andrews throws us for a loop. "I'm assigning partners based on this alphabetized class list." She holds up some sheets of paper. "When you hear your names, raise your hands so you know who you're working with. All right, let's start—Ames and Ardin."

Two arms go up. A girl with bright purple hair, and a girl wearing a Patriots cap.

"Axelrod and Bailey."

There are about a hundred people in the class, but

Andrews is efficient. She whizzes through names at a fast clip, and we reach the D's in no time.

"Davenport and Davis."

I raise my hand at the same time as Hunter. He shifts his gaze toward me, quirking his mouth in a half-smile.

Next to me, TJ sighs unhappily. He leans in to whisper, "Do you want me to legally change my last name to Davidson to save you from the hockey asshole?"

I grin at him. "It's okay, I'll survive."

"Grey and Guthrie," Andrews is saying.

"Are you sure?" TJ presses. "I bet you can switch partners if you said something."

"Killington and Ladde."

"Babe, it's fine. I don't even know the guy," I say. "You're the one who doesn't like him."

"I love him," Pax bemoans. "*I* want to play doctor with him."

But then Andrews calls out, "Lawson and Ling," and Pax brightens up when his partner raises a hand. It's a guy with wavy brown hair and a killer jawline.

"He'll do," murmurs Pax, and I swallow a laugh.

"These packages," Andrews says, gesturing to the stacks of orange manila envelopes on her desk, "contain detailed instructions about the assignment. One partner, please remember to grab one after the lecture. It'll be up to each team to decide who assumes which role."

Hunter twists around and gives me a finger gun, I assume to tell me I'm on envelope duty.

I roll my eyes. Already making me do all the work, I see.

Once everyone's assigned a partner, Andrews resumes the

lecture, and I take so many notes my wrist starts to ache. Shit, I'll need to bring my laptop next time. I usually prefer writing notes by hand, but there's a lot of material to unpack and she covers so much in such a short time.

After we're dismissed, I head to the front of the room to grab a manila envelope. It's got some heft to it. That might alarm some people, but I'm looking forward to this project. It sounds fun and comprehensive, even if I am paired with a jock.

Speaking of the jock, he wanders toward me, hiking his backpack over one broad shoulder. "Davis," he greets me.

"Davenport."

"Call me Hunter." His gaze does a slow sweep of me from head to toe. It lingers a little too long on my bare legs, still nice and tanned from a summer spent in Miami.

"I'm Demi." I notice TJ and Pax standing near the exit, waiting for me to finish up.

"Demi…" he says absently. He's still checking out my legs, and he visibly gulps before wrenching his gaze back to mine.

"Yes, that's my name." Why is he shifting his stance like that? I narrow my eyes at his crotch. Does he have an *erection*?

"Demi," he repeats.

"Uh-huh. Rhymes with semi." I shoot a pointed look at his crotch.

Hunter glances down. Then he snickers. "For fuck's sake, I'm not rocking a boner. That's just my pants."

"Surrrrre."

He slides one big hand to his zipper area and covers it with his palm, and the tent in the denim does seem to flatten. "New jeans," he grumbles. "They're still kinda stiff."

"Stiff, you say."

"It's the fabric. See? Touch it."

Laughter sputters from my throat. "Oh my God, I am not touching your dick."

"Your loss." Hunter smirks.

"If you say so, bud." I hold up the envelope. "So when should we meet up and go over all this stuff?"

"I dunno. You free tonight?"

I shake my head. "I've got plans. How about tomorrow night?"

"Yeah, I'll be around. When and where?"

"Eight o'clock at the Theta Beta Nu house?"

"Huh, really? I didn't take you for a sorority girl." I shrug. "Well, I am."

Truth be told, I only pledged because I didn't want to live in the dorms. Plus, my mother belonged to the Theta chapter at her college, and I grew up hearing about how her sorority days were some of the best days of her life. She was the life of the party back then, and still is.

"Okay then. I'll see you tomorrow night, Semi," he drawls before striding off.

3
HUNTER

"UGH. I MISS THOSE TITS SO MUCH."

"They miss you too..."

"Mmmm, yeah? What do they miss most about me?"

"Definitely your tongue."

"Mmmm. Let me see 'em, Hottie. Just a peek."

"What if one of your teammates walks in?"

"Then they'll be jealous of me till the end of time because I'm dating the sexiest woman in the world."

"Fine, I'll play. But only if you show me your dick."

"Deal. You first...aw fuck, baby...wait, maybe you should put the girls away—what if Hunter walks in? You said he was home."

"Oh, it's a non-issue. Hunter's a monk now. My bare boobs won't make an impact."

From the kitchen, I finally release the growl stuck in my throat. I *thought* I was coming downstairs to grab some dinner before my study date with Demi Davis. Instead, I just spent the past five minutes listening to the most nauseating Skype session in the world.

"Yeah, I'm a monk," I holler at the doorway. "Not a motherfucking eunuch!"

I march into the living room without giving Brenna any time to cover herself up. She doesn't deserve it. As a reward for enduring Brenna and Jake Connelly's video sexing, I deserve to see some boobs outside of porn.

But Brenna is already shoving her shirt over her chest, so all I get is a teasing glimpse of reddish brown nipples before they disappear from view.

"Move over, you evil devil woman." I drop my ass on the couch beside her and shove a forkful of wild rice into my mouth. I glance at the laptop sitting on the coffee table. "Hey Connelly. Nice cock."

The man on the computer screen gives a startled curse. His gaze snaps down to his right hand, as if it's just occurred to him he's gripping a rather impressive erection. A blur of motion and the sound of a zipper, and then Jake Connelly glares at me with intense green eyes.

"Spying on us, Davenport?"

I swallow my food. "Is it considered spying when you're naked Skyping in my goddamn living room?"

"*Our* living room," Brenna says sweetly, reaching over to pat my shoulder.

Right, like I could ever forget. Other men might be thrilled to shack up with three chicks, but it's not my ideal living situation. I like Brenna, Summer and Rupi individually, but throw the three of them together and the world becomes…loud. Not to mention they're always ganging up on me.

My former roommates, Mike Hollis and Colin

Fitzgerald, technically still live here too, but they're not around nearly as much as I'd like.

Hollis only shows up on the weekends—he stays with his folks in New Hampshire during the week for his job.

Fitz is a video game designer and has been taking on a lot of contract work since he graduated Briar. Sometimes that means traveling to the game studio's headquarters. Right now he's in New York working on a sci-fi role-playing game, and staying at Summer's family's Manhattan penthouse for the duration of the gig. Lucky Fitzy. The Heyward-Di Laurentis clan is filthy rich, so he's currently living it up in the lap of luxury.

"Connelly, get a move on. The car's waiting for us downstairs," another voice barks out of the laptop speakers. "We've got that charity photo op thing tonight."

Jake glances over his shoulder. "Oh shit, I forgot about that."

"What are you doing on—oh, hey Brenna!" A huge face appears on screen, a close-up so extreme that I can see up the guy's hairy nostrils.

When the man pulls back, I experience a rare fanboy moment, because holy shit—it's Theo Nilsson, one of the star players for Edmonton. I can't believe Nilsson just casually strolled into Jake's hotel room, and there's no stopping a pang of envy at the notion that Jake is actually out in the world playing hockey with some serious legends.

When I was a kid I dreamed of playing professionally, but as I got older I realized it might not be the best path for me. The lifestyle scares me, if I'm behind honest. So I didn't make myself eligible for the draft. Hell, I hadn't even planned on playing in college. I came to Briar set on earning a business degree and becoming an entrepreneur. But a friend and teammate who graduated a couple of years ago lured me out of my self-imposed retirement, and now here I am.

"I have to go, babe," Jake tells Brenna.

"Have fun getting your picture taken with all those thirsty puck bunnies," she chirps.

Nilsson barks with laughter. "It's a charity event for a senior citizen curling organization," Jake's teammate reveals.

She's unfazed. "Have you *seen* Jake?" she asks Theo. "Those old broads will be all over him. Puck bunnies transcend age."

As Brenna signs off, I shove a piece of grilled chicken into my mouth. "I can't believe that was Theo Nilsson," I say between bites.

"Yeah, he's really cool. We had dinner with him last week when they played the Bruins."

"Don't rub it in."

Brenna's trademark red lips purse in a saccharine smile. Even when she's home alone, she still takes the time to slather on that fuck-me lipstick. She's evil. "If you're a good boy, I'll invite you next time."

"I'm always a good boy," I protest. "Just ask my dick— poor dude wants to be bad and I ain't having it."

She laughs. "I feel like all this pent-up lust isn't good for your health. What if your balls explode and you die?"

I think it over. "Maybe it'll be like a thousand orgasms all rolled up in one explosion, and who would want to keep living after that? I feel like after you've experienced a thousand-orgasm explosion, there's nowhere to go but down."

"That's a good point." Brenna's dark eyes track me as I get up and head for the kitchen to rinse my plate.

"I gotta go now," I tell her, popping my head back into the living room. "See you later."

"Where are you off to?"

"Study thing at the Theta house."

"Ha! So much for the vow of celibacy."

"Nope. The vow's still intact. I'm just working on a project with a chick there."

"A project," she mocks.

"Yes, a project. The world doesn't revolve around sex, Bee."

"Sure it does." She licks her lips lasciviously and my mouth tingles in response. So does my penis.

She's right. Sex is everything and everywhere. A woman can't even lick her lips without my brain sinking right into the sexual gutter.

So far, I've found only one solution for controlling my libido: marijuana. And I can't even do *that* as often as I'd like, except for the occasional joint at a party. Weed mellows me out and reins in my carnal impulses, but it also makes me tired and slows me down during workouts. And there's no way I want to tempt the NCAA drug-testing gods. So, like sex, it's just another fun activity I get to avoid. My life is awesome.

"Anyway, I'm meeting some of the boys at Malone's afterward to shoot pool. Don't wait up."

"What? No invite?" She mock pouts.

"Nope," I reply and I don't feel the slightest bit guilty about it. I live in the estrogen zone, and sometimes it's imperative I escape it, even if it's just for the night. "No girls allowed. There's enough girls in this house already."

"Oh, you love it. Rupi makes you lunch every day,

Summer cooks you breakfast, and I'm always walking around in my underwear. Food and sexy material for your spank bank, Davenport. You're living the dream."

"If I was living the dream, I'd be banging all of you every night. At the same time."

"Ha! You wish. Go have fun with your"—Brenna uses air quotes—"project."

I give her the finger and leave, and fifteen minutes later I'm back on campus, parking my Land Rover on the tree-lined street that houses Greek Row. It's Tuesday night and the area is surprisingly quiet. Usually there's always some nightly party or event happening on Greek Row, but tonight I hear only the faint sound of music from a few of the fraternity houses.

I walk up the flower-lined path that leads to the front door of the Theta house. Nearly every window of the three-story Victorian is lit up. I ring the doorbell and a tall, skinny girl in sweats appears.

She arches an eyebrow. "Can I help you?"

"I'm here to see Demi." I lift the shoulder that's holding my backpack. "We're studying."

Demi's sorority sister shrugs, then turns her head and shouts, "Demi! Door!"

I enter the house, which has undergone a drastic makeover since I was here on the weekend. It's neat as a pin and smells like lemon cleaner, and there's no scantily clad chicks, drunken dudes, or puddles of beer all over the hardwood.

Footsteps echo on the wooden staircase, and the girl from psych class saunters down the steps, a lollipop sticking out of the corner of her mouth. Naturally, I zero in on her lips, which are glossy and tinged red from the candy she's sucking on. Her dark hair is up in a high ponytail and she's wearing plaid pants and a thin white tank top over a black sports bra.

She's really fucking cute, and I have to force myself to stop checking her out.

"Hi," she says, giving me a long appraisal.

"Mel, who was at the door?" someone shouts.

There's a burst of chatter, and then half a dozen girls spill out of the kitchen into the front hall. They all stop abruptly when they notice me. One of them openly undresses me with her eyes, while the others are slightly more discreet.

"Hunter Davenport," the ogler drawls. "Lord, you're even better looking up close."

I don't normally get shy or stupid around women, but they're all standing there appraising me, and it's fucking disconcerting. "Maybe you should give me your number?" I murmur to Demi.

"Why would I do that?"

"So that next time I can text you when I'm here and you can quietly come get me and we could avoid all of…this…" I gesture to our audience.

"What's the matter? Are you intimidated by a few girls?" Rolling her eyes, Demi leads me toward the stairs.

"Nah." I wink. "I'm worried about you."

"Me?"

"Well, yeah. If I keep coming over to see you, your sisters will start getting insanely jealous, and their resentment will eventually make them treat you poorly and you'll lose all of your friends. Is that really what you want, Semi?"

She laughs. "Oh no! You're right. From now on you

should climb in through my window. Like Romeo." Her tongue shifts her lollipop to the other side of her mouth. "Spoiler alert: Romeo dies."

She ushers me into a room on the second floor and closes the door.

I examine the bedroom. The walls are yellow and the bed is one of those four-post ones that looks like it should have a billowing canopy but doesn't. The bedspread is purple, and there's a stuffed panda chilling on one of the pillows.

Demi's desk is laden with textbooks. Chem, bio, and a math one I can't read the title of. I raise my eyebrows. If she's taking all of those in one semester, that's an intense course load and I don't envy her at all.

But my gaze is more interested in the large bulletin board over the desk. It's practically overflowing with pictures, and I move toward it to take a closer look. Hmmm, there are a helluva lot of dudes in these photographs. Some girls, too, but Demi's friend group seems to consist mostly of guys. Several photos feature Demi with the same raven-haired guy. Boyfriend?

"So, how are we doing this?" I ask, dropping my bag on her desk chair.

"Well, Andrews said we're supposed to treat these meet-ups like real therapy sessions."

"Right." I waggle my eyebrows. "You ready to play doctor?"

"Gross. I'm not playing anything with you, hockey boy."

"That's hockey *man*, thank you very much."

"Okay, hockey man." Demi digs into her schoolbag and pulls out the manila envelope we got in class yesterday. She sits on the edge of the bed with the envelope on her lap.

"All right, so I figured you would be the patient, and I'd be the doctor. That means you'd be doing the easier part of the write-up."

I frown. "What makes you think I need the easy part?"

"Oh, sorry, I don't mean to insult your intelligence," she says, sounding sincere. "But a friend told me you're a business major."

"So?"

"So I'm the psych major in this partnership, and I think writing the case study and doing all the diagnosis work would be more beneficial to me than you, since I want to make a career out of this. But if you really don't want to do the research element, we can draw straws."

I think about it for a moment. She does have a point about the career stuff. And I don't mind doing the research portion. "Sure, whatever. I'll be the patient."

"Perfect. Done."

"See how well we work together?" My gaze drifts to the small loveseat tucked beneath the window. "Sweet, it's like a real shrink's office." I stride over to the couch and cram my too-large body onto it, stretching my legs over the edge. Then I reach for my zipper. "Pants on or off?"

4
DEMI

I burst out laughing at the outlandish question. "Please, for the love of God, keep your pants *on*."

"You sure?" Hunter says, his fingers poised over the button of his jeans.

"Positive."

"Your loss." He winks and shoves his hands behind his head.

Davenport is entertaining, I'll give him that. He's also too attractive for his own good. My sorority sisters left drool puddles on the floor when he walked by them before. Most of them have a huge thing for jocks, so they'll probably burst into my room begging for details the second Hunter leaves.

He stretches out on my little couch and kicks off his shoes. He's wearing jeans that are ripped at the knees, a black T-shirt, and an unzipped gray hoodie. Muscular but not bulky, he's got a great body, and the heart-stopping face to go with it. And when he flashes me a cocky grin, I'm horrified to feel heat rise in my cheeks. That smile of his is dangerous. No wonder Pax is obsessed with this guy.

I open the large envelope and extract a stapled packet with the instructions for our assignment, as well as two other envelopes. One is labeled "DOCTOR," the other "PATIENT."

"Here." I toss the patient envelope at the couch. Hunter catches it easily.

Inside my envelope, I find a stack of papers, and flip through it. It's blank templates that I'm supposed to use for my "session notes." I skim the instructions bundle. We need to log a minimum of eight sessions, but we can do as many as we want. My session notes will apparently be included in the appendix for the case study I'll need to write. My package also includes diagnostic tools and tip sheets.

From the couch, Hunter chuckles softly. I glance over to see him skimming through papers. His stack isn't as big as mine, likely because his part of the project involves more research.

"We probably should've decided on our roles in class," I realize. "I don't know if we can do much of a session before you've brushed up on your fake condition."

But Hunter just shrugs. A wry note enters his voice as he studies his papers again. "It's cool. I know enough to wing it, at least for this first chat."

"You sure?"

"Yup." He slides the paperwork back into the envelope and drops it on his bag. Then he gets comfortable again. "All right, let's go."

As per Andrews' instructions, I'm not allowed to record the session. But I'm confident in my note-taking abilities. I crunch the last bit of my lollipop between my teeth, swallow the candy, and toss the little stick in the wastebasket.

Once we're both settled, we start going through the formalities. "So, Mister…?" I wait for him to fill in the rest.

"Sexy."

"Veto. You can do better than that."

"Big," he supplies.

I sigh. "Smith," I say firmly. "You're Mr. Smith. First name, um, Damien."

"Like the devil kid from that horror movie? Veto. It's bad karma."

"You're bad karma," I mutter. Jesus, it's taking forever just to record his fake name. At this rate, the project will never get done. "Fine, your first name is Richard, you picky dick."

He snorts.

"It's nice to meet you, Dick Smith," I say sweetly. "I'm Dr. Davis. What brings you here today?"

I half-expect another bullshit line, something about how this Dick needs to be sucked. But he surprises me. "My wife thinks I need therapy."

My eyebrows shoot up. Ooh, getting right down to it. I love it. "Is that so… And why does she think that?"

"Honestly? I don't know. *She's* the one who needs therapy. She's always losing her mind over something."

I jot down his phrasing. "What do you mean by that, losing her mind?"

"She overthinks everything. She bitches all the time. For example, if I'm home late from work, her brain immediately jumps to 'he's been screwing around.'" Hunter pauses irritably. "I guess for the sake of full disclosure, I should mention I cheated on her once or twice, and yes, she is aware of this."

Wow, this is like a soap opera. I'm already invested.

"All right…this cheating you mention." I make some more notes. "How long ago did it take place? And was it once, or was it twice?"

"The first affair was years ago, the most recent one this year. I was under a lot of stress at work."

I note that he ignored my question about how many times he'd actually cheated.

"Why do you think you cheated? Is there a particular reason that stands out?"

"It's hard to feel connected to somebody when they're constantly complaining and making demands. She fucking drove me to cheat. I mean, what else did she expect would happen if she kept acting like that?"

Ugh, what a prick. He holds his *wife* responsible for *his* cheating—

I stop the train of thought, reminding myself that I'm not supposed to be judge. I'm supposed to understand.

If I'm going to be a clinical psychologist, I'm sure I'll hear thousands of sordid tales of infidelity. I might even need to counsel someone who physically or emotionally abuses their partner. It's highly likely I'll encounter patients I despise, or who I might not be able to help.

My job isn't to condemn them; it's to hopefully help them reach self-awareness.

"So when you came clean about the affairs, did you and your wife agree to start over? Start fresh?"

Hunter nods. "She accepted responsibility for her part in what happened and agreed to forgive me. That means it's done, in the past. Her being suspicious of me all the time doesn't make me want to spend time with her. Trust me, she's not making it easy to be around her."

"I imagine so. But can you recognize why she might be behaving this way? Let's try to put yourself in her position. How do you think you'd react if your wife was unfaithful?"

"She'd never cheat on me," he says smugly. "I'm the catch in this relationship. She's definitely punching above her weight class."

You're the fucking worst, I want to say.

"I see," is what I say instead. And now I understand why therapists seem to cling to those two words. It's code for whatever expletives are ringing in your head.

Hunter and I talk for another twenty minutes about his fictional wife, her nagging, and his infidelity, and I begin to notice a trend in his responses. A complete inability to put himself in her shoes.

Lack of empathy, I write down, and draw a little star around it.

As he finishes another long-winded anecdote that paints his wife as the villain and himself as the innocent victim, I can't help but be impressed by how he just threw himself headfirst into this assignment. And he's doing *such* a solid job, which is…ugh, it's sexy as hell, if I'm being honest.

I'm about to ask another question when Hunter sits up. "Let's stop now. I've officially tapped out my knowledge about…my condition," he says vaguely. "Got to do some more research before we keep talking."

"This was fun," I admit. "Don't you think?"

"Yeah, it kinda was." He slides off the loveseat and raises

his muscular arms above his head to stretch them out. His T-shirt slides up as he does this, revealing abs of steel.

My jaw drops. "Oh my God. That is so unfair."

"What?" Hunter's dark eyebrows furrow.

"Have you seen your abs? Who the fuck has abs like that?"

His confusion gives way to a smug smile. "I play hockey. Every inch of me looks like that."

Once again, my cheeks feel a bit warm. I'm trying hard not to picture what the rest of him looks like beneath his clothes, but I have a feeling he's not exaggerating. His physique is bonkers.

I notice my phone light up on the nightstand and go over to check it. It's been on silent, and Nico texted twice during the past hour. One message thirty minutes ago, and another just now.

NICO: Hey bb I'm gonna have to bail on sleepover 2nite. Car died after work. Battery probs. Gonna get it towed to the garage in Hastings and pick it up in the a.m. b4 class.
NICO: R u mad

I type a quick reply.

ME: Not mad, babe. Disappointed, tho.

"Everything okay?" Hunter asks as he zips up his hoodie.

I shrug. "My boyfriend canceled on me. He was supposed to stay over tonight but his car battery died. I guess he needs a new one or something."

"Bummer. I'd invite you to play pool with me and the boys tonight, but I need a break from chicks."

"Yes, I imagine all the female attention must be excruciating." I think about the cute girl from yesterday, the one who went out of her way to make him lunch and he totally spurned her. "Come on, I'll walk you downstairs."

But before I can reach the door, Nico calls. "Oh, I need to answer this," I say as we leave the bedroom.

I have no choice, because whenever I miss a call or text from Nico, he has a tendency not to answer when I call or text back, even if it's half a second later. I don't get it. Way too many people do that. How are they not available five seconds after contacting me? I swear, it's like they send a text and then hurl their phones into the river.

"Hey," I say hastily. "What's up?"

"Just wanted to check in," Nico says. "I'm gonna shower soon and then I'll probably crash early."

"Why—oh, right, you need to pick up your car."

"Pick it up?"

"Because you got it towed to the shop…?" I remind him. From the corner of my eye, I notice Hunter curiously listening in. I urge him to walk faster as we descend the stairs.

"Oh no, actually, I got a jump from Steve. He had cables in his truck."

"Wait, so you got the car started?" *Then why can't you drive here*? I want to ask, but force myself not to.

"Yeah, I did. But I don't want to drive it again tonight in case the battery dies again," Nico says as if reading my mind. "I'm gonna get it checked out in the morning. But I'll see you tomorrow night, okay?"

"Sure."

"Love you, *mami*."

"Love you too."

I'm frowning as Hunter and I reach the front door. "The boyfriend?" he prompts.

I nod slowly. "I guess he got his car going with jumper cables, but the battery is still messed up? I'm not sure. I don't know much about cars."

"Sounds a bit shady," remarks Hunter. "Using the ol' car broke down excuse to avoid seeing someone."

"Really?" I challenge. "Do you often lie about your car breaking down to get out of a date?"

"Often? No. Have I done it? Yes."

I glare at him. "Well, not everybody is a liar like you."

He doesn't take offense. Just grins. "Gee. I didn't mean to hit a nerve."

"You didn't."

"Uh-huh. Anyway. My boys are waiting. Later, Semi."

I practically shove him out the front door. Maybe if I get rid of him fast enough, that little seed of doubt he created won't take root.

5
HUNTER

I'M THE FIRST ONE TO ARRIVE FOR THURSDAY AFTERNOON'S team meeting. I never used to be early for these things, but now that I'm team captain I'm trying to lead by example, so here I am, alone in the media room.

The Briar hockey facility is top-of-the-line, so we have a sweet A/V set-up. The large auditorium-style room offers three rows of tables with huge padded chairs, and a massive screen to watch game tape on. We've been studying film on Eastwood College all week. They're our conference rivals, and we're matched up against them for tomorrow's first official game of the season.

I'm not too worried. Eastwood's roster is not particularly strong this year—ours is. Even with Fitzy, Hollis and Nate Rhodes gone, the team still has a solid lineup. Me, Matty, an excellent goalie, and some of the hottest high school players Coach Jensen recruited for the freshman class.

After the team voted me to take over for Nate, our former captain, I called him up asking for tips on how to keep morale up, how to motivate the boys, how to actually *lead*, but he didn't have much advice. He said the dynamics change every year with the ebb and flow of new faces, and that I'd learn as I go along. It's simply a matter of navigating your way through thirty-odd egos, and keeping everybody pumped up and focused on the task at hand: winning.

Speaking of new faces, there are quite a lot of them this season. At the end of August we held open tryouts, an event that serves to showcase players who weren't recruited out of high school or those who try out for the hell of it. One of my new favorite teammates is the result of those tryouts—Conor Edwards, who saunters into the room as I'm settling in a chair in the front row.

Con's a self-proclaimed fuckboy, but he's not as douchey as you'd expect. He's actually quite decent, with a dry sense of humor that I appreciate.

"S'up, captain," he says before yawning hugely. He rakes a lazy hand through his sun-streaked blond hair, drawing my attention to the purple hickey on his neck.

He reminds me of Dean, the older brother of my roommate Summer, and a good friend (and former mentor) of mine. Dean was unapologetically sexual when he attended Briar. He didn't care if everyone knew he was constantly hooking up. And his manwhore ways didn't hurt his reputation either, because every chick who met him wanted to get naked with him. But his girlfriend Allie is the only one to ever steal his heart. They've been living together in NYC for the past couple of years.

Conor sits beside me. A few seniors stride in and settle in the top row. "Yo," they greet us, nodding hello.

We nod back.

Matt Anderson enters next. With Fitz and Hollis gone, I guess Matty's my best friend on the team now. He's the only black player on the roster, drafted by LA last year. I hope he officially signs with them, because it's a great franchise to play for.

"Hey," Matt says.

The room begins to fill up. We've got about two dozen starters, and then the rest of the roster is made up of benchwarmers and guys who still need a lot of development. And although Mike Hollis graduated, there is always, without fail, a Hollis type on every team. The lovable idiot, as Brenna calls him. The honor this year goes to a sophomore named Aaron, except everyone calls him Bucky because he looks like that character from the Marvel movies.

Bucky hates it, but the thing about nicknames is, they stick—whether you want them to or not. Just ask our senior left-winger Treeface, sometimes shortened to Tree or T, who one time four years ago got drunk and lamented how sad it is that trees don't have faces and can't see the birds who make nests on them. I'm pretty sure John Logan is responsible for that nickname.

Munching on a bran muffin he probably grabbed from the team kitchen, Bucky approaches the front row. "Did you talk to Coach about it?" he demands while chewing with his mouth open.

I play dumb. "About what?"

"The pig, dude."

"The pig," echoes Jesse Wilkes, a fellow junior. He was on his phone, but now he's focused on our conversation.

Fuck. I was hoping the subject would quietly be forgotten.

"No, not yet." *And I don't plan on it*, I want to add, but I haven't found a way to finagle out of this one yet.

The guys are insisting we need a team mascot, while I personally don't see the point. I mean, if we were somehow able to strap a pair of skates on a polar bear and have him perform double axels on the ice between periods, then, sure, great. Bring it on.

Short of that, who the fuck cares.

Coach's arrival spares me from humoring my teammates. He strides in and claps his hands sharply. "Let's not waste time," he barks. "Eyes on the screen."

Chad Jensen is a total hard-ass—he doesn't mince words or indulge us. When we're in this arena, we're required to be all business or else GTFO.

"Pay attention to Kriska on this first play," Coach orders as a hi-def video pops up on the projection screen. He's at his desk, using his tablet pen to circle Eastwood's goalie, Johan Kriska.

The freshman is rumored to be one of the best college goalies on the east coast. I've been studying the handful of his high school games that were televised, as well as all of Eastwood's preseason games. I need to be prepared when I face this kid. Not to sound cocky, but I'm the best forward on the team. And the top scorer, for sure, judging by last season's stats lines. Nate and I were tied for goals, but my former captain had me on assists. I guess that's another captainly requirement—*Don't hog the glory*.

I'm slowly compiling a list of captain dos and don'ts.

Despite his stellar rep, I'm not overly concerned about Kriska. I've already found a weakness. "His glove is slow," I pipe up. "Kid has trouble with the high shots. Maybe a thirty percent save rate, if that."

"Yes," Coach confirms. "That's why we've been running those concentrated shooting drills this week. But I'm sure they're prepping just as hard, and Kriska knows his own weaknesses. I want to see a shit ton of low shots on goal tomorrow. He'll already be overcompensating for the weak glove, and he may be so focused on stopping those shots that we'll catch him off guard and push one through the five hole."

"Good point."

We watch more of the tape. Someone whistles when Kriska makes one of the most gorgeous stick saves I've ever seen.

"Look at that," Coach says, pausing the game. "No desperation on his face at all. He's diving back into position to try to deflect the puck after getting completely hammered by those shots, and he's cool as a cucumber."

It is kind of impressive. Goaltenders don't use their sticks to make a save if they can help it. Pads, gloves, even their own bodies, are preferable. A stick save tends to be the result of pure luck, with the goalie scrambling like mad. But with Kriska, it appears effortless.

"We just need to find a way to rattle him," Matt speaks up.

I nod in agreement. I'm feeling confident, though. Last season we were killing it. It wasn't lack of skill that cost us. It was a fluke injury, along with Nate's ejection while defending my honor.

Another rule for the captain's handbook: *defend your boys*.

This year we lost a few good guys to graduation, but we gained a lot more. There's no reason why we shouldn't make it to the Frozen Four, not unless we're waylaid by massive team-wide injuries or do something to royally fuck up our chances.

The meeting wraps up when Coach claps his hands signaling that we can leave. Bucky instantly raises an arm and clears his throat. Loudly. He glances over to shoot me a meaningful look.

Shit.

Coach's head lifts from his laptop. "What's going on?"

"The captain has something to say," Bucky announces.

Jensen's shrewd dark eyes shift toward me. Those eyes are uncannily like Brenna's, complete with the perpetual glint of mocking. Then again, he's her father, so…

"Davenport?" he prompts.

"Uh…" Fuck fuck fuck. I'm about to sound like total moron. But I force myself to stand up and say, "Some of the guys want a pig."

Coach's eyebrows rise to his hairline. It's rare to catch the man off guard, but right now he looks flabbergasted. "A fucking what?"

I swallow a sigh. "A pig."

"A teacup pig," Jesse Wilkes chimes in.

"A fucking what?" Coach repeats.

"Here's the thing," I explain stupidly. "Bucky's sister and brother-in-law just got a pig from a breeder up in Vermont. Not a huge one, but a mini version. Apparently they make great pets? They're like dogs, except they eat and shit more."

"What is happening right now?" Coach shakes his head. "What are you saying to me?"

I take another stab at an explanation. "You know how some teams have mascots? The Darby College Rams have that billy goat that lives in the clubhouse behind their arena. Or the Coyotes down in Providence—they have a dog that's half-wolf and everyone takes turns housing him?"

"Tabasco," exclaims a senior D-man.

"I love that dog," Tree says happily.

"Did you know Tabasco can hump on command?" Bucky says, sounding impressed.

"Big fucking deal," Conor drawls. "I can do that too."

Loud laughter rings out.

Coach holds up his hand to silence everybody. "Are you idiots asking me if you can have a pet?"

"Pretty much." I give him a pleading look. "As the new captain, I've been asked to formally put forth the request."

"A room full of grown men are requesting a pet."

I nod.

"It'll be great for morale," Bucky insists. "Think about it, Coach. We could bring the pig out before games and he'll get the crowd all hyped up. Dude, it'll build so much excitement."

"How does a pig hype up a crowd? Is he going to sing the national anthem?" Coach asks politely.

"Come on, Coach, don't be silly," Con mocks. "Everyone knows pigs can't sing."

"You on board with this, Edwards?" Coach is skeptical. "You're Team Pig?"

Conor flashes a cheerful smile. "I literally could not care less."

"We're *all* on board," Bucky argues.

Coach's sharp gaze conducts a sweep of the room. "Jesus Christ. You dumbasses are serious? You honestly think that between the thirty of you, you can actually keep an animal alive?"

"Hey," Matt protests. "I've got two dogs at home."

"And where is your home?"

"Minneapolis."

"And where are you right now?"

Matt shuts up.

"You're all full-time college students with intensive athletic schedules—and don't even get me started on your social lives—and you think you can take care of a living creature? I call bullshit."

He's done the exact wrong thing. A bunch of competitive hockey players being told they can't do something? Suddenly even the guys that were indifferent to the pig are coming to their own defense.

"I could take care of a pet," objects Joe Foster, a new addition to the forward roster.

"Me too."

"Ditto."

"Yeah, come on, bro, give us a shot."

Coach's jaw tightens and twitches as if he's holding back a sea of expletives. "I'll be right back," he finally says, before stalking out of the room without explanation.

"Holy shit, you think he's going to get a pig?"

I turn toward the moron who asked the question. "Of course not," I sputter at Bucky. "Where the fuck would he find one? Hiding in the equipment closet?" I shake my head mutinously. "You just *had* to make me ask him, eh? Now he thinks we're insane."

"There's nothing insane about wanting the love of a pig."

Jesse hoots. "Guys, I know what to write on Bucky's tombstone."

"Fuck off, Wilkes."

My teammates are still bickering amongst themselves when Coach returns. With purposeful strides, he goes to the center of the media room and holds up an egg, which I assume he grabbed from the team kitchen.

"What's that?" Bucky asks in bewilderment.

Our fearless leader smirks. "This is your pig."

"Coach, I think it's an egg," one of the freshmen says hesitantly.

That earns him a look of disdain. "I know it's an egg, Peters. I'm not a moron. However, until the end of the regular season, this egg is your pig. You want me to sign off on a team pet, which, by the way, involves a shit ton of red tape with the university? Then prove to me that you can keep something alive." He waves the egg in the air. "It's hard-boiled. If it cracks, you killed your precious porker. Bring it back to me in one piece and then we'll talk pigs."

Coach grabs a Sharpie from the desk and scribbles something on the egg.

"What are you doing?" Bucky asks curiously.

"Signing it. And trust me, I know when my signature has been forged. So if this breaks, don't even think about trying to swap it out with another one. If this isn't the egg that comes back to me, then no pig." Coach plants the egg in Bucky's hand. "Congratulations, you have a team mascot."

Bucky catches my eye and gives me a triumphant thumbs-up.

If this is what being team captain is all about, I don't know if I really want the job.

6
HUNTER

WE'RE ABSOLUTELY WIPING THE ICE WITH EASTWOOD College on Friday night, and it has nothing to do with Kriska's weak glove. We're simply on fire and they are not. Kriska stops shot after shot, but five—count 'em, five— light up the lamp. I'd like to say I contributed more than one, but the hockey gods decided to spread the wealth. The first goal was mine, but the next four went to various teammates.

I don't know what happened to Eastwood's defense, but the D-men didn't show up to play tonight. Kriska is all alone in the net batting off pucks like Neo dodging bullets in *The Matrix*. Any time a Briar player gets a breakaway, the goalie's face turns snow white behind his mask, because he knows he's in trouble. The Eastwood D-men are either scrambling to keep up with us, or tangled up in the corners providing endless rebound opportunities for Briar.

Our fans scream their approval. This is a home game, so our school colors, black and silver, make up a massive expanse of the stands. Damn, it feels good to be back, to be breathing the crisp air in the arena. The chill tickling the back of my neck only heightens the adrenaline coursing in my blood.

I'm on the bench. Two minutes left in the third period, but there's no way Eastwood is scoring five goals in two minutes. I glance over. Con's beside me. We're on the same line this year, along with Matt, and the three of us are a forced to be reckoned with. This line is going to take us all the way to the finals.

"Je-sus, that was a crazy crosscheck," I praise him.

We're both out of breath. Our last shift was a penalty kill, during which Conor landed a bone-jarring hit on an Eastwood forward.

"Dude, my ears are still ringing from it." His grin gives off a toothy, wolfish vibe thanks to the mouth guard half dangling from his mouth.

"We needed you last season," I admit. "We didn't have a lot of goons." Meanwhile, our biggest rival Harvard had the goon of all goons, Brooks Weston.

But Conor only transferred this year from a college on the West Coast. He's a California boy, with his surfer hair and laidback attitude. Yet there's nothing laidback about him when he's smashing other dudes into the boards.

Coach keeps us on the bench as the clock ticks down, letting our third and fourth lines enjoy the action. We're in no danger of losing the game, and the extra ice time helps to develop them as players. The boys manage to hold Eastwood, and our first game ends in a shutout.

Everyone's in a celebratory mood as we file into the locker room to shower and change. Arrangements are made to go to Malone's, the bar in Hastings where the hockey crowd usually gathers.

"You in?" I ask Bucky.

"Yeah. Just gimme a couple minutes. Gotta make sure Pablo gets his dinner."

I choke back laughter.

On the top shelf of Bucky's locker, the team mascot is tucked away in its brand new coral-pink drink cozy. With the utmost care, Bucky reaches for Pablo Eggscobar.

Jesse, who's wandering by in a towel, spots the egg in Bucky's hand. "What the hell, man! Can't you see Pablo's hungry?"

"*Feed me,*" a singsong voice drifts from across the room, courtesy of Velky, our international student from Sweden.

In the day and a half since Pablo joined us, things have taken an evil turn. A few of the guys decided to be dicks about it and fuck with Bucky, texting him at random times throughout the day and night from the egg's point of view. Usually in all caps. Messages along the lines of: FEED ME! PET ME! LET ME OUT TO TAKE A DUMP!

However, like my friend Mike Hollis, Bucky is rubber and we're glue, and nothing anyone says or does ever bothers him. The fucker decided that sticking to a care schedule actually makes sense. Then he discussed it with Coach, and now we're all sworn by the honor system to treat Pablo like a real pig. Reasoning being that if we don't, then any time he's in our custody we'd toss him in a drawer and forget about him.

Bucky's the only one treating it seriously. The rest of us are just excited to mess with each other.

"Here, Pablo, eat your dinner," Bucky tells the egg.

The egg says nothing because it's a goddamn egg.

"I feel like I've traveled back in time to pre-school," Matt remarks. He shakes his head. "I'm not pandering to an egg, dude."

"Aw, well, that's too bad," Bucky answers smugly. "'Cause tonight's your turn with him."

"No, it's not. It's Conor's," Matty protests.

"Nope. Refer to the schedule." Bucky did a random draw this morning to determine who has custody of the egg and when. My turn is next week.

"This is fucking balls." Matt grabs the plush egg container from Bucky. "Swear to God, I'mma get wasted tonight and eat this motherfuckin' thing."

I'm chuckling as I leave the locker room, with Matt and Bucky in tow. Conor and the others are already gone. We meet up with them again at Malone's, my favorite place in town. Mostly due to its roomy booths, cheap beer, and sports memorabilia all over the walls, which at the moment are shaking from the classic rock song blasting through the bar.

Matt says something, but the loud chatter and blaring music drowns him out. He switches to sign language, nodding toward the bar and making a drinking motion with his hand, signaling he's going over there to order.

My gaze gives the main room a quick sweep, but doesn't land on anyone familiar. I weave through the crowd toward the arched doorway to the adjoining room, which houses the pool tables and some more booths along the wall. I spot a blonde head and then a brunette one. The Betty and Veronica of Briar University.

"There's Brenna and Summer in the middle booth." I raise my voice so Bucky can hear me.

His brown eyes glaze over. "Fuuuuck. She's so hot."

"Who? Brenna? Or Summer?"

"Well, both. But I was talking about Summer. That top she's wearing is...*fuuuuck*," he says again.

Yeah, her skimpy yellow halter top is hot, I have to acknowledge as we near the booth. But I'm gratified that the sight of Summer Di Laurentis no longer elicits a sexual response from me. Even celibate, I don't particularly want to sleep with her.

I had a thing for Summer when she first transferred to Briar, but unfortunately she had a thing for Fitz. And while I still believe my friend was shady in the way he handled the situation, I'm one hundred percent over Summer. She and Fitzy are happy together, and the more time I spend with her living in the same house, the more I realize she's not my type.

Summer's too easy, and I don't mean slutty. She's just not much of a challenge. She's easy to please, easy to figure out. Her transparency was initially why I liked her, but I can't deny it's more fun when a woman poses a bit more of a mystery.

Not that I'm solving any female mysteries any time soon. No sex means limiting my exposure to women, because I know myself. The more time I spend with someone, the more I want to fuck them. My roommates are the exception. And as of Monday, so is Demi Davis. My new classmate is fun to talk to, but the best thing about her is her boyfriend.

Brenna bolts out of the booth when she spots me. "Hunter! Jesus, what a game!"

"I know, right?"

"You superstar, you." She flings her arms around me, which is way more touchy-feely than Brenna usually is. But then I see the two shot glasses on the tabletop. Ah. She and Summer already started hitting the vodka.

"Seriously, I was on my feet the entire time cheering my lungs out," Brenna raves, and I know it's not just drunken praise. Brenna Jensen is probably the biggest hockey fan (and expert) in this entire bar. She's definitely her father's daughter, even landing an internship at ESPN. She works there on weekends, and afternoons when she doesn't have class.

"That was the ass kicking of the century," Summer agrees. "I wish Fitzy got to see it, but I was live-tweeting the entire time, so he can read the thread later."

I sit next to Brenna. Bucky slides in next to Summer. A minute later Matt reappears with a pitcher and a stack of plastic cups. Malone's has a new Friday night special—half-price pitchers, baby. I don't plan on going overboard tonight, because we have another game tomorrow. But a few beers won't hurt.

"Where's the nutty one?" Matt asks the girls.

"Who? Rupi?" Brenna snickers. "She's at home watching *Glee* reruns."

"Why didn't she come out?"

"She doesn't have a fake ID," I supply. "And she refuses to get one."

Summer speaks up, mimicking Rupi's high voice so flawlessly it's almost like she's in the booth with us. "I can't *break* the *law!* I will wait until I am of *age*, thank you very much!"

Brenna lets out a rueful sigh. "I honestly don't know how Hollis puts up with her. And vice versa."

"For real," Summer agrees. "All they do is scream at each other."

"Or make out," I counter.

"True. They scream or they make out." Summer shakes her head. "There's no in between."

"Is he still coming back on the weekends?" Matt asks, raising his beer to his lips. He takes a sip. "I haven't seen him in ages."

"He's home every weekend," I confirm. "But he spends most of his time with Rupi. Hollis in love is a scary thing to witness, bro. You need to come over this weekend and see it for yourself."

Bucky sets Pablo on the table so he can pour himself a beer. When Summer reaches for the egg, he swiftly smacks her hand away. "Pablo isn't a toy," he scolds.

"It's just an egg."

"*Just* an egg?" Conor drawls, approaching the booth to catch the end of Summer's amused response. "That's our fucking mascot, Di Laurentis. Show some respect."

"Oh, I'm sorry! I didn't mean to insult your *egg*."

He grins, and even Summer can't deny him a response. Her cheeks pinken, and Con's grin widens. Dude's well aware of what his smile does to women. He's probably been harnessing that power since grade school, like one of the X-Men.

But although Summer isn't entirely unaffected, she's still very much unavailable. "Stop smiling at me like that or I'll tell Fitz." She sticks out her tongue. "Then he'll show up at practice and kick your ass."

"I'm not allowed to smile at you? All right, then. How 'bout dancing? Can we dance?"

Summer ponders that. "Sure, that's allowed. But only because I like this song." It's some Taylor Swift track I don't know too well.

She hops up and drags Conor toward the cluster of people gathered near the small stage that's hardly ever used. I don't think I've ever seen a live band grace the stage at Malone's, but the tiny space in front of it is the closest to a dance floor that the bar has.

Brenna's eyes track Conor's easy gait. And his ass. "Geez, that boy is attractive."

"Don't you have a boyfriend?" Matt reminds her.

"So? I'm not allowed to acknowledge someone else is attractive? Come on. *Look* at him."

Matt, Bucky and I turn to scrutinize our teammate. He's got one hand on Summer's slim waist, the other holding his beer as they dance. When he leans in to whisper something in her ear, his gray eyes twinkle devilishly.

I mean, I'm not going to lie. Edwards is hot. We all know it.

"Ugh. Now I feel left out," Brenna whines, and the next thing I know she's shoving me out of the booth and tugging me to my feet. "Come on, hot stuff, dance with me."

Before I can blink, we're across the room and Brenna is squished up against me. And her body is so fire that I forget how to breathe. Skintight jeans are plastered to her long, shapely legs, her dark hair is thick and glossy, and her top is even more indecent than Summer's. So tight it looks like her full tits are trying to escape.

I don't want to touch her. I'm scared that if I do, that if my hands connect with a hint of bare skin or the slightest female curve, I might embarrass myself.

"What's the matter?" Brenna says. "You forget how to move?"

I offer a self-deprecating smile. "Trust me, you don't want me to move."

"Why's that…?" Understanding suddenly dawns. "Ohhh. Because you're out of commission." She purses her lips. "Are you scared that if our bodies touch, you'll get aroused?"

"I already am aroused," I grumble. "*Everything* gets me aroused, Bee. The feel of the wind on my face gets me aroused. Bumping into a table gets me aroused."

She throws her head back and laughs. "Oh, you really are in a state, aren't you?"

I groan. "The worst kind."

"You poor thing." She grabs my hands and plants them on her hips, then loops her arms around my neck.

And yup, my dick cannot distinguish between a girl with a boyfriend and one without. It promptly thickens behind my zipper.

"Fucking hell, Jensen, let's not do this. Please."

"Aw, come on. What's a boner between friends?" She starts moving to the upbeat T-Swift song, except three seconds later it ends and is replaced with that old T.I. track— "Whatever You Like." The one that's all about fucking, with a sultry beat that is way too dangerous for my aching nether regions.

"My boner doesn't understand that you're off-limits," I mutter.

"Can I tell you a secret?" Brenna says, and I almost pass out when she brings her red lips to my ear and seductively whispers in it. "Jake and I have an open relationship."

Immediately, my throat goes dry. "W-what?" I stammer hoarsely.

"I'm just saying…" Her hips sway. "If you ever want to break your vow…"

A bolt of heat shoots up my spine. "What the hell are you saying?"

"You know exactly what I'm saying."

She draws tiny circles on my nape with her fingernails. Meanwhile, T.I. is singing about things being wet and hot and tight and I'm in big trouble.

"Why don't we go home?" she suggests, wrapping her arms tighter around my neck. Our bodies are almost flush now. Her sexy voice is still tickling my ear. "We'll be really, really quiet. Rupi won't hear a thing."

My mouth is sawdust. From the corner of my eye, I catch Summer giving us an odd look. I've given up on dancing because my dick is way too hard. "Are you serious right now?" I demand. Because I don't buy it.

And I'm right not to.

"Oh my God, Hunter. Of *course* I'm not serious." Mischief gleams in her expression.

"So you and Connelly don't have an open relationship?"

"No!"

I stare at her. "What if I'd said yes? What if I'd kissed you?"

"Then Jake would catch the next redeye from Edmonton and your body would probably never be found."

"You're such a bitch," I sigh.

"Sorry." She's still laughing, but she has the decency to sound somewhat repentant. "I couldn't help myself. This celibacy thing of yours is fascinating. But…dude, if you're so hard up that you were actually considering hooking up with *me*? Then I don't know how you're ever gonna survive this."

Me neither.

"Whatever, c'mere," I grumble, tugging her against me. "Let's just dance."

"You sure?"

I nod miserably. "Yeah, why not. What's a boner between friends, right?"

7
DEMI

I follow Nico into the busy bar. We're meeting some friends at Malone's, which is the only bar in Hastings.

Nico and I don't come here often; if we're hanging out in town, we usually invite people to Nico's apartment and chill there. But my boyfriend was in the mood to go out tonight, and I wasn't about to complain. Malone's makes the *best* nachos in town. And the best chicken wings. The best burgers. The best—ugh, okay, the entire menu is stellar.

"Do you see Pippa?" I stand on my tiptoes and scan the crowded main room. "She texted that they're in a booth near the—oh, there she is."

Nico follows my gaze. "Who's she with?"

"Looks like Corinne and Darius and—oh wow, TJ actually showed up." I invited him to join us, but I hadn't expected him to come, because TJ's not particularly social. When we go for lunch or to the movies, it tends to be just the two of us. He's not big on crowds or groups.

Nico makes a face at the mention of TJ.

"Be nice," I chide.

"He's a *pendejo*, Demi." My boyfriend always reverts to Spanish when he's dissing someone.

"He is not. He's my friend."

"Friend? C'mon, babe, he's in love with you."

It's not the first time Nico's voiced that sentiment, but I don't believe it to be true. "He's not in love with me."

"Oh really? Then why's he always staring at you with moon eyes?"

"You're imagining it." I shrug. "And even if he *is* in love with me—so what? We both know who *I'm* in love with."

"Damn right we do." Nico curls a hand over the back of my head and pulls me in for a kiss.

To my surprise, he slips me some tongue and the next thing I know we're engaged in a mini make-out session in the middle of the bar. It draws catcalls from a group of guys in hockey jerseys, and I'm blushing as I pull back.

"What was that for?" I smile at my boyfriend.

"Just for being you." Nico takes my hand and brings it up to his lips. Like the Latin heartthrob he is, he brushes a kiss over my knuckles.

He's being extra sweet tonight, and in all honesty I love it. He turned down my sex advances last weekend because he was too tired, and then he bailed on me this week because of his car. I deserve to be spoiled a bit.

"Go join the group. I'll grab us some drinks," Nico offers before heading for the ridiculously long line at the bar.

As I walk toward my friends' booth, I glimpse a familiar face through the doorway that separates the main room with the adjoining one.

Hunter Davenport is dancing with a stunning brunette in a tight tank and blood-red lipstick. He's whispering in her ear. When he lifts his head to look at her, I don't miss the ruddy flush of his cheekbones and his heavy-lidded eyes. Uh-huh. Someone's getting laid tonight.

I wonder how his lunch girl feels about that…

The idea of dating multiple people sounds like a nightmare to me. Although, what sounds even worse is being the girl who is *dating* the guy who's dating multiple people. I'm a possessive bitch, thank you very much. My man's not allowed to see other women when he's with me. And if I ever do wind up having to date again, I'd stake my claim immediately and make sure to have the exclusivity talk before the dude is even allowed to hold my hand.

Like my mom always says, know your worth. Make them work for it.

But to each their own. Hunter clearly has a lot of luck with the ladies. The girl he's dancing with laughs at whatever he just said, and as he shakes his head in amusement, he catches sight of me in the doorway. He dips his chin in greeting.

I blow him a kiss. He grins and refocuses on his date, while I join my friends.

"Demi!" Pippa squeals, jumping out of the booth to throw her arms around me.

"Heya, chica." Pippa is my best friend at Briar. We met at freshman orientation, discovered we both grew up in Florida, and were instantly inseparable.

"Hey," our friend Corinne greets me. "I *love* that skirt."

"Thanks, it's like a million years old." I smooth my hands over the front of my distressed denim skirt. It's autumn, and

I'm still wearing short skirts and tank tops. I don't know whether to hate or love global warming.

I lean into the booth to smack a kiss on TJ's cheek. "I can't believe you're here," I tell him. "I'm so glad you came."

He blushes slightly and takes a huge gulp of his beer. Beside him is Darius Johnson, a good friend of mine and Nico's.

"Hi, D," I say.

"Hi, D," he mimics, and we both grin. When we first met, there was a bit of competition about who'd get to keep the nickname, but in the end we decided to share it.

"Where's the rest of the crew?" I ask. Wherever Darius is, there's usually at least three other basketball players not far behind. But they're nowhere to be found tonight.

"Briar won the hockey game," Darius explains. "They didn't want to deal with all the hockey fans. Those guys are nuts."

As if to prove that point, a trio of dudes choose that moment to drunkenly lumber past our booth screaming, "Bri-ar! Bri-ar!" One of them is waving his black-and-silver jersey in the air, which means he's stumbling through the bar shirtless. Classy.

Nico returns with a pink daiquiri for me, and a bottle of beer for himself. It's a Cuban brand that you can rarely find in the States and yet somehow Malone's actually serves it. It makes me smile, because I'm pretty sure my mom is the one who introduced Nico to that beer. I remember she let him taste hers at my fifteenth birthday party. He's been drinking it exclusively ever since.

"What have you been up to this week?" I ask Corinne as

I slide in across from her. "You never answered my text about unpacking. Did you still want help?"

"I know, I'm sorry. I was dealing with furniture shit. Moving is the worst," she complains.

Corinne just moved into a one-bedroom apartment in Hastings, only a few blocks from Malone's, in fact. It's rare to find housing in town, but Corinne knew the previous tenant, a fellow Econ major at Briar who abruptly decided to drop out. Corinne had an application in with the landlord of the small building before anyone else even knew the apartment was available.

"Moving isn't *that* bad," Nico teases her. "I mean, especially when you have three strapping young men helping you out." He wiggles his eyebrows.

I snort. Nico and two of his co-workers from the moving company helped Corinne last Sunday, hauling all her boxes and furniture from the house she used to share with five other girls.

"Did the strapping young men take off their shirts and flex their muscles for you?" I ask a blushing Corinne.

She bursts out laughing. "I wish. All they did was drink my beer and get my new carpet all dirty from their boot prints."

"She's lying!" Nico declares good-naturedly. "We wore booties over our shoes."

"And to answer your question," she says to me, running a hand through her mop of dark curls, "yes. I totally need help organizing everything. Maybe one night this week?"

"Sure. Just let me know when." I met Corinne through Pippa, and although we've never been as close, I like hanging out with her. She's a bit guarded, but when she relaxes she's actually pretty hilarious.

Nico takes a swig of beer before setting down the bottle and slinging his arm around me. He's so handsy tonight. He leans in and plants soft kisses on my neck until Pippa releases a loud groan.

"Come on, guys, enough with the PDA. You *just* got here. At this rate you'll be banging on the table by the end of the night."

"Sounds hot," Nico says, winking at me.

Lord, he is so good-looking. Originally from Cuba, Nico and his family came to Miami when Nico was eight. They moved in next door, and all it took was one look at Nico's soulful eyes and big dimples, and eight-year-old Demi was in love. Luckily, he felt the same way about me.

We talk about our classes for a bit, but I don't contribute much to the conversation. Truth be told, I hate all my courses this semester, except for Psych. Today in Organic Chemistry, we discussed organometallic compounds in such detail that my brain almost melted. I didn't mind my science classes in high school, but since I started college I'm slowly beginning to hate the sciences.

As I sip my drink, I absently listen to Nico and Darius chat about the basketball team. D is trying to convince Nico to be their equipment manager because their current one just bailed, but Nico's too busy with his work and class schedule. TJ remains quiet for most of the conversation, only speaking when I draw him out of his shell.

I don't care what Nico says. TJ's a sweetie. He's such a great listener, and he usually dispenses really solid advice. I wish he'd find a girlfriend, but he's so shy and it's hard for him to open up. I tried setting him up with one of my sorority sisters once, and she said he barely spoke a single word during their entire date.

"I'll be your equipment manager," Pippa tells D. "But only if I get to watch you guys shower. I feel like that's a reasonable requirement for—oh my God." She stops midsentence, gaping at the tall guy who saunters past our booth. "Forget it. I want to watch *him* shower."

I only manage to catch a glimpse before he passes. Shoulder-length blond hair, a red T-shirt. I twist around but can't see his face. His body is banging, though.

"Eyes up here," Nico chides, lifting two fingers up to his face.

I grin. "Oh, come on. Look at his butt. It's something else."

My boyfriend peeks out the booth just as the guy disappears through the corridor to the restrooms. "It's a'ight," he relents. "But that doesn't mean you're allowed to check him out."

"What are you gonna do, spank me?"

His chocolate-brown eyes narrow seductively. "Don't tempt me, *mami*."

Corinne gives a slight cough, while Pippa and Darius sigh dramatically.

"Sorry," I tell everyone. "We'll be good now, I swear."

"I don't want to be good," Pippa announces. "I want to be bad with that hottie. Who *was* that?"

TJ speaks up. "Hockey player, I think. He came from the hockey booth, at least."

"The hockey booth?" she echoes.

He nods toward the other room, where Hunter Davenport and his friends are piled into two huge booths. All I see are gorgeous girls, big athlete types, and a lot of food.

Speaking of food…

"Who wants nachos?" I ask as I grab the menu in front of Darius. "I'm ordering some for me, but I'm also thinking— ooh, there's a new app on here. Deep-fried spinach and mozzarella balls. Oh my fuck, yes. I'm in. I'll get an order of those, and then we're looking at the nachos, and maybe…the boneless wings?"

"Who is she even talking to?" Pippa asks my boyfriend.

He sighs. "Just let it happen, Pips. You know the drill."

I peer up from the menu. "Am I being judged right now?"

"Yes," Pippa tells me.

"One hundred percent, yes," Darius concurs.

"How do you eat so much and never gain weight?" Corinne demands.

"I'd never judge you," TJ assures me, grinning mischievously.

"*Thank* you, Thomas Joseph. The rest of you, guess what? You don't get to taste my spinach balls. You can sit here in envy while—"

"He's coming back," hisses Pippa.

Sure enough, the hockey player in the red shirt strides by again. This time I do see his face, and promptly understand why Pippa is drooling all over the table. He's got vivid gray eyes, and a beautiful smile that curves his mouth when he catches Pippa's gaze on him. He keeps walking, though.

"Oh my," I murmur, and Nico pokes me in the ribs.

"Definitely a hockey guy," TJ confirms with a nod. "But I can't remember his name."

"Hold on, I'll find out." I slide my phone out of my purse.

"What do you mean, you'll find out?" Pippa squawks.

I pull up Hunter's name in my contacts list. We exchanged numbers at my house on Monday night.

ME: Hey, hockey man. Who's the dude in the red t-shirt with the fuck-me face and tight ass?

Although I crane my neck toward the other room, I can't pick out Hunter amidst the sea of jocks. But on my phone screen three gray bubbles pop up to indicate a response is being typed.

"Who are you texting?" Nico demands.

"Hunter Davenport."

TJ looks up sharply. "You're texting Davenport?"

"Yeah, we're working on that project, remember? I have his number."

"Who's Hunter Davenport?" Corinne asks.

"Just a hockey player who thinks he's God's gift to the world," TJ tells her, smiling wryly.

"You don't even know him," I tease.

"I had a tutorial with him last year, remember? He treated the library like his own personal motel?"

I don't answer because Hunter's message just appeared.

HUNTER: Conor Edwards. Right-winger, #62. Why? You want his number?? Are we cheating on the boyfriend??? Tsk tsk.

Nobody's cheating on anyone, I type back, and when I sense Nico reading over my shoulder, I hammer the point home by adding, I love my boyfriend very VERY much.

Nico relaxes and drops a kiss atop my head.

ME: A friend of mine is eyeing him. Is he single?
HUNTER: Ya but I think he's already picked his flavor for the night. I'll come over and introduce them if you want?

I glance at Pippa. "You want an intro?"

Her jaw falls open again. "What! *No.* He's way too good-looking."

"You sure?" I wave my phone enticingly at her. "I got you an in."

"Am I *sure*? I've got a zit on my forehead and haven't washed my hair in four days, because I wasn't planning on meeting *Adonis* tonight. Come on, Demi, what the fuck is wrong with you?"

I snicker and text Hunter back.

ME: Maybe another night.

He responds with, Okey dokey, and the gray dots disappear.

"Coward," I tease Pippa.

"Whatever. You can't throw something like that on me at the last second. I'm not mentally prepared to hook up tonight."

I hadn't realized mental preparation was required for

casual hook-ups, but I suppose I'm clueless when it comes to modern dating. And I'm perfectly okay with that. Look at what's happening around me—Hunter juggling different girls, Pippa squirming nervously at the notion of being introduced to a hot guy. Dating seems insanely stressful.

Relationships, meanwhile, are nice and secure. The world of relationships is where I belong.

I link my fingers through Nico's and thank my lucky stars that I'm not part of that other, terrifying world.

8
DEMI

NICO WALKS ME TO CLASS ON MONDAY MORNING. HE'D spent the night, and I feel like we're back on track again as we stroll hand-in-hand down one of the many walkways that weave through Briar. Although the weather hasn't turned yet, the colors on campus are slowly beginning to change. I admire the massive trees that line the paths and dot the lawns, marveling at how pretty and quaint everything is. Sometimes it feels surreal. I lived in Miami until I was fifteen years old, so I'm accustomed to palm trees and colorful beach houses, not stately oaks and ancient buildings.

I remember putting up a huge stink when I found out we were moving to Massachusetts. My father had been offered a position at a prestigious hospital in Boston. Head of neurosurgery. Which is a HUGE DEAL. But I was a bratty, entitled teenager, and therefore I wasn't having it.

Dad, however, doesn't tolerate temper tantrums. Or rather, he lets me stomp and yell and bitch…and then offers a wry smile and pleasantly asks, *Are you done?* Because we all know he's going to get his way at the end of the day. He does the same thing with my mother. Mom personifies the stereotype of feisty Latina, complete with a generations-old family hot sauce recipe and a temper that's even more explosive than mine. But even Mom can't win against my father.

After my family moved to Boston, Nico and I endured three years of long distance, summers and holidays. And after graduation, I got into Briar and prayed to the lord above that Nico would too. I was secretly worried for a while there. He's not stupid, but Briar is a highly competitive Ivy League school, and Nico didn't have a basketball scholarship or any impressive extra-curriculars to bring to the table. He got good grades, but he wasn't the valedictorian of his class.

In the end, I think it was his admissions essay that won over the board. He wrote about his arduous journey from Cuba to America. Nico's father Joaquín had arrived in Miami ahead of his wife and son to work and get settled. Joaquín couldn't afford a flight to bring the family over, so Nico and his mom ended up traveling by boat. Which sank. No joke. They were adrift on a life raft for two days before a fishing vessel found them and brought them to safety. Eventually they became citizens, and Nico's sister Alicia was born in Florida.

His pride for this country definitely shone through in his essay. I proofed it for him. And when he received his admissions letter from Briar, I breathed a huge sigh of relief.

As we near the Faculty of Sciences building, I spot a familiar figure—Hunter, and he's with a stunning blonde.

With the temperature in the mid-eighties today, Hunter's companion is in a crop top and a filmy white skirt, her golden hair up in a topknot. She's as pretty if not more so than the brunette he was grinding up against the other night, as well as the cute girl who made him lunch. Lord. Mr. Popular only gets more popular.

I have no idea how he keeps track of all these chicks—three different ones in a week? I mean, good on him, but boy does it seem exhausting.

I lift my hand in a wave. Hunter waves back before saying something to the blonde.

"That's the hockey guy," I tell Nico. "Hunter."

Nico follows my gaze. "He does look very jocky."

I feel my pocket vibrate, and slide my phone out to read the incoming text.

TJ: Already inside. See u when u get here.

"Do you want to meet for lunch later?" Nico asks.

"Sure. Can we go to the dining hall in the Drama building? Pippa says they just started serving tacos."

He sighs.

"Did you hear me, babe? Tacos!" I don't understand why I'm the only one excited about this.

As we finalize our lunch plans, Hunter wanders over to us. "Morning," he says easily.

"Morning," I echo, before gesturing to Nico. "This is my boyfriend Nico. Nico, Hunter."

"Hey, man, how's it hanging?" Hunter sticks out a hand.

Nico gives it a hearty shake, his dimples digging a groove into his cheeks as he smiles warmly. "S'all good. I hear you're working on a project with this one—" He jerks a thumb at me. "Good luck, bruh."

"Uh oh. Please elaborate."

"Mess up even once, and the tongue-lashing you'll get…" Nico mock shudders, and Hunter snorts with laughter.

"She's a real nightmare, eh?"

"Seriously?" I demand. "You two are ganging up on me? That's not allowed."

They ignore me. "Any tips on how to handle her?" Hunter asks solemnly.

Nico thinks for a moment. "Give her a lollipop when she's cranky. All other times, just feed her, or plant her in front of a TV and put on a murder mystery."

Hunter nods. "Got it. Thanks."

"Screw you both," I say cheerfully.

Grinning, Nico gives me a peck on the lips. "A'ight, I got to go. I'll see you later, *mami*."

"Bye, babe."

"Doesn't *mami* mean *mother*?" Hunter inquires after Nico leaves. He furrows his brow.

"Well, yeah, that's the literal translation, but it's also a term of endearment. Mami, papi—it's like babe or sweetheart or whatever."

"Huh. Okay." Hunter pauses. "I give you permission to start calling me Big Daddy, then."

"Gross. Never."

He's chuckling as we enter the building. TJ waits at the door of the classroom, uneasiness flickering through his eyes when he sees me with Hunter.

"Hey. Where's Pax?" I ask, glancing around.

"No idea." TJ gives me a side hug and a peck on the cheek.

"Let's go in," I say.

Inside the lecture hall, TJ takes the seat beside me, while Hunter flops down on my other side. TJ raises a brow at the intrusion. We don't usually sit with other people. I just shrug and grin at him. I find Hunter amusing.

The room fills up and Professor Andrews arrives. Pax is still nowhere to be seen.

"Did Pax text you?" I ask TJ.

"Nope."

"Who's this Pax?" Hunter butts into the conversation.

"He's a friend of ours," I answer. "You talked to him last week—you called him Jax?"

"Oh, right. Jax. That little dude is hilarious."

"His name's Pax," I say in exasperation.

"Pax," TJ confirms.

Hunter chews on his bottom lip for a moment. "Are you sure?"

"Yes!" I can't control a burst of laughter. "His name is Pax Ling."

"Nah, I'm pretty sure he told me it was Jax. We must be talking about different dudes."

This guy's unreal.

TJ gives a soft snicker. Apparently even he isn't immune to Hunter's weird appeal.

Andrews commences the morning's lecture, which is an overview of personality disorders. Excellent. I'm happy we're starting off with PDs. I'm still trying to diagnose my fictional patient, and based on the notes I made during our first session I suspect I'm dealing with a personality issue.

He could be a sociopath, but the characteristic apathy was missing. Antisocial or narcissistic personality disorders are still on the table, and maybe borderline too, although Hunter hadn't described any mood swings or impulsive behavior, unless you count adultery. But his fake cheating came off as incredibly calculated and not at all impulsive. Hopefully he gives me more to work with in our next session.

Halfway through class, my phone vibrates.

PAX: Partied too hard last night and overslept. Take notes for me!

My nosy seatmate Hunter peers over my shoulder. "Is that Jax?"

"No, it's Pax."

"Agree to disagree."

I fight a smile and turn my attention back to Professor Andrews. She's discussing a case involving antisocial personality disorder she once encountered and how she reached the diagnosis. I'm obsessed with this course.

After class, TJ links an arm through mine and says, "Want to grab a quick coffee?"

"Actually"—I glance at Hunter—"maybe we could work on the project for a bit? I'm not meeting Nico till one thirty."

He shrugs. "Sure, let's do it. I'm done for the day."

"Rain check on that coffee," I assure TJ, giving his arm a squeeze.

"No prob. Text me later."

As TJ ambles off, Hunter stares after him, shaking his head ruefully. "Poor guy."

"What does that mean?"

"It means, poor guy. He's got a major crush on you, but

he's so deep in the friend zone it'd take the same rescue team that dug out the Chilean miners to save him. And even then I think they'd fail."

"He doesn't have a crush on me," I insist. What is everyone seeing that I'm not? "I've had a boyfriend for as long as I've known him."

"So? I've had crushes on lots of chicks with boyfriends. My dick doesn't discriminate."

"Yeah, I've noticed," I say dryly.

"What does that mean?" he mimics.

"It means in the one measly week I've known you, you already hooked up with three different women. Congrats, your penis must be extremely pleased."

"Oh, trust me, my penis is nowhere close to pleased." He runs a hand through his dark hair. "You want to go to your house?"

"Why don't we find a nice spot on the quad?" I suggest. "It's such a gorgeous day."

"Lead the way, Semi."

We follow the wide stone path toward one of the many manicured lawns that make up Briar's campus. We're not the only ones taking advantage of the warm weather. There are several picnics in progress, a soccer ball being kicked around, and a game of Frisbee being played in the distance.

We stop underneath a towering tree, its branches drooping over one side like a waterfall. It provides a small pocket of shade, broken up by rays of sunlight that slice through the gaps in the branches. Normally I'd plop right down on the grass, but my short skirt is a shade of beige that won't hide any potential grass stains.

I peer down at the ground. Well, this is a dilemma.

"Hold up there, girly girl." To my surprise, big tough Hockey Man strips out of his long-sleeved shirt, leaving himself in a tight wife-beater. He stretches the thin material of his shirt out on the grass. "My lady," he says graciously.

"Aw, thanks. That was surprisingly nice of you." I sit down, then lean back on my elbows and tip my head to gaze at the canopy of green above me.

"Why surprisingly?" Hunter demands.

"You didn't strike me as the chivalrous type."

"So you thought I was an asshole? Also, why do you think I'm hooking up with three chicks?" He sounds genuinely confused.

"Oh come on, don't play dumb." I proceed to tick them off with my fingers. "The girl who brought you lunch last week and practically begged you to love her. The one you were dancing with at Malone's. The one today, with the blonde hair and supermodel face…?"

Hunter starts to laugh. It's a deep husky sound that tickles my ears. "I'm not hooking up with any of them. They're my roommates."

"Your roommates?" I echo doubtfully.

"Yeah. The loud one is dating one of my friends, the blonde is dating another one of my friends, and the brunette from the bar has a boyfriend. And I live with all three of them."

"You live with three women?"

"Originally it was me, Hollis and Fitz, but they both graduated and somehow it was decided that Summer, Rupi, and Brenna would move in. No house meeting, no discussion, nothing. Nobody even asked for my opinion. Not that I'm complaining."

"You *are* complaining."

Hunter grumbles irritably. "Fine, I'm complaining. The girls are great, but I would've liked it if some of my other teammates had moved in instead. But this arrangement is more convenient for Hollis and Fitz. Hollis comes home on the weekends, and Fitz technically still lives there, but he's out of town for work a lot. Anyway, the moral of the story is—my dick hasn't been inside any of them."

"Well, I'm sure you get lots of action regardless."

"Nope."

"Yeah right." I twist my head toward him. "Have you *seen* yourself?"

He breaks out in a cocky grin. "Was that a compliment?"

"It was a statement of fact—you're hot. I know it, you know it, everyone on this lawn knows it." I nod pointedly at a group of girls sitting not too far away. Nearly every other second, one of them tosses a covetous glance in our direction.

"So, what, good-looking people *must* be having sex at all times?" Hunter challenges.

I snort. "You play hockey and you're attractive. Please don't tell me you're not having sex. I'm not an idiot."

"I'm not having sex."

He sounds dead serious, and I falter for a second. Then it dawns on me. "*Oh.* We've already started the session. Why didn't you tell me? I should be taking notes!"

A laugh pops out of his mouth. "We haven't started the session. I'm being serious. I'm celibate."

"Celibate?"

"Practicing abstinence," he clarifies.

"I know what celibacy is, Hunter. I just don't believe you."

"It's true."

"Liar."

"Honest to God truth."

"Prove it."

"*How?*" Hunter falls back on his elbows, his ripped body shaking with laughter.

I'm about to glare at him for laughing at me when I realize what an impossible demand it was. He can't prove anything, short of whipping out his dick and having sex with one of those girls over there.

"Okay," I muse. "I'll play along. Why are we celibate?"

"*We* are celibate because we need to focus on the hockey season."

"You can't focus on hockey and have orgasms at the same time?"

"Apparently not."

"Now I'm curious."

He offers a shrug. "I was kind of an idiot last year. I had this thing for Summer—"

"So what? Everyone loves summer," I cut in. Where the heck is he going with this?

That gets me a snort. "No, Summer is the blonde I was with earlier."

"The one who's dating your friend."

"Yes. But before she hooked up with Fitz, she and I shared a kiss on New Year's Eve, and, well, it's a long story and not very interesting. Basically Fitz said he wasn't into her and then went behind my back and dated her. I didn't handle it well."

"I don't blame you," I say, appalled on his behalf. "That goes against the bro code."

"Right?"

"And you still live with them?"

"Well, yeah. Fitz is a good guy. He was just stupid and in denial about his feelings. Afterward, I was kind of doing my thing and trying to forget about Summer. Basically drinking a lot, sleeping around. But then I ended up sleeping with the girlfriend of an opponent. I didn't know at the time," he adds defensively. "We played against his team in our conference finals, and that's when it all came out. The boyfriend freaked out and broke my wrist."

"Oh my God."

"We lost the game and the other team went to the championship and won." Hunter's features harden with resolve. "I'm not letting that happen again."

I chuckle. "I think 'not having sex' might be an extreme solution to a simple problem. Here's an alternative—don't bang girls with boyfriends."

"It's not only that," he admits. "I'm team captain this year. I want to be a good leader. I want to make up for what happened last year. I think it's just all-around better if I concentrate on the game and not on chicks or partying." He reaches into his pocket and checks his phone. "All right, should we do this thing? I've got about an hour before I need to go."

"What's in an hour?"

"I'm stopping by a teammate's house."

I perk up. "The hot one?"

"I'm the hot one, Demi." Then he winks. "You mean

Conor? Yeah, it's his house, so he'll probably be there. And don't you have a boyfriend who I literally met five seconds ago?"

"That doesn't mean your friend isn't hot. My girl Pippa liked him."

"Well, a word of caution—he's the sex machine that I was last year, so I'd probably steer clear."

"How long has it been for you?" I can't help but ask, because curiosity is a bitch.

"Since I fucked someone?"

"No, since you climbed Everest."

"April. So…what's that…five months?"

"You poor monk! That's an eternity!" I tease.

"I know." He lies down on the grass, using his backpack as a pillow. "It's awful, Semi. I miss sex."

"I had sex last night."

"That's a cruel thing to say."

"But it's the truth," I protest.

"I just told you about my poor aching balls and you're bragging about all the action your pussy is getting?" He heaves a dramatic sigh. "How was it?"

"The sex? Pretty good."

"Start from the beginning," Hunter orders. "Did he undress you or did you do a striptease for him? Did he—"

I hoot loudly. "Are you trying to live vicariously through me?"

"Yes," he moans. "I'm not getting any action. I can't watch porn because someone's always barging into my room or banging on the door if I *dare* to lock it—I swear those girls have no decorum. I'm relegated to jerking it in the shower."

He pauses. "Maybe I should look into buying one of those waterproof phones and bring it into the shower? That way I can watch porn and jack off to real-life girls."

"Those are *not* real-life girls," I argue. "Pornography is responsible for creating the most unrealistic expectations of women. Nobody looks like that, and real sex is never like that."

"What's real sex like, then?" he challenges.

"Real sex is unscripted. It's lots of fumbling, and foreheads banging against each other, and awkward positions where your arms and legs get stuck. It's laughing, cursing, multiple orgasms or no orgasms at all. I mean, it's fun, but it's also messy and certainly not perfect."

He scowls at me. "You're the worst. Now I'm thinking about all the sex I can't have."

"*You* brought it up."

"Did I? I honestly don't remember anymore. I don't know where sex ends and I begin."

I laugh. This guy is funny. And he's much cooler than I'd thought, definitely not the arrogant asshole I expected him to be.

I'm not gonna lie—Hunter Davenport is growing on me.

9

HUNTER

I slide into my Land Rover and instantly crank the A/C. Christ, how is it still so hot outside when we're halfway through September? Don't get me wrong, I hope it never ends, but I'm actually sweating after spending the past hour in the quad with Demi.

I drive out of the student lot and back to Hastings, where I speed past my residential street to another one a couple of blocks away.

I wasn't kidding when I told Demi I wish that someone had consulted me about the girls moving into the townhouse. I have nothing against them, but I'm in college, dammit. I want to hang out with the guys. I'm not in the market for a girlfriend this year and there's no reason why I should know so much about eucalyptus facemasks and what kind of tampons everyone in my house uses. Also, Rupi's and Brenna's cycles somehow synced up so now they get their periods at the same time. They're really mean when that happens.

I park in the driveway behind the beat-up Jeep that Matt shares with Conor. They're housemates, along with our teammate Foster and two seniors named Gavin and Alec.

When Matty answers the door, I welcome the familiar sounds of guys insulting each other and video game controllers clicking, and the aroma of pizza and stale beer when it's barely noon. This is college.

"Hey," I greet everyone in the living room.

Foster is sprawled in the armchair, balancing a beer can on his knee. Gavin and Alec are battling it out in a shooter game. The only notable absence is Conor, who's probably in class.

I'm not sure whose turn it is with Pablo Eggscobar, but he's on the coffee table in the drink-cozy harness that Bucky made for him, and he's rocking a new look. Someone used a black Sharpie to draw eyes and a snout right above Coach Jensen's scrawl, and voila—Pablo now has a pig face with Jensen's signature serving as his mouth.

Truthfully, I'm surprised he's still in one piece. Drunken college guys aren't exactly conducive to egg rearing.

"What's up, Pablo?" I greet the egg. He doesn't answer, because he's not real, but hey, at least I'm trying to make an effort.

Captain handbook rule number a thousand: *pick your battles*.

"Who's playing egg mom today?" I ask.

"Con. But he just went upstairs with some chick, so we're waiting for the right moment." Matt settles on the couch.

I flop down on the other end. "The right moment for what?"

Matt and Foster exchange evil grins. "For feeding time. Pablo is about to be hungry as fuck."

Gavin snorts without looking away from the TV screen.

I stifle a sigh. According to my sources, things have escalated since last week. Jesse Wilkes texted me yesterday bitching about how the other guys wouldn't stop calling him when he was out with Katie. It's officially become a game to inconvenience the egg carrier as much as possible.

"How long's it been?" Alec asks, his fingers moving like lightning over the game controller.

"Only about ten minutes," Foster replies. "They're probably still on foreplay."

"Hers," Gavin guesses.

"Or he's getting blown," Matt counters.

They all go quiet for a moment.

"Nah," Foster finally says, raising his beer to his lips. "He goes down on her first, then she blows him, then they fuck. That's the order of sex."

I start to laugh. "Oh really? Is that what the manual says?"

Matt snickers.

"That's the order I do it in," Alec chimes in. "Why? What do *you* do?"

"I don't fucking know. I don't chart out my sexual encounters like I'm exploring undiscovered islands in the Maldives." I roll my eyes. "There's no set order. You just see how it plays out."

"It always plays out the same way," Alec says stubbornly.

"It's true," Foster agrees. "Usually goes that way for me, too."

"Huh. Weird." When I think back on past hook-ups, they're honestly different every time.

Sometimes we stumble into my room and she's on

her knees with my dick in her mouth before I can blink. Once I was with a girl who wanted to kiss for all of three seconds before she turned around and offered me her ass, ordering me to screw her from behind. Longer sessions have begun with me kissing every inch of their bodies, or vice versa. Sometimes we even start with sex and end with foreplay.

"I don't know what you guys are doing, but I can't find a pattern in my hook-ups," I admit.

"Maybe it's a girlfriend thing," Foster suggests. "I dated the same chick all throughout high school and I'm using her as my point of reference."

"Three years with Sasha for me," Alec says with a nod, referring to his current girlfriend.

"Oh, it's definitely a girlfriend thing," Matt confirms. "Like, with Jesse. He and Katie have the most predictable sex life ever. When we were rooming together in the dorms last year, every time they put that stupid sock on the door I knew they'd need exactly forty-seven minutes to bang. I could probably plot out the exact time of orgasm."

"Sounds kinda boring." Although maybe having sex with someone you're madly in love with feels different somehow? I have no idea. I had a few girlfriends in high school, but none of them were ever *the one*.

"Okay. It's been twenty-one minutes," Foster announces. "He's either balls deep right now or she's got her mouth full. Either way, the dick is in play. I repeat, the dick is in play."

"You jackasses are the worst. As team captain, I should stop this," I warn.

They all wait expectantly.

A slow grin stretches my mouth. On the other hand, Conor gets so much action his ego could probably use some *coitus interruptus*. "But I won't. Go ahead. Do it."

Foster and Alec sprint up the narrow staircase. A moment later their heavy footsteps thud on the ceiling. Incessant pounding reverberates through the house as their fists attack Conor's bedroom door. It sounds like a SWAT team breaking into a crack den.

"Pablo's hungry!" Foster shouts.

"*Feed me*," Alec hollers.

On the other end of the sofa, Matt is shuddering from laughter.

An even louder commotion ensues. Angry cursing rings in the air, followed by the frantic footsteps of two huge hockey players racing down the stairs. Conor is on their tail, bare-chested, barefoot, with a pair of plaid boxers haphazardly sagging off one hip. His blond hair sticks up and his lips are a bit swollen.

"You fucking assholes," he growls.

"What?" Foster blinks innocently. He gestures to the coffee table. "Our pig needs his lunch. We have a *pet*, bro. Pet comes before pussy."

"Pet before pussy," Matt echoes.

Gavin tears his eyes off the video game and nods gravely. "The wise words of Thomas Jefferson."

"I fed him this morning," Conor protests.

Foster glares. "He eats three meals a day, you selfish jackass. Look at him—he's starving."

I glance at the egg and his stupid face, then bury my own face in my hands and quiver in silent laughter.

"Davenport!" Conor barks. "You're team captain. I'm filing a complaint against them."

I lift my head, lips still twitching. "What's the complaint?"

He jabs the air with his index finger. "I was fucking."

"That's not a complaint. It's a statement of fact."

Foster crosses his arms over his bulky chest. "Don't forget—you gotta take five whole minutes to make sure he eats all his food."

A vein throbs in Con's forehead as he snatches Pablo off the table. It looks like he's about to whip the egg against the wall, but at the last second he curses under his breath and spins around. Low mumbling comes from the kitchen.

I gape at Matt. "He's not going to prepare actual food, is he?"

"Nah, it's not in the rules."

"What exactly *are* the rules?"

"They're whatever we make them," Foster replies with a grin. "But basically, five minutes are required whenever Pablo is in play."

"But you can't abuse the system," Matt says.

"What system?" I sputter. "It's all nonsense."

"He eats three times a day, shits twice a day, and requires attention whenever one of us is bored and wants to harass whoever has him."

"But you can't play the attention card more than a few times a day," Foster adds. "With that said, texting between the hours of one and five a.m. is highly encouraged."

"This is all very reasonable," Alec tells me. "What aren't you getting?"

"Are you gonna do this to me when I have him?" I shudder. My turn is on Friday.

"Nah, we would never do that to you," Foster assures me. The others chime in.

"Never."

"Of course not."

"Never do that to our captain."

Goddamn liars.

———

On Thursday night, Demi and I manage to squeeze in a second study session for the week. Once again, we convene in her bedroom at the Theta house. She's sitting cross-legged on the purple bedspread, sucking on a grape lollipop. I'm sprawled on her little couch, regaling her with a juicy new tale in the sordid history of Dick Smith.

"So she promised to pick up a strawberry cheesecake along with the usual pumpkin pie. Meanwhile, everything else was coming together beautifully. The catering staff was top-notch. The table was set with the crystal my grandparents gave us as a wedding present. We had family coming in from Palm Springs and Manhattan. Thanksgiving in the Hamptons is always an important event."

Demi observes me carefully. I know she's trying to figure out where I'm going with this.

"But the pièce de résistance was going to be the strawberry cheesecake," I brag. "That was the first cake my parents ever sold when they opened that original little bakery on Burton Street, which they turned into a massive dessert empire. It was perfect—Mother would be so touched that I remembered, that

I'd gone out of my way to please her. God knows my brother Geoffrey doesn't care about her happiness."

Demi's lollipop pokes into the inside of her cheek. "Is this typical for you, taking great pains to seek the approval of your mother?"

"It had nothing to do with approval. I just told you, I wanted to make Mother happy."

"I see."

I huff in annoyance. "Anyway. Dinner was spectacular, and then it was time for dessert, and you know what happened? The servers come out with a fucking pumpkin pie and nothing else. No cheesecake. I was forced to paste a smile on my face, but inside I was seething. Kathryn apologized after dinner and insisted that all the bakeries in the area were either closed or sold out, but a fucking apology didn't help me in the moment. She made me look bad in front of the whole family, and then goddamn Geoff made a joke about pumpkin pie and how original that was, and I wanted to clock him. Happy Thanksgiving, right?"

There's a beat of silence. I glance over to find Demi shrewdly inspecting me.

"Wow," she says slowly. "There's a lot to unpack here. I guess my first question is—if all the bakeries were closed for the holiday, do you think it's fair to blame your wife for not being able to get the cheesecake?"

"She could've picked it up the day before," I say coldly. "There was no excuse."

She shakes her head a couple times, as if jarred out of the charade. "Jeez. You're good at this," she remarks.

I give an awkward shrug. "Right? You think I should quit hockey and get into acting?" It's a lame joke.

The actual punch line is, it's not a joke at all. The story I just told is the unfiltered truth. The only part I left out was how the asshole's son endured weeks and weeks of obnoxious boasting about that stupid strawberry cheesecake prior to Thanksgiving, and then years of bitter griping about the pumpkin pie following it.

Yup, that's my father for you, doesn't give a shit about anybody but himself. He wanted to look good and one-up his brother, and fuck all the closed bakeries and my horrible selfish mother for depriving him of his needs. Poor Mom was walking on eggshells for months afterward. That man is impossible to please.

When I opened my "PATIENT" envelope last week and saw the disorder I'd been assigned, I'd almost laughed out loud. Hardly any research required, as I'm wholly familiar with the symptoms and how it manifests. I've lived with it my entire life.

"Why was it so important for you to look good in front of your family?" Dr. Demi asks.

"What do you mean?"

She rephrases. "What was supposed to be a happy family gathering turned into a competition between you and your brother. I'm simply wondering why you engaged in it?"

"*I* don't turn shit into a competition, *he* does. He's jealous of me because I'm older and more successful. And, what, I'm supposed to let myself be humiliated when he tries to put me down? No way. I'm going to fight back."

"I see." A pause. "Do you feel like you have unreasonably high expectations of the people in your life, or an average level of expectation?"

I wonder what conclusions she's reaching. It's evident that Demi is highly intelligent. That's just one of the many reasons I enjoy hanging out with her. The main reason is that she's easy to talk to, and there's no pressure whatsoever to be anything but platonic. She has a boyfriend who she clearly loves, so there's no temptation on my end. Sure, her body is hot as fuck, and she has a habit of wearing tight tops that hug her perky tits and bare her midriff, but I'm able to admire her without fantasizing about tearing her clothes off.

Demi jots down more notes, then says, "'Kay, let's finish up. I've got dinner plans with Nico. But I think I'm starting to form an idea about your diagnosis."

"This really is fun," I admit. The irony is not lost on me that I'm having a good time describing—in detail—the way my father's brain works.

Dad isn't my favorite person, but I don't typically complain about him to anyone. My whole life, I just went along with the cookie-cutter perfect family thing we've got going on. Anything else would've felt self-indulgent. I mean, I'm a rich dude who grew up in Greenwich and attended elite private schools. Other people have it worse. Some of them suffer from actual physical abuse, which is far worse than simply being unable to meet the unrealistic standards of an egomaniac.

Nevertheless, it is fascinating to describe these events of my childhood from Dad's point of view. I don't know if I'm hitting the right notes, but more research on the subject will probably help me zero in on specific thought patterns.

"I'll see you next week," I tell Demi. "But I don't think I'm available on Monday, though."

"How about mid-week?"

"I should be around on Wednesday night. But not the weekend—we're playing three games."

"Okay, possibly Wednesday night," she says, "but that's usually my gym day."

"You go to the gym?"

"Of course. Why do you think I look this good?"

Naturally, my gaze is pulled right back to her tight, petite body. She can't be taller than five-three, but, man, her legs seem endless. Long and tanned and bare in her tiny denim shorts. I bet her ass is taut and perfect, a perfect little handful.

Oh shit.

It's happening.

I'm fantasizing about her.

Abort, dude, abort!

"Anyway." I wrench my gaze away, but not before she catches me.

"Oh my God, stop it. You're not allowed to look at me like that," Demi orders. "You're a monk, remember?"

"I wasn't looking at you like anything," I lie.

"Bullshit. You were giving me the Penis Eyes."

"I was not. Trust me, smoldering looks aren't my go-to move." I smirk. "If I was making a real move on you, you wouldn't be telling me to stop."

"You have an actual *move*?" A delighted smile lights up Demi's pretty face. Her skin is incredible. Glowing and flawless, and I don't think she's even wearing makeup. "Show me!"

"No."

"Please?"

"No," I growl. "You're not allowed to see my move."

"Why not?" she whines.

"Two reasons—you have a boyfriend, and I'm a monk."

"Fine. But for the record, I'm betting your move is lamer than lame." Grinning, she opens the top drawer of her desk. After some fumbling, her hand emerges with another lollipop. Cherry, this time. Or maybe strawberry.

"I think you're a sugar addict," I inform her.

"Nah, I just like having things in my mouth."

"Nope, not even touching that statement."

She glares at me. "It's called an oral fixation, Hunter. It's quite common."

"Uh-huh. If you say so."

And despite my best efforts to forget all about this conversation, thoughts of Demi and her oral fixation follow me all the way home and consume my sexed-up brain. And the next thing I know I'm locking the bathroom door and stepping into the shower, a tight fist around an erection hard enough to slice a slab of marble in half.

It's happening again.

I'm fantasizing about Demi Davis, and this time I ain't stopping it.

I picture her plump lips wrapped around that red lollipop, except within seconds the lollipop is replaced with the head of my cock. I'm nudging it between those sexy lips, and her tongue instantly darts out for a taste, because she's so hungry for it.

"*Mmmm,*" I imagine her murmuring. "*Tastes like candy.*" And I imagine myself saying that her pussy probably tastes even sweeter, which makes her moan and the throaty sound travels the length of my shaft and tightens my balls.

"Goddamn." My hoarse expletive echoes in the shower stall. I rest my forearm against the tiled wall as I work myself over with fast, desperate strokes. My dick is so hard it hurts. The steam in the bathroom makes it difficult to breathe. As I start fucking my own fist, my forehead sags against my arm and I suck in gulps of heated oxygen.

Oh man, this feels good. My cheesy scripted fantasy has dissolved in the steamy air. Now I'm stroking my cock to random images that flash through my mind—Demi sucking on me, Demi's cleavage spilling from those tight tops she wears, her tanned legs…spreading for me. Ah hell, I wonder what noises she makes when she comes—

I go off like a bottle rocket. Holy *hell*. My hips grow still as a rush of hot pleasure surges through my body. I shoot in my own hand, breathing hard, black dots flashing in my field of vision and my cock tingling wildly.

I feel only slightly guilty that I fantasized about Demi. And I think she'd forgive me if I told her. I mean, it was bound to happen. I'm in dire straits, five endless months without sex. By the end of the month, I'll be jerking it to fantasies of Mike Hollis.

I'm starting to get genuinely concerned for my sanity.

Loud pounding rattles the doorframe.

Startled, I almost wipe out in the tub.

"*Hunter!*" Rupi shrieks. "Get out of there already. You'll use up all the hot water and I want to shower before bed!"

A groan lodges in my throat, which feels raw and achy from all the heavy panting I just did. I'm still gripping my dick, but it's rapidly softening because that's what Rupi's voice does to penises.

"Go away," I growl at the door, but there's no negotiating with terrorists. If I don't submit to her demands, she'll probably go find a YouTube video on lock-picking, bust open the door, and forcibly pull me out of the shower.

I hate my roommates.

10
DEMI

I don't have class on Wednesdays, so I spend the morning studying for a bio test and completing a math assignment. This semester's workload is nearly double the previous year's, so I'm now waking up an hour earlier every day in the hopes that it'll help me stay on top of my classes.

And if I'm not already stressed enough, my father has decided that I should get a head start on studying for the MCAT exam. Last night he even sent a text offering to hire me a tutor. I told him I'd think about it.

Really, though, I just need to think of a diplomatic way to say, *Please, for the love of God, don't make me study for med school yet or I'll never survive junior year.*

In the afternoon, I hang out with Corinne at her new apartment in Hastings, helping her organize her closet. At my house in Boston, I have a sweet walk-in that's categorized by both color and style. My levels of anxiety reduce drastically when everything is neat and tidy.

"Thanks so much for doing this," Corinne says, a bit shyly.

I slide a heavy cable-knit sweater onto a hanger. "Of course. You know this kind of stuff is my jam. Plus we're friends. Friends don't let friends clean closets alone."

Her answering smile is brimming with gratitude.

Corinne's a tough nut to crack sometimes. She's very pretty, and there's a constant stream of guys chasing after her, but she's selective about who she dates. She's antisocial, quiet at times, but her sarcasm is top-notch and when she relaxes her guard she's a lot of fun.

"This apartment is super cute," I tell her. "I love how massive the bedroom is." It's almost as big as my room at the sorority house, and I lucked out in the random draw and snagged the master.

My phone buzzes on Corinne's double bed. I grab it and discover a message from Hunter.

HUNTER: Did you watch the Bruins game last night??

In one of our previous text exchanges, he'd been raving about some game on TV, and I'd mentioned I'd be sure to start watching hockey. I don't think he picked up on the sarcasm.

ME: Oh ya! It was INTENSE! I can't believe that player scored nineteen points!!!
HIM: You didn't watch it, did you?
ME: No. Sorry. Told you, I don't care for hockey.
HIM: I expected more from my therapist. Goodbye.

There's a long pause.

HUNTER: Fuck, wait, I texted for a reason. We still holding our session at the gym today?

ME: Yep. After I'm done with dinner. So around 8? Oh, and make sure you're wearing tight spandex pants so I can objectify you.

HIM: Obvs.

I grin at the screen.

"The hockey player again?" Corinne asks.

"Yeah." Chuckling, I shake my head indulgently. "He's so full of himself. But really hot. I'd set you up with him, but he doesn't have sex."

"Wait, what?"

"He's practicing abstinence for a while." I hope it's not a secret, but just in case, I don't offer any further details. "Hey, what's your Wi-Fi network? I'm trying to join it."

"Oh, I haven't set up the Wi-Fi yet. They're coming on Friday to do it."

I'm about to put my phone away when another message comes in.

TJ: Are we still on for dinner?

ME: Oh yeah. Sushi baby!!!!

I punctuate that with three fish emojis. TJ counters with a couple of shrimp, and then we're sending each other random sea-life emojis that make me giggle.

ME: Did you realize there's no lobster emoji?? WTH!

TJ doesn't respond, so I set the phone down and begin folding the pile of T-shirts on Corinne's mattress. "I feel like these should all go in your dresser," I suggest. "Hanging T-shirts is a waste of hangers."

"Agreed. Let's hang the stuff that might wrinkle, and then dresses, skirts—"

My phone buzzes again. TJ just sent a picture of a cartoon lobster with hearts in his eyes, and a speech bubble above his head that reads: "I WANT TO GET MY CLAWS INTO YOU!"

I burst out laughing. "Sorry," I tell Corinne. "TJ is sending memes."

"You have like a gazillion male friends. Meanwhile, I can't even deal with one." She shakes her head. "I don't know how you do it. All those fragile egos… They're all just little boys in need of attention." She gasps in delight. "You know who you are? You're Wendy with all the Lost Boys!"

"Sounds about right," I say dryly. "But I love my Lost Boys. They're a constant source of entertainment." I fold another T-shirt. "TJ and I are grabbing dinner in town tonight. We're trying out the new Japanese place that opened across from the theater. Wanna come?"

"I can't. I'm hosting a study group here later. It's just you and TJ? No Nico?"

"Nico is playing basketball with Darius and then meeting up with some guys from work for drinks. You probably met them when they helped you move."

"I met two." She thinks it over. "One was really cute, and one was really bald."

I snicker. "The bald one is Steve, and I think the cute

one…it was probably Roddy? Short for Rodrigo. But I think he has a girlfriend."

"Bummer."

"Yeah right. You don't even want a boyfriend."

"True."

I carry the stack of neatly folded shirts to Corinne's second-hand wooden dresser. "Come on, let's put all this random stuff away and then dive back into the closet. The closet is the fun part."

"The things that bring you joy…" She sighs. "You're so fucking weird, Demi."

I spend a couple more hours with Corinne, then walk the short distance into the heart of town. TJ meets me at the sushi place, which ends up being phenomenal, so naturally I text my boyfriend all about it on the Uber ride back to campus, because good food gets me excited and when I'm excited I must share it with Nico.

NICO: I think u devalue the currency of the orgasm whenever u call a meal "orgasmic."

ME: Well, I think you underappreciate good food. And that's practically a crime b/c you're Cuban and food is in your blood.

HIM: Nah.

ME: I'm telling your mom you said that.

HIM: Don't u dare.

ME: I'm hitting the gym soon. Be home around 9. Wanna come by after you're done with the boys?

HIM: Prolly not, bb. Think we're gonna go back to Steve's and have a Fortnite marathon.

I'm only a smidge disappointed. We didn't have plans, so I can't fault him for wanting to continue hanging out with his friends, the people he originally had plans with.

ME: OK. Have fun! Love you.
NICO: Love u too bb <3 <3 <3 <3

———

"I miss blowjobs," Hunter declares at the gym an hour later.

The forlorn assertion triggers a burst of laughter from me, which nearly results in me tripping on the treadmill. It's been a week since we've seen each other, and obviously his monk status is still solidly intact.

"I'm sorry to hear that," I tell him.

"Don't apologize to me, apologize to my dick."

Snorting, I dip my gaze south. Not gonna lie—his package is kind of impressive beneath his black track pants. I make a magnanimous gesture at his crotch. "I'm sincerely sorry for your recent troubles, Hunter's dick."

Hunter's dick's owner nods soberly. "He appreciates the sentiment."

This fucking guy. He is either the best or the worst. I still haven't decided.

With that said, he's definitely the worst gym buddy. For the past forty minutes, we've been side-by-side on our respective treadmills without altering the brisk pace. But now I'm waning. It's an admission of defeat when I flick my finger on the incline button to make the workout a bit easier.

Mr. Hockey Star has barely broken a sweat. A slight

sheen coats his forehead and that's about it. Meanwhile, I'm a sweaty mess. Thank God I'm not romantically interested in him, otherwise I'd be incredibly self-conscious and embarrassed about perspiring this much. Even Nico hasn't seen me at my sweatiest.

"Aww, does someone need a break?" Hunter mocks.

"Nope, just a flatter path."

"Wimp."

"Monk."

"You gotta stop using that as an insult. *Some* people consider my celibacy admirable."

"Says the guy who's moaning about missing blowjobs."

"Oh, like you wouldn't miss it if the boyfriend stopped going down on you."

"Not really," I say before I can stop myself. And I regret it instantly. I'm not a fan of locker room talk, especially involving my boyfriend. So what if Nico isn't an oral genius? That doesn't mean he doesn't possess other exceptional qualities.

Unfortunately, Hunter heard me loud and clear. Even as his head swivels my way, the rest of his body doesn't miss a step, his long legs eating up the treadmill. "Uh oh. My man Nico's not doing it for you with his tongue?"

"No, he is."

"Yeah? Didn't sound like it just now."

"Whatever, not everyone is great at oral," I grumble. "Practice makes perfect, right?"

Hunter appears to be trying not to laugh. "Haven't you guys been together for like ten years?"

"Eight," I say grudgingly. "We officially started dating when we were thirteen."

"And he still hasn't mastered the art of eating pussy?" Incredulity lines his tone.

"Don't be crude."

"Fine, would you like me to call it cunnilingus?"

Ugh, that word is truly unappealing. Who even came up with it? "Look, I'm not saying he's awful at it. Honestly, I think it's me. I'm just not interested in it."

"Have you ever gotten oral from anyone else?"

"No."

"Then how do you know it's you?" Hunter challenges. "A hundred bucks says he just sucks at going down on chicks. How much time does he spend down there?"

My cheeks are on fire. "Not a lot." I hurry on in Nico's defense, "I think he's too impatient to get inside me."

"But the anticipation is half the fun," Hunter protests.

I shrug. "It doesn't matter. Even if it *is* him, he does amazing things when he's in me, and his finger game is pretty sweet. We can't all be good at everything, right?"

"I can," Hunter says smugly.

"Mmm-hmmm, I'm sure you're phenomenal in bed. Men who brag about their sexual prowess always are."

"I am. Too bad you'll never find out."

"Me and every other girl, Monk."

He rolls his eyes. His pace remains brisk. How is he carrying an entire conversation without getting breathless? Me, I'm struggling to talk and run at the same time. Damn athletes.

"Anyway, despite his very disappointing failings, Nico seems like a cool dude," Hunter relents. "He's funny."

"He's hilarious. And yes, he is a cool dude."

"Minus the subpar oral skills, of course."

"They're not subpar. They're par."

"What an endorsement!"

"Oh, shut up."

"You shut up." Hunter flashes that devilish grin of his. "Don't worry, I won't tell him you said that. It would crush his ego."

"Everything you and I talk about falls under doctor-patient confidentiality," I say firmly.

"You got it, Doc."

A woman in tight workout gear meanders over and starts doing squats directly in our line of sight. One might think her choice of location is unintentional, if not for the fact that in the mirror across the room, her thirsty gaze is super-glued to Hunter.

He notices the admirer and gives me a wink. She's not the first female to try to catch his attention this evening, and I'm sure she won't be the last. It's ironic that he's celibate, because any chick in this fitness center would happily have sex with him. In the gym. In front of everyone.

"I can't believe Nico's the only person you've ever slept with," Hunter muses.

"What's wrong with that?"

"Wrong? Nothing. It's just surprising."

"We've been together forever—when would I have had the opportunity to sleep around?"

"You never cheated? Ever?"

"Never. There were some breaks over the years, but I never slept with anyone else."

He cocks one eyebrow defiantly. "You're saying you didn't hook up at all during those breaks?"

"I kissed some guys," I admit with a shrug.

"Because *that* isn't the vaguest response I've ever heard."

"God, you're so frickin' nosy. Fine. I kissed three other guys, and there may have been some petting during one of those encounters."

"Light or heavy?"

"Light. Didn't go beyond second base. He wanted to do more, but I felt like I was betraying Nico."

"Really? You should've gone for it. Because I hate to break it to you, but I *guarantee* that Nico was going beyond second base."

"I know he was. He and I are honest with each other. Plus, on one of the breaks I saw him making out with some girl at a party. That's what led to me fooling around with the light petting guy." I hesitate. "And I know Nico slept with someone else, at least once."

"At least?" Hunter's sneakers slap the treadmill as he increases his pace. Ugh. He's running faster now! And he's still not even breathing hard. It's unbelievable.

I'm moving at a snail-paced walk by this point, and I'm not even on the cool-down setting. "I know there was one hook-up for sure, because he told me about it. But… I think he cheated on me once," I confess, and then chastise myself for it.

It's one thing to critique your boyfriend's oral skills, but opening the closet and letting the skeletons tumble out? That's crossing a line.

"Do *not* tell anyone I said that."

Hunter is smart enough to recognize I'm serious. "You really believe he cheated on you?"

I jerk my head in a nod. This isn't a subject I particularly enjoy dwelling on. "The summer before senior year, I visited him in Miami and a bunch of us went on a camping trip to the Everglades. Well, not really camping. More like glamping."

"Booooo!" Hunter exclaims instantly, giving me two thumbs down.

The woman who's shaking her butt in our faces glances over her shoulder to see what the commotion is, but Hunter doesn't even look her way.

"Nope, nope, nope," he announces. "You're not allowed to be one of those girls, Semi."

"I don't believe in outhouses, okay? I prefer camping in a place with walls and a toilet and Wi-Fi and—"

"That's not camping!"

"Exactly. It's glamping, like I said."

"Boooooo!"

"Will you *please* stop booing me?"

"Just when I was starting to like you, I find out you're a spoiled Miami brat who refuses to sleep in a tent."

"Do you want to hear the rest of the story or no?"

His expression quickly turns eager. "Oh, I really do. But only if you want to tell me."

For some inexplicable reason, I *do* want to tell him. I'd only ever confided in one other person about it: Amber, my best friend in Miami. And she told me I was being paranoid.

"One of our friends brought his cousin Rashida on the trip, and I'm telling you, this chick would *not* stop flirting with Nico. It was starting to piss me off, so I—" I stop abruptly.

"You what?" Hunter demands.

I make a grumbling sound. "I may or may not have told her that if she didn't stop hitting on my man, I'd drown her in the lake and leave her body for the gators."

For the first time in sixty-two minutes, Hunter's gait stutters. He grabs the handrail to steady himself, but the laughter shaking his body doesn't subside. "Fuck. You're a psychopath, Davis. I knew it."

"Nah, I stole that killing method from an episode of *Cheerleaders Who Kill*. I'm not creative enough to plan a gruesome murder. Anyway, this Rashida chick was so predatory and so obvious about it that she needed the reminder that he had girlfriend. God knows he wasn't acting like it. I felt like he was encouraging the flirting, which annoyed me even more. We started arguing about it and Nico got pissy, announced he was taking a walk, and disappeared for a few hours."

"A few *hours*?" Hunter narrows his eyes. "Let me guess, Rashida disappeared about the same time?"

"Good guess. She claimed she drove into town to buy snacks, and the cupboard in the cabin *was* restocked, so maybe she did. But I still found it suspicious."

"Hell yeah, it was suspicious."

"I confronted Nico and he insisted he was alone in the woods and hadn't seen or spoken to Rashida in hours. He told me I was being ridiculous and overreacting, and freaked out on me so hard that I felt guilty for making the accusation and ended up apologizing to him for a whole year afterward." I frown deeply. "I want to believe he didn't do anything, but…"

"But you don't," Hunter finishes.

"I don't. And I feel like an asshole for it."

"You shouldn't. Always trust your gut, Demi. If people

are acting shady it's usually because they've done something shady. And the fact that he lost his shit and yelled at you speaks volumes. Guilty people attack. Innocent people don't."

"Maybe, but…whatever, this was years ago. We were kids." I shrug. "We're in our twenties now and it's in the past."

"Is something like that ever truly in the past?" Hunter's voice becomes gruff. "I feel like an incident like that would always lurk in the back of my mind. Like, let's say Summer changed her mind and decided she liked me and not Fitz after all? It'd be niggling at me for our entire relationship— *does she actually want me, is she thinking about him right now*, that kinda shit. I think it's better to…" He makes a snipping motion with his fingers. "Cut it off. Start fresh. If a well runs dry or goes bad, you dig a new one, right? You don't drink from the poisoned water."

I snort. "You know much about wells, Connecticut boy?"

"You don't need firsthand experience with something to use it as a metaphor." Hunter's expression turns pensive. "But, look, Nico does seem like a decent guy, and he's obviously in love with you, if that makes you feel better."

"It does, actually." I appreciate impartial third-party observations. They mean more than the false assurances and platitudes you tend to receive from people who love you.

Another girl passes by. Her stride slows drastically when she notices Hunter. He's finally sweating, his damp shirt clinging to the most impressive chest I've ever seen. His pecs are perfectly defined, and his arms are spectacular. I don't blame any of these women for going gaga over him.

Hunter spares a glance for his admirer, then gravely looks

my way. "You have no idea how nice it is to hang out with someone who doesn't want to fuck me."

"Oh my God, that's the most conceited thing I ever heard."

"It's true." He waves his hand around. "Look at them, Semi, look at them all! They're all so fuckable and they all want me. Meanwhile, you're like this beautiful neutral creature with no desire to bang me. It's glorious."

"They're *all* fuckable? I feel like that's an exaggeration."

"We've already established my dick doesn't discriminate. Even you don't have immunity."

I swivel my head. "What the hell does that mean?"

"Ah. Nothing." He's obviously hiding something as he presses a few buttons on the machine to trigger the cool-down setting. When he glances at me again, his expression is sheepish. "I have a confession to make, but you have to promise not to be mad."

"I will never promise that. Ever."

"Seriously?"

"Seriously. Tell me at your own peril."

"Fine. I jerked off the other night—"

"Congratulations. Did your penis tingle when you came?"

"I wasn't finished."

"So you didn't come?"

"I meant I wasn't finished speaking," he growls. "I jerked off the other night…fantasizing about you."

My jaw drops.

Um. What?

"Oh. My. God." I stare at him in utter disbelief. "Why would you ever tell me that?"

"Because I felt guilty about it. Like I needed to go to church and confess."

I can feel myself blushing, and I suspect I'm redder than a tomato. Yes, I have many male friends, but this is the first time one of them has confessed to pleasuring themselves while fantasizing about *me*. I mean…it's flattering, I guess? If TJ or Darius or—

I shudder at the mere thought of it.

Okay. Interesting response. The idea of my other guy friends masturbating to me is extremely unappealing. But the idea of Hunter stroking his cock and fantasizing about me is…

My thighs actually clench together at the dirty image.

Oh my God.

No.

Nope.

In. Ap. Propriate.

Hunter heaves a big sigh. "I feel so much better now that I got that off my chest."

"Well, *I* don't!" I can't get the image out of my mind now, and that is so, so wrong.

His dark eyes twinkle. "Take it as a compliment."

"No, thanks."

He uses the hem of his shirt to mop up the sweat on his brow, which means he literally just flashed his entire chest to me and the rest of the gym. His washboard abs are glistening.

"Anyway, aside from the teeny little hiccup of me yanking it with you in mind, I'm truly digging this thing we have." He gestures between us. "Promise me this will never change."

"That what will never change?"

"That you'll never want to sleep with me," he says dramatically.

The sheer arrogance… I release a sigh of my own and reach over to pat his stupidly muscular arm. "I promise I will never want to sleep with you, Hunter."

11
HUNTER

I'VE BEEN AVOIDING GREEK ROW PARTIES SINCE THE THETA Beta Nu lingerie torture fest, but the boys insist on hitting a frat party after our game on Saturday. We played at Suffolk, so the bus doesn't drop us off on campus until past eleven. Then we have to drive to Hastings, because we all live off-campus and the guys want to change. Or, in Foster's case, grab his weed.

Hard partying during the season is minimal, but drinking and the occasional joint isn't unheard of. I know several hockey guys who do coke, but Coach Jensen runs a clean program at Briar. Every now and then someone hits up a concert and does MDMA, but it's not a frequent occurrence. We're all wholly aware of the NCAA's strict (and random) drug-testing protocol.

Instead of choosing a designated driver, we take an Uber back to campus because everybody's planning on having some drinks to celebrate winning our games this weekend. But our schedule has been light so far. Next week we're facing some tough matchups, including Boston University, and they're undefeated this season. But it's early yet.

Conor is next to me in the backseat, with Foster on his other side. Con's scrolling through his phone. Probably browsing his digital black book.

I'm on egg duty tonight, so I wore a collared shirt with a pocket that I could stick Pablo in. "Look at this manwhore," I tell the egg. "You ever see anything so disgusting?"

Conor's head lifts from the screen. "Oh, can it. I've heard the rumors about you, Mr. I Boned Every Woman on Campus Last Year."

He's got me there. "Who are you talking to?" I ask curiously.

"This chick Michelle. She's meeting us at the party."

He resumes his texting, so I follow suit, because Foster is also on his phone and I'm tired of being ignored. I message Hollis, who's home for the weekend and wanted to party with us tonight. He and Rupi were arguing about it when I left. He wanted to go, she wanted to stay home. Girlfriends, amiright?

ME: Dude, just sling that little hellcat over your shoulder and come out. You know you want to...
HOLLIS: I really really want to. Been soooo long since I went to a party :(((Is this what it's like having a gf? Constant snuggling?

I'm typing a response when another message pops up.

HOLLIS: I didn't mean that. Having a girlfriend is the most rewarding experience in a young man's life. Girlfriends are to be treasured.
ME: Rupi, did you steal Mike's phone?

NO, is the response, and I start laughing because it's so obvious that she did. Corny words aside, Hollis has never texted in full sentences in his life.

ME: Throw the man a bone, Rupes. He wants to go to a party, not a weeklong EDM festival. Basically means having a beer or two and grinding up all over you to shitty music. Be nice to him for once.

No reply. My phone remains silent all the way to campus, not lighting up until the guys and I are sliding out of the Uber.

HOLLIS: U are da fucking man, Davenport! SEE YOU THERE!!!!!!!!

Well. I did my good deed for the day.

A crowd gathers outside the Alpha Delta house. This terrific weather we've been experiencing is still holding up, and although it's almost midnight the air is balmy and people are in shorts and T-shirts. The frat even set up a snow cone machine on the front lawn. I love college.

Conor thumps me on the arm. "Michelle says she's out back." He winks. "In the hot tub."

Foster pales. "Oh, Jesus, no, do *not* go in that hot tub. You're gonna get syphilis of the leg."

"What the fuck are you talking about?"

"Don't you remember that gross rash on Jesse's leg? During preseason? Yeah, he got it from soaking in the Alpha Delt hot tub, AKA Bacteria Central."

"It's true, he did," Bucky confirms. "I don't think anyone ever checks the pH levels or whatever the hell you're supposed to do." He wags a finger at me. "Don't bring Pablo anywhere near it."

"Yeah, you might boil the fucker," Foster guffaws.

"He's already hard-boiled," I argue. "He can't get any *more* boiled."

"So?"

"So I could crack him open right now and he'd be delicious."

"Dude, don't do that," drawls Conor. "That egg has changed so many hands these past couple weeks *it* probably has syphilis."

I snort and pat my breast pocket. "Congrats. You get to live another day, Mr. Eggscobar."

The four of us walk around the side of the house and through the gate. The backyard is massive, housing a kidney-shaped pool, a large expanse of lawn, and the infamous hot tub. Luckily, the tub is full, so even if we wanted to get in, there'd be no room. Chicks are doubling up on guys' laps, and each other's.

Several partygoers let out a huge cheer at our entrance. "Briar hockey!" someone shouts, raising a red cup.

"Briar hockey!" the crowd shouts back.

Not gonna lie—it's awesome being campus celebrities. The football team hasn't done well for nearly a decade, but the hockey program has always been excellent. We kick ass on a frequent basis, and we've got no shortage of fans.

Guys come up to slap me on the shoulder. Girls begin swarming, one of whom makes a beeline for Conor.

The nice thing about Conor is that he's a "one at a time" sort of man. When he sets his sights on a woman, they tend to remain on that woman. Granted, his focus doesn't last more than a week or two. When it comes to hooking up, Con even gives Dean Di Laurentis a run for his money. But for the time being, his interest is directed solely at the cute blonde elbowing her way through the mob.

Conor slings an arm around her shoulder. "Hey babe."

"Hi!" Her lips are stained red from the cherry snow cone in her hand. She raises it to Con's mouth and chirps, "Want some?"

"Fuck yeah." And he growls and chomps off the top of it like a savage.

Michelle giggles, and the other girls disperse unhappily as they realize they won't be reeling in the big fish tonight.

Conor introduces me to Michelle and we chat for a bit, while Bucky and Foster dart off to grab us drinks. Michelle inquires as to why there's a bulge in my shirt pocket, which forces us to explain the Pablo situation. You'd think she'd be horrified by the sheer scope of our immaturity, but instead she laughs in delight and tells Conor how adorable he is. He gives her the Penis Eyes and before long they're making their way inside the house, likely in search of some privacy.

"Hockey man!" a loud voice exclaims, and I turn to see Nico sauntering over.

I blink in surprise. "Hey," I greet Demi's boyfriend. "Fancy meeting you here."

We exchange a macho fist bump. "All these dumbasses here won't quit cheering—I assume you just won a game?" he asks with a grin.

"Yup, yup."

"Nice. I guess Briar's unstoppable tonight—the basketball team won, too. Fucking *destroyed* Yale. We all just came from there."

"Is Demi with you?" I peer past his shoulder.

"Nah, she's at home. It's boys' night." He gestures to a small group a few yards away, and I note that it includes more than boys. Quite a few scantily clad women are hanging all over Nico's friends.

My brain suddenly summons Demi's confession on the treadmill the other night. How she secretly believes, even years later, that Nico cheated on her in high school.

And now, running into him at a frat party with a bunch of chicks in tow, my internal alarm system is triggered.

But maybe I'm being a jerk. Just because he's hanging out with some girls doesn't mean he's stepping out on Demi.

"Anyway, I spotted you from over there and wanted to say hello," Nico says, raising his cup in a toast. Except he does it so abruptly that liquid spills over the edge, and the potent odor of vodka reaches my nostrils. His clumsy hands and hazy eyes tell me he's pretty drunk. "Catch you later, 'kay?"

"Cool. Cheers." I lift my own cup.

Nico strolls back to his friends. I'm mollified to see that he doesn't stand next to any of the girls, but is immediately engrossed in conversation with a short, balding guy in a black tank top. I don't care if Nico catches me watching him—I'm just looking out for Demi. She's a good egg.

"Just like you," I tell Pablo, patting my pocket.

"I. HAVE. ARRIVED!"

The majestic shout is courtesy of Mike Hollis, who

emerges onto the patio from the back door, both arms raised in a victory pose. Rupi scampers at his heels like an annoyed kitten.

Despite being incredibly obnoxious, Hollis was quite popular when he attended Briar. Old teammates and a slew of fans wander over to say hello and he accepts their welcome and their praise as if he's Meghan Markle greeting the commoners.

Rupi spots me and marches up. She's clad in traditional Rupi attire: a knee-length, high-waisted skirt and a prim, buttoned tee with a high neckline.

"I *really* wanted to watch *Riverdale* tonight, Hunter," she huffs.

I throw an arm around her tiny shoulders. "Sorry, Rupes. But sometimes we need to make sacrifices for those we love."

A huge smile practically breaks her face in two. "Oh my gosh, that was the sweetest thing you've ever said. I *knew* you were a secret softie."

"Don't tell anyone. You want a drink?"

"I can't. I drove us here."

"I thought you didn't have a license."

"No, I don't have a *fake* license. Ugh, Hunter, you don't know me at *all*."

I suppose I don't, and I gotta admit—I'm A-OK with that. Rupi is exhausting on a good day.

"Is that Pablo?" Her expression brightens. "I didn't know we had him this weekend," she adds, as if discussing the custody arrangement of a human child. "Let me hold him!"

I extract the pink bundle from my pocket and pass it to Rupi. "Go nuts," I tell her.

We mingle for the next hour or so. Foster passes me a joint and I take a deep drag before handing it back. I feel good. Loose, relaxed. Happy to just chill with my buddies and dance with Rupi to the crappy pop music blasting from the outdoor speakers. For the first time in ages, I'm not thinking about sex. Women try to catch my eye. Several come over to flirt with me. But I'm not feeling it. No libido for me tonight. Weed has that effect on me.

"Pablooooo!" Hollis crows. He'd been chatting with some dudes from the lacrosse team, but now he rejoins us near the deep end of the pool. "Hand 'im over, babe."

"Leave Pablo alone," Rupi chastises, protectively holding the egg to her bosom. "You're too drunk to hold him."

"I am not! C'mon, pass 'im to me."

"No."

"Fine, then I'll just…TAKE HIM FROM YOU!" Like a ninja, Hollis snatches the egg from his girlfriend. Only, she's right—he's too drunk to be holding small objects. His big paw fumbles with Pablo, who flies out of Hollis's grip and goes sailing.

Directly into the pool.

Bucky cries out in horror. Hell, even I'm momentarily stunned. We all stare at the little bundle bobbing in the water, which appears blue thanks to the lit-up pool tiles. Nobody moves.

"Did we just kill him?" Foster demands.

"Can pigs swim?" Rupi asks anxiously.

"No idea," I admit. Pablo is still floating in the pool.

"Quick, someone Google if pigs can swim," Bucky orders. Rupi's already on her phone. "Oh my gosh," she says a moment later, her voice rippling with relief. "They can! It says here that some pigs take naturally to water, like dogs. Others hate getting wet. You can train them to swim." She examines our aquatic egg. "If it was a real pig I don't think he'd be able to get out of the pool by himself, though. There's no steps in the shallow end."

"Yeah, he ain't climbing that ladder," Foster agrees.

All eyes turn to me.

"What?" I say.

"You're in charge of him tonight. You need to get him out."

"Pardon me?" I stare at the empty pool, which an hour ago was teeming with people. Now it's almost two a.m. and there's no swimming to be had. "I'm not jumping in the pool, you fuckers."

"We never trained him to swim," Bucky argues. "Right now he's treading water. Soon he'll be dead."

"This has gone too far," I say firmly.

Except, to my genuine shock, everyone stands their ground, even Foster. Bucky crosses his arms tightly.

"Fuck's sake," I snap. "You're seriously gonna make me do this?"

I'm cursing up a blue streak as I strip out of my shirt. Shoes and cargo shorts come off too, because I'm not sitting soaking wet in an Uber on the way home.

I step toward the edge of the deck. "You assholes don't deserve me as a captain," I mutter, and then I dive into the water in my boxers.

Luckily, the temperature is like bath water, and as I swim for Pablo, I force myself to think good thoughts about my team.

Captain rule number a million: *Patience. Always be patient.*

With Pablo in hand, I climb up the ladder, dripping water all over the concrete deck. "Here," I mutter to Foster, shoving the egg in his hand. "I'm going upstairs to dry off and change."

Rupi's unhappy gaze fixes on my underwear. "Hunter, I can see the outline of your penis."

Yup, because the boxers are white, and they're soaked and sticking to my flesh. I scowl at Rupi before gathering my discarded clothing and stalking into the house.

It's late and the party is winding down, so there's no line at the main floor bathroom. But the door is locked and when I knock on it, an agonized voice slurs, "Go 'way, I'm busy in 'ere."

So I trudge upstairs and try the one in the hall. Door's shut, but I jiggle the knob and find it's unlocked. I push the door open in time to hear a husky groan and see Conor Edwards fisting both his hands in a tangle of blonde hair.

"Ahhh fuck, I'm coming," he rasps, his hips pumping. And on her knees Michelle swallows every drop.

Jesus!!

I quickly slam the door, not caring if they heard it. I've witnessed friends hooking up before, but never had the honor of staring into their heavy-lidded eyes fuzzy with bliss as they climax. Goddamn Conor. Hasn't he ever heard of a lock?

My gaze turns toward a bedroom at the end of the all. I know the guy who lives there—Ben something or other. And he has a private bath. My wet body is dripping water on the carpet. I need a towel and a wastebasket to toss my boxers in. Ben's bathroom, it is.

But I've only taken one step down the hall when Ben's door swings open and I witness yet another thing I shouldn't.

Only this time it's worse than Conor coming in some chick's mouth.

Much, much worse.

12
HUNTER

I'M UP AT SIX A.M. ON MONDAY. WE HAVE MORNING SKATE at seven and I need to eat, because I always have breakfast before practice. And then a second breakfast afterwards in the hockey facility kitchen. Like a hobbit.

Hollis is already awake. He needs to make the drive back to New Hampshire today. Sometimes he leaves on Sunday night, but some weekends he simply can't sacrifice one single second with his fair maiden Rupi and leaves early on Monday. I guess this was one of those weekends. But he's in for a bitch of a commute at this hour.

"Hey," I say as he staggers into the kitchen.

He grunts in response.

I head for the coffeemaker. I need a dose of caffeine to jumpstart my brain. "Want some?" I offer.

That gets me another grunt.

I decide to treat it as a yes. A couple minutes later we're drinking our coffee while I scroll through my phone to check the meal plan for the week. Our nutritionist Karly has the team on a strict diet. Granted, we break it all the time, but as Karly always warns, ignoring her meal plans only does ourselves the disservice in the end.

I skim the options on the list and decide on an egg white omelet loaded with veggies. "You want breakfast?" I ask Hollis. "Omelets."

He nods. "Yeah, one for the road might be nice. Actually, make that two."

"You want two omelets."

"I'm hungry."

"I'll start with one and then we'll see if there's time left. Coach will be pissed if I'm late." I slide a cutting board and a knife across the counter. "Get dicing."

Hollis chops mushrooms and green peppers while I prep the eggs. As we cook, the rest of the house remains eerily quiet and the sky's still dark beyond the kitchen window. The darkness makes it feel like nighttime, and my brain is unwittingly transported back to Saturday night.

Fuck.

Nico absolutely slept with that chick I saw him exiting the bedroom with.

Or at the very least, he had his pants off with her.

And when you have a serious girlfriend, your pants should never come off in the presence of another woman.

The thing is… I didn't actually catch him red-handed. I caught the potential aftermath. And I'm not about to stir up trouble in the relationship of someone I barely know. Demi doesn't trust me enough yet to take my word for it. If I went up to a friend, like Dean, for example, and said, "Hey, Allie's cheating," he would believe me. Because Dean knows I'd have no reason to lie or play games. But Demi doesn't know that.

She would question my motivations, maybe even suspect me of trying to sabotage Nico so I could have her for myself, which isn't the case.

"Hey Mike," I say as I pour the first omelet mixture into the hot pan.

"Mmmm?" He's busy chopping up a red pepper now.

"I've got a hypothetical for you."

"All right. Hypothetical me."

"What?"

"You know, like *hit me*, only with the word hypothetical instead of—whatever, just fucking say it."

"All right. Let's pretend someone you know is in a long-term, committed relationship, and you caught their boyfriend or girlfriend cheating on them. Well, *possibly* cheating. You're not a hundred percent certain, but the circumstances were very suspicious and…" I set down the spatula on the counter. "You know what? Screw it. I *am* a hundred percent certain. I know when a dude just got sucked off. I literally saw Conor ejaculating three seconds before that."

"Davenport." Hollis speaks in a voice so ominous that I'm almost nervous to turn to face him.

"Yeah?"

"Are you trying to tell me that you saw Rupi sucking Conor Edwards' dick?" Hollis rumbles like an angry bear, his face redder than the pepper on his cutting board. "When the *fuck* did it happen? Was it at the party? Was it when she went to fix her hair—"

"Relax," I interrupt. "I'm not talking about Rupi. Are you insane? That girl would never cheat on you. She's obsessed with you, Hollis. She's your stalker. You're dating your stalker."

"That's the nicest thing anyone's ever said to me."

"I'm talking about a friend from class, okay? I'm pretty sure her boyfriend cheated on her. The question is, do I tell her?"

"Nope." Zero hesitation from Hollis.

"Why not?" I use the spatula to transfer the first omelet from the pan to Mike's plate, then get to work on my own breakfast.

"Because you don't want to stick your nose in other people's biz. Trust me."

"But he's cheating on her."

"So? That's his biz, not yours."

"It's also her business," I point out.

"It can't be her business when she doesn't know about it," Hollis counters.

I pause. "So you subscribe to the whole 'what she doesn't know won't hurt her' camp? Really?"

"I'm just saying, is some rando from class worth you getting involved in a third-party relationship? Child, please."

"Please don't say *child, please*."

He ignores me, taking a huge bite of the omelet. "Look, if it was one of us," he blabbers with his mouth full, "then I'd say hell yeah, you have a duty to say something. But how well do you know this chick?"

"Not well. We're still getting to know each other."

Hollis finally swallows his food. "There you go. So even if you do tell her, she won't believe you, bro. If someone I'm 'still getting to know'"—he uses air quotes—"accused Rupi of cheating, I'd say child, please—"

"I'm begging you to stop saying that."

"—and I'd think they had an ulterior motive."

Mike Hollis, of all people, is rationally confirming my own doubts. But maybe men are naturally cynical? I'm sure if I polled any of the women living in this house whether they'd want to know, the answer would be YES! In a heartbeat.

"You don't want to get involved," Hollis warns. "Trust me, man. Stay as far away from this situation as you can."

———

Morning practice is fast-paced. I'm sweating like a dog, and panting like one as I skate hard toward the net. We're running two-on-ones, designed for the defensemen to attempt to stop a forward on a breakaway. But I'm way faster than Kelvin and Peters. During the entire drill, I've managed not only to outskate them, but to score on net every time.

Until now. I wind up my slapshot and unleash the puck, only for the goaltender to pluck it out of the air with his glove. It's Trenton, our backup goalie.

He lifts his mask and flashes a toothy grin. "How do you like them apples, captain?"

I whistle in admiration. "That's a wicked glove you got there. If you were a bit faster with the pads, you'd be giving Boris some real competition for the starter job."

Rather than look defeated, Trenton's eyes gleam with fortitude. "Then I'll get faster," he vows.

Oh yeah, he's got that hunger. The kid's gonna be starting games in no time.

I skate toward the bench. Coach blows his whistle, signaling practice is over. Our defensive coordinator O'Shea asks a couple of D-men to stay behind to run one more drill, but the rest of us are free to go. Good, because my stomach is grumbling. Time for second breakfast. But first I need to wash all the sweat off me.

Our showers have the sweetest set-up. Each one is its own individual stall separated by waist-high partitions, so we can see each other's heads but not our junk, just the way I like it. In the stall next to mine, Con is dunking his head under the spray, smoothing his longish hair away from his forehead. He's got a bite mark on his left shoulder. This fucking guy.

"Hey, about this weekend," I start, deciding to poll more people about my dilemma.

But Conor misinterprets. Chuckling softly, he turns to grin at me. "Yeah, sorry 'bout that. I forgot to lock the door." He raises a brow. "You should've joined us."

I'm helpless to stop my dick from twitching. Bad enough that I'm not having sex with the parade of women throwing themselves at me at parties—now I'm being invited to three-somes? The universe has a lousy sense of humor.

"Nah, I'm not talking about the BJ. I needed—"

"*Feed me!*" The anguished shout reverberates in the shower area, making Con and me jump.

"For fuck's sake," Conor says, turning toward the doorway.

Matt and Treeface are standing outside Jesse Wilkes' stall, the latter waving Pablo around in the air. I'm not worried about the egg falling into one of the showers, because it's been established that pigs can indeed swim.

Jesse remains unfazed by the intruders. He simply squirts shampoo into his palms and lathers up his hair. "You can wait five minutes, Pablo," he says cheerfully.

Matt glares at him. "Would you really do that if he was real? If your pet pig was standing in the doorway begging to be fed?"

"Hell yeah, I would. I've got three golden retrievers at home. They eat when I tell them to eat."

Laughter bounces off the acoustics in the room. He's got a point. I had a Jack Russell growing up and he ate twice a day, like clockwork. My control-freak father wouldn't have it any other way.

Man, I miss that dog. I was ten years old when he died, and I remember crying my eyes out in my bedroom until Dad came in to inform me that real men don't cry. Good chat.

"But he's *starving*," Tree says in accusation.

Jesse just gives them the finger before continuing to wash his hair. He's even whistling.

Although…he's shampooing rather fast… In fact, I barely have time to blink before he's shutting off the water and darting through the doorway.

Conor grins at Jesse's retreating backside. "Dude. I think they're actually starting to believe it's a real pig."

"Right?" But I can't deny that Pablo has developed a life of his own. Even I can't be certain he's an egg anymore. I think he might be a real boy.

"Anyway," I say as I rinse off. "I need advice."

"Hit me," Conor replies, because that's a normal response from a normal person. I don't understand why Hollis— annnnd there's no point trying to figure out Hollis. It's like trying to understand the wind.

Toweling off, I quickly outline the situation. Unlike Hollis, Con *does* hesitate. He thinks it over for several beats before providing an answer.

"I'd tell her."

"Yeah? Even though she might punch me in the face?"

"Well, sure, the messenger always risks getting shot, but is it better to leave her in the dark? What if you run into her and the boyfriend? What do you do, pretend everything is cool and that you don't know he's a total douchebag?"

"I'm with Con," Foster pipes up from my other side. He's been listening in this entire time. "You gotta tell her, man. And hey, if it turns out you're wrong? You say *I'm sorry, I was trying to be a good friend and look out for you, and I made a mistake.*"

Which is precisely what this boils down to—me wanting to be a good friend. I hate the idea of Demi being played for a fool. Nico seemed like a good guy the first time I met him, but he was emitting some real slime vibes at the party. On the other hand, I hardly know the dude. Maybe he's just a bit slimy. Doesn't make him a cheater.

I poll a few other teammates in the locker room, and the consensus seems to be to tell Demi the truth. But it isn't until Jesse texts his girlfriend for her opinion that I'm fully swayed to the side of morality. In all caps, Katie texts back a resounding:

TELL HER RIGHT EFFING NOW, YOU HEARTLESS MONSTER!!!!!!

I guess I have my answer.

13
DEMI

THERE'S A TEXT MESSAGE FROM HUNTER WHEN I STEP OUT OF Biology class late in the afternoon. He's supposed to come by tonight for a fake therapy session, but apparently now he's cancelling.

> **HUNTER**: Need to cancel tonight. Last-minute thing in Boston.
> **ME**: Didn't we LITERALLY just talk in class earlier and confirm?
> **HIM**: Yes, and then I LITERALLY just got a text from a friend and now I have to cancel.
> **ME**: I demand to know why.
> **HIM**: Bruins game.
> **ME**: Is there really a game or are you just lying to get out of studying? Cuz you were acting super strange this morning. Even TJ noticed.
> **HIM**: I wasn't acting strange and there really is a game. Google it.
> **ME**: I will choose to believe you. How are you getting there?

HIM: Teleporting, obviously.
ME: Jackass. Are you driving?
HIM: Ya. Why?
ME: When are you leaving? Maybe I can catch a ride with you??

I'm hopeful as I await his response. A free ride to Boston would enable me to visit my parents, who I haven't seen since Labor Day weekend. It's already mid-October, but I haven't had much free time to make the trek into the city. I don't have a car, an Uber would be too expensive, and the bus takes way too long.

Rather than texting, Hunter calls me. "Why do you need to go to Boston?"

"My parents live there. Our house is near Beacon Hill."

"Fancy."

"You're one to talk, rich boy. So can I catch a ride with you?"

"Sure. I'm leaving around six, but if you want a ride back with me, it won't be till eleven-ish."

"That's fine. Pick me up from here?"

"Yup yup."

"Please don't say yup yup. I don't like it."

"I don't care. See you in an hour."

He hangs up on me and I grin at the phone. Hunter amuses me. He makes a nice addition to my roster of male friends. The Lost Boys, as Corinne would say.

I take a quick shower and then put on a green sundress and the gold hoop earrings my parents gave me for my birthday in August.

I hate these earrings with a passion. They're big hoops, and if it were up to me, big hoops would be banned in this country. But I slide them on now because I want Mom and Dad to think I wear the hoops on the reg. They have the tendency to act all wounded if I don't fawn over their gifts.

Hunter texts when he's outside, and I'm not surprised to find a shiny black Land Rover parked at the curb. I slide into the passenger's side and settle on the sleek leather seat.

"Hey," he says. He's wearing a black-and-yellow jersey, his dark hair slicked back from his face.

"Are you wearing hair gel?"

"Are you wearing enormous hoop earrings?"

"I asked first."

"Yes, I'm wearing gel."

"Your head is *glistening*."

"Yeah, but at least it's staying in place. Whenever I watch live hockey, I get agitated and run my fingers through my hair until it's fucking falling out—I figured gel would help prevent that. Your turn."

"My turn what?"

"The hoops, Semi. I could probably fit my entire glistening head through one of those monsters." He chuckles faintly. "I guess you can take the girl out of Miami but you can't take Miami out of the girl?"

"Wrong. I despise these earrings. They're more my mom's style," I admit. "She's all about the big hoops, and she thinks everyone should dress and accessorize exactly like her. But I prefer tiny studs—you know, so there's no chance of them getting caught on anything and ripping my ear off, leaving a bloody hole in the side of my head."

"That's a really cynical view of hoops."

"They're a safety hazard. I stand by that."

"So you pretend to like them to please your mommy and daddy?" He's mocking me.

I bristle, but only slightly, because there's truth to that statement. Especially the daddy part. My father is a scary man. The kind of man who is so impressive you constantly feel the need to impress him back.

"Why didn't Nico drive you tonight?" Hunter asks suddenly, and there's a strange note in his voice.

He was using that same tone this morning too. Every time I whispered something to him during Andrews' lecture, he responded in that weird tone and then avoided my eyes.

I glance over, but he's focused on the road and his face is devoid of expression. "Nico's working tonight."

"People move at night?"

"Sometimes, yeah. He actually gets paid more for night moves."

"*Night moves* sounds like the name of a porno."

"I think it might be a song," I say, trying to recall. "I could be wrong, though. Anyway, he gets paid time and a half for any jobs after six, so if a late shift comes up, he always takes it."

"Makes sense." Hunter nods. A few beats of awkward silence ensue. First time it's ever happened to us. Then again, we don't know each other super well, so an awkward silence was bound to make an appearance sooner or later.

"Let me sync up my Bluetooth to your car," I say, reaching for the touch screen on his dash. "I'll find us a fun driving playlist."

He instantly swats at my hand. "No way," he says. "No woman is allowed to have that much control over me."

I laugh. "What control? It's Bluetooth. Bluetooth is harmless."

"Nope. Maybe tonight it's harmless. And maybe tomorrow you'll be remotely controlling my car."

"How would I even do that?"

"By hacking into the system and driving my Rover off a cliff." He sounds smug.

"I want to drive you off a cliff *now*," I threaten. "Just let me sync up, dammit." And then because I'm a jerk, I go through the process of pairing my phone to his car. Whistling the entire time.

When I'm done, I graciously ask, "What would you like to listen to?"

He glowers at me. "I can't believe you just did that."

"If you don't pick something, I'll put on Disney soundtracks."

Hunter capitulates. "Got any old-school hip hop mixes?"

I nod in approval. "Coming right up." I click on a popular playlist and we spend the remainder of the drive locked in a competitive rap battle to Cypress Hill and Run-DMC. By the time we reach the city, my throat is hoarse, and Hunter's face is lobster red from laughing.

"You got mad rhymes, Semi!" he says gleefully. "We need to make a YouTube video."

"Oh God, never. I have zero interest in being in the spotlight. Unlike you."

"Me?"

"You like the spotlight, no? Won't you be playing professional hockey when you're done college?"

Hunter surprises me by shaking his head. "No, I didn't declare for the draft and I don't plan on signing with a team after I graduate. Teams have come knocking on my door since high school, but I always tell them I'm not interested."

"Why the heck not?"

"I'm just not. I don't want that kind of national attention."

I wrinkle my forehead. "But aren't you really talented? The girls at the house said you're the best player on the team."

"I'm okay."

I appreciate the modesty. But all it tells me is that Hunter must be a lot more than *okay*.

"I'm not interested in the pros, Demi. Not everyone wants to be famous."

It's a peculiar answer and I don't quite buy it, but the British lady on Hunter's GPS is chirping that our destination is up ahead on the right.

I smile as we drive down the street I've called home since I was fifteen. Even after six years on the east coast, my mother still isn't in love with Boston, whereas I liked it the moment we moved here.

Miami is loud and colorful and undeniably fun, but just because I'm half Latina doesn't mean I want things to be loud all the time. We lived in Little Havana, a mostly Cuban community full of art galleries and coffee shops and cigar stores on every street corner. It's a bustling area, almost the polar opposite of Boston's conservative Beacon Hill neighborhood.

My new city, while not as IN YOUR FACE as Miami,

has its own unique character, from its brownstones and tree-lined streets to Boston Common and Newbury Street. Plus, despite contrary opinion, I find the accents downright charming.

"Here we are. Have fun with your parents," Hunter says.

"Have fun at your game."

I'm pleased to notice that he waits until I reach the front stoop before pulling away from the curb. Real gentlemen are hard to find these days.

My mother shrieks happily when I walk through the door. She's the loudest person on the planet. My friends insist that she's a clone of Sofia Vergara from *Modern Family*, and they're not far off the mark. Although Mom's not Colombian like the character, she's drop-dead gorgeous with a voice that could shatter every plate in a china store.

Blabbering on in Spanish, she hugs me tight enough to restrict my airflow, then drags me down the hall toward the kitchen. "Where's Dad?" I ask.

"On his way home from the hospital. He just finished surgery, so expect Grumpy Papa tonight."

I'm used to Grumpy Papa. Some surgeons ride a high after they operate, but Dad is always exhausted after a long surgery, and he gets cranky when he's tired. Like a toddler. But he deserves to be cut some slack, because—hello—he just saved somebody's life. Brain surgeons are allowed a free bitchiness pass, as far as I'm concerned.

"Are you hungry?" Mom demands, then answers her own question. "Of course you are! Sit down so I can feed you, *mami*. How is school going?"

"Good." I fill her in on my classes and the project with

Hunter, while she unloads Tupperware containers from the fridge.

If my visit hadn't been last minute, I have no doubt she would've cooked me a feast. Instead, I'm relegated to the leftovers from whatever feast she cooked for Dad yesterday. And it's *spectacular*. Soon the cedar work island is laden with dishes, most of them Cuban, with a few of Dad's American favorites sprinkled in.

My mouth waters as each new item emerges from the microwave. There's shredded beef seasoned to perfection with veggies and olives and served on brown rice. Cuban chicken stew with raisins to give it a bit of sweetness. Stuffed peppers. Fried beans. The roasted potatoes and garlic carrots that Dad likes.

"Oh my goodness, Mom," I declare while inhaling her food. "I've missed your cooking *so* much." Pieces of rice fly out of my mouth as I talk.

"Demi," she chides.

"Hmmmm?" I mumble through a mouthful of spicy beef.

She flips her glossy brown hair over one shoulder. "Of all the traits you could've inherited from your father, his poor table manners is what it had to be?"

"What? You should take it as a compliment that we both enjoy your cooking."

"Maybe you can enjoy it with your mouth full," she suggests. "And leave some carrots for your father." She slaps my hand when I try to stick my fork in the carrot container.

Speaking of my father, he appears in the doorway without warning. I hadn't heard him come in. Granted, that's probably because I'm chewing so loudly.

"Hi baby," he says happily. Enormous arms encircle me from behind as he places a kiss on the top of my head.

"Hey Daddy." I swallow some more rice.

He greets my mother, which is always a fun sight to see. Standing at six foot five, Dad is a bald black guy with arms like tree trunks, palms like oven mitts, and long but surprisingly delicate fingers. Or I guess not surprisingly, seeing as how nimble digits are required when poking around in somebody's skull. And then there's Mom, who's all of five feet, with huge boobs and shiny hair and the Latin temper she passed on to me. They're the cutest couple ever, and I adore my little family. Being an only child means I don't have to share anything with a sibling, including my parents' attention.

Dad joins me at the counter and digs into the leftovers. Mom, who has trouble staying still, eventually sits down too and nibbles on an olive while Dad tells us about his surgery. The patient was a construction worker whose skull nearly got crushed by a falling steel beam. He wasn't wearing his hardhat, and now he might have permanent brain damage. It's heartbreaking. Which is one of the reasons I'd never want to be a surgeon—that and I don't have the hands for it. My fingers get trembly when I'm nervous, and I can't imagine a more anxiety-inducing situation than sawing into a human being's skull.

The topic once again shifts to my classes, which I list for my father. "Organic Chem, bio, math, and Abnormal Psych."

"Organic Chemistry was always a favorite of mine," Dad reveals, sipping on a glass of water Mom gets for him.

"It's my least favorite," I confess. "Right now I'm having the most fun with the psychology class. It's so fascinating."

"Are you taking physics next semester?"

I grimace. "Unfortunately."

Dad laughs. "You'll enjoy it," he promises. "And then wait till med school! Everything you learn there will be fascinating. Have you given more thought to that MCATs tutor? I have a good one lined up—just say the word."

I swallow, but it does nothing to alleviate the lump of pressure that constricts my throat. "Maybe next semester?" I counter. "I'm worried my grades will dip a little if I add another study commitment to my schedule."

"It'll only be a few times a week."

A few times a week? Oh my God, I thought I'd only have to see this tutor once, *maybe* twice a week.

"Let me see how it goes with midterms and then we can reevaluate?" I hold my breath, praying he'll accept the compromise.

Luckily, he does. "All right. But I do think the head start will help you a lot. The med school application process can be stressful."

"Honestly..." I find some courage, then continue, "Sometimes it feels overwhelming when I think about it. Med school, I mean."

"I won't deny it's a lot of work, and a lot of sleepless nights. But that makes it all the more rewarding when you graduate and start calling yourself Dr. Davis."

"You're Dr. Davis."

"There can be two," he teases.

I hesitate again. "You know, I could still call myself doctor if I got a PhD in psychology rather than med school."

His shoulders immediately stiffen. "Are you considering that avenue?" There's an edge to his voice, along with surprise-tinged disapproval.

Yes, I almost blurt out. Because it's the more appealing avenue, in my eyes. What do I care about biology or anatomy? I'd way rather be taking courses like psych theory, cognitive and behavioral therapies, research methods, personality development. AKA far more interesting areas of study.

And yet I can't say any of that out loud. My father's approval matters to me. Maybe too much, but that's how it's always been.

So I backtrack as fast as I can. "No, that was just a joke. Everyone knows people with doctorates aren't *real* doctors. Like, come on."

Dad booms with laughter again. "You got that right."

Then I shovel more food into my mouth so I won't have to keep talking. This doesn't bode well, though. With senior year coming up, I've been giving more and more thought to what I want to do after I graduate. Med school had been the plan, but grad school is also tempting. Truth is, I find psychiatry to be so…clinical. There's such a large focus on medication management of patients, and I can't seem to gather much excitement at the notion of prescribing meds and monitoring dosages. I suppose I could specialize in something stimulating, like neuropsychiatry and treat patients with Alzheimer's and MS. Or maybe work in a psychiatric unit of a hospital.

But I want to focus on treating the behaviors of patients, not only the symptoms. I want to talk to people, to *listen* to them. But my father never would get that. And this proves it. I mean, I just stuck my toe in the water and an alligator bit it off. That doesn't exactly make me want to broach the subject again.

14
HUNTER

"DUDE! IT'S BEEN AGES!" DEAN LOOKS INSANELY HAPPY TO see me.

Dean took me under his wing when I was a freshman and he was a senior, and I think part of him still views me a bit like his protégé. To be honest, he's the one who taught me the bad habits that landed me in trouble last season. "How To Pick Up Chicks" by Dean Heyward-Di Laurentis should be a prerequisite course for all horny college boys. The guy knows what he's doing.

Of course, it helps when you have supermodel-chiseled features, golden hair, sparkling green eyes. Summer is like the girl version of Dean, which is a bit unnerving considering I've jerked off to fantasies of her before.

"It's good to see you," I tell my old friend. "How's it going?"

"Pretty damn good. My roster is *killer* this year." Dean coaches a girls' hockey team at a private school in Manhattan. He'd actually gotten into Harvard Law, but at the last moment accepted a teaching position instead. I guess you could say he's a high school gym teacher, but he also coaches hockey and volleyball, and coaching is where his true passion lies.

"Nice. I should try to catch one of your games if they don't conflict with my sched. Do you ever have road games? Anything in Boston?"

"Actually, there's a tournament here next month. I'll let you know the dates. But you should definitely come. Allie showed up to the last game and the girls lost their shit. They love her show." Dean's girlfriend, Allie Hayes, is an actress on a popular HBO show. It even won a bunch of Emmys recently. Allie wasn't nominated for her role, but they won for Best Drama, which is impressive as fuck.

"Is Allie here?" I ask, searching for her blonde head.

Dean nods. "She's up in the box with Grace, chatting up a storm. All the girlie talk got too much for me, so I said I'd wait for you out here." He gestures to the front entrance of the massive arena behind us.

The air is electric tonight, as it always is for a home game. All around us are black-and-yellow jerseys, interspersed with the red-and-white ones worn by the fans representing Detroit, tonight's opponent.

It's utterly surreal to think that I'm friends with not one, but two of the men on the ice tonight. Garrett Graham is the star of the team, the leading scorer in the entire league, and arguably one of the greatest hockey players of all time. I can't believe I played one year of college with him.

The other friend is John Logan, another college legend. It's Logan's rookie season with the team. Before this, he was playing for the Bruins' farm team, so this is like his big promotion. So far, he's done well in the first few games of the season, and I'm excited to watch him and Garrett play live again. These days I catch their games on TV, but it's not the same.

"Is Fitz still staying with you guys in Manhattan?" I ask Dean as we head inside.

"Not at mine and Allie's place. He's at my fam's penthouse, doing work for that Brooklyn game studio. He has the whole penthouse to himself this time, which I think is a huge relief for him."

"Oh, it is. He told me he was staying there with your dad last month."

Dean chuckles. "Yup, the two of them living it up in the bachelor pad, while Summer's in Boston and Mom's in Greenwich. Jesus. I can't imagine having to shack up with Allie's father. He'd probably murder me in my sleep and bury my body in a block of cement under their brownstone. No one would find it until years later, when someone decides to rebuild the house and jackhammers the foundation."

"Oh come on, I thought you and Allie's dad were cool."

"For the most part. But he still calls me 'rich boy' and always asks me what designer I'm wearing." Dean sighs glumly. "So now I just wear rags when I'm there so that I don't get made fun of."

I swallow a laugh. Stories about Allie's father never fail to entertain me. I haven't met the man, but he sounds hilarious. "Does your dad like Fitzy?" I ask curiously.

"Are you kidding me? Dad will love anybody Summer brings home. She's his princess and can do no wrong. She could legit bring home a serial killer and Dad would be sitting there asking to see pictures of the victims." Dean imitates his father's voice. "Oh, you used a hacksaw to chop off the head? Neat! Can you show me how to do that?"

This time I can't contain my laughter. "You're exaggerating."

"Not exaggerating in the slightest, dude. Remember that guy in high school? You'd know him—you were in the same year. Rickie? Ronnie? The one with the face tattoo?"

"Lawrence," I say with a groan.

"Man, I was *way* off."

"That guy was such a loser. Summer went out with him?"

"It was during her rebellious stage. Mom told her she couldn't do something, I can't remember what, so Summer got all huffy and that weekend she brought Face Tattoo to our family picnic. Mom almost died. Meanwhile Dad's asking him about the inspiration behind the *face tattoo*."

"It was…stars?" I ask, trying to picture Lawrence's tats.

"Birds," Dean corrects with a snort. "Winding around his neck and going up to his cheek and forehead."

"Sounds hot."

Snickering, we take the escalators up to the private boxes reserved for VIPs. I flash the guest credentials Dean handed me downstairs, and the guards wave us through. Our box is the one for Wives and Girlfriends. I love it. We're considered WAGs tonight, but the only actual girlfriend present is Grace Ivers, a senior at Briar. She and Logan live together in an apartment between Hastings and Boston.

I don't know Grace very well. In fact, I don't think we've ever had a conversation. But she greets me warmly and gives me a quick hug.

I know Allie a lot better because of Dean, and her hug

is tighter and lasts much longer. "Hunter! You're looking so good! You've gained like fifty pounds of muscle."

"Not quite." I smile. "You look great. I'm digging the shorter hair."

She smooths a hand over her blonde bob. "Really? Dean says it makes me look like a pixie."

"So? Pixies are hot. Did you guys take the train in from New York?"

"Yeah. We were both free tonight and decided, what the hell. Might as well support the boys."

"Good call." I wander over to the massive window overlooking the rink. The players are warming up at the moment. I search the ice for Garrett's and Logan's jersey numbers. I spot Logan first. Grace's eyes are glued on him too, as she comes up beside me.

"How's he doing this season?" I ask. "I haven't studied his stats line too closely."

"He's doing well. Not as well as he'd like to be doing, but he got two assists in the game against Philly. Boston has some pretty amazing defensemen already, so John's not seeing as much ice time as he wants." Grace sounds unhappy. I'm not sure if it's on Logan's behalf, or if there's more to it.

"Uh oh, is he taking it out on you?" Allie demands. Evidently she glimpsed that same flicker of discouragement in Grace's eyes.

"No, not at all. But he's just a bit on edge. And I'm busy at the radio station, so our schedules often conflict." She shrugs before offering a halfhearted smile. "Every relationship has its speed bumps in the road. We'll be fine."

"True," Allie agrees. "But if you need me to knock some

sense into him, let me know. I'll get my boyfriend to beat him up."

"Wait," Dean balks, channeling Mike Hollis. "*I'm* your boyfriend."

I snicker.

Dean sets his jaw. "I'd never beat up Logan for you, Allie-Cat. He's my BFF."

"I thought Garrett was your BFF," she taunts.

"I thought *I* was your BFF," I whine.

He sighs. "Jesus fucking Christ, you're all my BFFs, okay?"

"Hey, where's Hannah?" I ask, referring to Garrett's girlfriend, Hannah Wells. The last time I was in the WAGs box, she was also present.

"Holy shit, did you not hear about Wellsy?" Dean demands.

"What about her?"

"You know how she's been working with that famous producer? The one who's also worked with Rihanna and Beyoncé and a bunch of other huge names?"

"Yeah, but I thought she wasn't making her own music. Isn't she writing songs now?"

"She is," Allie confirms. "And one of her songs is going to be performed by—get *this*! Delilah Sparks! They're in the recording studio as we speak, laying down the track. Hannah says it might actually be the single on Delilah's next album."

"Wow. That is impressive." It's really cool seeing what everyone's been doing after college. Dean teaching and coaching. Allie on TV. Hannah rubbing elbows with superstar recording artists.

But…and maybe this is just the little boy in me…for me,

watching Garrett and Logan skating in a packed TD Garden, representing our city, trumps everybody else's careers.

All I ever wanted was to play professional hockey. It was my childhood dream. When I first told my parents that dream, I think Dad was pissed, because in his mind he'd been grooming me since birth to work for his company and eventually take it over. But when it turned out I was really damn good and had a more than realistic shot of making a shit ton of money as a pro hockey player, suddenly Dad was on board, encouraging my budding career.

So, yes, I wanted it. Badly. But then... I changed my mind. I realized that the NHL lifestyle is not for me. It's too decadent, too destructive if you're not careful, and I truly don't know if I trust myself to be part of it.

Still, knowing I won't be down on that ice one day doesn't take away from the excitement of watching my friends skate. Everyone in the box is cheering their lungs out, and a wave of screams rocks the room when Garrett creates a rebound that lands on Logan's stick. Logan snaps it up and scores his first goal of the season. Grace is on her feet, screaming herself hoarse, her face shining with pride.

I wonder if I'll ever find a woman who looks at me like that. A woman who, when presented with "speed bumps" in our relationship, works with me to smooth them out instead of simply driving away. I might not want a girlfriend this very second, but I can't deny that I hope to find something—no, someone—real in the future.

On the other hand, some relationships are total shit. I mean, look at Demi. She's head over heels for her boyfriend, and he's going around getting his dick wet at frat parties.

And I *still* haven't told her the truth. I had all day to do it, for chrissake. We sat together in Abnormal Psych this morning. We spent an hour in the car together on the way up here. Yet every time I opened my mouth to tell her, I couldn't get the words out.

I'll say something on the drive home tonight. I have to.

I'm just going to suck it up, blurt it out, and let the chips fall where they may.

———

Like a coward, I wait until the last possible second to broach the subject with Demi. After picking her up from her parents' house, I let her chat for the entire drive home, nodding and smiling while internally gathering my courage. The last time I found myself in a situation like this, it blew up in my face like a grenade. Every fiber of my being wants me to keep my mouth shut, but I like this girl, and I think she deserves to know.

I guess I'm not a great actor, because Demi finally calls me on my behavior as I turn onto the main road toward campus.

"Okay, what is *up* with you?"

"Nothing," I lie.

"I'd think I was boring you, but I know for a fact that I am *not* boring. I'm a fucking excellent conversationalist and I just told you a story about the time I met Gigi Hadid in South Beach AKA the best meet-cute of the century."

I crack a smile. "You're certainly not boring," I agree.

"So why are you acting weird?" Demi sounds aggravated.

"I…" Inhale. Exhale. Here goes. "I need to tell you

something, and I've been debating all day whether or not to do it."

"What is it?"

"Uh."

Silence commences.

"Okay. Cool. Great chat, bro!"

I quickly backtrack. "You know what, it's not important." *It's none of my business*, I tell myself. Whatever Nico's doing is his own business.

"I'm joking," she insists. "Tell me what going on."

"Uh."

Silence recommences.

"Come on, Monk, am I going to have to beat it out of you?"

"I'd like to see you try."

"I'm a lot stronger than I look." She frowns. "Are you really not going to tell me?"

"Nico," I blurt before I can stop myself.

And I instantly want to punch myself in the face, because Demi is like a shark that just caught a sniff of blood.

"What about him?" she demands.

"Nothing." Goddammit, why did I even bring it up? And why is it taking so long to reach Greek Row? I need an escape plan, ASAP.

"*Hunter*," she says sharply.

"Fine. Just…don't shoot the messenger, okay?" I release a quick breath. "I ran into him at a party this weekend at the Alpha Delta house. Saturday night?"

Demi toys with one of her hoop earrings as she thinks about it. "He went out with his work friends Saturday night.

I thought they were in Hastings, but I suppose they could've gone to that party."

"They were definitely there. I don't know if it was with the work buddies or not, but Nico was there. He and I even spoke."

"Okay. So he went to a party. Big deal."

"That's not all he did."

Her features sharpen again. "What do you mean?"

"I mean I saw him upstairs with some chick."

Once again, silence falls over the car. Shit. I should not have brought this up at all.

"All right," she says slowly. "You saw him with a girl. What were they doing?"

"They were exiting a bedroom."

"Were they naked?"

"Well, no, they were both fully clothed. But…" I don't want to say it, but I force myself to spit it out. "He was zipping up his pants."

"Oh."

"Obviously that doesn't mean they were doing anything," I add hastily. "Maybe they both needed to use the bathroom and he forgot to do up his fly after taking a leak. But, speaking as a guy—"

"As a fuckboy, you mean."

"Whoa." I'm taken aback by the verbal assault. She must really hate me right now. "Should I remind you I haven't been sexually active in months?"

"Should I remind me how sexually active you were last year? You said so yourself, remember? So maybe you're just associating your own behavior with whatever you think you saw Nico doing." Her lips tighten. "Maybe they were using the bathroom. Maybe they were hanging out or talking or whatever. You don't know for certain that something happened."

"That's exactly what I'm saying to you," I grumble. "I don't know if anything happened."

We reach the fork in the road that leads to Greek Row, and I eagerly flick the turn signal. I've never been happier to see a sorority house and I'm not even banging anyone inside of it.

"Look, I'm sorry," I mutter. "I shouldn't have said anything."

Demi doesn't answer. Her profile is as tense as the current state of my shoulders.

I stop in front of the Theta house. I avoid her eyes as I put the Rover in park. "But I figured I should tell you. You know, just in case."

"Tell me what? That my boyfriend was talking to some girl?"

"No, that he went upstairs with her, that they were alone in a bedroom, and that he walked out zipping up his pants. Get your head out of the sand, Demi. Men in relationships don't do that kind of shit."

I instantly regret my harsh tone. But rather than go silent or meek, Demi's eyes turn molten. "You don't know anything about my relationship, Hunter."

"I know that you already suspected him of cheating on you once."

"Yeah, when we were kids. He's matured since then."

Has he? I want to challenge. I keep quiet, but the

unspoken question hangs in the air, and Demi hisses in response to it.

"He *has*," she insists. "And you know what? I don't appreciate you jumping to conclusions, and I don't appreciate all your fear mongering!"

"Fear mongering?" I can't help but snicker. "Jesus Christ. All I'm telling you is that I saw the dude zip up his pants. Do with that what you will."

15
DEMI

HE WAS ZIPPING UP HIS PANTS.

Hunter's words buzz in my brain as I stalk into house. Despite the late hour, a bunch of my sorority sisters are still up, watching a horror movie. The living room is dark, and I glimpse bowls of popcorn and hear a lot of shrieking at the screen. But I don't join them. I'm not in the mood.

Instead I go to the kitchen and stick my head in the fridge. I need a snack. Pronto. When I'm agitated, I eat. It's a habit I probably need to squash, because great metabolism doesn't last forever, but my mom is in her forties and can still eat whatever she wants, so I'm hopeful for the future. I grab a block of cheddar and angrily start cutting the cheese into cubes.

I don't care what Hunter says. Nico couldn't have cheated. Yes, he was out on Saturday night with his friends. And fine, maybe they did wind up at a frat party. But that doesn't mean he did anything shady. For all Hunter knows, Nico was hanging out with Pippa. I'm pretty sure Pippa went to that party, too.

I put down the knife and grab my phone, wasting no time texting my friend.

ME: Hey, were you at the Alpha Delt party on Sat??

As I wait for Pippa's response, I pile the cheese cubes onto a plate and then rummage through the pantry for a box of crackers. I dump a bunch of those on the plate too.

When my phone buzzes, I dive for it.

PIPPA: Ya. Why??
ME: Did you see Nico there?
HER: No. Was he there?
ME: Maybe? Someone says they saw him.
HER: Hmmm. Well I did leave kinda early, like around 11. Do you know what time he got there?
ME: No clue. But just to be clear, you didn't see him when you were there?
HER: Nope.

I bite my lip. All right. So he wasn't with Pippa. That doesn't mean anything.

PIPPA: What's going on, D?
ME: Call me?

She calls less than five seconds later. I carry my cracker and cheese plate upstairs to my bedroom, balancing the phone on my shoulder. "Do you think Nico's cheating on me?" I demand in lieu of hello.

"Cheating on you? Is that a joke?"

"No. Someone saw him in a compromising position with another girl at the party."

Pippa laughs. "Bullshit."

A tiny sliver of hope pierces into me. "You think so?"

"I know so. Come on, babe. That boy is *obsessed* with you."

"That doesn't mean he's not cheating."

"Trust me, there's no way he would do anything to jeopardize your relationship. He's constantly going on and on about how you guys are going to get married someday. I can't see him throwing everything away for some random hook-up."

I can't, either. And, she's right. Nico does have the tendency to boast about the amazing future we're going to have. Why would he be planning a future with me if he's hooking up with other women?

"Who told you about this?" Pippa asks.

"Hunter," I confess.

"The hockey player?"

"Yes. He was at the party and he saw Nico leaving one of the upstairs bedrooms with a girl. Apparently he was zipping up his pants."

A brief silence meets my ear. Then Pippa says, "No. I still don't buy it."

"You don't?" The hope in my chest grows, joined by a rush of relief. "So, what, you think Hunter is lying?"

"Probably."

"What's his motivation to lie?"

"I bet he wants in your pants."

"We're just friends," I say. And I can't stop picturing the

tortured expression on his face when he told me what he saw. It's obvious he didn't want to say anything.

Or…he could've been putting on an act, pretending that it pained him *so much* to tell me, but really it was all a plot to, as Pippa said, get in my pants. I mean, Hunter fully admitted to having a sexual fantasy about me once. *And* he's a self-proclaimed former manwhore. Why should I trust anything he has to say about women and relationships?

On the flip side, I've known Nico since I was eight years old. He's my best friend.

"Nico loves you," Pippa says as if reading my mind. "I think Hunter is lying or else he misinterpreted what he saw."

"So you think I'm being crazy?"

"I think you're being crazy."

"Thanks, chica." I sigh. "Should I say something to Nico?"

"I don't know, babe. It might start a fight, but if you need to do it for your peace of mind, then yeah, you should. But don't frame it like an accusation," she advises. "Maybe treat it more as a joke? Like, *omigosh hon, can you believe that?*"

"That's a good approach."

We hang up a few minutes later, and I'm left sitting on my bed with a snack plate in my lap.

I stare down at the mountain of cheese and crackers, but I don't have much of an appetite anymore.

———

NICO: Good morning, bb. Meet for breakfast?

I stare at my boyfriend's message for a good five minutes before assembling enough courage to respond.

> **ME**: Sure. But I just woke up, so I need time to get ready. Pick me up in 45?
> **HIM**: Sounds good :) I'll msg u when I get 2 campus.

I'm nervous as I get ready. I decided I'm definitely going to confront him about what Hunter told me. I have no choice, because if I don't, it'll eat away at me like a slow-moving cancer, until I won't even be able to look at him without wondering if he cheated.

Hunter has to be wrong, though. Like Pippa said, he's either straight-up lying or he misinterpreted the situation. I'm hoping for the latter, because I enjoy our friendship and I don't like the idea that he's secretly been running a long con to get me into bed. That would be really shitty.

Nico texts when he's outside. I step onto the porch and am greeted by his handsome face and beautiful dimpled smile. I find myself relaxing. I adore that smile, and I adore that face. He's… well, he's my first love. I'm always going to see him and have this giddy, schoolgirl reaction. And just because I've had some doubts about our relationship, some suspicions along the way, doesn't mean we're not a good couple.

"Hey *mami*." He pulls me toward him for a hug, followed by a deep, tongue-tangling kiss.

I want to say it's a lot of passion this early in the morning, but Nico is always this passionate. It's the Cuban in him. He's all about bold claims and romantic gestures.

"You look good enough to eat." He smacks his lips together comically and I laugh.

"So do you. But I think I want some real food first."

"You always want real food."

"True."

He snickers. "How was Boston last night?" he asks as we step off the porch.

"Good. My parents were bummed you weren't there."

"Me too. But I had to work." He takes my hand. "Hopefully we can get up to see them before Thanksgiving."

"I doubt it. I've got midterms, and in the beginning of November the sorority is planning that fundraiser for the animal shelter."

His fingers loosely clasp mine as we walk towards the curb.

"Nice, you have your work truck," I say. It's one of the white pick-ups from the moving company, with their black and red logo stenciled onto the side.

"I know it's only a ten-minute walk, but do you mind if we drive to Carver? I only have an hour."

"Your first class isn't until two," I remind him.

"I know, but I need to go to work for a few hours. I told Frank I'd do a small job before class." He opens the passenger side door for me, then hurries around to get into the driver's seat.

"You asked Frank about next Friday, right?"

Nico starts the engine. "Next Friday, like two weeks from now?"

"Yeah, it's Corinne's housewarming. You were supposed to tell Frank you couldn't work that night."

"Oh, right." Nico nods, and a hunk of black hair falls on his forehead. I reach over to brush it away. "Sorry, I forgot because it's so far away. But yes, I did talk to him. He promised I'd be outta there by seven."

"Good." I buckle my seatbelt. "Isn't her new place so cute?"

"Honestly? I don't remember what it looks like," he says with a grin. "I've moved boxes into so many houses and apartments that they all blend together in my mind. Oh hey, I got you something."

That piques my interest. "You did?"

"D and I were grabbing burgers in the city the other day, and the place had one of those gumball machines, except instead of gumballs it gave out little toys and trinkets. Cost me a buck, but"—Nico grins broadly—"I knew I *had* to get this for you."

He pops open the small compartment in the center console and sticks a hand inside. Things rustle and keys jingle as he rummages around.

Finally, his hand emerges with a plastic yellow egg. "Here you go."

Highly curious, I pry open the two plastic pieces, and a small baggie falls into my lap. I break out in a grin. The bag contains a pair of cheap, plastic earrings—enormous red hoops with black polka dots.

"Because I know how much you *love* the big hoops," Nico teases.

"Aww, you're the worst." But I can't stop grinning because this gift means Nico was thinking of me when he was out with his friends, enough to stick a dollar bill into some kiddie machine so he could get me these silly earrings.

"I love them," I say, and then dramatically fling my arms around him and kiss his cheek.

"Also, they're plastic," he says helpfully. "So if they do get caught on anything, they'll probably break apart before your earlobe gets ripped off."

This boy knows me well.

He pulls away from the curb and it takes literally a minute to drive three parking lots over to the one behind Carver Hall. I have a meal plan since I technically live on campus, but Nico doesn't, so he has to pay for his breakfast. He gets French toast, and I fill my plate with bacon, eggs and toast from the buffet. Then we find a cozy table in the back of the chalet-style dining hall. The room has an impossibly high ceiling, oak paneled walls, and round mahogany tables scattered throughout.

Ten minutes into breakfast, I finally raise the subject. "Hey, so I wanted to ask you something."

"Hmmm?" He takes a bite of French toast.

"It's just…and honestly, I am *not* accusing you of anything, so please don't take it wrong way."

That gets Nico's attention. His fork snaps down on his tray. "Accusing me? What's going on?"

"Um, well. Someone mentioned something to me and I wanted to discuss it with you."

"Discuss what?"

Shit, what am I doing? Do I really want to discuss this in public? What if it goes horribly wrong?

But I already boarded the train and now I've gotta ride it all the way to crazy town. "Somebody saw you at the Alpha Delta party last weekend. With a girl."

"Somebody saw me with a girl... Can we be a little more specific?"

"They saw you coming out of an upstairs bedroom with her, and you may or may not have been zipping up your pants."

His dark eyes flash angrily. "Who said this exactly?"

"That's not important."

"Like fuck it isn't. I want to know who's spreading lies about me."

I study his expression. He seems genuinely upset, and his denial didn't ring false to me. Yet for some reason I don't want to throw Hunter under the bus, so I lie about my source. "It was a random girl at the party who told one of my sorority sisters, who told me. How I found out isn't important. I just wanted to be sure...you're saying you didn't do anything?"

"Of course not."

I hear nothing but sincerity in his voice. "Were you at the party, though?"

"Yeah, I went with Steve and Rodrigo and a couple other guys from work. I told you I was chilling with them that night."

"Right, but you didn't tell me you were going to a frat party down the street from me."

"I said the boys and I were hanging out, and we were. We went to a few different places," Nico says irritably. "Eventually we wound up there, but it was late and I didn't see the point in calling you. I had a few drinks, joked around with the guys, and the only chick I spent any time with was Roddy's sister Carla—that's probably who they saw me with. I took her up to use the bathroom. The line for the other bathroom was ridiculous, so we snuck upstairs."

This all sounds plausible. I've been in the Alpha Delta

house before, and I've seen how popular that lone downstairs bathroom is.

"Carla did her business, I did my business, and then we left the room. I don't remember zipping my fly." His jaw tightens. "But if I did, it's probably because I forgot to zip it up after taking a piss."

He doesn't sound defensive. He's defending himself, yes, but I'm not getting any sense that he's trying to convince me of something.

"Whoever told you this crap obviously read something more into the situation."

"That's what I figured. I only brought it up because…" I shrug. "Well, because it's good to always be open and honest with each other."

"I agree." His body language is still a tad stiff as he picks up his fork and resumes eating. "But I don't like the idea of people talking trash about me."

"There was no trash talking involved," I promise. "Just one friend watching out for another friend."

"One friend trying to stir up shit, more like it. Which chick said this to you?"

"I told you, I don't know the girl at the party."

"But which one of the Thetas said it?"

"It doesn't matter. She brought it to my attention because we look out for each other, but for what it's worth she also didn't think there was anything to the story," I lie.

Nico looks pleased. "Good. And I'm glad you don't believe that bullshit, either." He reaches across the table for my hand, interlacing our fingers. "You know I would never do that to you."

16
DEMI

I'M TEMPTED TO CANCEL MY SESSION WITH HUNTER THE following Monday. We haven't spoken since Boston last week, our only contact being when he texted to ask if we were still on for tonight. I feel like he was hoping I'd cancel. But this class is important to me, and I want to do well on our project. That means sucking it up and continuing to see him every week.

Maybe Hunter truly was looking out for me when he threw Nico under the bus, but for the past week everyone I've spoken to has assured me whatever happened with Nico and that girl was completely innocent. When we were at one of the campus bars a few nights ago, Darius had pulled me aside and said, "Listen, I wasn't even there that night and I can still tell you it's bullshit."

I appreciated hearing it from Darius. Nico's work friends all backed him up too, but I don't know them as well as I know D. Also…I'd never say this out loud, but I find Steve and Roddy and those guys seriously douchey. I suspect they'd have Nico's back regardless of his guilt or innocence, because they're all about the bro code. Darius, however, is a good friend to both of us, so I know he wouldn't lie to me.

Meanwhile, Nico has been extra attentive since I confronted him. Coming dangerously close to what I'd consider sucking up. I'm trying hard not to hold a cynical view about it, and even harder to put this behind us. He told me nothing happened and I said I believed him. That means letting go of any negativity, and not mistrusting him or questioning his motives.

I'm on edge as I wait for Hunter to arrive, stress-eating a bag of potato chips.

HUNTER: Josie let me in. I'm coming up.

He knocks on the door a moment later. I call out, "Come in," between my loud crunching.

Hunter appears, his thumbs loosely hooked in the pockets of his ripped jeans. They're not skinny jeans, but they're fitted to his long legs, while his black Under Armour shirt is tight to his sculpted chest. His dark hair is tousled, and his cheeks are red.

"It's windy out there," he mutters, dragging one hand through his hair.

"It's supposed to thunderstorm tonight."

"Good. It's mid-October—how is it still so hot out there?"

"Global warming," I supply.

"Yeah, it's a real problem."

Oh boy. This is not going to be fun. We're discussing the climate. And he's not looking at me, but at his Timberland boots. The ease and humor that normally flows between us is nowhere to be found.

When Hunter takes his designated seat on the loveseat, he doesn't lie down like he usually does. His big, muscular body remains seated—and tense. "Whatever, let's do this."

I grit my teeth. "You could sound a little more enthused."

"So could you," he shoots back.

I shove the chip bag on my nightstand. Fine. I guess this is how it is. I flip open the binder I'm using for the project and turn to the latest blank log.

After having done this a handful of times, I think I'm solidly in the Narcissistic Personality Disorder camp. "Dick Smith" fits all the diagnostic criteria from the DSM-5. But the problem with an NPD diagnosis is that narcissists customarily don't *know* they're narcissists, meaning that any analysis is only as useful as the info coming in. And the fact that narcissists have a tendency to rewrite events in their minds makes the whole process even more challenging.

This means the therapist needs to ask the right questions. Weed out important tidbits and search for any emerging patterns, such as the patient describing an interaction that doesn't match their reaction to it. And don't get me started on treatment. I mean, if a narcissist can't recognize he's a narcissist, how on earth do you treat his narcissism?

Ugh. I'm not super thrilled with this one. I would prefer something more straightforward, like an anxiety disorder. At least those suffering from anxiety tend to be aware they have a problem.

"So why do you think you're in therapy?" I ask my fake patient.

"I told you, my wife wanted me to go."

"So you don't think you need therapy."

"Nope." Hunter crosses his ankles and gazes up at the ceiling. "There's nothing wrong with me."

"There doesn't need to be something wrong with you, or anybody, for you to benefit from therapy."

"People who see shrinks are weak. Only reason I'm doing this is to keep my marriage together."

"And why do you want to do that?"

He scoffs. "Because no one in my family gets divorced. Divorce is another sign of weakness. An indication of your inability to work hard enough to achieve a goal."

"The goal here being, saving your marriage."

"Yes."

"Because if you get divorced, you'll look bad in front of your family and colleagues?"

"No, because I love my wife. I want to keep everything together for her and my son."

"Your *son*?"

Oh my God. Plot twist! I've been waiting weeks for a curveball like this.

Instantly, my pen is poised over my paper, ready to take copious notes. "This is the first time you mentioned a son."

"I had no reason to. The problems in my marriage have nothing to do with him."

"Yes, but it would still be fruitful for me to get a better sense of your family unit," I point out. "I need to know all the facts."

Hunter watches me through slitted eyes. "I see. So knowing all the facts *is* important?"

I tense at the jab, which is obviously directed at me, Demi, and not the fake Dr. Davis. "When the facts are true or relevant to the discussion, then yes. When someone is stirring up trouble for no reason, then no."

"For *no reason*?" The muscles in his jaw harden. "Whatever. Fine. You want to hear about my son? I'll tell you about my son. He's a little prick."

I'm taken aback by the vehemence in his tone. "Why do you say that?"

"The kid's a snitch. If it weren't for him, my wife would have no idea about that goddamn affair with my assistant. He's the one who told her."

"I see."

"He showed up at my office one day over summer break. He came by to say hello and caught me banging my secretary on the desk." Disgust twists Hunter's features. "Did he try to get an explanation from me? Ask what his mother may have done to drive me to such extreme actions? Absolutely not. Instead he took off, ran home, and told his mother what he saw."

There is something scarily...realistic about this story.

Hunter's visible resentment tells me this is more than playacting. "How old was he?"

"Fourteen. A fourteen-year-old punk who thought he was a man, the big hero who was gonna rescue his mom. Joke's on him, though. Kathryn didn't care. Of course she wasn't going to leave me. Look at me—rich, attractive. She can't do any better than me. My son thought he was doing the right thing, but as it turns out, nobody gave a shit about his opinion."

Hunter angrily shakes his head. "And it scarred the kid, because it turns out his mom already *knew* about that affair, and the previous affairs before it, and she begged him to just look the other way because his father was *such* a good man and a good dad and a good provider. When he tried to argue, she called him a troublemaker and made him feel like he'd done something wrong by telling her the truth. And so years later, when he saw something else he knew might hurt another woman, he wanted to keep his mouth shut." He's glaring at me now. "And it took a fucking lot for him to say anything. He asked his friends if he should, if they would want to know, and in the back of his mind a little voice was saying *don't get involved, it's only gonna blow up in your face again*, and look what happened—it fucking did."

Silence crashes over the bedroom. Hunter is visibly furious. I don't know if it's with me, or with himself, or with the world. He scrapes his fingers through his hair again, stone-faced.

"Hunter," I start carefully. "You…told your mother that you caught your father cheating? And…so wait…all these things you've been describing during our sessions, they actually happened to you? Your dad is the one who…"

I trail off in confusion, as my brain cycles through our sessions in an attempt to parse out which stories were real and which ones he fabricated to suit the assignment. Obviously his father was the inspiration for the narcissist he'd been pretending to be, but how much of it was an act?

"Whatever," Hunter mutters, rising to his feet. "I was trying to be a good friend, but you know what, screw this. We're done for the day. See you next week."

I'm helpless to do anything as he storms out of my room. I want to go after him, but my mind still feels muddled. Too many facts are scrambling my brain. I flip through my notes, reading over the Thanksgiving story, all the affairs, the wife's lack of a backbone and my patient's cruel dismissals of anyone he views as inferior. Is this Hunter's family? How much of it was embellished?

The one thing I'm certain was real, was the agony in his voice when he recounted telling his mother what he saw, and being told he was a troublemaker for trying to protect her.

And I said the same thing to him, accusing him of stirring up trouble.

Fuck. Sighing, I scrub my palms over my face, as guilt twists my stomach into knots. Maybe Hunter's motives were one hundred percent pure, after all.

But...he's still wrong, dammit.

———

On Friday we go to Corinne's housewarming. She's low-key so she didn't want a party, but Pippa and I talked her into it and she agreed on the condition that we kept it small.

Nico grabs me, Darius and Pippa from campus. As his girlfriend, I'm granted permanent shotgun, which means Darius and his six-foot six-inches frame is banished to the backseat.

"C'mon, D," he gripes. "My body deserves shotgun and you know it."

"If you're nice, I'll let you have it on the way back." I pull out my phone to text Corinne, only to discover it's completely dead. Shit. I forgot to charge it before I left.

I twist around to address Pippa. "Can you let Corinne know we're on the way?"

"On it."

I slide my iPhone back into my purse. Nico drives one-handed, his free hand planted firmly on my thigh. At a couple points during the drive his thumb seductively rubs my bare knee, and at one red light he even slides his fingertips under the hem of my skirt. I give him a look that says, *You're incorrigible*, and he winks in response.

There are already several people at Corinne's place when we arrive. It's an interesting mix tonight: a couple of basketball players, a girl from Corinne's yoga studio in town, and some guys from her math class. She's an Economics major and a math geek, and so are her three classmates. One of them is actually wearing a suit and tie, which makes me grin.

"You know you're at a party, right?" I tease after we're introduced. His name is Kyler and he's a senior.

"The tie's too much?" he says wryly.

"Just a bit."

As Kyler and I chat, Nico appears at my side and takes my hand. He does that sometimes, staking a physical claim when I'm with another guy, as if to say *she's mine*. I used to think it was cute. Sometimes I still do. Other times, like tonight, when I'm trying to walk around the room and talk to people, his being glued to my hip is an encumbrance.

And, frankly, annoying.

Corinne set up a refreshment table in the small dining/ living area. The party is BYOB, but she bought a variety of chasers and a couple bottles of tequila. I'm planning on drinking tonight, so I don't waste any time organizing the first round of shots.

"Come on, guys," I urge, waving everyone over.

Nico's all for it. He's more of a rum man, but he happily pours a waterfall of tequila over the row of shot glasses I lay out. I start handing them out, and then the eleven of us raise our glasses. "To Corinne, and her awesome new place!" I toast.

"To adulting!" Pippa adds.

"To adulting!"

The tequila burns a fiery path down my throat and instantly I'm warm all over. Someone turns up the music, and Nico and I drift over to the couch.

Pippa is sitting in Darius's lap, his long fingers toying with her hair. They're not a couple, but they flirt shamelessly when they're together. I tried setting them up a long time ago, but it didn't work out for whatever reason. I think neither of them wants a serious relationship, so their flirty arrangement suits them both.

Corinne stands nearby chatting with Kyler, and the others are gathered near the drinks table. Darius snatches the remote off the glass table when he notices what's on TV.

He swiftly turns up the volume. "Aw shit, I love this movie!"

"You realize it's for chicks, right?" Nico informs him.

"If it's for chicks then why is Scarlett Johansson in it?" D challenges. "Cuz I highly doubt chicks jerk off to ScarJo as often as I do."

Laughter breaks out. Kyler the math guy blushes. He's kind of cute. I wonder if he and Corinne are into each other. He's standing very close to her.

"Where do I know this actor from?" Pippa asks as a handsome guy appears on the screen. "He was in that movie about a cellphone, wasn't he?"

"That's the vaguest shit I ever heard," Darius says, poking her in the ribs.

"You know the movie I'm talking about, right, Demi?"

I peer at the screen. "Is that Chris Evans?"

Pippa nods. "And I swear to God, he was in that cellphone movie. It's an older movie with…that British guy, and that lady, and…"

Darius hoots loudly. "Fuck's sake, P, stop being so vague."

"Wait, I think I know the movie you mean," I tell Pippa. "Shit. I can't remember the title, either. Babe, let me use your phone to look it up?"

Nico reaches into his pocket and hands me his iPhone. It doesn't require a passcode to unlock, which only serves as another reason why Hunter's cheating accusations fall flat to me. Why would Nico willingly relinquish his phone if he were hiding something?

Nico's data plan is shit, so rather than pull up a browser, I open his settings first. "Hey, what's your Wi-Fi network?" I ask Corinne.

"Cwiley22," she calls back. "Password is lower-case A, upper-case F—"

"That's weird," I interrupt, "it connected on its own."

An uneasy feeling tickles my tummy as I glance at Nico.

"Huh." A frown creases his brow. "You know what, my phone must have saved your network when the boys and I were here moving you in," he says to Corinne.

"Oh, that must be it," she replies.

I nod slowly and open a web browser to search for—what am I searching for again? Oh, right. Chris Evans. But my fingers are trembling as I Google his filmography.

Something's bothering me and I can't figure out what it is. I mean, I already knew that Nico and his co-workers moved all of Corinne's boxes from the dorm to the apartment, and transported her new furniture. He never hid that, and neither did she. And of course she would've given Nico her Wi-Fi password if he'd asked. And he would've asked, because his data plan sucks and if he was here for a couple hours and wanted to use his phone, he'd definitely—

Then it hits me, the reason why my stomach is churning and twisting itself into knots.

Corinne didn't have Wi-Fi until nearly a week after she'd moved in. When I came over to help with her closet, it still hadn't been set up.

There's no way it could've been up and running when Nico was there days and days before.

My entire body suddenly feels cold.

"Demi. What's the movie we're thinking of?" Pippa asks impatiently.

My breathing is labored as I glance at the phone screen. "It was called *Cellular*," I mumble.

"Ha! Damn, you were right about it being a cellphone movie," a laughing Darius says to Pippa.

"I told you so."

As everyone starts chatting again, I drop the phone in Nico's lap. His deep brown eyes study me carefully. "Babe?"

I'm having a tough time finding my voice. I truly don't know what to say. Corinne is still talking to Kyler, but for some reason I *know* she's listening to me and Nico.

I draw a shaky breath. Why did his phone instantly connect to her Wi-Fi? That would suggest he's been back here since moving day, but why would he ever need to be? She's my friend, not his. I can see him hanging out with Pippa without me, but not Corinne.

The tequila gurgles in my stomach. Fuck. Am I going to throw up?

"Demi, what's wrong?" Nico urges.

I weakly meet his gaze. "Corinne only set up her Wi-Fi a week after she moved in."

For one fast second, panic flits through his expression. But it happens so quickly that I can't be sure.

"Okay, that is weird, then," he says, pursing his lips. "I wonder why it just connected like that."

"Yeah, I wonder," I say tightly.

Our hushed conversation draws Pippa's attention. "What's going on?" she asks.

"Nothing," Nico says instantly.

But Pippa knows me well. One look at my face and she's already sliding off Darius's lap.

"What's going on?" she repeats, her sharp gaze moving from me to Nico and then back to me.

I open my mouth but nothing comes out. Slowly, I turn my head toward Corinne. She's looking right back, and the guilty cloud in her eyes is all it takes for me to bolt to my feet.

The room spins for a moment. With three shots of tequila swimming in my gut, now I really am in danger of vomiting.

I choke down the bile coating my throat. "You have *got* to be kidding me," I spit out. "How long?"

Corinne takes a step toward me. "It's not what you're thinking—"

"How long have you been fucking my boyfriend,

Corinne?" My head swivels toward Nico. "How long have you been fucking her?"

The entire room goes dead silent. On the TV screen, ScarJo is bickering with Chris Evans and suddenly the movie doesn't feel so cute and funny anymore. It feels like a slap in the face, these stupid people falling in love when I've just been blindsided by my boyfriend of eight years.

"Oh shit," Darius murmurs. His voice is low, and he seems as stunned as I feel. I don't think he knew about this. I don't think anyone did, except for Hunter.

Hunter tried to warn me. He found the courage to tell me what he saw at the party and—

I abruptly turn to Corinne again. "Was that you at the frat party?" I demand.

She blinks. "What?"

"A couple of weekends ago, the party at the Alpha Delta house on Saturday night—were you there with Nico?"

She rapidly shakes her head. "No, I swear I wasn't. I'm in a study group with Kyler and Ahmed and we meet Saturday night."

She gestures to the two guys, who are quick to back up her alibi. "We were all together," Kyler says awkwardly.

"Then how long has this been going on?" My voice is cold.

"It only happened once," she blurts out. "Just one time, I swear."

My stomach roils again. I don't want to hear anymore. I'm done.

Gulping hard, I spin on my heel and stomp toward the door. Nico chases after me, his pleading voice echoing through the small apartment.

"Demi, please, stop! Let me explain."

"Explain what?" I roar, whirling around. "You cheated on me with my friend! And then again with some other girl at the party! Who was she? How many goddamn women are you screwing?"

"I didn't cheat on you. She's lying—"

"Hey!" Corinne flies forward. "I am *not* lying!"

I flick my gaze her way and glimpse a flash of outrage. It's directed at my boyfriend.

"I'm not lying, Demi," Corinne says quietly. "It happened."

And I believe her.

"Pippa," I say in a wobbly voice. "Get me an Uber. Now." I'm fighting tears, because my phone's dead and I'm trapped here in this stupid apartment with my traitorous friend and my cheating boyfriend and I just want to crawl in a fucking hole and die.

"On it," Pippa tells me.

"Demi." Nico tries to grab my arm.

On instinct I swing my other arm and clock him in the face.

His head rears back, a bitter curse ripped out of his mouth. My fist caught him on his left cheekbone. With a wounded expression, he cups one hand over it. "You hit me."

"You bet I fucking did, and you deserve a whole lot more, you fucking asshole."

"Uber's two minutes away," Pippa announces.

I jab my index finger into the center of Nico's chest. "Do *not* follow me," I warn him, and then I run out the door.

17
HUNTER

It's Friday night and my roommates and I are playing an inane board game called Zombies!™ Exclamation mark included.

Hollis is home for the weekend, which means we get to listen to him and Rupi bicker over the latest development in the game. Hollis just drew a Sacrifice card—this requires him to sacrifice someone in our collaborative group in order for the rest of us to get closer to safety. Only problem is, the most advantageous move would be to get rid of Rupi. If she dies, we don't lose much. Everybody else is too valuable to the group. There are two crossbows in my arsenal, for chrissake. What does Rupi have? Nothing.

"Dammit, Mike, finish her off," Summer bursts out, and damned if I don't crack up hearing someone as angelic-looking as Summer advocating for the fake killing of one of our friends.

"Summer!" Rupi gasps in utter betrayal.

"What?" she says defensively. "The whole point is to get the most people to the research station. There's only one

Sacrifice card in the deck. Only one person in the group is gonna die and it has to be you."

"Has to be you," Brenna agrees, taking a sip of the hot chocolate that soon-to-be deceased Rupi prepared for us.

"Mike," Rupi warns. "If you kill me, I swear to God…"

"Babe," he says.

"Mike."

"Babe."

"Mike."

"Babe," he sighs, and then places the Sacrifice card in front of her pile.

Rupi shrieks loud enough to shake the coffee table. "I *cannot* believe you did that!"

"I had no choice," he protests. "It was best for the group."

"What about what's best for *me*?"

"You're being very selfish right now, babe."

"Why? Because I want my boyfriend to protect me from harm? I don't believe this! After we're done with this game, I'm going to—"

"You *are* done with the game," Brenna interrupts dryly. "He killed you."

Rupi huffs and flounces off in traditional Rupi fashion. The girl is a drama queen.

Luckily, she found true love with a drama king. Hollis stands up and throws his frazzled arms up in the air. "Do you see what you made me do?" he accuses the rest of us. "This is why I never play board games!"

He hurries after Rupi.

"And then there were three," Brenna says indifferently, flipping through her arsenal cards.

"We can't go on without him," I tell her. "He's the only one who has the antidote for the second mutation. Oh, and the only one who can skin a rabbit."

"We'll redistribute all the assets," Summer suggests.

"Nah, I think the game's over." I drop my cards on the board and lean back against the couch cushions.

"We need to stop playing games with them," Brenna remarks as she picks up her mug.

"Definitely," Summer concurs. "They're the worst."

I reach for my own hot chocolate and gulp it down. My head wasn't in the game, anyway.

For the past five days, Demi Davis has consumed my thoughts. I feel like shit for snapping at her, but if my severe tone wasn't bad enough, I followed it up by info-dumping my dismal relationship with my father on her. I could practically see the gears in her brain working over all the things I'd told her since the semester started, trying to discern which ones were true.

Sadly, the majority were. I embellished a few details, to be sure. Dad generally isn't cruel to my mother, nor does he speak to her with the same disdain I used during the fake therapy sessions. I was trying to exaggerate certain narcissistic tendencies to make it easier for Demi.

But all the events I described occurred in real life. I did catch my father banging his secretary when I was fourteen years old. I did tell my mom, and she did tell me to not interfere in their marriage. Just be a good boy and stay quiet because Daddy takes care of us and what kind of life would we have without him.

That was the day I realized my mother has no self-worth and my father has too much of it.

Still, an angry trip down memory lane was no excuse to take it out on Demi. I knew there was a chance she wouldn't believe me when I told her about Nico. I shouldn't have mocked her about getting her head out of the sand, insinuated she was a naïve fool.

She called you a fuckboy.

Ugh, true. She was as much of a dick to me as I was to her. We're both dicks.

Fuck. I should try to clear the air. I look toward the side table where I left my phone. But no. Texting is garbage. A text conversation about this would feel too impersonal.

"You know what." I hop off the couch. "I have to go."

Summer glances over. "Are you sure? We could start a new game."

"Nah, I think the zombies can have this one. I'll be back later."

"Where are you going?" Brenna asks.

"To see a friend."

"Ha!" Mocking laughter rings out. "I knew the celibacy wouldn't last."

"Not for sex," I clarify. "It's the girl I'm working on that project with. We got into an argument the other day, and I want to smooth things over."

"You know you can just text her," Summer says helpfully.

"You know you can mind your own business."

"All right then."

I haven't been drinking, so I make the ten-minute drive to campus and turn onto Greek Row. I can't find a spot in front of the Theta house, but there's a stretch of empty curb a few houses away. I park the Rover and that's when I hear the yells.

Oh shit.

I quickly jog down the lane, skidding to a stop cartoon-character style when I spot Nico on the lawn of the Theta house, shouting up at the second-floor window.

"Come on, Demi! Please!"

The man sounds utterly destroyed. I'd probably feel genuine sympathy for him if not for the fact that I know precisely what's going on. He cheated on Demi at the party. There's no other reason why he'd be outside Demi's house, begging her to let him in.

"Please, *mami*, I love you! I fucked up, okay!"

I lurk near the hedges that separate the sorority house from its neighbor.

"Go away!" comes a high-pitched voice.

It's not Demi. I peer up and see two girls at the window, their figures backlit by Demi's bedroom lights.

"She doesn't want to talk to you. Go away," one of them yells.

"We'll call the police if you don't," the other one warns. "You're disrupting the peace. People are trying to sleep."

"It's nine o'clock on a Friday and this is Greek Row!" Nico growls. "Nobody is fucking sleeping, Josie! Just tell her to come down."

"She doesn't want to see you, you cheating prick."

Yup. I called this one.

"Demi," he wails. His voice actually cracks, and this time I *do* feel for the guy.

I know narcissists—I lived with one my whole life—and they don't usually experience remorse. If they do show any regret, it's probably an act. Yes, Nico could be putting on that act, but my gut says he isn't. He seems genuinely heartbroken.

He made his bed, a voice in my head points out.

"Demi! I'm going to stand out here all night until you let me in! *Please*. We've been together forever! You owe me a conversation. You owe me a chance to explain—"

A shriek of epic proportions slices through the night air. It's shrill enough to give Rupi Miller a run for her money.

Demi appears at the window, shoving her sisters out of the way. "I owe you?" she thunders. "I OWE YOU?"

Nico instantly recognizes his mistake. "No, I didn't mean it in that way—"

She cuts him off. "You cheated on me with one of my friends! And then you cheated on me *again* with some random chick at a party!"

Oh, Nico, you stupid bastard.

Any sympathy I had for him is long gone. I'm solidly on Team Demi. I mean, I always was, but now I don't care how gutted the guy appears to be. He deserves it.

"We're done," Demi screams out the window. "Do you hear me, Nicolás? We're *done*."

"Baby, don't say that."

"You're right—we've known each other forever. I've been loyal to you forever. But you're incapable of reciprocating that loyalty. So please, just go."

"We can work through this," he pleads. "Please, give me another chance. Let me earn your trust back."

"*Dude!*" a random voice shouts from one of the neighboring houses. "You're pathetic! Bitch wants you to leave!"

Demi ignores the interruption. "There's no earning my

trust back," she calls to Nico. "We're done. I don't want to be with you anymore. I don't want to be with a liar and a cheater. I'm worth more than what you've given me."

She's right about that. And call me a perv, but I'm disgustingly aroused by the sight of her right now. Her cheeks are flushed and her dark eyes are blazing like hot coals. She's got a hand on her hip as she glares down at Nico. Fierce and confident. Scorned but not defeated.

"We're not done," Nico says.

"We're done," she repeats.

"*You're done, bro,*" someone else hollers, and then other voices from Greek Row chime in.

"*Go home, asshole!*"

"*You're killing my buzz!*"

Nico only has eyes and ears for Demi. "You don't mean it," he informs her.

Idiot. Men really need to stop telling women what they mean or don't mean. The one lesson I've learned over the years is that a woman doesn't appreciate it when you put words in her mouth—or your dick in someone else's mouth.

"Oh, trust me, I mean it." Demi abruptly disappears from the window.

For a moment I think it's over. But then she reappears, her arms full of clothes.

"Let me help you clean out your drawer before you go," she says angrily.

I choke on a laugh as items of clothing come sailing out the second-floor window onto the lawn. A Celtics hoodie. Some T-shirts. A pair of boxers float down.

"You don't deserve a drawer in my house! You don't

deserve anything anymore. I'm done with this. Take all your stuff and get out of my life."

Once again I think it's all over.

But then Nico, stupid *stupid* Nico, utters the dumbest shit he could've ever uttered. "Don't you dare throw my PlayStation out the window, Demi!"

If that ain't a challenge.

She whirls around again, and this time she doesn't come back.

Huh. Okay. Maybe she decided to spare the PlayStation. Nico seems to think so, because his entire body relaxes. He glumly walks forward and begins picking up the clothes on the lawn.

He still hasn't noticed me, and I'm not about to make my presence known. It'd be like approaching a lion with a thorn in its paw.

Just when I decide all is well—when the night is quiet and Nico's scattered items have been collected—the front door of the sorority house flies open and Demi emerges. Holding a tangle of cables, controllers, and a slender black PlayStation.

Nico's head snaps up. "Thank you!" Looking relieved, he holds out his hands as if he truly believes he's getting the game console back unscathed.

"Thank you? No, thank *you*," Demi shoots back. She's spitting fire again. "Thank you for wasting eight years of my life." She hurls one controller to the ground. "Thank you for lying to my face." The second controller smashes on the concrete walkway. "Thank you for disrespecting me."

When she reaches the curb, the only item she's left holding is the PlayStation.

I hold my breath. The other components could easily be replaced. This console itself can't.

"I never want to see you again. You've ruined this. You ruined our friendship, you ruined our relationship, you ruined *everything*."

Crash!

The PlayStation collides with the sidewalk, breaking into several pieces.

Nico has the nerve to say, "I can't believe you did that!" Which prompts Demi to take a swing at him, and that's when I jump away from the hedge.

She manages to get one sharp blow in before I haul her away from him, trying to corral her like a wild horse.

She might not be a teammate, but I think this still qualifies for paragraph four, line eight of the captain's log: *Don't let your teammates commit murder*.

"Hey, hey, stop," I order.

"Hunter? What are you doing here?" She blinks a few times before her eyes go feral again. "Let me go. He deserves an ass kicking!"

"Yes, he does," I agree, and Nico scowls at me. "But karma will do that job for you, trust me."

"Hunter, let me go!" Now she's grunting, gritting her teeth, attempting to punch her way out of my grip. So I fling her over my shoulder in a fireman's carry. "Hunter!" she screeches in outrage. "Put me down!"

"No. I'm not watching you get arrested for assault tonight, okay?" I kick away a piece of Nico's PlayStation, while trying to contain a struggling Demi. "You're already guilty of property damage."

"I don't care!" she says stubbornly. "Now I want to do bodily damage."

"I know you do, Semi, but trust me, he ain't worth it."

But the riled-up woman in my arms is still flapping her arms like a trapped bird trying to get free. I spare a dark look at Nico before marching off toward my Land Rover. Only when I reach the vehicle do I set Demi down. The moment her socked feet meet the sidewalk, her steely demeanor seems to crumble. Suddenly she turns into a vulnerable girl, tears welling in her eyes.

"He humiliated me," she whispers.

"I know, babe. C'mere." I open my arms, but she ducks her head shamefully.

"No. I don't want a hug," she mumbles.

"Fine, then get in the car."

"Why?"

"You're coming over to my place and we're getting drunk. You could use the distraction."

Demi hesitates. She glances in the vicinity of the Theta house, where Nico is slowly walking toward his pick-up truck. Then she tears her gaze away and opens the passenger's door of my Rover.

We're on the road a few seconds later. Demi doesn't say a single word. She keeps her gaze straight ahead.

"I'm so sorry," I say gruffly.

She finally speaks, her voice trembling with each word. "No, I'm the one who's sorry. You were right—about everything. And I snapped at you and called you a fuckboy." She sniffles. "I feel horrible about that. Please tell me you accept my apology."

"Of course I do. It's all good with us, Demi. I promise."

She still refuses to look at me. "*He* was the fuckboy. He cheated on me. More than once, with more than one person."

"Yeah, I gathered."

I turn onto the main road that leads to town. It's a straight ten-minute drive, and then I'm pulling up into the driveway behind Summer's silver Audi. The lights are still on in the living room.

"Come on, you look like you need that drink."

Fat teardrops slip out the corners of her eyes. She blinks them back fast. "Okay."

We walk inside. Demi reaches down as if to remove her shoes before realizing she's not wearing any. Pink and gray striped socks cover her small feet. She stares at them for a moment as if questioning whether they even belong to her.

"Yo, Hunter? That you?" Hollis calls from the living room.

"Yeah," I call back.

"Good timing—we're about to start a new game."

I guess he and Rupi ironed out their insane differences. "I brought a friend with me," I answer as I unlace my boots.

"Oooh," teases Brenna. "Is it a sexy friend?"

I examine Demi. All I see are quivering lips, smudges of mascara under red-rimmed eyes, and a shell-shocked expression.

"Fuck off," she says ruefully.

I snicker. "Sorry, but sexy isn't on your side right now."

When we enter the living room, the girls take one look at my guest and jump to their feet. "Are you okay?" Summer blurts out.

Brenna glares at me, then turns to Demi. "What did he do to you?"

"Oh, screw off, Bee."

Demi laughs through her tears. "Be nice to him. He just stopped me from physically assaulting my cheating boyf—*ex*-boyfriend," she corrects.

"Ugh! Cheaters are the worst kind of dirt bags," Summer declares.

"The worst," Hollis agrees.

"You poor thing," Rupi clucks, tugging Demi toward the couch.

In the blink of an eye, she's surrounded by the girls, who immediately start pressing for details.

"If you guys don't mind, I'd rather not talk about it," Demi admits. She gulps a few times, then gives a half-hearted smile and points to the board game on the coffee table. "What are we playing?"

18
DEMI

"I've barely seen you these past couple weeks." Disappointment and compassion war in TJ's eyes, but after a beat he reaches across the table and gives my hand a squeeze, showing that his compassion won out. Which is a relief, because I'm simply not equipped to reassure him right now. My mental health comes first, and I've been AWOL for reasons that have nothing to do with him or our friendship.

"You didn't miss much. I haven't been great company." I pick at the edge of my banana muffin.

"You're always great company," TJ says with a smile.

"That's sweet of you to say."

"It's the truth. How are you doing?"

"Better. I mean, my boyfriend cheated on me, so I'm not throwing any parades right now, but I'm also not tempted to commit violence and blow up his apartment." Which, considering my behavior following Corinne's housewarming, is certainly progress.

I honestly think I blacked out that night. I remember everything I did, but the memories feel removed and are filtered through a red haze. Throwing Nico's clothes out the window, smashing his PlayStation, punching him in the face. The clearest of the memories are the ones involving Hunter and his roommates. That silly board game we played had succeeded in calming me down, and therefore I'm forever indebted to Zombies!™

"Have you spoken to him?" TJ asks. "Or do you still have his number blocked?"

"Still blocked." I had no choice but to do it. Nico was calling and texting so often it was becoming intolerable. "But he did show up at the house last week," I admit.

TJ frowns deeply. "You didn't tell me that."

"There was nothing to tell. He knocked on the door, and Josie and the others threatened to castrate him if he came by again."

"Good. And don't forget, my offer still stands—I'll beat him up for you if you want."

I give a dry smile. "He's not worth it. Besides, I don't want you getting hurt." TJ isn't scrawny, but he's five-eight with a lanky build. Nico would murder him in a fight.

His hand tightens over mine.

"I didn't mean it in a you're-a-wimp sense," I backpedal. "I know you're not. I just mean he's not worth the effort. Besides, you'd have to get in line. Pax is already doing extra arm days at the gym to bulk up, so that he can, and I quote, 'fuck him up and not in the good way.'" We both snicker. "And Darius isn't speaking to him at all."

"Wow. Really?"

"Yep. Say what you will about D, but you know how he feels about monogamy." Darius is also very religious, so he doesn't condone anything that treads the line of immorality. "Oh, and we can't forget about Hunter. He would love to knock Nico around."

Speaking of Hunter, my phone buzzes a minute later with a text from him. I click on it to find a picture of an egg in a tiny hammock. A second message simply says: @PabloEggscobar.

Oh my God.

Pablo has his own Instagram account now.

TJ leans in curiously. "What's that pic of?"

"They have a pet egg." I put the phone down, shaking my head.

"What? Who?" TJ sounds confused.

"The hockey team. Their mascot is a hard-boiled egg that they all take turns caring for. I think it's some sort of team-building exercise? Hunter wasn't very articulate about it."

"Won't it go rotten and start stinking?"

"Already has. These days it's wrapped up in cellophane and kept in the fridge overnight, but the plastic wrap hasn't suppressed the smell completely. Hunter had the egg on him last week and I kept catching whiffs of sulfur."

"That is so weird. I'll never understand jocks."

"Honestly, I don't think it's an across-the-board jock thing. I think it's a Briar hockey player thing. They're all nuts, Hunter included."

"Then why do you keep texting with him?" TJ asks lightly.

"Because we're friends." I shrug. "My friends are allowed to be nuts."

And Hunter, for all his strange habits, has been an

amazing friend to me since my relationship was blown to smithereens. Also, his roommates are my new favorite people. Brenna is a total smartass and I love her. Summer and I don't have much in common, but she makes me laugh. And Rupi is…Rupi. Her relationship with Hunter's friend Hollis fascinates me. I truly can't tell if they're madly in love or hate each other's guts. Maybe a mixture of both? Either way, they're highly entertaining.

I'm learning that keeping busy is the best remedy for a bad break-up. This means concentrating on midterms, math quizzes, chem labs, psych readings, anything that occupies my brain. And when my brain gets tired, I distract myself with friends. Drinks with Pippa, movie nights with my sorority sisters, hangouts at Hunter's house. So far, it's helping.

"When does your bus leave today?" TJ asks over the rim of his cup. A teabag string hangs over the edge. He's not a coffee drinker, so it's herbal teas for him.

"Seven-thirty." I groan. "Ugh, I'm not looking forward to Thanksgiving. My parents are going to have simultaneous heart attacks when I tell them about Nico."

"Wait, you still haven't told them you guys broke up?"

"Nope. It'll be a Thanksgiving surprise."

"That sucks. They really like him, eh?"

"Like him? That's like saying frat boys *like* kegs. They're obsessed with him, view him as a son-in-law. They're going to be devasta—" I stop midsentence when a familiar person enters the Coffee Hut.

Corinne.

My spine snaps into a straight, inflexible line. Corinne tried calling several times after her housewarming. When I ignored her calls, she sent a text asking if we could talk. I sent one back saying that when I'm ready to talk, I'll reach out myself.

Well, it's been two weeks and I'm nowhere near ready.

She freezes like a deer in the headlights when she notices me. Then she recovers her composure and—dammit, she's walking toward us.

"Hide me," I plead at TJ, but it's too late. Corinne reaches our little table, a nervous smile on her face.

"Hi," she says softly.

"Hi." My voice is tight.

"I know you said we'd talk when you're ready, but... well, the holidays are coming up, and then we'll be back and it's final exams, and then spring break..." She shrugs wryly. "Maybe we should just clear the air right now?" She lets the request hang in the uncomfortable air between us.

TJ gives me a questioning look, as if to say, *should I step in?*

I respond with a slight shake of the head. "Fine," I tell Corinne. To TJ, I say, "Do you mind? You're supposed to go meet your roommate soon, anyway. Right?"

He nods. "Yeah, it's no problem." He eyes Corinne warily as he stands up.

She goes to grab a coffee, her black curls cascading down her back. She's wearing a puffy navy-blue winter coat, which she takes off as she gets in line.

"I really don't want to do this," I tell TJ.

"I know, but you can handle it."

"I'm not so sure about that."

"You can handle anything," TJ promises. "You're fearless.

But if you truly need an out, text me SOS and I'll ditch Ryan and come right back."

"You da best."

He touches my shoulder, his palm lingering before he withdraws it. A moment later, the bell over the door jingles as he exits the coffeehouse.

When Corinne returns, we endure another awkward silence. I stare at her, because I'm not going to be the first person to speak.

"I'm so sorry," is her opening line.

How original. "Yes, you already told me that."

"I know, and I'm just going to keep saying it until maybe you'll believe that I mean it."

"Oh, I believe you mean it. But it's easy to ask forgiveness. What *shouldn't* have been easy for you was sleeping with your friend's boyfriend."

Shame colors her cheeks. She gulps, offering a quick nod. "I know. I made a mistake. And if you want to ask me any questions about it, I promise every word I say will be the truth."

"Okay, I'll bite." My tone is more frigid than I intend it to be, but I can't control it. "How many times did you sleep with him?"

"Once," she says instantly. "It wasn't long after the move. He came by one night to help me hang a shelf."

I strain to recall when that could've been. Probably one of the nights Nico was working late. I wonder how many times he lied to me over the years. God. This entire conversation is so embarrassing.

"We had a beer, and you know I don't handle alcohol very

well—that's not an excuse," she hurries on. "I'm not blaming the alcohol, but I *was* buzzed. And he was, you know, he was Nico. He's charming."

"Yes, he is," I say tersely. It's the dimples. Those dimples never fail to disarm women.

Corinne stares at her hands, wrapped around her coffee cup. "He kissed me, and I knew kissing him back was a bad idea, but I wasn't thinking clearly and then he said—" She stops.

"He said what?"

"He told me you guys were having problems but that you didn't want anyone to know."

My jaw drops.

"And he said…" She blushes. "He said your sex life was non-existent."

"Non-existent?" I'm seething again. "We were having sex regularly." I just didn't realize he was also having sex with everyone else.

"I'm sorry. I really don't want my excuse to be that I was a stupid girl, but I was. I was stupid and insecure, and I hadn't had a boyfriend in so long and suddenly this charming, gorgeous guy was paying attention to me, flirting with me, telling me all these terrible things about you."

"And you believed him?" I'm hurt by the notion.

"No," Corinne admits. "I *wanted* to believe him, because then it'd give me justification to not feel bad. But I did feel bad. I felt awful—before it happened, during, and after. And then he actually tried to see me again, in secret. I felt sick and said no way in hell. I wanted to tell you the truth, but he said he'd deny it if I did, and paint me as a slut who tried to seduce him."

I don't even know what to believe anymore. In his subsequent texts after our showdown at my house, Nico spammed my phone with his explanations, his excuses. And that was precisely what he told me—that Corinne came on to him, and he was too drunk to fend off her wicked advances.

"I don't know if this helps or not, but..." Corinne takes her phone out of her bag. "These are all the text exchanges I had with him."

She slides the phone across the table and I reluctantly pick it up. The first thing I do is click on Nico's contact page to ensure that his name is assigned to the right number. People are liars, and technology is easily, and frequently, manipulated these days. But it's the right number.

I don't want to do it, but I force myself to read the text thread. And there it is, in black and white. Or rather, gray and blue. My loving boyfriend, asking my friend when they were going to have sex again. Corinne's not lying. The entire exchange is disgusting.

NICO: Still thinking bout u. when r we gonna do it again? ;)

CORINNE: Never. I never want to do it again, Nico.

HIM: Srsly? playing hard 2 get all of a sudden?

HER: No. I feel sick to my stomach. I want to tell Demi what happened.

HIM: WTF? R u kidding me?

HER: No, I'm not. I can't sleep, I can't eat. I feel like the worst person on the planet. She's one of my closest friends. I don't have a lot of those. What we did was so freaking stupid and I'm so ashamed of myself. I'm throwing up every night. I have to tell her.

HIM: Not gonna happen, Corinne. She's gonna think ur a liar

HER: No, she won't.

HIM: Ya she will, cuz I'll tell her ur lying.

It goes on for a while longer, and Corinne is right. She insists on coming clean, Nico warns her what he'll do if she does.

I set the phone down. My eyes are stinging, but I refuse to cry.

"I'm really sorry," she whispers. "And I know our friendship is irrevocably changed. All I'm asking for is forgiveness and maybe another chance. When you're ready, of course."

I nod slowly. "I accept your apology, and I will work on the forgiveness part, but...I can't do it right now. I'm not there." Her feeling genuine remorse after she slept with my boyfriend doesn't alter the fact that she slept with my boyfriend.

"I understand."

"But I am glad we finally talked," I say, and I truly mean it. I'm not one of those girls who will blame the "other woman." Yes, Corinne demonstrated poor judgment and total disregard for our friendship, but she wasn't the one sleeping with me, the one professing love for me, the one telling me we were going to get married. Corinne was a bad friend, but Nico's betrayal cuts so much deeper.

"Anyway, I have to go." I scrape my chair back. "I need to pack for Thanksgiving."

"Are you going to Boston?"

"Yes. I'm leaving tonight and coming back Sunday. Are you seeing your family in Vermont?"

"No, we're doing a friends' Thanksgiving in Hastings." She hesitates. "Pippa will be there. I hope that's okay."

I swallow a sigh. Pippa's been walking on eggshells lately, trying not to mention her friendship with Corinne to me. Fuck Nico for complicating everything.

Men are such garbage.

———

My parents are thrilled to have me home, even if it's only for a few days. There's already a full buffet on the table when I arrive, and it's only the three of us tonight. Tomorrow we have a ton of family coming in from Miami. Dad's an only child like me, but Mom's side of the family is enormous. I expect tomorrow to be super noisy. Two of my mother's three sisters are coming with their brood, and all my cousins are younger than me, so there'll be a tiny mob of eight, nine and ten-year-olds running around. Mom's only brother Luis and his wife Liana just had a baby boy, who I cannot wait to meet. I love babies.

Tonight is basically the calm before the storm.

"Oh lord!" My mouth is legit watering when I glimpse the feast Mom laid out. I'll be leaving a trail of drool on the way to the table. "Mom, you are the greatest treasure in the whole world."

"Thank you, *mami*." She plants a kiss on my forehead and then pushes me into a chair. "Now, eat! You look so thin, Demi. What's going on? What's wrong?"

I give a slight frown. My appetite disappeared after the break-up and it's only now returning, but I hadn't thought I'd lost any weight. All my clothes still fit.

Since lying to my mother is impossible, I reply with, "Let's wait for Dad. I'll tell you both at same time."

"*Dios mío*! I knew it. Something *is* wrong. Tell us what!? *Marcus*!" she screams at the doorway, and my eardrums promptly shatter. I'm surprised the paintings don't fall off the dining room walls.

My father takes his time coming downstairs. He's learned to differentiate between Mom's various screams and volume levels, and has clearly deduced this is not an emergency. When he finally strolls into the room, he greets me with a hug and kiss. "Hi, baby."

"Hey, Daddy." I stab a deep-fried crab cake with my fork and plop it down on my plate.

"What's going on?" He glances at Mom as he takes his usual chair at the head of the table.

"Demi has something to tell us."

His gaze swings back to me. "That so? What is it?"

"Can you let me finish this yummy crab cake first?" I chew extra slowly, relishing the taste, then spear some Cuban-style shrimp from one of the serving dishes. I quickly pop a shrimp in my mouth. "Mmmmm. Did you pan-fry this in pineapple? And garlic? It's so good."

I'm stalling and Mom knows it. "Put down the shrimp, Demi."

Ugh. "Fine." I lay my fork on the plate, swallow, and wipe my mouth with a napkin. "Mom, maybe you should sit down too."

They're both alarmed. "*Dios mío!*" she cries again. "You're pregnant! Marcus, she's pregnant!"

My eyebrows shoot up in alarm. "What! No! I'm not pregnant. Jesus. Sit down already." I hastily add, "Please."

Suitably chastised, Mom settles in the chair next to my father.

I clasp my hands on the tablecloth and clear my throat, as if I'm about to deliver a really depressing lecture. "Okay, first of all, to reiterate, I am *not* pregnant." I give them a warning look. "But this does have to do with Nico, and I need you guys to remain calm—"

"Is he all right?" Mom says in horror. "Is he in the hospital?"

"No, he's not in the hospital, and I literally just asked you to be calm. Could you please promise to let me finish speaking before commenting?"

Dad waves a big paw. "Go on."

"Promise," I order.

They both mumble a promise to stay quiet.

I release a breath. "Nico and I broke up a couple weeks ago."

When Mom's mouth snaps open, I slice my hand down to karate chop the air. Her mouth closes.

"I know this isn't something you want to hear," I continue, "and believe me when I say I didn't expect it to happen. As far as I knew, we were happy together and our relationship was on track."

Dad growls. "What did he do?"

I let this particular interruption slide. "He cheated on me."

Silence falls.

"Was it… was it a drunk mistake at a party?" Mom actually has the nerve to sound hopeful.

"Even if it was, that's still unforgivable," I say firmly.

"Well, it's far more forgivable than if he—"

"Three different girls," I interject, and her mouth slams shut again. "One of them was my friend, one was the sister of his coworker, and the third was a random girl he met at a bar when he was out with friends." He fessed up to the third indiscretion via one of his text diatribes. "Four, if you count the girl he cheated with in high school—" Another lovely text confession, although that one was more of a confirmation. "So, no, there's no hope and no forgiveness. I'm officially done with him. Maybe one day I'll be able to be his friend again, and the only reason I'd even consider that is because of our families, not for myself."

"Oh, Demi," Mom says sadly.

"Obviously I'd never ask you guys to stop talking to Dora and Joaquín, but…" I hesitate, wringing my hands together. "I know we invited the Delgados to visit for Christmas, but—and I'm begging you here—maybe we can ask them not to come…?"

Dad, who reacted protectively when I revealed Nico's infidelity, now looks uneasy. "But everything has already been planned, sweetheart." I know my father well—he doesn't want to look bad in front of his friends.

"I get it, but I'm asking you, as your only daughter, to please put my well-being first when it comes to this. I can't spend Christmas with Nico and his family. I just *can't*. The breakup is still too fresh and it would be so awkward. It would…it would hurt me," I say softly, and then avert my eyes because I hate showing vulnerability in front of my dad. He's so strong that falling apart in front of him feels like a crushing failure.

But the words have the desired effect. With tears clinging to her eyelashes, Mom stands up and comes over to hug me. "Oh, *mami*. I am so sorry."

As I hug her back, I watch my father, who's still trying to rationalize Nico's actions. "You truly don't think you'll give him another chance?"

"No," I reply through clenched teeth. "I can't."

Dad's expression flickers with unhappiness. "I've known that boy since he was eight years old. He always had a good head on his shoulders."

"I thought so, too."

"Surely there's more to this story. Perhaps Nico—"

"He cheated on me, Daddy."

"And I'm not excusing it," he says quickly. "I promise you I'm not. All I'm saying is, maybe there's more to the story. Maybe Nico is having emotional problems we're unaware of, or substance abuse issues, or—"

"Or maybe he's just a fucking asshole," I snap.

Dad's eyes narrow. "Language."

"No, I'm not going to watch my language, and I'm not going to stand here while you seriously try to persuade me that my serial-cheating ex-boyfriend is worthy of another chance. No way, Dad. I'm not getting back together with him and I'm not excusing that kind of behavior. We're over."

"Maybe in the future—"

A cry of desperation is ripped from my throat. "Oh my God, no! We're done. And please, *please* don't invite them for

Christmas." My stomach churns as I imagine having to spend the holidays with Nico's family. I always thought my father had my back, but at the moment it seems as though he's genuinely torn between me and Nico. And I'm his *daughter*.

Without another word, I stomp out of the kitchen and hurry upstairs to my bedroom. It's not ten seconds later when my mother appears in the doorway.

"Demi, baby." She sees my wet eyes and holds her arms open, and like a little kid I fall into them.

"Why is he being so stupid?" I mumble against her huge boobs.

"Because he's a man."

My answering giggle is muffled.

"Do you want to talk about it some more?" Mom offers, rubbing soothing circles on my upper spine.

"No, there's nothing else to say. But what I'd love for you to do is go downstairs and tell Dad to stop whatever the hell this is. Tell him if he wants Nico back, he can date him himself."

She laughs quietly. "I will pass that message along. And I want you to know, yes, we are having a tough time believing that Nicolás could do something like this, but the pain in your eyes tells me that boy hurt you very badly, and anyone who hurts my baby…" She trails off ominously, her brown eyes becoming deadly slits. "Are you sure we can't invite them for Christmas so I can poison their food?"

"No," I say glumly. "I like the rest of his family too much." A sigh slips out. "And I don't want him dead, either. I think he probably feels terrible about what he did. But that doesn't mean I'd ever take him back. Do you know how humiliating it is knowing he was sleeping with other women? Meanwhile, he was lying to me about it and buying me dumb gifts and making me feel like—" My voice cracks and I stop talking, because there's no point in continuing.

It's over between Nico and me. And I truly don't want him back. In fact, since I blocked his number it's almost like a weight was lifted off my chest.

"Ugh. Mom, I just want to be alone for a bit," I admit. "Do you mind putting aside a plate for me so I can eat it later?"

"Of course, *mami*. If you need me I'm only a shout away, okay?"

Once she's gone, I lie on my bed and stare at the ceiling. The room was dusted and cleaned in anticipation of my arrival, and it smells like pine and fresh linens. Mom knows how to make everything feel homey.

I roll over and toy with the edge of a throw pillow. This truly sucks. I hate how entangled mine and Nico's families are. I'm always going to have this constant reminder of him, when all I want to do is put him behind me. Truth be told, I'm ready to move on. Or, at the very least, I'm intrigued by the idea of being with somebody new.

Sighing, I open Instagram and mindlessly scroll through my feed. I make sure to follow Pablo Eggscobar, who still only has one pic up. I wonder if that little rope hammock was homemade. I can't imagine where they might've bought one. Hastings isn't exactly teeming with miniature egg clothing and accessories boutiques.

Hunter texts during my scrolling session, a welcome distraction from social media.

HUNTER: You make it to the city all right?

ME: Yep. I'm here now. But it was the worst bus ride EVER. The guy beside me kept showing me pictures of his ferrets.

HIM: Ferrets???

ME: Ferrets.

HIM: Semi, I think you sat beside a serial killer. Next time please text me a pic of your seatmate so I have something to show the police.

I laugh to myself, and type, Are you in Greenwich? I know he was making the drive there after his morning practice.

HIM: Yeah. Drove up with Summer and Fitzy. He's spending Thanksgiving with her fam.

ME: And for you, it's just you and your parents? No uncle/aunt/cousins/grandparents?

HIM: Nope. Just the three of us. Oh joy.

ME: Is it that bad?

HIM: My father yelled at the caterer for only putting out one communal gravy boat on the table instead of small individual ones for each person. I heard her crying in the kitchen afterward.

Oh Lord, that's brutal. And I can't believe his family gets *catering* for Thanksgiving. My mother would literally rather face an execution squad than entrust someone else to cook Thanksgiving dinner.

ME: That = fucked up. Though if it makes you feel

better, my father's being insufferable right now too. I
just told them about Nico, and Dad tried to convince
me to give him another chance!!

HIM: Seriously??

ME: Yep. He's obsessed with him.

HIM: Do you *want* to give him another chance?

ME: 100% no. Actually, I was just thinking before you
texted that I might be ready for...drum roll please...a
rebound.

HIM: Oooh exciting. Those are fun.

ME: Are you volunteering for the job?

Wait. What?

What the hell did I just type? And to add to my sudden
case of agitation, Hunter responds with an LOL.

ME: WTF does that mean?

HIM: It means laughing out loud.

ME: I know what LOL means! But why are you
laughing at me?

HIM: Because you were joking...?

ME: What, rebounding with me is a laughing matter?
You don't think I'm cute?

HIM: You're more than cute.

I can feel myself blushing. This entire conversation is
ridiculous. Of course Hunter wasn't volunteering to be my
rebound, and now I'm just fishing for compliments because
I'm insecure that my ex-boyfriend couldn't keep his pants
zipped. Literally and figuratively.

HIM: Can we be real? Are you legit asking me to be your rebound?

My thumb hovers over the letter *y*. I could just press it, and then the letter *e*, the letter *s*. But that means opening the door to something that could blow up in my face. Hunter and I are friends. I find him attractive, but this is the first time I've considered being more than friends.

I don't get the chance to type those three letters, as Hunter sends a follow-up.

HIM: Because you know I'd have to say no, Semi. I'm out of commission.

I don't even try to make sense of the disappointment that flutters through me. My emotions are all over the place these days.

ME: I know. I was basically joking.
HIM: Basically?
ME: 60/40 joking.
HIM: So 40% of you wants to get with this?
ME: Get with what?
HIM: With me. You want to get all up in my dick biz.

Laughter sputters out of my mouth. Suddenly I don't feel so disappointed anymore.

ME: If you say so. Anyway, pointless discussion. Like you said, you're out of commission.

I put the phone down and slide into a sitting position. Interacting with Hunter never fails to cheer me up. I'm still grinning, and my appetite has officially returned. Luckily, there's a feast downstairs with my name on it.

It isn't until much later, nearly midnight, that I hear from Hunter again. I'm just getting into bed when the message lights up my phone.

HUNTER: If I wasn't, I'd be all over you, Demi.

19
DEMI

I feel surprisingly refreshed after Thanksgiving weekend. It was nice to see all my cousins and my crazy family, and Dad eventually did calm down about the Nico situation. He said he was sorry for not acknowledging my feelings, and I accepted his apology. Then he spent nearly an hour trying to badger me into hiring an MCATs tutor for next semester, until finally I flat-out told him I wasn't interested in even *thinking* about that exam until next year. He didn't like that idea one bit. So I appeased him by saying I'd take another science class over the summer to free up next year's schedule for med school studying. That idea, he *loved*.

I get it, I really do. My dad had a tough upbringing. He grew up dirt poor in Atlanta and worked his ass off to climb out of the gutter. Because he's genius-level smart, he excelled in high school, graduated early and got a scholarship to Yale. That's when he met and married my mother, who was originally from Miami. She wanted to move back after graduation, so Dad went with her, working at Miami General for nearly two decades before we moved to Massachusetts.

Dad's intense drive and unparalleled work ethic got him to where he is now, and he's instilled in me the value of hard work since the day I was born. When I was a teenager, he insisted I do volunteer work and community outreach so I could see how many people go without the privilege I was born into. He wanted me to understand how blessed I am. And I do understand, absolutely.

But the pressure of living up to my father's high standards can be exhausting.

And although Dad didn't bring up the Nico subject again this weekend, that didn't stop him from dropping several subtle comments over the weekend about how people are flawed, how human beings make mistakes. It was never specifically about Nico, but I knew exactly what Dad was trying to imply.

Well, too bad. Dad will just have to get over it. His boner for my ex-boyfriend will eventually deflate and hopefully get hard again for whoever I date next—and if *that* isn't the grossest analogy I've ever used, then I don't know what is. I don't want to think about my father getting hard over anyone. I don't want my father to have a penis, period.

As for the rebound idea I floated with Hunter via text, I'm finding myself more and more open to the idea. In fact, I'm kind of excited about it as I walk to class on Monday morning.

I'm wearing a parka with a fur-lined hood, an oversized messenger bag over one shoulder, fur-lined boots, and holding a steaming coffee cup in my hand.

You know that saying—dress for the job you want? Well, I dress for the *season* I want. It's the end of November and it still hasn't snowed, and I'm growing tired of this weird in-between period where there are no leaves on the trees but no snow on the ground. It's eerie and I hate it.

Pax, TJ and I chat about our Thanksgivings until Professor Andrews arrives. Hunter texted early this morning that he wouldn't be in class today. Apparently he has a physical with the team doctor.

I see him later that night, though, when he comes over for our—sob—final therapy session. My session logs are filled with notes. Hunter's done with all his research. Now it's just a matter of him writing the technical paper, and me writing the case study and detailed diagnosis, but those aren't due for a few more weeks.

"Since we're officially done, am I allowed to tell you your diagnosis?" I ask him.

"Hit me," Hunter says with a grin. He's sprawled on the loveseat, his hands propped behind his head, his arms bare. He runs hot, according to him, so every time he's in my room he strips down to a wife-beater or T-shirt, showing off those sculpted arms.

"Congratulations, you suffer from Narcissistic Personality Disorder, with a hint of antisocial PD."

"You're good."

"Thank you. I figured it out after like the second session, but NPD is actually super hard to diagnose properly," I say, which leads to a short discussion about the disorder and what Hunter learned during his research. He concurs that NPD cases are tough, especially because narcissists are so skilled at manipulating people, including psychologists.

"My father had our therapist eating out of his palm," Hunter admits.

I try to mask my eagerness. I hadn't wanted to bring it up myself, but I've been thinking a lot about our last session. Hunter's breakdown. His revelation that we'd been discussing his own father this entire time. My breakup with Nico had dominated my thoughts after that session, but now it's in the forefront of my mind as I cautiously study Hunter.

"I'm really sorry you had to go through all that crap with him," I say in a quiet voice.

He shrugs. "Whatever. Other people have it worse."

"So? My boyfriend cheated—other women might have a husband of thirty years who cheated and six kids at home. Does that diminish my own experience, because someone has it worse? There's always someone with a shittier life than yours. That doesn't turn the shit in *your* life into roses."

He exhales sharply. "That is very true, and you're too smart for your own good."

I chuckle. "I know. And I mean it, I'm sorry for everything your father has put you through."

"Thank you." His tone ripples with…awe, maybe? I can't tell. But it's evident he's genuinely appreciative of my words.

Then I realize what he'd said before—*our therapist*—and surprise jolts through me. "Wait, your father actually went to therapy? Willingly?"

"Willingly, hell no. It was one of those extremely rare times when Mom tried to stand up for herself. She told him if he didn't change his behavior, she would leave him. I mean, nobody bought that, but I guess she sounded serious enough that he capitulated. So we went to family therapy. Mom thought Dad and I also needed to clear the air between us, so I was forced into it. Christ, the whole thing was a shitshow."

"Why's that?"

"He completely manipulated the therapist during his individual sessions. I don't know what he told her, but when we saw her as a family, she was squarely on Team Dad. She spoke as if Mom and I were the evil perpetrators and he was the victim. It was unreal."

"Wow. I'm so sorry, babe. I can't even imagine having a parent like that. Parents aren't supposed to be the selfish ones. I mean, we're the kids. *We're* the selfish ones."

Hunter offers a sad smile. "In my house, my father is the only person who matters. You're lucky—your dad might want you to get back with your ex, but at least he doesn't treat you like a piece of property."

That is a very good point. Empathy continues to swell in my belly. I want to go over and give him a big hug, but I suspect he'd feel embarrassed.

"What's going on with all that, anyway?" Hunter asks, changing the subject. "Have you spoken to Nico?"

"Nope, and I don't plan on it, not for a long time."

"And the rebound situation?"

My heart skips a beat. "Well. You won't give me one, so I guess I'm on the hunt."

He looks startled for a second and then he laughs. "Come on, you said you were basically joking about that."

"Right."

But was I?

I suddenly find myself staring at him. With his classically handsome features, Hunter Davenport is objectively one of the best-looking men I've ever met.

If we're talking *sub*jectively, then…ugh, then *yes*. I think he's incredibly hot. He has a sexy mouth and a killer smile. And dimples. What is it with me and guys with dimples? It's like my sexual kryptonite.

My gaze travels the length of his body. He's wearing jeans, and I wonder what he's packing underneath them. Considering women are constantly throwing themselves at him, he must have some good dick game. And check me out, talking about dick games as if I know what good dick actually entails. My list of lovers is a resounding ONE.

"So. Just because we haven't checked in for a while— you're still a monk?" Somehow I muster up a casual tone.

"Yup yup."

"*Don't* say yup yup."

"I can't believe I've lasted this long." His expression becomes tortured. "We're at seven months, almost eight."

"When does this celibacy vow expire? I mean, you don't plan on keeping it forever, right?"

"Nah, till the end of the season."

"And then what? You'll go wild in the summer? You still have your senior year at Briar," I remind him.

"I know." He groans. "Honestly, I'll probably go nuts in the summer and fuck anything that moves." Another groan. "My balls hurt all the time, Semi."

I grin. "Aw, do you want me to make it better?"

"Stop teasing."

"I'm not teasing."

Am I? Lord, I don't even know anymore. What I do know is that I desperately need that rebound.

"I need that rebound," I say out loud.

Hunter purses his lips. "I don't know if I like the idea

anymore. You hooking up with some random dude is… worrisome." He holds up a hand. "And stop saying you want me to do it because we both know you don't mean it. Besides, this dick's broken." He points to his groin as if I don't know where a penis is located.

"Well, then it has to be a random guy. I can't hook up with one of my friends—that's just a recipe for disaster."

"Exactly!" Hunter says triumphantly. "Ergo, stop trying to rebound me."

"Is that a verb?"

"It is now."

"Anyway, so you're out because of the broken dick. Pax is gay—"

"Yeah, Jax isn't a good candidate."

I roll my eyes. "TJ is too—"

"—in love with you," Hunter finishes.

"He's not in love with me. But he's too good of a friend and he's super sensitive. I could see him getting emotionally attached."

"Got it. So you want a guy who won't get emotionally attached."

"Pretty much."

"Are you on Tinder?"

"I've been dating the same guy since I was thirteen. Of course I'm not on Tinder."

"Then you should be. It's the easiest way to find a no-strings hook-up or friend with benefits. Come to think of it, that's probably a better fit for you. You need a FWB."

"Why's that?"

Hunter offers a shrug. "I think you'd feel sleazy after

a one-night stand. Like you said, you were with the same guy since the age of thirteen. You're used to a certain level of intimacy."

He has a point. "So you think I need someone who I'll see more than once."

"Yup yup—"

"Don't say yup yup."

"—this will be fun. Come on, let's download the app." With a wolfish grin, he climbs onto my bed and flops down beside me. A moment later, we're downloading—ugh—Tinder.

"I only have an hour or so for this," I warn. "I'm meeting TJ for dinner tonight."

"In town or on campus?"

"Carver Hall."

"Then we have plenty of time. Carver's like down the street from you." Hunter watches as I load the app. "Oh, this is so exciting. I get to live vicariously through you."

"When your dick was functional, were you ever on any of these apps?"

"Nah. Do you realize how easy it is for me to get sex, Semi?"

"You're such an egomaniac."

"No, I'm a hockey player. I could literally walk out my front door and there'd be a woman standing there ready to screw me."

He's probably right. I'm still not much of a hockey fan, but I have been making an effort to pay attention when it's on. My favorite part of hockey is when the half-naked men get interviewed in the locker room after the game. So I can definitely see the appeal.

"Also, we're in college. Dating apps aren't really necessary since everyone's always partying and being social. It's easy to meet people on campus."

"Then why am I setting this up?" I grumble.

"Because we're fishing for a specific kind of meeting. When you want a particular thing, you filter out everything else. Yeah, you could sit in a bar, wait for different guys to approach you, and try to figure out what they're looking for. But this way you go into it knowing exactly what they want."

"Fair enough." Excitement tickles my belly as I set up the account. I use my phone number to log in, because I don't want my social media linked to this craziness. When it's time to load my profile picture, Hunter slides closer and watches me scroll through my camera roll.

He smells fantastic. It's a woodsy, masculine scent and I'm tempted to bury my face in his neck and inhale. However, I think that could be construed as sexual harassment.

"How about this one?" I click on a photo that I think I look super cute in.

Hunter balks. "Seriously? Who are we trying to attract here? Young Republicans? No. The first profile photo needs to show some skin."

"What do you mean, skin? Like a nude?"

"Of course not, dumbass. I don't think that's even allowed. But you sure as shit can't use *this* picture. You're wearing a turtleneck—and that long flowy skirt? You look lumpy, Semi. Do you want the first picture potential suitors see of you to make them say, *hey, who's this lumpy chick*?"

"You are *such* an ass."

"No, I'm realistic. I'm not trying to be skeevy, but come

on. These dudes don't care about your personality. They care about your looks. They're literally swiping through photographs deciding if they want to meet you based on those photos."

"Okay, fine. How about this one?" In this next photo, I'm clad in a tight tank top and denim shorts. My boobs look great and my hair is loose and flowing over one shoulder.

"Better." Hunter nods his approval. "Stick that one in for now and then we'll rearrange the order." He steals the phone from my hand and takes over scrolling duties. "Ah, fuck yes, you definitely want to include this one."

"No way. I'm in a bikini."

"Exactly. And you look goddamn edible. You're searching for a guy to fuck you, Demi. *This* would make me fuck you."

Heat rises in my cheeks. Oh lord. He is sitting way too close to be dropping F-bombs like that. And why does he smell so good? Has he always smelled like this? I don't think we've ever sat this close before. Our thighs are touching, and one muscular arm is pressed up against the sleeve of my thin sweater. I can feel his body heat through the material.

"You would really fuck me if you saw this picture?" I study the bathing suit I'm wearing. It's a red string bikini that reveals *a lot* of skin. The picture was taken in South Beach, courtesy of my friend Amber.

"Oh yeah," Hunter confirms, and I notice his eyes have actually glazed over.

"Are you trying to picture what I look like underneath the bikini?" I accuse.

"Yes."

I lightly punch his shoulder. "Hey, I already offered you

the rebound. You declined. Therefore you're not allowed to fantasize about me now."

"Fine," he grumbles.

We select a few more pictures. Hunter insists I need a full-body shot, a face shot where I'm staring directly at the camera, and a shot in which I'm smiling with teeth, because apparently not showing teeth means I've got the mouth of an old British man. He also lays down the law about Snapchat filters, and any selfies taken from above. According to Hunter, that's the "deception angle."

"For the last photo, how about this one with me and my friends?" I suggest. "That way the guys can see I'm a social person."

"You can't use that picture. You're with a bunch of guys. It's intimidating."

"Why?"

"Are you joking? They look like huge basketball players."

"Well, yeah. Because they are."

Hunter rolls his eyes. "By posting this, you're pretty much saying these are the kind of guys you can pull. Any guy who doesn't look like that will be way too scared to swipe on you."

"You are scarily good at this," I inform him.

"It's common sense, Semi. Now let's write your profile. We want to keep it short. My recommendation? Three letters. D. T. F."

"No way."

"Uh-huh. So I'm wrong about your intentions?"

"No, but I'm sure if we put our heads together we could find a more diplomatic way of saying it," I say dryly. "How about this?"

I write:

Recently single. New to this and not looking for anything serious right now.

"Not bad," Hunter relents. "And maybe we should add a few interests. Here, let me." He snatches the phone again, chortling as he types.

When he passes it back, I can't stop a laugh.

Fascinated by child psychopaths, unhealthy relationship with food, will break your PlayStation if you f*%k with me.

"That makes me sound like a lunatic," I say.

"Look me in the eye and tell me that *none* of those things are accurate."

"I fucking hate you."

Then I delete what he wrote and change it to: crime show enthusiast, food lover, all-around awesome person.

Once again, Hunter concedes. "I like it. All right, hit *next* to finalize the account."

I obey his command, then offer a nervous grin. "Now what?"

"Now we swipe."

20
DEMI

I HAD NO IDEA THERE WERE SO MANY MEN IN THE WORLD. Obviously, I was aware the global population is in the billions, but how are there *this many* guys on this app, all within a sixty-mile radius of me? It's way too much data. I'm on sensory overload as my finger flicks past profile after profile.

Like Dan, who enjoys kickboxing.

Or Kyle, who's here for a good time, not a long time.

Or Chris, who wants me to "just ask."

Or another Kyle, who describes himself with three eggplant emojis.

And another Kyle! This one likes to eat out. Hint hint, nudge nudge.

"Ewww! Why are all the Kyles so repulsive?" I demand.

Hunter thinks it over. "Coincidence," he finally answers.

"Coincidence? That's your best guess?" I can't stop laughing. This is the most fun I've had in ages. I swipe to the next profile and gasp. "Oooh, I like *him*. Let's swipe right on Roy."

Hunter examines the potential suitor's photos. He whistles softly. "Fuck yeah. Check out those obliques. I'd do him."

"Glad we're in agreement." I grumble in disappointment when Roy and I don't match. The last three guys I swiped right on, I matched instantly with.

"Don't let it get to you," Hunter says helpfully. "A guy with a body like that has options."

Literally two seconds later, a bubble pops up announcing I matched with Roy.

"Ha!" I say in triumph.

Hunter grins. "Looks like you made the cut."

"What about this guy?" I ask about the next profile.

"He's wearing sunglasses and a hat in every picture. He's either bald and ugly, or a murderer. Though I'm sure the latter would be enticing for you."

"Oh, for sure. I'd sell my firstborn to be able to psycho-analyze a killer."

"It worries me that I can't tell if you're joking."

We swipe for a bit longer, but all the faces are melding together. I'm starting to get bored and the messages are starting to pour in. "Let's talk to some of these matches and weed out the ones we don't like," I suggest.

But it doesn't take long to realize we're dealing with a quantity over quality situation.

"Christ, these messages are lame," Hunter groans.

What's up beautiful?

You're so hottttt.

9 inches, at your service.

"Hard pass," I declare, and promptly unmatch Mr. 9 Inches. I open the next message and give it a skim. The guy, Ethan, wrote an entire paragraph introducing himself. "Jeez. Check this one out."

Hunter reads the message and whistles. "No way. He's too thirsty. I don't like him."

"Me neither." We seem to be on the same wavelength when it comes to the vibes we're getting from these men.

Finally, I reach Roy's message.

> Hey Demi! I know this sounds cliché, but you've got beautiful eyes. How's your night going?

"I like him," I announce.

Hunter chuckles. "Isn't it sad that all they have to do to gain our approval is possess basic conversational skills and not talk about their cocks? Shows how low of a bar we're dealing with here."

"You're right—that's sad as fuck. What should I say back?"

"Tell him you like his man-vee."

Ignoring the suggestion, I type, Thanks! Your eyes are pretty nice too. So is the rest of you ;)

Hunter mock gasps. "Demi, you hussy!"

I grin and send a follow-up message.

> **ME**: My night is okay. Doing some schoolwork. How about you?
> **HIM**: My night would be a lot better if we were having a beer together :)

"Oh, he is good," Hunter remarks.

HIM: What do you say? Should we meet up for a drink tonight?

"Ask him to go to Malone's," is Hunter's advice.

"What? Right now? We've literally exchanged three messages."

"So? You're not looking for a pen pal or a sexting buddy. The point of this is to get a date, right? You need to meet in person to know if there's any chemistry."

"But does it have to be tonight?"

"Why not?"

"I have plans with TJ."

"Then ask to meet up tomorrow. But trust me, a guy with an ass like that doesn't last long on the meat market. I'd marry him in a heartbeat."

I chew on my bottom lip. I suppose I could reschedule with TJ—he and I see each other all the time. And it might be nice to go on a date with someone new. I haven't done that since high school, during one of my breaks with Nico.

"Okay," I decide. "I'm meeting Roy tonight."

"That's the spirit!" Hunter raises his hand.

We high-five, and then I nervously type out a response to Roy. We make arrangements to meet at Malone's in an hour. Hunter offers to drive me.

Next, I message TJ.

ME: I need a rain check on dinner. I have a......DATE. Gasp! Can you believe it? How's tomorrow night?

I see him typing, but it takes almost a full minute before the message arrives.

> **TJ**: No prob. Tomorrow works.
> **ME**: Okay perfect. You da best.
> **TJ**: xoxo

There's an army of butterflies wreaking havoc on my stomach. "Oh God," I tell Hunter. "I'm so nervous! And I only have an hour to take a shower and figure out what to wear."

"Go take the shower. I'll pick an outfit for you." Hunter's already striding toward my closet.

"Clothes," I warn, wagging my finger at him. "Please pick *real* clothes, Hunter."

He's cackling as I close the bathroom door.

———

By the time we arrive at Malone's, my palms are sweaty and my heart is beating dangerously fast. Am I actually doing this? Suddenly I don't feel so ready.

Hunter parks the Land Rover in the tiny lot behind the bar. He cuts the engine and turns to appraise me. "I do good work," the jackass says with a pleased nod.

I'll allow him the outfit—he picked a pair of dark blue skinny jeans, a soft gray sweater that hangs over one shoulder and shows some skin, and black suede boots with short heels. It's a cute outfit and I look cute in it.

But the accessories? He doesn't get any credit for those. "I hate these earrings," I gripe, carefully arranging the big hoops so that they don't catch in my hair. "You *know* this. And yet you still peer-pressured me into wearing them."

"Because you look hot in them," he protests. "Trust me, they up the outfit's hotness factor from a nine to an eleven. Just quit complaining and wear them for tonight. One night."

"Ugh. Fine." As I slide out of the SUV, I'm surprised to see Hunter do the same. "You're coming in with me?"

He gives a nod. "Don't worry, I'll sit at the bar. I'll stick around until I'm sure he won't murder you. Just pretend I'm not there."

I'm genuinely touched. "Thank you. You're a good friend."

We round the side of the building toward the entrance. I can't believe I'm going on a date. A Tinder date, to boot. That's pretty much code for "*maybe I'll have sex with you tonight.*"

Wait, tonight? I can't have sex with anyone tonight. I just realized I forgot to shave my legs.

Dammit, why didn't I shave my legs?

It's fine, it's only a drink, I reassure my panicky self.

We enter the bar and I conduct a quick scan of the main room. It's busier than I expected for a Monday night, but college students go out drinking any night of the week, I guess. My pulse accelerates when I notice a tall, muscular guy pushing away from the bar.

His eyes widen appreciatively when he spots me. "Demi?" he calls out.

"Roy?"

"That's me." He smiles, flashing a pair of dimples. Oh no, he has dimples. I'm in trouble. "There's a free table over there," Roy says warmly. "Shall we?"

"We shall." Ugh, that was *so* dorky. I'm bad at this.

A smattering of high, standing tables make up the main room. Two are empty, and we choose the more secluded of the pair. I glance over my shoulder. Hunter winks and nods in encouragement, then wanders toward the bar stools.

"Sorry for being so forward, but you are even hotter in person." Roy openly checks me out, so I don't feel bad doing the same.

His shirt is outrageously tight, probably tighter than any piece of clothing I own. I can clearly see the outline of every muscle, and his nipples. Hard little beads poking out for all to see. I'd always been indifferent to man nipples, but Roy's body-hugging shirt brings so much attention to them that I can't look away. I force myself to redirect my gaze to the TV screens above our heads. One is playing Monday night football, the other shows an NHL game.

"Do you like sports?" Roy asks.

"I'll watch football if it's on. I'm not too into hockey, although I have a friend who plays. And my ex-boyfriend played basketball, so I had no choice but to pay attention to the NBA." Dammit, you're not supposed to bring up another guy when you're on a date. That feels like a major no-no.

Okay, I'm *really* bad at this.

But Roy doesn't seem fazed. "I never played any sports." He gestures to his huge, muscly body. "I know, I know, doesn't look like it, but I got this physique from working out."

"So you're, like, a gym guy?"

He nods vigorously. "Seven days a week. How about you? Do you go to the gym?"

"I use the one in the student fitness center a couple times

a week. But I don't do more than use the treadmill, lift some weights, nothing fancy."

A waiter comes up to take our order. Roy asks for a Bud Light. I'm not in love with beer, but I don't feel comfortable drinking anything harder. My nerves are tickling my tummy and making my fingers tremble.

"I'll have a Bud Light too," I finally decide.

Once the server is gone, Roy picks up where we left off. "Have you used the pool in the fitness center? It's great for swimming laps."

"No, I haven't. Like I said, my workouts are pretty mild." I shrug. "I have a great metabolism."

"Working out has nothing to do with metabolism. Fitness is about health. Healthy heart rate, healthy mental state, healthy bones." He goes on about the benefits of exercise for several minutes, until my eyes start glazing over.

Finally, I interrupt him. "You kind of lost me there, bud."

Roy offers a sheepish smile. "Sorry. I'm really passionate about fitness."

"I can tell."

"Let's talk about other stuff." He rests his forearms on the table. A heavy silver watch adorns his left wrist, and it sparkles under the light fixtures. "So you're looking for something casual, huh?"

Oh boy. This topic is even more awkward. I'd way rather talk about his biceps curls. "Um, yeah. I mean, I recently broke up with my long-term boyfriend, so…"

"So you're on the rebound," he supplies.

I nod.

"Me too," Roy confesses.

"Really?" His profile bio didn't mention that. "When was your break-up?"

"A couple days ago."

A couple *days* ago? And he's already on Tinder? At least my break-up can be measured in weeks.

"That's very recent," I say carefully. "Are you sure you should be, you know, doing this?" I gesture between us.

Roy's right hand fiddles with his bulky watch. "Truthfully? I don't know. But I need to get over her, and I figured this is the best way. Putting myself right back out there, you know?"

Uneasiness trickles up my throat.

"Can I ask why you and your ex broke up?"

I answer truthfully. "He cheated."

"Oh man, that sucks. Were you together long?"

"We've known each other since we were eight. First kiss at twelve. Officially boyfriend and girlfriend at thirteen." As I recite the details, I'm startled to notice the lack of accompanying emotions. My heart didn't even clench when I listed each Nico milestone.

"Wow," Roy marvels. "That's a lot of history."

The server returns with our beers, and I gratefully accept my bottle. I'm not entirely sure how this date is going, but I'm leaning toward *not well*.

We clink our bottles together. "Cheers," I say.

"Cheers." He takes a long swig.

I do too, and it requires all my willpower not to blanch. I hate the taste of beer. Why did I even order this? What a stupid decision. I wonder if I should flag down the waiter and ask for a glass of water.

"So we're both unlucky in love." Roy observes me over the rim of his bottle.

"Guess so. What happened with your girlfriend?"

"She said I didn't spend enough time with her." He swallows another quick sip. "She thinks she should be my number one priority and that I focus on trivial shit instead of her."

I think it over. "Well, she has a point and she also doesn't. Obviously your partner needs to be a top priority, but we're in college. We also need to prioritize our classes, our assignments, our social lives—"

"No," he interrupts. "She means the gym. She thinks I'm addicted to the gym."

I can't stop my gaze from lowering to his pecs. The ones that are straining against his shirt, fighting to break free. *This shirt cannot hold me*! those pecs are screaming.

I think maybe Roy's ex is right.

"But screw that," he says irritably. "She should be proud of all the work I put into looking like this. Other dudes pump themselves full of 'roids, HGH. They poison their bodies. But me? This is *all* natural. My body is a temple."

A snort rings out from behind me. For fuck's sake. Is someone eavesdropping on us?

I turn my head—and sigh when I recognize the familiar profile. It belongs to Hunter, who's lurking at the neighboring table. He was supposed to be at the bar, dammit.

My discomfort only grows at the knowledge that my friend is listening in. But maybe it doesn't matter, because it's also becoming painfully obvious that Roy and I will *not* be entering into a Friends with Benefits arrangement.

"I don't get why I have to choose," he's grousing.

I fix him with a serious look. "Did you love her?"

"With all of my heart," he says passionately.

"Then how is it even a choice? Cut back on your gym time, you dummy."

Another snort.

"It *is* a choice," he argues. "An impossible choice."

"Oh, come on now. That's an exaggeration. You can't love the gym more than a woman. You can't get married to the gym, Roy. You can't have babies with the gym."

The floor beneath my feet is vibrating, and I don't know if it's from the heavy bass track blasting from the speakers, or because of Hunter shaking uncontrollably with laughter.

"You have a point," Roy says, albeit begrudgingly. "But I don't see why I should give up my passion."

"She's not asking you to give it up. She's clearly asking you to find a balance," I answer pragmatically.

"A balance," he echoes.

"Yes. Listen. What's your girlfriend's name?"

"Kaelin."

"I think Kaelin has a point. If you truly view her on the same level as the *gym*, then she's right to be upset. Kaelin is a human being, Roy. The gym is just a room full of machines."

Behind me, Hunter howls.

I ignore him. "I think you need to examine your priorities," I advise. "A rebound isn't the right move for you. Granted, it'll be a rebound with a ridiculously hot woman—"

"The hottest," he agrees, and my ego takes comfort in that.

"But it's not the right move," I repeat.

He sips his beer. "What's the right move then?"

"Calling Kaelin and asking her to get together and talk. And maybe actually *listen* to what she's telling you. She's not trying to control you. She simply wants to be with you." I really hope I'm not misinterpreting this, and that Kaelin didn't dump him because he's clearly in love with the gym, and I do mean in love in a sexual way. But heck, it warrants a conversation, seeing as how he's obviously not over her.

"I know this is totally rude…" Roy reaches into his back pocket and pulls out a twenty-dollar bill, way too much money for two shitty beers. "But do you mind if I bail on you?"

"Absolutely not. Go get 'er, Tiger." I accept the twenty. Might as well use it to buy me and Hunter a round.

Speaking of Hunter, he appears at my side the moment Roy disappears. "That was the craziest fucking date I've ever spied on," he declares, his jaw half open.

"Tell me about it. Is this what it's like to be back in the saddle? You just have to ride a bunch of donkeys?"

"Dude. First of all—the way that man was jacked, he's a majestic steed, not a donkey."

"And second of all?"

"Oh, I don't have a second point."

I sigh. "I can't believe that just happened."

"Well, you didn't do yourself any favors by being such a *therapist.*"

"How is that a bad thing?"

"It is when you're trying to hook up. You're supposed to ride the man's dick, Semi, not convince him to get back together with his girlfriend."

"You're right. I really do suck at this," I moan.

Hunter pulls the Bud Light out of my hand and sets it on the table. "Let's get this garbage out of the way. We will *not* be drinking Bud Light tonight."

"We?"

"Your date bailed. I'm all you got, babe. I'll go and grab us some actual beer."

Hunter is gone all of three seconds before another guy approaches me. He has a shaved head, an oversized hoodie, and very white teeth.

"Hey, beautiful. Want some company?"

I'm about to say no, but he's already sidling up beside me.

"What happened to your friend?" White Teeth asks.

"He's getting our drinks. So if you don't mind—"

He leans in closer, and I instinctively lean back. I don't like it when people infringe on my space cushion.

"What's the matter?" White Teeth drawls.

"You're in my space cushion," I retort. "I'd appreciate it if you moved."

He furrows his brow. "What do you need space for? We're getting to know each other."

To my sheer relief, Hunter returns with our drinks. He takes one look at the intruder and levels him with a hard glare. "No," Hunter says coldly.

"No what?" White Teeth sounds annoyed.

Hunter widens his stance. "This ain't happening. Get lost."

I smile at Hunter's menacing pose. Apparently he's my new protector.

My very attractive protector.

Dammit, I need to stop thinking about how hot is. He

doesn't want a rebound with me. He already made that clear.

It would be *so* much easier if he agreed to it, though. I'm attracted to him, and, more importantly, I trust him. But I'm not making a play for my friend, especially when he explicitly stated he's not into it.

The Space Cushion Encroacher stalks off in a huff, while Hunter stares after him in amusement. "That was easy." Then, with an extravagant gesture, he presents me with a tall can of beer. It's called Jack's Abbey House Lager.

"It's in a can," I remark.

"Yeah, cans are making a big comeback in craft beer circles. You're really living now, babe."

"Ergh. I probably should've told you to grab me a vodka cran or something fruity. I'm not a fan of most beers." I pause in thought. "Actually, I can't think of a single beer I like. They all taste the same to me: bad."

"Trust me, you'll like this one. It goes down *so* smooth. Just try it."

As Hunter watches expectantly, I take a big swallow of his magical beer.

"Well?" he demands.

My gaze drops to my suede boots. "It tastes exactly like the other one."

"Are you *joking* right now? You think Abbey House and Bud Light taste the *same*? I'm so ashamed of you right now."

"I told you, I'm not a beer girl."

"You're a disgrace."

"*You're* a disgrace."

Hunter grins as I stick out my tongue at him. He sips

his own can of pretentious beer, then says, "I'm sorry it didn't work out with Mr. Muscles."

"It's fine. To be honest, it was nice to get out of the house. And it's good practice, right?"

We do some people-watching as we savor our beers. Well, Hunter savors. I just hold my nose and swallow. We crack each other up by creating fake backstories for various bar patrons, and in no time at all I've forgotten all about being ditched by Roy. I have more fun with Hunter, anyway.

Around nine-thirty we leave the bar and head for the parking lot. As I'm zipping up my parka, one of my earrings nearly gets caught in the hood and I curse under my breath.

"I hate these stupid things," I complain as I move the hoop aside. "They're a menace."

"You're a menace."

Yes, this is our thing now. It makes us snicker every time, which I suppose indicates that either our shared sense of humor is immature, or we are.

Hunter starts the Rover and reverses out of the parking spot. "I'm taking you home?" He glances over.

"Yep, thank you." I buckle my seatbelt, laughing when I notice that *my* Bluetooth is the device that connects to his car.

"You didn't un-sync!" he accuses. "You promised me you did."

"I lied to you, Hunter." Chortling, I load a playlist that includes a bunch of Whitney Houston ballads, which I know he doesn't like.

"You're evil," he says as he drives us away from town.

"Sorry, I can't hear you. Whitney is singing."

Then, just because I can, I sing along to "Greatest Love

of All" until Hunter threatens to leave me on the side of the dark, deserted road if I don't shut up.

"Hey, could you turn off my butt heater?" he asks. "My ass is on fire."

"Sure." I'm holding my phone, so I go to plop it into the cup holder. But the Rover hits a pothole at that exact moment and the phone slips from my hand and tumbles to Hunter's feet.

"Chrissake, Semi. Grab that before it gets stuck under the gas pedal."

"Chill out. Hold on." I lean toward him and stretch out my arm, but the moving car sends my phone skittering across the floor mat. "Dammit, I can't reach it. Can you try to kick it toward my hand?"

"No. I'm fucking driving."

"Just try."

Groaning, he tries to poke the phone with his left foot, and the SUV swerves slightly.

"Okay, no, stop doing that," I order. "Focus on driving. I'll do it."

I unbuckle my seatbelt and crawl over his lower body. My hand begins wiggling around in the vicinity of his calves. The car swerves again.

"Pay attention to the road!"

"Trying to," he grinds out. "But you keep bumping my leg." I bend over as far as I can, until my head is squished in Hunter's lap. I stretch out my arm again, and—yes! My fingers collide with the phone and I swiftly close a fist around it.

"Got it!" I announce, and then I move to sit up and—

I can't.

"Demi," Hunter orders. "Move." The car rocks slightly to the right.

I try to lift my head again, and a jolt of pain shoots through my ear. "Oh my God," I wail. "I told you. I fucking *told* you."

"Told me what? Jesus, get up—"

"I can't!" My voice is muffled against the fly of his jeans. "My earring is stuck."

"Stuck on what?"

"On you! On your jeans! I don't know what." The position I've found myself in has my head wrenched to the side, so all I can see is Hunter's knees, and his foot on the gas pedal. Rather than attempt an escape, I keep my head planted flat on his thigh.

"Try to unsnag yourself," he pleads.

I refuse to budge. "No. It'll rip my earlobe off, Hunter."

"It won't."

"It will." Honest-to-God tears well up in my eyes.

He growls in frustration. "It's not gonna rip your—fuck, you know what, hold on. Let me pull over," he says.

And that's when we hear the sirens.

21
HUNTER

THIS IS A DISASTER. I'M GETTING PULLED OVER BY THE COPS, and Demi's head is stuck in my lap. She's draped over me like a blanket, her face inches from my crotch, and I know that the second the officer reaches the driver's side window, he's going to think…

Jesus Chris, he's going to think she's blowing me.

"Why did they pull us over?" she hisses.

"Must've seen us swerving all over the road." Shit, this is a nightmare.

I shut off the engine. As I wait for the cop to approach the window, I make a frantic attempt to pry Demi off me.

"Ow!" she wails.

"Sorry," I mumble. "I'm trying to get you free." Her earring is caught, all right, but I'm not sure on what.

I think it's one of my belt loops? But how the hell did it get embedded like that? Maybe it snagged on a thread? I'm not making a lick of progress, and every time I try to tug the hoop free, Demi whimpers in pain. I can't believe I'm even thinking it, but…she might lose that ear.

I don't know whether to laugh or cry.

"Someone's coming," she whispers as footsteps thump on the pavement.

"License and regist—" The police officer stops midsentence.

I sigh in resignation.

"What in the hell is going on here? Sit up, Miss," he commands. "Now, please."

"I can't!" moans Demi.

The cop's stern eyes fix on me. "I'm going to need you and your girlfriend to get out of the car and place both your hands on the hood."

"I'm not his girlfriend," Demi says, as if *that's* our most pressing concern, being mistaken for a couple.

"We can't," I answer through gritted teeth.

"Look, kid, I realize this is a cool thing you college boys like to do—"

A *cool thing* we do?

"—but lewd behavior is grounds for arrest. Not only that, you were driving recklessly and endangering other drivers."

I peer out the windshield at the dark and completely empty road. "What other drivers? There's nobody here but us. A single car hasn't driven by since you pulled us over."

"And we're not being lewd," Demi protests. "I'm stuck!"

"Stuck," he echoes dubiously.

I sigh. "She dropped her phone and tried to pick it up, and now she's stuck."

"Stuck," he says again. Then he shakes his head as if deciding he doesn't want to buy what we're selling. "Miss, this is the last time I'm going to ask—please sit up."

"I can't."

The officer reaches for his belt.

"Jesus!" I blurt out. "You don't need your weapon!"

"What weapon!" Demi starts wiggling in my lap, renewed in her efforts to set herself free.

If the officer wasn't there and it was the two of us, all that wild undulating would summon a heated response out of my dick. But the cop *is* here, so my dick is limp and I'm seconds away from breaking out in manic laughter. Which won't go over well with the increasingly irritated officer.

Turns out, he was only reaching for a radio. "I'm going to need some backup on Ninth Line and Highway Forty-eight. Suspects were pulled over for reckless driving and perform-ing oral sex while in a moving vehicle and are now resisting arrest." Static crackles.

"I'm not performing oral sex!" Demi growls. "Trust me, I would *love* to perform oral sex on him, but he's celibate."

I'm sorry, what?

Did she just say she would love to perform oral sex on me?

"Seriously, Demi? You're saying you actually want to bl—do that?" My mind spins like a carousel. During all this talk about rebounds, I truly believed she was joking when she suggested me as a candidate. That's why I never let myself… get my hopes up, I guess?

"I told you I want a rebound, and I wanted to have it with you." Her voice is muffled and her fingers continue to fumble with her ear.

But we'll need to discuss Demi's desire to blow me later. I need to get through to this stubborn officer first.

"Sir," I say calmly. "Please. I understand what this looks like, but we are not engaging in lewd behavior. We're both clothed. My dick's in my pants."

"Where is your license and registration?"

"In the glove box, but I can't reach—"

A shout of triumph echoes in the car, and suddenly Demi's head pops up like a jack-in-the-box.

"I did it!" She's frantically rubbing her left ear.

"Holy shit," I say when she moves her hand. Her earlobe is bright red and swollen to three times its size, and there's blood staining her fingertips.

She's right. Hoop earrings should be banned.

"See!" Relief lines her voice as she gazes imploringly at the officer. "His pants are zipped. We weren't doing anything wrong. And we only drank a beer each. Well, two for me."

I swallow a groan.

Goddammit. Drinking hadn't even been part of this equation. And now, thanks to her, it is.

The cop is officially done humoring us. "I'm going to need both of you to get out of the car. Now."

———

"*This* is the drunk tank?" Demi asks an hour later.

She looks thoroughly unimpressed with the holding area of the only jail in Hastings. The large cell currently houses three people—us, and a middle-aged man with a bushy beard, sleeping on one of the benches. He's twitching in his sleep, and one foot taps against the bars every few seconds.

Yup, we're behind *bars*, and it's all thanks to the big hoops.

"Maybe it's nicer when you're actually drunk?" she hypothesizes.

I laugh as I slide my back down the cement wall and sink onto the metal bench. Beneath my feet is a dirty linoleum floor. Above my head the fluorescent lights are way too bright.

"You know this is all your fault," I say cheerfully.

"*My* fault?" Her brown eyes fill with indignation.

"I told you what would happen if you synced your Bluetooth to my car."

"This is *not* my Bluetooth's fault."

"Oh really?"

"Really. I dropped my phone."

"Still your fault."

"Oh shut up."

"You shut up." I scoot closer to her, until we're sitting about a foot apart. "How's your ear?" I ask gruffly.

From what I can see, it's still pink and swollen, but it doesn't seem to be bleeding anymore. The dried blood caked onto the lobe triggers a pang of guilt, because I'm the one who talked her into wearing those earrings tonight.

"It's sore," she admits. "But at least it's still attached to my head."

"At least that," I agree. "I'm sorry I made you wear the big hoops."

"It's all right. Now you know." She releases a bleak sigh. "Sometimes you must witness the tragedy firsthand in order to understand it."

"Yes," I said gravely.

My lips twitch until finally a laugh slips out. She joins in, stretching out her legs and tapping her suede boots on the linoleum.

"I wish I had a lollipop," she says.

"I wish I had my freedom."

That summons another laugh from her. "God. I can't believe we're in jail. For lewd behavior, of all things."

"And my dick wasn't even out!"

"I know, right?"

The lone deputy in the holding area glances in our direction, and I glimpse a glimmer of amusement in his eyes. He's been at his desk for the past hour, typing on a computer.

I have no idea where the arresting officer disappeared to, although we weren't technically arrested. Nobody read me my Miranda rights, anyway. No Miranda rights? Ha! I've seen enough *Law and Order* reruns to know that any judge in his right mind would dismiss this case in a heartbeat. Unless the judge is having a bad day.

Personally, I think Officer Cranky was having a shitty night. Demi and I didn't do anything wrong and he knows it. Our breathalyzers barely registered a thing.

"What's the punishment for lewd behavior?" she asks curiously.

"No clue."

"Excuse me—sir?" She hops up and approaches the bars. "What's the punishment for lewd behavior? Is it death?"

Once again, he seems to be fighting a smile. "For first-time offenders, usually a fine."

"Perfect," she chirps. "My co-conspirator is filthy rich. He can write you a check."

"Hey, don't look at me," the desk jockey says with a grin.

"Wait until Officer Jenk returns—he's the one you need to talk to."

"Officer Jerk, more like it," Demi grumbles.

I snicker. "Nice."

She addresses the deputy again. "Aren't we supposed to get a phone call?" she challenges.

"She's right," I say, sauntering up to the bars. "I'd like my phone call, please."

"Sure. Whatever." The young cop walks over and unlocks the cell door. He gestures for me to step out before sliding the bars back into place with a sharp click.

"Who are you calling?" Demi demands.

I turn to answer her, but the sight of her gripping two iron bars and peering at me from inside a cell… It's too good. I'd regret it my whole life if I let this opportunity pass.

"Am I allowed to take a picture?" I beg the cop.

"Don't you *dare*," Demi warns.

He grins. "Go for it." I think this is the most fun he's had in a while. Riding a desk is probably boring as fuck.

I fish my phone from my pocket and snap a picture of Demi, who looks like she wants to murder me. Then, to rub salt in the wound, I turn around to take a selfie, with Demi's outraged face in the background, her fingers curled around the bars.

"That's my Christmas card, right there," I tell her, giving a finger gun.

"I hate you."

No you don't, you want to blow me.

I can't stop the wicked thought. And I can't quite fathom it, either. Was she actually serious about wanting me to be her rebound? She's so sarcastic that I assumed she was messing with me.

Maybe it's a good thing I was in the dark about it. Hell, it'd probably be better if I still was. I promised myself I wouldn't hook up this year, and the temptation to break that vow for Demi is overwhelming.

The deputy leads me over to his desk and points to the landline.

"Can't I use my own phone?" I hold it up in reminder. I mean, he literally just allowed me to take a picture.

He shakes his head. "Against protocol."

"Okay, well, that doesn't make any sense, but whatever." I shrug and grab the handset off its cradle. Then I dial one of the few numbers I know by heart.

"Hey Coach," I say after his brusque hello.

"Davenport?" he asks suspiciously.

"Yeah. I hope I didn't wake you." The digital clock across the room reads 10:37. Not crazy late, but we have a six-thirty a.m. morning skate, so there's a chance he was already in bed. "What's going on?" he barks in my ear.

"Not much." I stall, wondering the best way to frame my predicament.

"Is this about the fucking egg?" Coach sounds annoyed. "Did something happen to it?"

"Nah, Pablo's good, thanks for asking. Well, at least I think he's good—he's with Conor tonight, so…yeah…anyway…" I exhale. "There's no easy way to say this, so I'm just going to Band-Aid it. I'm in jail right now and I'm hoping you might be able to come here and talk to the officers and, you know, do your thing?"

"My thing?"

"Yelling at people," I clarify.

There's a brief silence, followed by, "Is this a prank? Because I don't have time for that shit."

I swallow a laugh. "I'm dead serious. A friend and I got pulled over in Hastings tonight. It was a total misunderstanding—we weren't drunk and there was no lewd behavior despite what Officer Jerk might say—"

The desk cop chuckles softly. Man, I wish he was the one who pulled us over. He probably would've high-fived me and let us go.

"Coach?" I prompt.

Another silence trickles by.

"I'm on my way."

22
HUNTER

"Where is he?" Demi asks impatiently. "I thought you said he lived ten minutes away."

"He does. And it's literally only been *one* minute since I called." Rolling my eyes, I rejoin her on the uncomfortable metal bench. Our cellmate remains fast asleep, now snoring softly. His foot keeps twitching, and there's no mistaking the odor of stale booze that wafts our way.

Demi presses her lips together, as if trying not to laugh. "This is the best date I've ever been on," she says sarcastically. "I mean, the romantic ambience alone…"

A snort slips out. "Only thing missing is the Whitney Houston ballad. Oh, and your actual date—you know, the dude who ditched you for his girlfriend. Or maybe the gym. I honestly can't be sure. It was such an impossible choice."

It's her turn to snort. "Meh. Whatever. You're a way better date."

Grinning, I sling one arm around her and tug her closer, and she rests her head on my shoulder. The sweet scent of her hair floats up into my nostrils. I breathe deeply, trying to pinpoint the scent. Jasmine, I think. She feels nice and warm pressed up beside me. I wonder what she's thinking about right now. If her thoughts align with mine.

I almost groan in disappointment when she lifts her head. "I really mean it," she informs me.

"Mean what?" Shit, my voice sounds way too husky. I promptly clear the gravel from my throat.

"You're a fun date."

"This isn't a date."

She tips her head in challenge. "Then why are you giving me the Penis Eyes?"

"I'm not."

"I know Penis Eyes when I see 'em."

A laugh tickles my throat. This girl is something else. She cracks me up. And she's so fucking beautiful. Her skin always looks so soft and luminous that my fingers itch to stroke it. Her hair looks silky to the touch too. It falls in a straight, shiny curtain over her shoulder, the one that's bared by her loose sweater. A few dark strands fall over her left eye.

My lips feel dry. I lick them, and heat flares in Demi's expression.

"You've got hair in your eyes," I say roughly.

I reach out to gently brush it away. My thumb lingers on her cheekbone as I tuck the hair behind her ear, the one that's normal-sized.

She gives a sharp intake of breath. "Oh my God. Was that it?"

My eyebrows crash together. "Was what it?"

"Was that your move?" Delight dances in her eyes.

"Licking the lips, brushing hair off my face, that little thumb rub. That's totally the move. Right?"

I flash a cocky smile. "Depends. Did it work?"

"Yes," she says frankly, and now it's my breath that hitches.

Her honesty is such a turn-on. And although I didn't plan on busting it out tonight, that *was* my move. It just happened naturally.

"Davenport," booms a loud voice.

My head snaps toward the bars. Footsteps thud down a hallway and then Coach's thunderous face appears in the doorway. Officer Jenk tails him.

"Unlock that door." Coach issues the order to the desk jockey, who jumps to his feet at the arrival of Coach and his colleague.

Weirdly enough, the younger deputy actually reaches for his heavy key ring before remembering that Coach is not his superior, nor a cop. "Jeff?" he says, glancing at Officer Jenk.

His name is Jeff? Jeff Jenk?

Poor bastard. Maybe that's why he's in such a bad mood.

"Do it," Jenk says curtly.

Coach gives me and Demi a brisk once-over as we emerge from the cell. "You all right?" he says curtly. "Did anybody manhandle you?"

"No," I assure him, touched that he'd asked. "Nobody knocked us around at all, but thanks for worrying."

"I'm not worried about you, you idiot. I'm worried about your fucking shooting hand. We have a game in four days." His accusatory eyes shift toward the officers. "If his slapshot is even a tenth of a second slower than usual, I'm going to hold you personally responsible, Albertson."

"Sorry, Coach," the desk jockey mumbles.

I stare at them both. "You two know each other?"

"Yeah, kid used to play for me. Sammy Albertson, class of 2012."

Damn, now I really wish Albertson was the one who pulled us over. I could've just name-dropped and gone on my merry way. Just my luck that I got the cop with the chip on his shoulder.

"And you," Coach says, turning to a sour-faced Jenk. "Unless the kid's dick is out and inside someone's mouth, it ain't considered lewd conduct. Make wiser choices next time."

"Tell your player that," Jenk says snidely. "He can't be swerving all over the road."

"I was stuck," Demi pipes up. "Hunter was trying to—"

Coach raises a hand to silence her, and, like all of his players, Demi falls in line. "Any paperwork we need to sign?" he barks at Jenk. "Any fines to pay?"

"No, I'm letting them off with a warning as a courtesy to—"

"Good, let's go," Coach interrupts. He nods his head, and Demi and I scamper after him like baby geese following their mommy.

Outside the tiny station, Coach zips up his coat. It still hasn't snowed once this winter, but the temperature is finally turning frigid. Coach's breath escapes in white puffs as he says, "Your Land Rover wasn't impounded because the tow truck's ETA was a couple of hours, so it's still on Ninth Line. I'll drive you over to it."

"Thanks, Coach."

"And I want you to go straight home, you hear me?"

"Demi lives on campus," I say, shaking my head. "I need to drop her off first."

"I'll do it," he snaps before stalking toward the curb, where his Jeep is parked.

Demi turns to me in alarm. "Should I be worried he might murder me on the drive home?" She pauses. "I can't remember if my show has an episode called *Coaches Who Kill*."

"You're probably okay."

"*Probably*?"

I shrug. "He's more pissed at me than you. I'm the one who dragged him out of bed."

"True." She flips up the fur-lined hood of her parka, and plants one hand on her hip. "And for the record, none of this would have happened if you'd agreed to rebound me."

"It still would've happened." I smirk at her. "Only difference is, you would've actually been blowing me." I instantly regret saying that, because the thought of my dick stuffed in her mouth is so torturously enticing I almost groan out loud.

"No," she counters, "we wouldn't have been anywhere near your car. We would've been warm and cozy in my bedroom, with no Tinder profiles and no distractions. Just you and me and a big comfy bed and my mouth on your penis. I want you to think about that!" she taunts as she flounces off to Coach's vehicle.

Right. As if now I'll be able to think of anything *but*.

———

And think about it I do. All week long.

Normally I'd be pumped and focused on the upcoming

game, but by the time Friday rolls around, I can't even remember who we're playing against. My concentration is shot, not only because Demi's gotten under my skin, but from the constant ragging I've been getting from my teammates all week.

I had no choice but to fess up about the jail incident, because Brenna had breakfast with her father the morning after and Coach Jensen decided to be an ass and told his daughter. And obviously Brenna opened her big mouth, and now I'm Hunter Davenport, the guy who got arrested for receiving a blowjob while driving. The worst part is, I didn't even get the blowjob.

Demi's also been teasing me about it, only she's taking things a step further than my teammates. Since experiencing my "move," she's launched a campaign to end my celibacy, as evidenced by the text she just sent.

> **DEMI**: Have a good game tonight! I hope you score! Speaking of scoring, have you considered breaking your vow?

I sigh at the phone. See? I should be mentally prepping for the game right now. I'm in the visitors' locker room at… Boston College. Right! That's who we're facing tonight. I should be thinking about the game, not Demi Davis.

> **ME**: I told you, it ain't happening.
> **HER**: You wouldn't even consider it? For lil ole me?

Someone smacks me between the shoulder blades. "Hey, now. Stop fantasizing about the road head, captain."

I turn to find Matt grinning at me.

"Seriously, though, *nice,*" he praises.

"You've said that to me at morning skate every day this week."

"Yeah, because it's *nice*. Always wanted road head."

"Me too," I say dryly. "Like I've been telling *you* every day, nothing happened. Demi's earring got stuck on my pants."

"I've gotten road head," Conor drawls as he unbuttons his white dress shirt.

"You've gotten head everywhere," I shoot back.

"That's not true. I've never gotten…" He strains his brain trying to offer up a blowjob-free location.

"Having a little trouble there?" Matt hoots.

Chuckling, I peel off my own clothes and begin to suit up. My phone dings again and I realize I didn't respond to Demi.

> **HER**: Sorry. I'll stop talking about this. I know it makes you uncomfortable.
>
> **ME**: No, sorry, I'm just gearing up. Gotta go, talk later.

I add a kissy face and then tuck the phone in the pocket of my discarded pants. Once I'm in uniform, I sink down on the bench to put on my skates.

Conor sits beside me. "What are you doing after the game? We were going to have some people over. You in?"

"Sure. I've got nothing else going on."

He slants his head pensively. "Are you seriously not doing this sex thing or are you fucking with all of us?"

"Not since April," I confirm.

"Christ. That's intense. I'd probably lose my mind if I couldn't bust a nut."

"I never said I'm not busting nuts." I release a gloomy sigh. "I'm just doing it solo."

"Still. Sounds like a hellscape."

I can't help but snicker. "It's not that bad. I'm actually getting used to the perpetual blue balls."

"Jesus!" Bucky interrupts, walking over with a Saran-wrapped stinky Pablo in one hand and a cellphone in the other. "Have you *seen* this shit? Pablo's Insta account reached ten thousand followers. Someone just DM'd asking if we'd do a sponsored post for an age-defying moisturizing cream."

My jaw drops. "Is that a joke?"

"No joke." Bucky shakes his head in disbelief.

"Age-defying cream?" Alec pipes up, looking confused. "How do you defy age?"

"And what the hell does that have to do with an egg?" Conor cracks. "Are we supposed to slather moisturizer on his little pig face and pose him for a photo shoot?"

Bucky grins. "I'll message them back and find out."

Coach strides into the locker room to deliver his pregame pep talk, which typically consists of a sentence or two, tops, before he turns it over to the captain or assistant captains to pump everybody up. This evening's "pep talk" offers the usual sentiments—kick their ass, don't embarrass me, don't bring shame onto your house, et cetera et cetera. Then I give a little speech and we all file out onto the ice.

The crowd is deafening, and I don't even care that only a third of the seats consist of Briar fans. The screams and cheers and even the boos fuel my blood. I fucking love this sport. I love the ice, the speed, the aggression. I love the physicality of it, the way every bone in my body jars and my teeth rattle when I'm slammed into the boards. Those are messed up things to love, but that's hockey.

I remember the game Fitz and I watched in our living room last night. Edmonton versus Vancouver. Jake Connelly scored one of the most beautiful goals I'd ever seen. And I remember the longing I felt, an ache that actually tightened my throat, because while college hockey is great, it's nowhere near as fast and competitive as professional hockey.

And if the pros were simply about being out there on the ice, I'd sign up in a heartbeat. But that life comes with strings I'm not interested in. It comes with women and glamour and press conferences and constant travel. Constant temptation. And Davenport men don't fare well in the face of temptation.

So I'll just have to content myself with *this*, right now, skating out on the ice with my friends, kicking ass. Because this is what it's all about.

———

The bus drops us off on campus around eleven, and from there I hop into my Rover and drive myself and a few teammates back to Hastings. I deliver them to Matt and Con's house, then head home to park my car. I'm planning on walking back to Matt's. That way I can drink more than a couple of beers.

At home, I change out of my dress clothes—we're required to wear jackets, ties, and trousers for all away games. It's almost a shame to strip out of my suit, because I rock it like nobody's business. I can thank my father for that. He pulls off the CEO look better than anyone. Probably why he's so popular with the ladies.

A little *too* popular.

"Hunter, you heading out?" Brenna pokes her head into my bedroom. As usual, there was no knocking involved.

"Yeah, I'm going to Matty's. Want to come?"

"I might pop over later. I'm Skyping with Jake first."

"Tell him I said hey. Oh, and tell him I'm jealous of that goal he scored yesterday. It was a beauty."

"Right? I've never been more turned on in my life."

"I honestly think Edmonton has a shot of winning the Cup this year."

"Same. They're unstoppable."

I zip up my hoodie. "When I was in Boston last month, Garrett was saying he hopes they don't have to face each other in a playoffs series." Christ, I don't even know who I'd be rooting for in that scenario. Garrett, I guess. No. Jake. Or maybe Garrett. Fuck, it's an impossible choice. Like picking between the gym and your girlfriend.

Brenna wanders off, and I go downstairs to put on my coat and boots. I'm about to slide my phone in my pocket when it beeps in my hand. I check it and find a text from Tara, a girl I hooked up with last year.

TARA: Hey, sorry for texting out of the blue like this—random, right? Nice win tonight. Just wanted to give you a heads up, tho. Some guy was asking about you.

ME: I might need more details than that LOL

HER: After the game, some guys came over and one

of them was grilling me and my girls about where you
were. I said probably on the team bus.

ME: Wait, this happened in the city?

HER: Yeah, outside the BC arena.

ME: OK, that's weird. Thanks for the heads up.

HER: No prob, hon.

She punctuates that with three hearts. *Red* hearts. Every
guy on the planet is aware that red hearts mean business. An
invitation to start something up if I want to. But I don't.

I walk out the front door, and I'm nearing the sidewalk
when my phone beeps again. This time I find a message from
Grady, the little brother of one of my teammates.

GRADY: Hey. Hunter. Got your # from Dan. He told
me to text about this—some dude was looking for you
at BC.

ME: Yeah, I just heard. Any idea who it was?

HIM: Never seen any of them before. The main guy
kinda looked like a young Johnny Depp?

ME: Doesn't ring a bell.

HIM: Anyway, I heard someone mention to them
that you might be at Matt Anderson's house tonight.
Wanted to let you know in case he tracks you down.

ME: Thanks. I appreciate it, man.

Okay. I don't like this at all. Two different warnings that
a bunch of strangers were asking about me? Strangers who
raised enough alarms that Tara and Grady both felt the need
to reach out to me.

And fuck, I'm glad they did, because when I reach Matt and Con's street, I immediately notice the group twenty feet ahead, loitering by the curb. If I hadn't been forewarned, I might've waltzed right up to them thinking they were partygoers.

Instead, I slow my gait, giving myself time to scope out the guys. There are five of them. They're not particularly huge in terms of height, but they're all pretty beefy. One is bald and stocky and appears vaguely familiar. The tallest one has his back to me, but he turns around when he hears my footsteps.

"Nico," I say guardedly. "Hey."

I haven't seen or spoken to Demi's ex since the night she went all Carrie Underwood on his stuff. And on closer examination, he kind of does resemble a young Johnny Depp, but with a darker complexion.

"What's going on?" I ask when he doesn't return the greeting.

"You tell me."

I resist the urge to roll my eyes. "I'm not sure what you mean."

"Really? Because rumor has it you were out with Demi on Monday night." Barely concealed rage reddens his face. His fists are clenched at his sides.

Nico's friends creep forward. Not close enough to pose a physical threat, but enough that my shoulders snap into a rigid line.

"Yeah, we went to Malone's for a drink." I omit the part where Demi was going there to meet another guy. Nico is already on edge.

"I heard it was more than a drink." His voice trembles with anger. "Heard you got thrown in lockup together."

Fuck's sake.

I open my mouth to respond, but Nico hisses like a venomous snake. "Heard you got pulled over with your *dick* in her mouth."

"That's not what happened." My tone is calm, even.

"You feel like a big man, Davenport, disrespecting my girl like that?"

"I'm not disrespecting anyone—"

He's still talking. "Using her? Forcing her to blow you?"

"I didn't force her." I quickly amend that when I realize what it implies. "Nothing happened, man. It was a misunderstanding, and the cops let us go. But even if something *did* happen, you'd have no right to be pissed. You guys aren't together anymore."

"We're not together right now," he qualifies. "We'll get back together. We always do."

"Is that so," I drawl.

"You don't know a damn thing about our history."

"I know you cheated on her at a frat party."

Nico's eyes flash. "She tell you that?"

"Nah, I saw you, man."

A brief silence travels between us. Then Nico hisses again. "Wait, it was you? You're the asshole who told her about the chick at the party?"

"What the hell does it matter? She was going to find out anyway, Nico. She was already going to find out about your *other* screw-up because you're too stupid to delete a Wi-Fi password."

"Who the fuck you calling stupid?"

He charges at me, and I dodge him, taking several steps

back. "I'm just saying, you did this to yourself. If you want someone to blame, go look in the mirror."

"You ratted me out." Nico glances over his shoulder at his buddies, each of whom has his arms crossed. "This *puta* ratted me out, can you believe that? You're a real prick, Davenport."

"I'm the prick? You cheated on your girlfriend."

"You broke the bro code," he spits back.

"You're not my bro." I take another backward step. "Are we done here?"

Before I can blink, his arm shoots out. He grabs the collar of my winter coat, tugging me toward him. His face is inches from mine, the white puffs of his alcohol-scented breath chilling my face.

"Nico," I warn.

A spiteful smile stretches across his angry face. Beyond his shoulders, I spy his buddies closing in on us.

"Get your hands off me," I say in a deadly voice.

His smile widens. "Or what?"

23
HUNTER

"The way I see it, there's five of us and only one of you." Nico chuckles, his dark eyes glinting with impending violence. "Sure, you're the hockey guy. I bet you can fight real good. But can you take all five of us?"

I know I can't. I glance toward Matt's front door. It's closed, and the pulsing music thudding in the house tells me that even if I shouted for backup, nobody would hear me. My best hope is that someone decides to brave the early December chill, come out to smoke a cigarette or a joint, and throw me an assist.

But what I'd prefer happen is that I defuse this bomb before it goes off in the first place.

"Look, Nico. You seem like a cool guy. You made a mistake, and there's no need for violence, okay? Even if I didn't tell Demi about the party, she would've found out through her friend. But you're right—what I did went against the bro code. I should've kept my mouth shut."

"Damn right you should have."

"So I'm sorry for that, okay? With that said, you *really*

need to take your hands off me." Adrenaline is already surging in my bloodstream. Nico's right—hockey players are no strangers to fighting. I've gotten into scraps on the ice, and off of it. I can hold my own in most physical confrontations.

But not when it's five against one.

"Sorry, jock boy, but you're not getting off that easy." Nico chuckles.

"For chrissake, man, you're gonna punish me when *you're* the moron who cheated on your woman—"

The first blow cuts me off and sends my head rearing back. His fist crunches against my jaw, a jolt of pain shooting down my neck. Just as I straighten out, two of his buddies are suddenly behind me, locking my arms behind my back. Presenting me like a juicy carcass to a pissed-off hyena.

Nico cracks the knuckles of his right hand, then the left. "All I'm saying is, us men need to stick together. And the fuckers who don't, deserve to get their ass whupped."

His second punch collides with the corner of my mouth.

I taste blood. I spit it out onto the pavement. "Get your punches in," I tell him in a resigned tone. "If that's what makes you feel better. But it's not gonna bring Demi back and it's not gonna change the fact that you're a sack of shit—"

The next blow gets me in the ribs.

Fuck.

My side is already sore from a hit I took in the game tonight, and now my entire ribcage is throbbing and I'm goddamn pissed. The anger brings another jolt of adrenaline that enables me to scramble out of the iron-hold on me. I elbow one of Nico's friends in the throat, manage to land a punch in another one's stomach, but then my body is thrown back like a rag doll, and they all swarm again.

"What the hell!" someone shouts from the porch.

The cavalry has arrived.

Matt comes tearing down the frost-covered lawn. More shouts and angry curses fill the night as six more hockey players race toward the curb. Someone grabs me and shoves me aside. Nico and his cronies retreat, creating about three feet of distance as the two groups face off with each other. My bottom lip is caked with blood. Nico's ragged breaths exit his mouth in rapid puffs.

"Go home," I tell him.

"Fuck you," he snaps.

"You really don't want to stick around, Nico. You're the one who's outnumbered now, and there's already been enough violence tonight, okay?" I drag my forearm over my mouth to sop up the blood. "Just get out of here."

"Stay away from my girl."

She's not your girl, I want to say, but I resist the urge to provoke him.

Beside me, Conor takes a slight step forward. "Leave," he drawls, and despite the laidback tone, his expression is deadlier than I've ever seen it.

It has the desired effect. Nico spits on the ground, and then he and his friends stalk off toward a nearby truck. I watch them go, hoping that the shitshow is truly over and this wasn't just the first act.

———

I'm cleaning my face in the hall bathroom when I hear the commotion beyond the door. My shoulders instantly tense. Nico had better not be back—

"Is he in there? Hunter, are you in there!"

I relax at the familiar voice. "In here," I call out.

I'd left the door slightly ajar, and Demi wastes no time pushing it open. She appears in all her fierce glory, hands on hips, eyes on fire.

"I'm going to *kill* him!" she thunders when she sees my face. "Are you okay? I cannot *believe* he did this!"

"How'd you find out what happened?" I frown. "And how'd you get here?"

"I called a campus taxi right after Brenna called."

Frickin' Brenna. With impeccable timing, she'd shown up just as we were all trudging inside after the fight. She must've phoned Demi before she'd even taken off her coat.

"You're bleeding," Demi frets. "Brenna said you weren't badly hurt."

"I wasn't," I assure her. "My lip split open again because I was laughing at something Conor said."

Guilt floats through her expression. "I am so sorry. How did he even know you were here?"

"Apparently he was at Boston College earlier, asking random people where I was. I think he and his friends were drunk."

Demi's entire body vibrates with anger. "I'm unblocking him so I can yell at him."

"Don't. You blocked him for a reason. And it's fine, I'm fine."

"Are you sure?" She reaches for my face. I try to swat

her hands away, but she's not having it. "Let me look at it, dammit." Her fingertips tenderly graze the side of my mouth.

A shiver runs up my spine.

Her bottomless brown eyes lock with mine. "This is it? Just the busted lip?" Her hand sweeps up my face to gingerly examine my cheekbone.

I wince. "He got me there too, but that one'll just be a small bruise."

"I can't believe he did this," she says again.

"Nah, I get it. He heard about our dalliance with the cops last night and jumped to conclusions."

Her jaw drops. "How on earth did he find out about that?"

"It's gotten around," I admit. "Coach told Brenna, so now the entire team knows about it, and people talk. He lives in Hastings, right? Hell, he could've heard someone talking about it at the diner."

"Maybe." She curses. "Ugh. You're bleeding again. Sit down, will you?"

I dutifully lower myself onto the closed toilet lid. If she wants to fuss over me, then I'm going to let her.

She shoves some toilet paper under the sink faucet, then presses the wet wad against my lip to soak up the blood.

"Let's leave this on here for thirty seconds or so," she murmurs. "Hopefully the pressure will stop the bleeding for good."

I try not to smile. "You know I could be doing this myself, right?"

"Just let me do it, Hunter. Please. This is all my fault."

"It's not your fault."

She kneels on the floor and damned if that position

doesn't send a flurry of dirty images to my brain. If a woman's on her knees in front of me, it's usually because she's about to undo my pants and take my cock out. My eyes dip to Demi's pink lips. I imagine the tight suction of them around the head of my cock and suddenly it becomes difficult to swallow.

I jerk my gaze away from her mouth.

"What?" she says urgently. "Are you okay?"

"I'm fine," I croak. Christ. My dick is harder than stone.

"What's wrong? You look like you're in pain! Is this hurting?" She reduces some of the pressure.

"It's all good. Don't worry about it."

Demi bites her lower lip. Fuck, I need to stop fixating on those gorgeous lips. But I can't. They'd probably feel so soft and warm pressed against mine.

We should not be alone together right now. I'm still hopped up on adrenaline from the game, from the fight.

"I don't know whether to believe you or not," she mutters.

"I'm fine. Trust me, I've suffered worse from playing hockey."

She removes the toilet paper from my lip. It's soaked red, and she makes a face before tossing it in the wastebasket. "The bleeding stopped," she says.

"That's good."

Her fingertips run over my cheek again.

"Demi," I say thickly.

"Yeah?"

"Please stop touching me."

She looks startled. "Why?"

"Because no one's touched me like that in ages. You realize this is essentially torture?"

She presses her lips together as if resisting a smile. "It's turning you on?" Her knuckles graze my cheekbone, the one that isn't bruised. "This? This is turning you on?"

"Yes," I say through gritted teeth. "Therefore—please stop."

My protest sounds hollow to my own ears, so I'm not surprised when an impish glimmer fills her eyes. "What if I don't want to?"

"Well, it's not about what you want, now is it?" In one swift motion, I lock her wrist with my right hand and move it away from my face.

Only, I make the mistake of putting it near my knee, and now her fingertips are centimeters from my thigh. I almost expect her to move her small palm in a caress, but she keeps it still. A slight crease appears in her forehead as her gaze fixates on my mouth.

"Am I bleeding again?" I ask hoarsely.

She slowly shakes her head.

"Then why are you staring at me like that?"

"You got beat up because of me. I feel bad."

I study her preoccupied expression. "Really, that's why you're staring at me?"

Her brown eyes abruptly come into focus. "Well, no. That's just me feeling bad. I'm staring at you because I want to kiss you."

I inhale sharply. "You shouldn't do that."

"I'm not going to, not unless you're into it. But that doesn't mean I'm not thinking about it. We're making out hardcore in my head right now." She blinks innocently. "It's amazing, in case you're wondering." Her eyes twinkle. "I urge you to reconsider."

A beautiful girl is begging me to kiss her. How is this even a quandary? But I promised myself I wouldn't hook up during the season. It might not be the most noteworthy vow any human being has ever taken. I'm sure others have made sacrifices for much nobler causes. But this was important to me. *Is* important to me.

"Is that a no?" she prompts when I remain quiet.

"It's a…" I trail off helplessly.

Demi leans toward me. "If you don't want it, stop me," she whispers, but I'm powerless to stop her, because I want it as bad as she does.

"Just one taste," I mumble, and holy fuck, I was right— her lips *are* soft. They feel like heaven as she gently rubs them against mine in the sweetest of kisses.

The moment our mouths make contact, a hot shiver rolls through me and settles between my legs. My dick is thick, heavy against my thigh. Motherfucker. This kiss is *everything*.

She moans, and the throaty sound creates tiny vibrations that quicken my pulse. Her tongue tentatively prods the seam of my lips, and like an idiot I part them to let her in. The meeting of our tongues summons desperate noises from both of us. Hers is a whimper of happy surprise, mine is a tormented groan. Demi's hand curls over my cheek as her tongue teases and explores. She tastes like candy, literally, and I wonder if she was sucking on one of her lollipops earlier. I savor the sweet flavor and thrust my fingers through her dark hair.

I officially forget my surroundings. I register the faint sound of music, but my pounding heart drowns it out. I am so turned on it's not even funny. The kiss goes on and on, a tangle of tongues and the mingling of heated breaths, not ceasing until the moment I taste copper in my mouth.

"Ugh." This time I groan unhappily. "Demi, stop." When she pulls back, I see her lips are tinged with my blood. "I'm bleeding again and now it's all over you."

"Really? I didn't even notice." Her voice is breathy. "Oh my *fuck*."

"What?" I grab more toilet paper from the roll and dab my lips. "Is it terrible?"

"No, I'm saying oh my fuck because…" She shakes her head in wonderment. "That was a good kiss."

I can't disagree. "It was."

"I want to do it again."

I haul her up to her feet. "Bad idea."

"Come on, Monk, let's do it again. I know you enjoyed it." She directs a pointed look at my crotch.

"Of course I enjoyed it. I haven't been with anyone in like eight months."

A part of her seems to deflate, and I realize I'd said the wrong thing. "You're saying you would've enjoyed kissing anyone? I'm nothing but a pair of lips?"

I let out a breath. "No. You're much more than that. But you can't pressure me into being your rebound."

"I'm not trying to pressure you," she argues.

"Seriously? You just stuck your tongue in my mouth and now I'm harder than stone. You knew it would tempt me."

"Oh my God, you *gave* me the green light. You said you wanted a taste, and I can't help it if kissing me gets you hard. Jeez, it's okay to get a boner every now and then."

A loud guffaw echoes in the doorway. I glance over to

find an amused Conor watching us. "Yeah, captain. A boner's not gonna kill you."

Demi is smug. "Exactly."

I'm grateful for the distraction, until I notice Conor assessing her with his trademark Penis Eyes. "And you are?" he asks slowly.

"The reason I look like this," I answer for her, jerking a finger at my face.

"Ah, the ex-girlfriend and infamous provider of road head."

"Oh, give it up," I grumble. "There was no road head. It was a misunderstanding."

"Uh-huh. That's what they all say, bro."

Demi grins at Conor. "Sadly for him, this time it's true. Nothing happened except that I was nearly the victim of ear mutilation. I could've died."

"Chrissake, Semi, you wouldn't have died."

"There are important arteries in your ear. What if I bled out?"

"I don't think there is a single motherfucking artery in an ear," I growl.

Chuckling, Con gives her another flirtatious appraisal. "All right. So if you're not with my captain and you're not with that loser who beat him up, that mean you're single?"

"Yep," she says, flicking a mocking look my way.

"Excellent. Then how about I get you a drink?"

"Sounds great." She steps toward him, then glances over her shoulder, as if expecting me to stop her from grabbing a drink with Conor.

But I just lift one shoulder indifferently.

And she walks away.

24
HUNTER

DEMI: Did you win your game today?

ME: Yup yup.

HER: Don't say that. But good. I'm glad you won.

ME: You were worried we'd lose?

HER: I thought maybe you'd be too banged up from Nico.

ME: Ribs were a little sore, but I powered through.

HER: Are you home now?

ME: Ya, but not for long. Heading into the city soon. Friend of mine coaches girls hockey and they have an exhibition this weekend.

HER: You played hockey all day and now you're going to watch hockey all night?

ME: Got a problem with that?

HER: You need a life.

ME: I have one. It's called hockey.

I TYPE A FOLLOW UP, BUT HESITATION RIPPLES THROUGH ME. My fingers hover over the *SEND* button. I can still taste her on my lips, and I'm afraid to be around her again.

But we're friends. If I actively avoid her after one kiss, what the hell kind of friend am I?

I hit *SEND*.

ME: Wanna come?

She clearly struggles with her own moment of hesitation, because she takes equally long to respond.

HER: Sure? Anyone else coming or is it just us?
ME: Just us. Unless you want me to invite Conor...?

Is there a font for *snide*? I'm fully aware that nothing happened between them last night, but watching Con flirt with her still grated. And Demi was flirting back. She'd mauled me in the bathroom and then gone off with my teammate and took a tequila shot off his abs.

Although in her defense, I'd all but shoved her into Conor's arms by pretending I couldn't care less what she did with him.

HER: Invite whoever you want. I'll Uber to your place so you don't have to make the drive to campus. It just started snowing.

———

Demi shows up forty-five minutes later, bundled up in her parka, gloves and a bright-green scarf. I'm guessing her favorite color is green, because she wears it frequently. It looks good on her. Brings out the flecks of amber in her dark brown eyes.

"So who's this friend we're meeting?" she asks as I flick on the windshield defroster in the Rover.

She was right about it snowing, but sadly it's only light flurries. Nothing's sticking to the ground, and I find myself wondering if winter might skip New England altogether this year. So far we've received only one major snowfall and it all melted away by the morning. If we don't get a white Christmas, I'm going to be bummed. It's the only thing that makes the holidays in Connecticut bearable.

"Dean Di Laurentis," I answer. "He's a former teammate, graduated a couple years ago. Oh, and he's Summer's brother."

"Eek. Does that mean he's as...dramatic as Summer?" Her tone is the epitome of tactful.

"Nah, he's definitely more chill. They could be twins, though."

For once, Demi lets me listen to my own music library during the ride. I think we're both remembering what happened the last time we used her Bluetooth. Still, she makes sure to skip any song she can't dance to or doesn't know the words to.

Neither of us brings up the kiss. I'm thinking about it, though. I wonder if she is. I sneak glances at her, but she's too busy singing along or bopping her sexy torso to the beat. She's the cutest fucking thing and I want to kick myself for rejecting her.

Dean's girls are playing at a community center near Chestnut Hill. The parking lot is surprisingly packed *and* costs twenty bucks to enter. I can afford it, but it's the principle of the matter.

"*Twenty* bucks," I mutter under my breath as we get out of the Rover. "That is a travesty."

"You're a travesty."

Snickering, I check my phone to read an incoming text from Dean.

DEAN: G and Logan are here too. Behind my bench.

Huh, really? How are they swinging *that*? Garrett is one of the most recognizable hockey players in the country. Last time I saw him, he admitted he scarcely goes out anymore because he's constantly getting recognized. Logan is in his rookie season, so he can probably still maintain a low profile, but G's the star of the team.

When we arrive at our seats, I discover that the two Boston players are terrible at disguises. They've opted for baseball caps, and Garrett's wearing a pair of square hipster glasses on the bridge of his nose.

I burst out laughing. "Fake glasses? Seriously?"

He smirks. "Worked, didn't it? You did a double take."

"Not because I didn't recognize you—because you look stupid."

Logan snickers.

I introduce them to Demi, who, thanks to her complete ignorance of the sport, doesn't make a big fuss over them.

"Are Hannah or Grace coming?" I ask. I hope the answer's yes, because it would be nice if Demi had some chicks to chat with during the game. I doubt she'll pay a lick of attention to what's happening on the ice.

"Gracie's writing a paper," Logan replies. "She wanted to

get it done before winter break so she doesn't have to work over the holidays."

"And Hannah's still at the studio," Garrett says. "She said she'd try to meet up with us afterward, if we go out anywhere. What have you been up to?"

"Oh, Hunter's been super busy," Demi answers for me. "He got arrested, got his ass kicked…busy busy bee."

Logan snorts. "I didn't want to ask about your lip, but now that the subject's been brought up…"

"My ex-boyfriend beat him up," Demi informs him. "I take full responsibility for it."

"Yeah, and you should take full responsibility for the jail thing, too," I say in accusation.

"*You're* the one who made me wear the big hoops!"

"This is confusing to me," Garrett says frankly.

We don't get a chance to elaborate—Dean just spotted us and he's slapping a palm on the Plexiglass to say hello.

"That's Dean," I tell Demi, who for once is speechless.

"Oh," she finally remarks. "Wow."

I narrow my eyes. "What does that mean?"

"It means he's insanely attractive."

"Yeah, and he knows it," Garrett says with a sigh.

The first period kicks off, Dean's army of fourteen-year-olds taking the ice. The puck drops, and the center wins the faceoff, deking out two opponents before passing to one of her defense-women. Dean's girls are good. Very, very good. The refs, on the other hand, are hot garbage.

"What the hell was that?!" Logan shouts, flying to his feet. "They were offsides!"

On the bench, Dean is red-faced from outrage. "Offsides!" he thunders, but the ref merely skates past him.

"Lord, he's even beautiful when he's angry," Demi breathes. "Guys, how are you not acknowledging this?"

"We lived with him for four years," Garrett says dryly. "We're well aware of his appeal."

"Do you think life is different when you're that attractive?"

I lean over to pinch her side. "We should ask *you* that. You're the supermodel."

"Aw, thanks, Monk."

"Monk?" Garrett echoes.

"Because he's celibate," Demi clarifies.

G grins. "That's still going on?"

"Yup yup—"

"Don't say yup yup," Demi interjects.

"—you know me, willpower of steel."

The rest of the game, while fast-paced, is not at all competitive. Dean's team crushes their opponent, scoring five goals to the other team's one. I note that Dean is a terrific coach, praising his players each time they return to the bench. With one girl, he leans in to whisper in her ear for a long time between line changes, dispensing his wisdom. When she's back on the ice for her next shift, she almost scores off a teammate's rebound. Even without a goal under her belt, she's beaming at Dean when her line skates off. That's the mark of a great coach—he can make you feel invincible whether you win or lose.

After the ass-kicking, we meet up with Dean in the lobby. "I'm just coordinating with the other teachers about getting the girls back to the hotel," he says. "I gotta ride the bus with them, but I want to go out afterward. I can meet you guys somewhere."

"You don't have to stay with the girls?" Garrett asks.

"God no. Parent chaperones, baby. I've done my job, and now I need to get the fuck out. I've been surrounded by teenage girls for the past two days." Yet he says it jokingly, and I know he's proud of his team's performance this weekend. "You in?"

"Where are you thinking?" Demi asks him.

"Hmmm. Well, Saturdays are Latin night at the Exodus Club."

She rolls her eyes. "Why did you look at me when you said that? Because I'm Latina?"

He rolls his eyes back. "No, because you asked me the question, baby doll. So what do you say?"

Demi glances at me with an unspoken *Can we*?

"Sure." I shrug. "Why the hell not."

———

Hannah Wells meets us outside the club. There's a line down the block to get in, but Dean has no qualms about striding to the bouncer and dropping a name in his ear. *Dude, you can't make Garrett Graham wait in line*, I suspect he's saying. And a second later we're waved past the velvet rope.

Our little group follows a nearly pitch-black corridor toward the sounds of thumping bass and Spanish guitar. There's a coat check at the end of the hall, which we make use of, handing over our winter gear.

"So I hear your songwriting career has taken off," I tease Hannah with a smile.

"I'm doing okay," she says modestly.

"You were in the studio with Delilah Sparks tonight. That's more than *okay*."

"Right? I can't even. It's still so surreal."

When we enter the club, an array of strobe lights assaults my vision. The music blares and the temperature is scorching. Three seconds in, and I'm already sweating through my Under Armour T-shirt.

Demi links her arm through mine. "Do you salsa, Monk?"

"Nope." She's wearing a skimpy tank top, and the heat of her body sears into me. Christ. I wish she'd never kissed me. I've been horny as fuck ever since.

"Let's grab some drinks," Garrett suggests.

"Shots?" Logan says hopefully.

"*One* shot."

"C'mon, G, we've got four days off. Let's take advantage."

Garrett throws a muscular arm around his long-time girlfriend. "Oh, trust me." He winks. "I'll be taking advantage of it."

Hannah grins.

They do one round of shots, but I abstain. I'm the DD, so I want to keep a clear head tonight. What if we get pulled over again? What if this time Demi decides to suck my dick in the car for real?

A man can hope.

We spend the next few minutes shouting to each other over the music. When the current song changes, Demi shrieks in delight. It's "Despacito," the Bieber version, and the entire club goes wild.

"Come salsa with me," she begs, tugging on my arm. "This is my song!"

"Nope," I say firmly. "I don't salsa."

"I do," Dean announces, holding out his hand.

"You salsa?" She gawks at him before turning to me. "He's beautiful *and* he salsas? What on earth am I doing here with *you*?"

She's joking, but I still glare at her. "He's taken."

"Super taken," Dean confirms. "But I'm a salsa master thanks to my girl. Allie-Cat and I took lessons."

Demi takes his hand, and I swallow a sigh as I watch them saunter toward the dance floor.

"She's cool," Logan tells me.

"I know. We're good friends."

"Just friends?"

I shrug. "She got out of a relationship a month ago."

"So?"

I twist the cap off my water bottle and take a hasty sip. I'm not sure why I put that out there. Then I shift my gaze to the dance floor and almost choke on my water.

Goddamn Dean. Since when does he salsa dance? And he looks damn good doing it. Dean might've skipped out on law school to become a gym teacher, but the man still oozes money. He's wearing khakis and a crisp white shirt, its top two buttons undone and the sleeves rolled up. His blond hair falls onto his forehead as he spins Demi around as if they're on *Dancing with the Stars*.

"Check out that footwork," Garrett marvels.

They're even drawing stares from the other dancers. Demi's in leggings, leather boots, and a red tank, but the way her hips are moving, I can totally envision her in a bright sundress and high heels, the ones with straps that wrap around a woman's ankles. Maybe a flower in her hair. Red lipstick painted on those pouty lips.

Annnnd now I'm acting out my own salsa-themed porno in my head. Which Dean brings to life when he lifts one of her legs and props it on his hip, and they do a sexy little grinding move before he spins her around again. Demi's cheeks are flushed, her eyes bright with joy. Dean whispers something in her ear and she starts giggling.

Jealousy constricts my throat. Obviously I'm being ridiculous. There's always chemistry when two hot people are dancing, it's inevitable. But the sight of Dean's hands on Demi's body makes my blood boil.

"What the hell is a *despacito* anyway?" I grumble. "Is it like a desperado?"

Hannah bursts out laughing. "It means slowly."

"Whatever. It's a shitty song." I don't really believe that. If anything, I'm indifferent to the damn track. I just wish it would end already. I promptly glare daggers at the dance floor again.

"Just friends?" Logan asks knowingly.

The sigh I've been holding slips out.

"Aw, he has a crush," teases Hannah.

"Nah," I lie. "I'm putting sex and dating on the backburner this year. I want to focus on hockey."

"I get it." Garrett nods a couple times. "But there's more to life than hockey, Davenport." He's gazing at his girlfriend as he says that. Hannah is his entire world. I have no doubt he'd give up anything for her, even a flourishing career.

"I know there is, but I made myself a promise. You know, to try to grow as a person and all that shit."

The guys laugh loudly, while Hannah offers an admiring smile. "I actually think that's commendable," she says. "We get so caught up in sex and relationships, sometimes it's good to take some time for yourself."

"But sex is so good," Logan protests.

He's right. Sex is goddamn incredible, and right now Dean and Demi are engaged in a vertical version of it on the dance floor. My stomach twists again.

"You should cut in," Garrett suggests.

I'm about to maintain that I can't salsa, when the DJ changes up the music again. A slower, sultry beat reverberates through the club. "Havana" by Camila Cabello. I can work with that.

"I'll be right back." I stride forward, leaving my companions in the proverbial rear view mirror.

I can hear them laughing behind me, but I don't give a shit. I make a beeline for Demi. "Beat it," I tell Dean.

It's a joke.

But also not a joke.

And he knows it. Grinning, he slaps my shoulder and goes off to join the others.

Demi stares at me, one eyebrow quirked. "Wow. Was that a show of dominance?"

"Nah."

"Really? So you banished my dancing partner for no reason? What am I supposed to do now?" She snaps a hand on her hip. We're surrounded by other dancers, but neither of us moves.

"Well. I guess I'll just have to do," I say, extending a hand toward her.

She breaks out in a smile. "Took you long enough."

I yank her toward me, grabbing hold of her waist. Demi rests one hand on my shoulder, and places the other one at my nape, her fingers curling loosely around my neck as we begin to move to the beat.

Luckily, our lower bodies aren't touching, so I'm spared the agony of feeling her rubbing up against me. The experience would be too confusing for my dick.

Except great. Now she's rubbing up against me.

Cue: dick confusion.

I try to ease my hips away from her sexy body, but that earns me a huff of exasperation. "You have to actually dance back, Hunter. You can't just stand there."

"I'm dancing back," I protest.

"Your body is two feet away! Where did you learn to dance? Puritan camp? Why did you even bother cutting in?"

I shrug.

Demi thinks it over for a second. Then she releases a triumphant laugh. "Oh my God, you were jealous! You didn't like seeing me dancing with Dean!"

Another shrug.

"Ha!" She's so much shorter than me that she has to tug my head down to bring her lips to my ear. "Admit it," she whispers.

My lips travel toward *her* ear. "Fine," I whisper back, and I'm gratified to feel a shiver run down her body. "Maybe a little jealous. But it wasn't real jealousy."

"What the hell does that mean?"

"It was body jealousy."

"That's not a real thing."

"Yes it is. Bodies get jealous when they see other bodies close together."

"Right. Keep telling yourself that."

I kind of need to, to preserve my own sanity. I can't let myself develop feelings for Demi. I mean, obviously, I like her. She's amazing and we have fun together. As *friends*.

I don't want our friendship to be ruined.

But Demi seems hell-bent on setting it on fire.

"I have a secret," she teases, gesturing for me to lower my head again.

"Yeah?" My voice comes out stupidly husky.

Her breath tickles my earlobe. "I'm about to do something you're not going to like."

Like a fool I ask, "What's that?"

And rather than answer, Demi angles her head and slants her mouth over mine.

The kiss is as delicious as the last time. She tastes like tequila and a hint of cherry, probably from the red candy she had in her mouth at the game. Her tongue had kept poking it into her cheek, making it look like she had a creature moving around in there.

I laugh at the memory.

She pulls back breathlessly. "What is it?"

"Nothing. I was just thinking about your candy obsession and…forget it." I just kiss her again, and her tongue eagerly slides into my mouth.

Just feeling it touch the tip of mine unleashes a greedy, caveman side I never knew I possessed. I shove my hand in her hair and drive the kiss deeper. She gasps against my lips.

I'm fully aware we're in the middle of the dance floor sucking on each other's tongues. I hear music. I register people around us. I don't know if they're dancing or staring at us. I don't care. All I care about is kissing her. And touching her.

I slide a hand down her slender back and cup one firm ass cheek. Ah Christ, I want to rip off those leggings. I want to smack her perfect ass. I want to slip a finger inside her and find out how wet she is for me.

Demi breaks the kiss again. "Let's get out of here," she pleads.

The sheer desire swimming in her eyes brings me back to my senses. "No," I croak, abruptly leading her away from the dance floor.

"Why not?" is her frustrated response.

"Because I don't want to complicate our friendship."

"We've been making out for the past five minutes, Hunter! It's already been complicated!"

"No, it hasn't. That was…just kissing." The best kissing ever. My body is still throbbing from it.

Accusation sharpens her face. "I feel like you're purposely trying to be difficult."

"I'm not," I say unhappily. "Look, I made this decision before I even met you. And I want to stick by it. I want to prove to myself that I can actually stick to a goal I've set and not let sex blow up my whole life again."

"That won't happen," she insists. "The team is doing great. You're winning all your games."

"Yeah, because my head is clear. And now it's about more than celibacy. I *like* you. This friendship is everything to me and we both know damn well that sex would screw it up.

So I'm sorry, okay? I'm not giving in to temptation again." I shake my head in defeat. "I can't."

Unhappiness flickers in her eyes for a moment. Then it transforms into a glimmer of determination. "Fine. I won't hit on you anymore. But only if you make me a promise."

"Demi—"

"After the season ends—" She slants her head, defiant. "*I* get to be the one you cross the finish line with, friendship be damned."

25
DEMI

A FEW DAYS BEFORE THE BREAK STARTS, I MANAGE TO squeeze in a coffee date with TJ, who meets me at the Theta house. It's chilly outside, but we both agree a winter walk through campus would be lovely, so we set off in the direction of the Coffee Hut.

"Are you mad at me?"

TJ's wounded tone has me glancing over in surprise. "Of course not. I've just been crazy-busy. I'm working on the case study, cramming for finals, planning the sorority's holiday party with Josie, organizing a Secret Santa for everyone in my Biology tutorial. Life is nuts right now."

"No, I know. I just miss you."

"Aw, I miss you too." I link my arm through his.

"Are you around tonight?" he asks. "There's this skating thing at the rink in Hastings."

"What skating thing?"

"It's, like, a winter fair? It's the first year the town is holding it. I thought it would be cool to go. Drink some hot cocoa, skate for a bit, get our picture taken with Santa."

"That sounds fun. I love fairs. Oh—but I have Hunter's game tonight."

"Hunter's game?"

I nod. "Briar's playing against...you know what, I didn't even ask who they're playing. But it's a home game, and I promised him I'd go. It'll probably end around nine-thirty, ten? How long is the fair open until?"

He opens a browser on his iPhone, and I notice the Town of Hastings webpage is already loaded up. "It says here it goes till midnight."

I brighten. "Okay, that works, then. I should be done by ten-ish, and that'll give us a couple hours at the fair. Sound like a plan?"

"Sounds great." He smiles, a rare sight to behold.

I can't deny that TJ isn't the easiest person to get to know. He keeps his emotions locked up tight, but once he warms up to people, he's actually super sweet. He can be moody at times, which is probably why I can't spend long chunks of time with him. That doesn't mean I don't like him, though. I also can't spend an inordinate amount of time with Pax, whose melodramatic nature eventually drains my patience.

TJ and I navigate the winding path, snow crunching beneath our feet. The ground is icy, and he tightens his hold on my arm as we encounter a particularly precarious section of the path.

"They need to salt this," he gripes.

"Right? I nearly face-planted just now."

We're about fifty yards from the Coffee Hut when TJ brings up the subject of Hunter. "You two hang out a lot," he remarks.

I can't decipher his tone. I feel like it might contain a hint of disapproval, but I'm not certain. TJ can be so hard to read sometimes. "Well, yeah. We're friends."

Friends who kiss.

I keep that tidbit to myself. Hell, I don't know why I'm even still thinking about it. I kissed the guy twice and would happily kiss him a hundred more times. But Hunter rejected me twice and doesn't want a single kiss more.

Ugh, and he wouldn't even promise that we could resume the kissing when the hockey season ends. He just reiterated that our friendship is too important, and we proceeded to spend the rest of the night hanging out with Dean and his other friends, pretending we hadn't just sucked each other's faces off.

It's so vexing. Frustrating. I don't believe it's an ego problem on my end, because I'm confident I wouldn't have much trouble finding someone to have sex with me. Half the men on Tinder would offer themselves up.

But I don't want those men.

I want Hunter Davenport.

I haven't allowed myself to delve too deeply about precisely *what* I want from him. To keep kissing him, for sure. And sex, absolutely. The mere thought of our naked bodies tangled together gets me hot.

I'm not looking beyond that. But I do think he's wrong—I think we *could* be friends with benefits without it complicating anything.

Couldn't we?

"I just think it's weird," TJ says, jolting me from my troubled thoughts.

"Why is it weird?"

"I dunno. He's such a fuckboy."

"Not really."

"Yes really. I told you about catching him in the library last year, remember? Any guy who fucks chicks in public is slimy."

"One, that's not at all an accurate barometer of slime— lots of very respectable people possess exhibitionist tendencies. Weren't you paying attention to Andrews' lecture about sexual compulsions? And two, that happened last year. Hunter's different now. He's not even dating at the moment."

"Yeah, probably because of the herpes."

I give TJ a sharp look. "That's a rude thing to say."

He shrugs. "The truth isn't always pretty."

Now I roll my eyes. "What truth? You're saying Hunter Davenport has herpes?"

"I think that's what it was? I don't remember exactly, but I'm friends with this chick in my dorm and she said Davenport gave her an STI this past spring. She used the word outbreak, so I just assumed herpes—but do the other ones give you outbreaks? What do chlamydia and gonorrhea do?"

"I don't know." I frown. "Are you being serious right now?"

"Honest to God."

My stomach does a queasy little flip. TJ is a decent guy, and he doesn't typically spread rumors, so I'm predisposed to believe he did hear something. But there's no way it's *true*. Hunter doesn't have a sexually transmitted disease.

Well, I mean…he could.

Something else suddenly occurs to me. Is *that* why he's not sexually active? Because he's embarrassed about having something and passing it to someone else?

It's possible, I guess. Either way, I'm uncomfortable discussing Hunter's private business with TJ, who clearly doesn't like him.

"Whatever. This is not a conversation we should be having," TJ says before I can. "It's really none of our business."

"You're right," I agree.

"I shouldn't have even said anything. But I wanted you to be aware, just in case. Since you're spending so much time with him."

———

Later that night, I drag Pippa to the hockey game with me and Brenna. Mostly because I'm worried Brenna will be so absorbed in the game that I won't have anybody to talk to. Like me, Pippa isn't a hockey fan. Neither of us could properly explain what's currently happening on the ice. I just see big hulking boys skating very fast and wielding sticks.

Hunter told me his jersey number is 12, so I attempt to track those two digits with my gaze. I think he's doing well? Then again, he hasn't scored any goals, so maybe he's doing poorly?

I truly don't know how to measure hockey success. Nico played basketball in high school and used to score a ton of points in every game. But when I ask Brenna why nobody is scoring, she explains that hockey isn't as point-laden as basketball. Apparently some games might end with only one goal between both teams. Or even a tie of zero.

Speaking of Nico, Pippa asks about him during the first intermission. "Did you ever hear from Nico after he attacked Hockey Boy?"

"Nope."

"Has he tried to contact you?" Brenna asks curiously.

"No idea. I told you, I blocked him on everything, even email. I'm sure he's figured that out by now."

"Oh he has," Pippa confirms.

I look over sharply. "You've spoken to him?"

"Me, personally? No. But Darius is speaking to him again."

That brings a frown to my lips. I was texting with D the other day, and he didn't once mention he's back in contact with my ex.

"Darius said Nico is losing his shit. The guys had to forcibly stop him several times from showing up at your house. D told him it was asking for trouble."

I make a mental note to call Darius later for more details.

"But yeah, he's definitely not over you, or handling this breakup well." Pippa gazes at the ice, where the Zamboni is shuffling along to smooth out the shiny surface. Then she switches gears from my cheating ex to the friend he cheated with. "Corinne says you two are texting again."

I nod. "She sent me a funny meme the other day and we had a short convo."

"For what it's worth, she still feels terrible about everything."

"She should," I mutter, but my anger toward our friend isn't as powerful as it used to be. Even my anger at Nico has dimmed.

"I really hope you two can be friends again one day, so we can hang out the way we used to. Maybe over the holiday break the three of us could have a girls' night?"

A sigh flutters out. "I mean, we could try."

"Hold up—you're *texting* and making *hangout* plans with the chick who slept with your boyfriend?" Brenna demands. Her mouth is wide with disbelief, drawing attention to her trademark red lips. It's the only splash of color amidst her black turtleneck, leggings and leather boots.

Pippa shakes her head wryly. "Seriously, Demi, you're so fucking forgiving and understanding it makes me want to punch you."

"Really? Those two wonderful qualities of mine make you want to *punch* me? Also! You literally just suggested we do a girls' night. You're encouraging me to be friends with Corinne again."

"Yeah, but by agreeing to it you're setting a bad example for the rest of us. You know, the grudge holders."

Brenna grins. "I hold a mean grudge, I'll tell you that."

I roll my eyes at both of them. "I want to be a psychologist. That means I ought to practice what I preach, right?"

The second period gets underway when the referee skates up to the faceoff and drops the puck.

"How does he not get hurt?" Pippa demands.

"Who, the ref?" Brenna asks.

"Yes! Look at that little guy! He's way too close to the action. One of those huge monsters could smash into him at any second and break every bone in his body."

"I know it looks dangerous, but the refs know how to stay out of the way," Brenna assures her.

A cheer rocks the arena and I squint hard, trying to understand what I'm seeing. #12 is flying past the blue line at the center of the rink. "Oooh, that's Hunter! And he's all alone."

Brenna supplies the hockey lingo. "He's on a breakaway."

Oh gosh, he's tearing toward the opposing net, his stick snapping up in preparation for his shot. As my heart lodges in my throat, I find myself shooting to my feet.

"Holy shit, you're into hockey!" Pippa accuses, staring up at me in shock.

"Into it? No. But did you see that shot?" Hunter missed, but it was still ridiculously thrilling to watch.

Pippa narrows her eyes. "Ohhhhh," she finally says. "I get what's happening. You're not into hockey. You're into the hockey *player*."

"No," I lie. Then I groan. "Well, maybe a little."

Brenna lets out a hoot. "That means *a lot*. Have you found the key to his chastity belt yet?"

A laugh pops out of my mouth. "No, sadly. It's still locked up tight." I hesitate for a beat. I haven't told anybody about kissing Hunter, but I suspect that's about to change. I need advice, and there's no better time like the present.

So while Brenna and Pippa sit there grinning at me, I confess to the two kisses, which I think of as Bathroom Kiss and Salsa Kiss. "Salsa Kiss involved a butt squeeze," I confess. "But then he stopped it from going any further. I think I might need to accept he's not interested."

"Bullshit," Brenna says.

Pippa nods in agreement. "If he wasn't interested, he wouldn't keep kissing you back."

"And then *stopping* it," I reiterate. "He's dead set on trying to be a good team leader and make hockey his priority."

"Sleeping with you isn't going to destroy the team." Brenna rolls her eyes. "That's just nonsense."

"Maybe, but I can't force someone to sleep with me. There's this thing called consent?"

"Nobody's telling you to force him," Pippa says. "But it couldn't hurt to give him a nudge?"

"I've done more than nudge. I kissed him twice. He shut me down twice. And after Salsa Kiss, I told him I wouldn't hit on him again until he's done with the season."

"Then don't hit on him." An evil glint lights Brenna's eyes. "You need to change your tactics here, babe. Stop going after him. Make him come to *you*."

"How?"

"Make him jealous. Flirt with one of his buddies."

"Oooh, Operation Jealousy!" Pippa chimes in. "That's totally what you need to do."

Make him jealous… I guess I already did that, the night I danced with Dean. And it worked, I realize. I wasn't openly flirting, but the mere act of dancing with another man triggered Hunter's possessive instincts.

"Isn't there always a party after these games?" Pippa asks. "You should do it tonight."

"I can't. I have plans with TJ. Oh shit, that reminds me! I need to text him my ETA. When is the game over?" I ask Brenna. I'm worried I'll end up being late, because even though we got here at seven-thirty, they didn't drop the puck until past eight. There was a lot of preamble first, including a ceremony honoring a middle-aged alumnus who supposedly set a bunch of records back in the day.

"The second period just started. So you have at least another hour, hour and a half. And maybe another half hour for the boys to shower and change?"

Shit, that puts us closer to eleven. And if I want to say hi to Hunter once he's out of the locker room, it becomes even more unlikely I'll get to Hastings at a reasonable time. Shit.

I unlock my phone and pull up my text thread with TJ.

ME: Hey, so I totally got the times wrong. Apparently I'm not out of here til 11. I don't think there's a point in showing up at 11 if the fair closes at 12. Is it on tomorrow night too?

TJ: Not sure. Can't you duck out of the game early?

ME: I would, except I'm here with Pippa and Brenna, and I promised Hunter I'd come find him after the game.

There's a long delay. And still no response.

ME: I'm so sorry. Please don't be mad. Our meet-up was a last-minute thing, anyway, remember? I already had plans to go to the game.

HIM: I know. It's fine, D. Have fun at the game.

He's clearly annoyed. I don't blame him for it, either. But I'm also growing weary of reassuring him all the time. TJ asks me to hang out nearly every single day. We're friends, sure, but I don't even see Pippa every day, and I consider her my bestie. Hell, I didn't even see Nico every day and we were a *couple*.

Regardless of all that, I do feel bad about not being able to make it to the fair. I shouldn't have agreed to two sets of plans in one night. Any time you do that, timing always

overlaps in some stupid way, and now I've disappointed one
of my good friends.

> **ME**: I'm really sorry, hon. This is on me. I shouldn't
> have made plans on top of plans. It turned into a
> dumb double-booking thing, and I apologize for that.
> I'll call you tomorrow and we can plan a friend day
> that fits both of our schedules, okay? Xo

He responds with xoxo followed by an, Okay.

Whew. I'm glad I patched that one up. Now it's time for
more pressing matters.

"I'm not meeting TJ," I tell the girls. "So I guess I'm good
to party later. What's my game plan?"

"Flirt and seduce," Brenna advises. "Pick his hottest
friend—I'm thinking that's Conor, or Matty. Get your flirt
on, and make sure Hunter's watching."

"Then what?"

She shrugs. "If he takes the bait, hopefully there'll be a
chastity belt on your bedroom floor tonight. If he doesn't…
hell, hook up with Conor or Matty, then."

I balk. "But I hardly know them."

Pippa snorts. "You are the most sheltered college woman
on the planet. It's okay to fool around with guys you haven't
known since you were eight years old, D."

I stick out my tongue at her.

"I'm serious. You're allowed to experiment. For all you
know, you were having the worst sex of your life with Nico,
only you thought it was mind-blowing because you didn't
know any better. Let yourself know better."

"Nico and I had good sex." I pause. "Well, aside from the subpar oral." Because who am I kidding? It was never even close to par. "But I never really saw the appeal, anyway. With oral, I could take it or leave it."

"But that's the most important part!" Brenna says in outrage.

"If I do end up with Hunter tonight, should I be worried about…um…you know, sexually transmitted diseases?" TJ's warning continues to lurk in the back of my head like a cat burglar.

"As in, does Hunter have one?" Brenna thinks it over. "Nobody's ever said anything to me about that, but obviously I can't know for sure." She wrinkles her forehead at me. "But that's why you have the conversation before the clothes come off."

"The conversation?"

"Disclosure," she explains. "Diseases, birth control, any weird kinks you want to disclose. Like, if a guy has a foot fetish, I need to know about that shit up front so I don't throw up on him."

Pippa breaks out laughing. "Oh God, that's a great point. All foot fetishes must be disclosed prior to sexual relations. And don't even get me started on the guy in sophomore year who wanted me to pee on him."

I resist the urge to bury my face in my hands and moan in despair. I am so out of my element here. I've only slept with one person. I lost my virginity to him, and we were in a long-term relationship for years. There was never any need to have "the conversation."

And I never, ever had to wonder if he *wanted me to pee on him.*

I never thought of myself as naïve or inexperienced. I thought I was a ballsy, smart-talking chick from Miami who owned her body and her sexuality. But maybe it's time to grow up a little. I *do* need to think about things like STIs and new partners.

And if everything goes my way tonight, that new partner is going to be Hunter Davenport.

26
DEMI

THE AFTER PARTY IS HELD AT CONOR'S HOUSE. I KNOW from my last visit that he's got four roommates and they're all hockey players. In fact, most of the male bodies in the townhouse tonight belong to hockey players, which means there isn't much space to maneuver. I'm talking muscles galore.

A crappy EDM song blasts in the air, making my temples throb. Never been a fan of electronic dance music. Nico and I attended a couple of raves in Miami, but it wasn't my thing. When we were there, he tried to convince me to do MDMA, and I said hell no, which surprised most of his friends.

It's funny, but people expect me to be more reckless than I actually am. I mean, I'll dance at the drop of a hat, no matter where I am. I'll talk to strangers in the CVS checkout line. And sure, if someone asked me to go skydiving or bungee jumping I'd consider it. But I've never cared for the drug scene or the kind of dangerous activities our Miami friends were into. Whenever I visited, Nico spent a lot of time racing cars.

Illegally, of course, which meant I was looking over my shoulder the entire time waiting for the cops to show up.

So no, recklessness isn't a trait I usually possess. But I'm going to be reckless tonight. I'm going to tease my friend and hopefully convince him to break his vow. I guess that probably makes me a jerk, but a part of me wonders if Hunter is overcompensating for something. Last year he acted in a self-destructive manner, hooking up with random girls, drinking too much. But I don't believe that's inherently his nature. I think he was simply reeling from Summer's rejection and the perceived betrayal from his friend.

If you ask me, sex isn't the reason his hockey season imploded last year, nor do I think the *lack* of it is responsible for the team's success this year.

I'm starting to believe it's a matter of trust. As in, he doesn't trust himself to make good decisions in the moment. But I don't think avoiding any situations that require difficult decision-making is the solution.

My gaze drifts in Hunter's direction. He's across the living room, deep in conversation with Matt Anderson. Meanwhile, I'm in the corner like a loser, sucking on one of the many lollipops stashed at all times in my purse. Hunter left me to my own devices once we got here, but this isn't my crowd and I don't miss all the dirty looks I'm receiving from the hockey groupies, as if I'm trespassing on their property.

I don't particularly understand the sports groupie mentality. The fact that they make it seem like I'm trying to *steal* something from them tells me that they don't care about the men they're coveting, only the status those men bring to the table. I look at Hunter and see Hunter. They look at him and see HOCKEY PLAYER.

"What's the matter? Not having fun?" Conor wanders over and joins me in the doorway.

It's impossible to look at Conor without noticing how incredibly attractive he is. He sort of resembles Hunter's friend Dean, except in a surfer-dude way whereas Dean should be posing in cologne ads or underwear spreads.

"Eh, I just don't know anyone." I shrug, absently twirling the stick of my lollipop between my thumb and index finger.

"You know *me*." He flashes a crooked grin.

"True."

He nods toward Hunter. "And Davenport."

"Also true. But he's busy at the moment."

"Well, I'm not." Conor slants his head. "Come dance with me. We can entertain each other."

Normally I wouldn't turn down a dance offer, but my bladder is full from the two sodas I drank at the game and the vodka cranberry one of Conor's roommates made for me.

"I would, but I have to pee so bad," I admit. "If we dance I'd probably pee all over you." Then again, maybe that's his kink. As I learned tonight, that's actually a *thing* people do.

He laughs. "All right, how 'bout you take care of that little problem first, and then we'll reevaluate."

I check behind us, noting the line for the downstairs bathroom. "How 'bout you keep me company while I wait in line?"

"I'll do you one better." He winks and holds out his hand. I take it.

And when I notice Hunter frowning in our direction just

before we exit the room, I can't fight a smug smile. I hadn't intended on it happening right this second, but looks like Operation Jealousy has officially commenced.

Upstairs, Conor opens a door and gestures for me to enter. "I've got the master bedroom with the ensuite. My toilet is yours, milady."

I snicker. "Thanks, milord."

In the bathroom, I toss out my lollipop, then lift up my dress and do my thing. I feel slightly stupid wearing a short dress in the middle of winter, but we stopped off at Brenna and Hunter's house after the game, where Brenna convinced me to ditch my leggings and sweater for one of her dress-es—a long-sleeved, ribbed sweater dress that barely reaches my knees. Black, of course.

As I wash my hands, I hear the murmur of voices beyond the bathroom door. A female one, and more than one male. I emerge to find Matt sprawled on the bed next to a girl with dark braids. "Hi!" she says when she spots me. "I'm Andrea."

"Demi."

"Come sit down," Conor calls from the small couch. The master is big enough to contain a double bed, a dresser, sofa, and huge flat screen TV. Conor's on one end of the couch, fiddling with a video game controller. Hunter is on the other end, uncapping a bottle of amber-colored liquid.

"Whiskey?" I say, wrinkling my nose. "We're drinking whiskey now? What happened to your precious beer?" When we got here, he'd made a big deal about how Matt had picked up a case of Dampf Punk for them. Obviously, I inquired as to why anyone would pick such a stupid name for a beer, at which point he'd given me the finger.

"We're all out. The only thing that's left is the watery keg." He makes a face. "Come do a shot with me, Semi."

I hesitate. If I start doing shots, I might lose my head. On the other hand, I could use the liquid courage. Truth be told, I have no clue how to go about seducing somebody.

"Is it still cool if I crash on your couch tonight?" I ask him.

Hunter nods. He removes his baseball cap to run his fingers through his dark hair, then shoves the cap back on.

I join him on the couch. "Okay. Let's do it."

While Conor is busy setting up a skateboarding game, Hunter pours a shot and swallows it back.

I watch the strong column of his throat as he gulps the whiskey. I want to kiss him right there—right at the base of his throat. I wonder if I'd feel his pulse fluttering beneath my lips.

He passes me the shot glass. I eye it suspiciously. "What? I don't get my own?"

"There's only one up here. If you want your own, go downstairs and get one." Hunter lifts an eyebrow. "What, you afraid of catching my cooties?"

"Your tongue's been in my mouth. If you have cooties, I'm already infected."

That makes Conor chuckle. "Pour me a shot, too."

"Me first," I say, lifting the glass to my lips.

I drink, and the alcohol instantly makes my eyes water. Eeek. I'm not used to whiskey, I guess. I can sling back tequila like a pro, but something about this whiskey is getting me buzzed harder and faster than usual.

Hunter pours another one, and I pass the shot to Conor.

He swallows it, then starts a game. I watch as his skateboarder performs a series of tricks on a concrete half-pipe.

"Hey, that's in Jacksonville!" I exclaim as I study the familiar setting on the screen.

"Kona Skatepark," Conor confirms. "You been there before?"

"A few times. My ex"—Lord, it's still so weird saying that—"was friends with a lot of skaters. Have you ever been to Florida?" I ask him.

"Nah, I'm a West Coast boy."

"California?"

Conor nods. "Huntington Beach."

"Never been," I admit.

"You should come visit me this summer. I'll show you around."

Hunter rolls his eyes. "Watch out, Semi. He's making his move."

"I'm not making any moves," protests Conor. "I'm just sitting here like a good little boy, playing my game." He presses a few buttons on his controller, then gives me a cocky smile. "Unless you want me to make a move?"

I think it over. "Maybe."

Hunter makes a grouchy noise. "Demi. I think I'm gonna have to cut you off."

"I've literally had one shot!"

"And it's clearly clouded your judgment if you're openly flirting with this dumbass."

On the bed, Andrea overhears him and giggles. "Um. You can't *not* flirt with Conor Edwards. He just brings out that side in women."

"What about me?" Matt complains, and I notice they've inched so close to each other they're practically cuddling. "What side do I bring out in you?"

She whispers something in his ear. Matt chuckles in response, and I lose interest.

Conor passes the controller to Hunter, who leans forward and rests his forearms on his thighs. His forehead creases in concentration as his player performs a series of kick flips. I don't recognize this next course, and to be honest my patience threshold for watching video games has officially exceeded its limit.

Meanwhile, I don't miss that Conor has moved closer to me. He smells good, like sandalwood and citrus soap. His hair's slightly damp from the shower he must've taken after the game. He's wearing a T-shirt and cargo shorts, and he's barefoot.

A perpetually high body temperature must be a hockey player thing—Hunter stripped out of his hoodie almost the second we arrived at the party, leaving him in his trademark white wife-beater.

"So." Conor sounds thoughtful. "We've established that you want me to make a move."

"I said maybe," I remind him. Coyly.

"'Kay… What'll it take to turn the maybe into a hell yes?"

"I don't know. Make me an offer and let's see what happens."

"Hmmm." His long fingers travel up my sleeve and toy with a strand of my hair. "How 'bout the best sex of your life?"

Hunter snorts. His focus remains on the screen.

"What else you got?" I lightly rest my hand on Conor's knee, and this time Hunter's gaze flicks over.

"How about the best massage of your life?"

"Dude, you gotta stop using superlatives. Only sets you up for failure." Hunter tosses the controller in Conor's lap. "You're up. I have to take a leak." He staggers to his feet and ducks into the bathroom.

Conor doesn't start a new game. Rather, he sets the controller on the floor and angles his body toward mine. His silvery eyes glint knowingly. "So, you and the captain have a thing going on?"

"We kissed a couple times," I confess, my tongue loosened by the whiskey. "But he doesn't want to do anything more."

"Ah right. The vow of celibacy."

"Yep."

"Is this why you're hitting on me?" He cocks his head, and his lips are curved in a mocking smile. "You're hoping he'll be jealous enough to cave?"

"I'm not hitting on you."

"Let's not do that."

"Do what?"

"Lie to each other." Chuckling, Conor captures my chin with his thumb and forefinger, forcing eye contact. "You want my help or not?"

My throat goes dry. I swallow a few times, but it doesn't help. "You think we can get to him?"

"Baby," he drawls. "I can get to anyone."

27
HUNTER

When I step out of the bathroom, Demi and Conor are still on the couch, but Matt and Andrea are gone. I'm not particularly thrilled about Demi and Con's proximity to each other. She's sitting so close to him she might as well be in his lap.

I can't say anything, though, because I made my own position clear last week. I told her I just want to be friends. Which means, if she wants to flirt with my teammate, I'd be a real asshole to try to stop her. And I'd be a selfish team captain if I cock-blocked one of my guys.

That's rule number five thousand, draft three of the captain handbook. *Your teammate's dick comes first.*

Despite their blatant flirting, they don't ask me to leave. And like a chump I don't leave, despite the fact that I'm very noticeably the third wheel.

Conor murmurs something that makes Demi giggle.

I bristle. "What are you whispering about over there?"

"Nothing. Pass the bottle?" Con holds out his hand.

I look at Demi. Her cheeks are flushed, but whether it's from too much alcohol consumption, I can't be sure.

"It's for me," Con says knowingly.

I lean over to hand him the whiskey and he takes a swig directly from the bottle.

He hands it back to me, and I take a swig too. Maybe that's what I need to do—get stupidly drunk. Because it's inevitable that Demi will find her rebound tonight and if it's not with Con I'll eat my hat. And why not? Despite his ladies' man reputation, I've never heard a single woman express she felt used by him or didn't have a good time.

"So you guys have kissed," Con says suddenly, his gray eyes fixing on me. "How'd that go?"

Phenomenally. "It was all right," I say out loud.

Demi's outraged gasp makes me smile. "Just all right? Fuck off, Monk. My kissing is more than all right. I'm an excellent kisser." Her eyes dare me to defy her.

"She's an excellent kisser," I admit.

She beams at me. "And you want to do it again…?" she prompts.

"Nope."

Conor snorts. "Damn, dude, you're no good for a woman's ego."

"Trust me, her ego is doing just fine."

"It is," Demi confirms. "I'm very confident in my overall awesomeness as a person."

"Yeah?" Conor has his arm around her now, while the fingertips of his other hand teasingly stroke her bare thigh.

Despite its long sleeves, Demi's black dress is indecently short. I don't remember her wearing it at the game. When did she have time to change?

It's getting hard to breathe. I'm not drunk enough for

this. And I'm definitely not drunk enough when Con's hand slides upward, his knuckles grazing Demi's right breast on the way to her neck. He starts stroking that, too.

Her breath hitches. "Did you just cop a feel?"

"No." His tongue is caught between his teeth as he offers a lewd grin.

"You grazed my boob."

"Yeah, a graze, not a feel."

"Same thing. Right, Hunter?"

I don't answer. My mouth is bone-dry. I remember making out with her in the club in Boston, how badly I'd wanted to cup her tits with both hands, tease my thumbs over her nipples until they were harder than icicles. But we were in public and I didn't do it. And even in private, I still can't do that.

Maybe watching Conor do it will provide me with some sort of satisfaction? Is secondhand boob-groping a thing?

But Con's focus is no longer on Demi's perfect tits. He lowers his mouth, and Demi squeaks in surprise.

I stiffen at the sight of his blond head buried in her neck. She, on the other hand, softens like warm butter. Her body practically melts into Con, and she even slants her head to grant him easier access to suck on her neck.

It's no longer difficult to breathe—it's impossible. Jealousy pounds a steady drumbeat in my blood. But so does arousal. I should get up and leave, ASAP. Anything short of that is self-torture.

But my ass remains glued to the couch cushion.

Conor lifts his head, his eyelids heavy with lust. "I want to kiss you," he whispers to Demi, who inhales deeply.

I curl my fingers over my knee to stop them from clench-ing into a fist.

Con flicks me a brief look, winks, and then lowers his mouth to Demi's.

Mother*fucker*.

She welcomes the kiss, parting her lips for him, and I almost curse out loud when I see his tongue enter her mouth.

I grit my teeth. Finally finding my voice. "I'm just gonna go…"

Demi breaks the kiss and plants her hand on my thigh. "Stay."

Oh sweet Jesus. Yeah, there's definitely no oxygen in this room anymore. "Nah," I grind out. "I feel like you guys might need some privacy."

Conor licks his bottom lip. "When you were in the can, I was telling Demi about that time you walked in on me getting sucked off. She said it was the hottest thing she'd ever heard."

I glance sharply at Demi, whose lips curve seductively. "The hottest," she says in a throaty voice. "Why didn't you join them?"

"That's what I said!" Con nuzzles her neck again. I know the moment he sucks on her flesh, because she gasps in delight.

When he raises his head again, he quirks up an eyebrow and his gaze locks with mine, as if to say, *I'm down for anything. How about you?*

I don't know what the hell I'm feeling. I know that I'm hard as a rock and that I shouldn't be.

I know that Demi is threading her fingers through

Conor's shoulder-length hair and pulling on the blond strands to tug him forward.

I know that when I see their tongues touch, I want to rip his out of his mouth and wear it around my neck like a war trophy while I fuck Demi right in front of him.

And that's when I snap. The scorching jealousy in my blood rivals the primal need flooding my body. I snarl like a territorial dog and jump to my feet, forcibly pulling Demi up with me.

"Nope. Nope nope nope nope *nope*."

Her eyes widen. "What the hell!"

Conor merely chuckles.

"We're leaving," I bark at her, as my pulse careens and my breaths come out ragged.

"But—"

I silence her protest with a growl. "You want your rebound? I'll give you your fucking rebound. Let's go."

28
DEMI

I don't remember getting to Hunter's house. Not because I'm drunk and unaware of my surroundings, but because I'm so full of anticipation I can't think or see straight. Hell, I can't hear straight, either—the only sound registering is the incessant thudding of my heart.

Getting Hunter to cave was so easy. Although I won't lie—for a moment there I was worried I'd crossed the line from making him jealous to completely driving him away. I can't deny it felt good kissing Conor, but nothing rivals the dizzying excitement of stumbling into Hunter's bedroom and glimpsing that ravenous look on his face.

He kicks the door closed. Locks it. Then he's advancing on me like a predator. He stops when our bodies are less than a foot apart. "Are you sure about this?" His voice is low. Husky.

"Yes." I swallow. "Are you?"

A ragged breath puffs between us. "Yeah, unfortunately."

My jaw drops. "Really, Hunter? The idea of having sex with me is *sooooo* unfortunate—"

He cuts me off with a kiss and I've already forgotten what I was bitching about.

I am obsessed with this guy's kisses. Hot, passionate, just enough tongue to not be overpowering or slobbery. He knows how to draw moans from my throat, how to seduce me with his firm, talented mouth. And as his tongue slicks over mine seductively, his big hands drift down to my ass, caressing the line of flesh where the hem of Brenna's dress ends.

"This dress is way too short," he hisses in my ear before sliding his hands underneath and squeezing my ass. My butt cheeks might as well be bare, with that dental-floss thong between them.

"Short is bad?" I ask breathlessly.

"It is when you've got Conor Edwards' hand on your thigh."

"Jealous?"

"Yes." No denial, just pure hunger in his dark eyes as he yanks the sweater dress up and over my head. He whips it aside, then steps back to admire my thong and skimpy bikini bra.

"Take the bra off," he rasps. "Show me those tits."

My fingers shake as they undo the front clasp. The bra flutters to the floor. Now I'm standing topless in front of him, my heart pounding.

He admires me for a moment. Then he licks his lips and moves close again, filling his palms with my aching breasts. When his thumbs sweep over my nipples, I whimper. They're so hard they actually hurt.

"Your tits are perfect, Demi."

I can't speak. I'm too busy watching his face as he plays

with my breasts. Each caress makes my heart beat even faster. I'm sure he feels the rapid *thump-thump* beneath his exploring hands. I almost weep when he stops, but then those rough hands travel lower to grip the thin strap at my waist. He shoves the thong down my legs. I'm naked now. Hunter's still fully dressed.

He's just staring at me, and the need burning in his eyes is too much. My core clenches tightly. "Do something," I whisper.

"I shouldn't," he says gruffly, and yet he grabs his shirt by the collar and pulls it off.

His bare torso taunts me. Smooth golden flesh with a smatter of hair between his heavy pecs. Sculpted abs tapering into a trim waist. He has a treasure trail that disappears into the waistband of his black cargo pants and I want nothing more than to follow that trail with my tongue and see what it leads to.

I want to kiss his chest, drag my tongue over every ridge, every tight sinew. But I'm too scared to move. Scared that if I break the spell, he'll put a stop to this.

Without a word, he undoes his pants and lets them drop on the floor. His belt buckle jangles when it hits the hardwood. Next, he tugs his white boxers down his muscular legs. His dick swings up, long and thick.

Like one of Pavlov's dogs, saliva floods my mouth. "Oh my goodness. That thing's been under there this entire time?"

He gives a choked laugh. "Yeah. A man's cock is typically attached to his body."

I can't take my eyes off it. It's a lot bigger than Nico's.

Hunter takes a step closer, then another one. When our

bodies are almost flush, his dick brushes against my stomach, leaving a streak of moisture near my belly button.

He looks down sheepishly. "Just realized something."

"What is it?"

"I'm going to come the second you touch me."

I narrow my eyes. "You're being hyperbolic."

"Trust me, I'm not. I haven't been with anyone since April."

My lips twitch in humor. "So you're saying I'm not going to enjoy this?"

"That's not what I'm saying at all." And before I can blink, he lifts me up in his arms.

My legs instinctively close around his hips, arms looping around his neck. He kisses me deeply as he stalks to the bed and lowers me onto the mattress. My head collides with a pillow. I blink again and suddenly his calloused hands are roaming my body. When he cups my pussy, a jolt of pleasure ricochets through me.

"*Fuck*." Hunter moans against my neck and I wonder, is there any sound sexier than a man moaning? If there is, I can't name it.

The hoarse sound is so frickin' hot, and I can't help but compare this encounter to any of my encounters with Nico, who was so quiet during sex that sometimes, if the room was pitch black, it felt like I was in the bed alone.

But Hunter makes noise. He whispers how sexy I am. Groans when his palm glides over my very wet core. Hisses when the tip of his finger slides inside to feel even more wetness. I love how vocal he is. I love the needy haze in his eyes as he raises himself up on his elbow and peers down at me.

"You're so beautiful." His lips find my breasts again, and one nipple is drawn into the hot, wet suction of his mouth.

I shiver. "Feels nice," I murmur.

"That's the goal." He continues to suck my nipples until I'm gasping in pleasure.

It feels so ridiculously good, and I get impossibly wetter. By the time his muscular body shifts down the mattress so that his head is positioned between my legs, I almost apologize for how aroused I am. I'm pretty sure I left a wet spot on his bedspread. That's fucking embarrassing, but he doesn't seem to mind.

He absently rubs my clit, watching me from beneath surprisingly thick eyelashes. "I'm not getting up until I make you come," he informs me. "I'm going to lick every goddamn inch of you, and I'm going to do it right." A sexy smile curves his lips. "That means you telling me what you like…"

"I already told you," I say awkwardly, "oral isn't that important to—"

He kisses my pussy, and my hips buck off the bed.

"That," I gasp. "I like that."

He gives me another soft kiss, then another, and then his tongue joins the mix and the sensation of it gliding over my clit is both pure torture and exquisite ecstasy. "Start slow," I whisper. Then brace myself, because this is usually the moment when an overeager tongue flicks hard and quick over my clit until I'm squirming to make it end.

But Hunter proceeds to bestow the sweetest, slowest licks upon my delighted pussy. Kissing, teasing, exploring. His palms sweep over my quivering thighs in a soft caress before snaking underneath me to squeeze my ass. He lifts me up slightly and brings me closer to his greedy mouth. Oh my *God*. I think I like oral sex. It was never me at all.

His low groan vibrates in my core. "You taste so fucking good. I could do this for hours." He starts going faster, laving my clit with his tongue, and I ease away a bit. "Not good?" he murmurs.

"Not yet," I mumble. "Too much too soon."

He resumes the slow pace, whispering dirty words against my core. "Got it. How about I suck on this for a bit," he gently rubs my clit with his thumb, "I think that'd feel really, really good, baby. What do you think?"

"I don't know," I croak. "Why don't you give it a try?"

He gently captures my clit between his lips, gives a light suck, and oh my *goodness* it's the best feeling in the world.

Hunter continues to tease me with long, languid licks, interspersed with open-mouth kisses that always end with the sweet sucking of my clit and me rocking my hips in sheer desperation.

"Hmmm," he chuckles against my pussy. "That's how we do it, then."

"Do what?" I'm too turned on to think.

"That's how we make you come. Slow and steady, and just when you can't take it anymore, I suck on this hot little clit and your body fucking sings…" He lifts his head and grins up at me. His lips are shiny and swollen. "I figured you out."

I want to say it's not that difficult, but I know from previous experience that my body is a hard nut to crack.

Humming with satisfaction, Hunter goes back to driving me crazy. As he works me over with his tongue, I slide my hands through his hair. I'm not the girl who can come in three seconds. It takes time for me, but he doesn't complain. If anything, the noises he's making grow hungrier and hungrier, and when his finger slides inside me and my pussy eagerly clamps around it, he groans loudly.

I gaze at his long body stretched out before me, his muscular thighs, his taut ass. I catch a flash of movement and realize he's got his dick in his free hand. It's rock hard, but he's not stroking it. He's squeezing it, as if he's trying not to come. Knowing he's *that* turned on from going down on me triggers a rush of hot pleasure. My hips start moving faster.

"Oh fuck, baby, yes. I want to feel you coming on my tongue. Give it to me."

The command is hoarse, dirty. "Finger," I choke out, and he pushes one finger back inside as his lips close around my clit.

The orgasm sweeps through me in a scorching wave of pleasure. It's the first time I've climaxed with someone other than Nico, and that's scary and exhilarating and I can't stop moaning as I grip Hunter's hair and shake with release.

When I go calm and still, he plants a soft kiss between my legs and whispers, "Ah fuck, that was so hot." Then he kisses his way up my body and nuzzles the crook of my neck.

His dick is heavy against my hip, the heat of it branding my flesh. I reach down to grip it and Hunter's agonized groan makes me laugh. "You're going to have to let me touch it eventually," I point out.

"I know. I'm just already embarrassed about what's gonna happen."

"You can do it," I encourage. "I believe in you."

He trembles with laughter. Then he starts to roll over, and

for a second I wonder if he's going to slide his dick inside me without protection. But no, he's just rising to his knees and leaning over my body to grab a condom from the nightstand.

The square packet is a sobering reminder of the conversation we didn't have before ripping each other's clothes off.

"Um." I gulp. "I know this is awkward, but…I don't have to worry about any diseases on your end, right…?" I let that hang.

His response rings with reassurance. "I'm one hundred percent clean. I get tested regularly on the team. I can show you my latest results, but they're a month old."

"We should get tested together," I suggest. "Actually, I—" I halt, suddenly horrified. "Oh my God, I should've gotten tested immediately after finding out about Nico. Dammit, Hunter! He was sleeping with other girls. What if I'm the one with the disease?"

He chuckles ruefully. "Well, there's nothing I can do about it now, because I just went down on you for a half hour. But tell you what, we'll use a condom now and then if we ever want to do this again, we'll take a trip down to the health center together."

"Sounds like fun! Couples STD testing!"

He barks out a laugh. I'm glad he found that amusing and didn't comment on the word *couples*. It was just a figure of speech, anyway. I know what this is and what it isn't.

As Hunter grips the base of his dick so he can roll the condom on, I begin to applaud. "Look, you didn't come from doing that!"

"Yeah, well, you know, the diseases talk usually kills some of the mood."

"So you're saying you're not in the mood anymore?"

He secures the condom, and his erection sticks out like an iron spike. "Does that look like I'm not in the mood?"

I giggle.

"I'm just saying, now I might be able to last a little longer."

"Good. Get in me already." And then we're kissing again and he's on top of me. I'm still wet, and more than ready, when he enters me.

The moment his full length is buried deep, Hunter releases a streak of desperate curses against my lips. "Oh, fuck, you feel so good."

He withdraws, then plunges back in.

"Fuck fuck fuck fuck *fuck*. Why is sex so good?" His lust-soaked expletives heat the air between us.

"Sex or sex with me?" Yep, apparently even during the act of copulation, I resort to fishing for compliments.

"Sex with you," he says hoarsely.

"So it wouldn't be this good with anybody else?"

His head jerks as he shakes it, his dark hair tickling my cheek. "I don't know if it's ever been this good."

I'm sure that's probably his eight-month drought talking, but I like to think maybe it's me.

He starts to move, and I meet him thrust for thrust by lifting my ass. As he plunges into me over and over and over again, we kiss frantically and make helpless, tortured noises against each other's lips. It feels amazing. I don't think I'm going to come again, but I already got my orgasm and now I get to watch Hunter as he comes apart before my eyes.

Anguish creases his forehead. He bites his lower lip, then slowly releases it. He curses. He groans. His eyes are hot with lust.

He fucks me for longer than I expected, and I realize that his chest is trembling and his features are taut because he's trying desperately not to lose control. So I scrape my nails down his back and squeeze my inner muscles around his dick. "Let go," I urge.

He moans. "You sure?"

"Uh-huh. There's nothing hotter than watching you right now. Give it to me."

Heat flares in his eyes and then his hips snap forward. The tempo quickens. His breaths come out in short pants, until he gives a final thrust and I can feel the orgasm shudder through his body. When he peers down at me, he looks sleepy and sated and it's so damn sexy.

"That was good," I mumble.

"So good." His head drops again, his mouth prodding at me as his lips seek any sort of contact. They connect with my chin, and he kisses it before burying his face in my neck.

"I'm sorry I made you break your vow," I whisper sheepishly, as I hold him tightly against me.

"I'm not," he whispers back.

29
HUNTER

"Hey, is Matty here?" I ask when Conor opens the door the next afternoon. It's one-thirty, Demi left my house thirty minutes ago, and I'm in desperate need of advice.

Con shakes his head. "He went home with Andrea last night. Hasn't come back yet. The rest of the guys are still passed out. And I'm about to lift some weights. Come on, you can spot me."

"Sure, what the hell." I step inside and take off my coat and boots.

"How was last night?" Conor asks with a knowing grin.

Incredible, I want to say. Magnificent. Tremendous. Mind-blowing. Stupendous. There aren't enough adjectives to describe how good last night was. It was the best sex of my life, hands down.

When I woke up this morning and saw Demi lying naked in my bed, so sweet, so irresistible, I couldn't help myself again. I made her come with my tongue, and then she gave me a handjob that made me see stars. After I spilled into her hand, she winked, brought one of her fingers to her mouth to lick it up, and I almost came again.

That girl is…incredible. Magnificent. Tremendous—okay, not enough adjectives again. She's so sexy, and I'm attracted to everything about her. And yet as much as I want to sleep with her again, I'm also pissed at myself. I walked over here to talk to Matt about it, but looks like Conor will have to do.

We go down to the basement, where the guys have a makeshift gym. It's not much—treadmill, a bench press, a rowing machine, and some free weights and resistance bands. Con heads for the bench and strips out of his T-shirt.

Groaning, he slaps his rock-hard stomach and says, "Do I have a booze belly? I feel like I'm bloated."

"Are you fishing for compliments? Because your abs are tighter than a gymnast's ass," I grumble as I help him get the weights. I raise a brow when I see what he's lifting. "A hundred pounds? Slacker," I taunt.

"Hung-over," he grunts. "I'm starting off slow."

I snicker. "Hung-over how? I'm pretty sure I drank all your whiskey."

"I cracked open another bottle after you left," he says with a grin. "Stayed up till three in the morning drinking with a really hot redhead."

"Uh-huh, I'm sure all you guys did was drink."

"Well, no. I got laid—obvs."

I roll my eyes. "Obvs."

It doesn't surprise me that he went from kissing my girl to hooking up with another one. And I doubt he did it to soothe his bruised ego—Con's ego could sustain a direct missile hit.

If he hooked up, it was because he was horny from kissing Demi, not because he needed a confidence boost after Demi went home with me.

"How about you, captain?" he asks.

I play dumb. "How about me what?"

"You never answered how last night was for you. Am I the only one who got laid?" He lies down on the bench and holds up his palms so I can deposit the barbell into them.

When I don't answer, Conor barks out a laugh. "Come on, man, it's not a trick question."

"Fine. I got laid," I admit.

"Shocking! Never saw that coming!"

"Fuck off," I sigh.

He lifts a brow. "Why so glum? Did you blow your load too fast because of the celibacy thing? Or was it just bad sex in general?" He frowns. "That's surprising, 'cause she looked like she'd be a lot of fun." As he lifts and lowers the barbell, all the muscles in his arms bulge and flex.

"She is fun. And the sex was great," I say roughly.

"Then why do you look so pissed?"

I gaze down at him unhappily. "Because I broke my vow."

"Fuck the vow."

"I wanted to stick by it," I say in a tired voice. "You weren't here last year. My partying is the reason we didn't beat Harvard."

Conor rolls his eyes. "If you truly believe that, then you're an arrogant prick. One player doesn't make a team."

"It wasn't one player, it was two. Our captain was out, too. Nate and I were the top two players on the team."

"Well, shit happens. Some teams lose their top three, four, five, to injuries. It's just bad luck."

"I guess." I'm still unconvinced. I release another sigh. "I just wanted to be a good captain this year."

"Dude, you are a good captain. I mean, look at the shit you tolerate. Bucky and Jesse wanted a *pig*, and you made yourself look like a complete idiot in front of Coach to make it happen for them. Cut yourself some slack."

"You're just saying that because you cut everybody slack. You're a surfer dude—your whole life is slack."

He laughs, which trips up his even breathing for a second. He inhales deeply and resumes lifting. When he's done with his set, I put the bar back in place and give him a second to catch his breath.

"I'm just worried it'll fuck us over," I confess. "I'm worried we'll go on a losing streak now."

"You really need to chill, dude." Con's tone grows serious. "Look, Demi's cool. I like her."

I narrow my eyes.

That gets me another laugh. "I don't like her like that. I mean, don't get me wrong, if you weren't in the picture, I'd be all about her. But—one, you are in the picture. And two, I'm not looking for a relationship."

"I was in the picture last night too," I say darkly.

Con looks like he's trying not to roll his eyes again. "Do you honestly think I'd mack on your girl?"

"You did mack on my girl."

"Yeah, to light a fire under your ass, you idiot."

I falter. "What do you mean?"

"I was never going to go through with it. Neither was

she." Conor is chuckling as he stretches out on the bench and gestures for me to spot him again. "I'm surprised you let it go as far as you did. She and I figured there'd be some flirting and nothing more. Didn't realize I'd need to stick my tongue down her throat for you to get the memo."

"You guys *planned* it?" I feel outraged, but at the same time, I'm also…touched? Yeah, I think I'm actually touched. But I guess that makes sense after what happened with Summer and Fitzy. I told Fitz I was into Summer and he made a move anyway. It's kind of a relief to know Conor wouldn't do that to me.

"Like I said, Demi's really cool," he tells me. "Women like that don't come along often, so trust me when I say you need to lock it down, ASAP. If you don't make an effort to keep her, you'll lose her. She'll have a boyfriend again in no time, and then you'll look back on it and realize what a total dumbass you were for letting her go."

———

I last about six hours before I cave and shoot a text to Demi.

> **ME**: Want to hang out tonight?

To my relief, she answers immediately.

> **DEMI**: Come over?
> **ME**: Be there in 20.

It's difficult not to break every traffic law on my way to

campus. I force myself to stick to the speed limit, which means I'm twitching with impatience by the time I reach the Theta house. The sorority president, Josie, lets me in. She doesn't look surprised to see me. The Thetas are used to me being around, thanks to mine and Demi's psych project.

When I walk into Demi's room, I find her on the bed, sitting in front of a mountain of schoolwork. The mattress is covered with textbooks, papers, notes, binders, and highlighters.

"Did you rob a school supplies store?" I ask pleasantly.

"Studying for my bio exam," she moans. She peers up at me with big brown eyes. "I hate science, Hunter. I hate it."

Sympathy rises inside me. "I'm sorry." She's visibly distressed, a drastic contrast from the way her face lights up when we're working on our psych project.

"I think I'll do okay on bio and math. I'm more worried about Organic Chem. The exam is the day before winter break, and I'm nowhere near ready for it. I need like ten thousand more study sessions in order to ace that class."

"You'll ace all of them," I assure her. "I have faith in you." And I have faith in her work ethic. This girl works her ass off. I've seen how invested she is in psychology, and I know she puts the same amount of effort into all her classes.

"Are you sure you have time to hang out?" I ask. I'm standing awkwardly at the foot of the bed, because there's no room for me on there. "Should I even be here right now?"

Demi glares at me. "I'll kill you if you leave."

I can't tell if she's joking. That's the problem with being into a chick who's into murderers.

She gets up and methodically gathers her study materials.

She stacks the textbooks on her small desk, then the binders, the pages of notes. All in neat little piles. Her organizational skills are as cute as the rest of her.

When the bedspread is clear, she glances at it for a moment before turning to me, a blush on her cheeks. "I've been thinking about you since the second I opened my eyes this morning," she admits.

"Obviously." I grin, cocky as fuck. "You opened your eyes this morning to my tongue between your legs."

"Mmmm yeah." She shivers happily. "I'll rephrase—I've been thinking about you since I left your house today." She hesitates. "Have you been thinking about me?"

"God, yes." No hesitation on my end.

Her expression brightens. "Really?"

"Oh yeah."

"Oh. Okay. That's good. Because I wasn't sure if you wanted last night to be a one-time thing."

Our eyes lock.

"I don't think once will be enough," I confess.

"Me neither," she agrees solemnly, and the next thing I know, our mouths are fused together.

The kiss makes my head spin. I fucking *love* kissing her. I love how eager her tongue is, how warm her lips are. I love the way she whimpers when I tug her body close to mine.

I break the kiss to lick my lips. "Have you been sucking on something cherry? Or is that strawberry?"

"Cherry gummies," she confirms. "But…I'd way rather be sucking on something else now…"

Grinning broadly, she pushes me onto the bed and starts

pulling my clothes off. A second later, I'm buck naked and sprawled on my back, while Demi crawls down my body.

She kisses her way south, her lips leaving shivers in their wake. My cock rises in full salute, pleading for her attention, and when she curls her fingers around the base, a bead of moisture pools at the tip.

With a devilish smile, Demi laps at the pearly drop with the tip of her tongue.

The tortured groan she draws from my throat is so loud I half expect an army of Thetas to bang on the door asking if everything is okay.

Demi lifts her head. "You make the hottest sounds in bed."

"That's because you do the hottest things in bed." Then I watch from under heavy eyelids as she sucks on the tip of my cock before lavishing wet kisses on my shaft.

Eventually my eyes flutter closed and I lose myself to sensation. The sweet scrape of her tongue, the hot suction of her lips. The blowjob is slow, tentative, as she determines what I like.

I guide her with husky commands. "I like it rougher than that," I whisper, and I reach for her fist, wrap my hand around it, and tighten her grip.

"Really? Like that?" she says in surprise. "I feel like that would hurt!"

"It doesn't hurt," I assure her.

She tests her grip again, squeezing hard, and I shudder in pleasure. "What if I break your penis?"

A choked laugh flies out. "You're not going to break my penis, I promise."

Demi gives a hard stroke, then sucks on my tip again and it's the best feeling ever. I thread one hand through her hair and start thrusting upward. This is way too good. My balls draw up tight and my vision wavers. *Way* too good.

"I need to be inside you," I grind out.

She gets up and crawls toward the nightstand, and the sight of her on her hands and knees is too tempting to ignore. I rise up on my knees behind her and slip a hand between her legs. She's so wet. When I slip a finger inside, her pussy clamps tightly around it.

Moaning, Demi bucks back against my touch. I add another finger, and now there's two moving inside her, summoning breathy noises from her lips. "Oh my God. Feels so good."

I finger her with lazy, teasing thrusts until my body can no longer take it. "Condom," I mutter, and Demi slaps one into my palm.

My dick throbs as I roll the latex onto it. I stop for a second to admire Demi's perfect ass. It's jutting in the air, practically begging for me to—

"Eek!" she exclaims when my palm connects with her smooth flesh.

"Sorry," I say, quickly soothing the sting with a soft caress. "Your ass is so smackable, you don't even know, babe."

"Do it again."

A grin lifts one corner of my mouth. "You like to be spanked?"

"Maybe?" She wiggles that sexy ass and my palm once again lands in a sharp smack.

"Oh my *goodness*," Demi mumbles. "Do it again—but this time when you're inside me."

This girl is incredible.

I'm harder than steel as I position my dick at her opening. I slide inside her and spank her ass at the same time, and Demi moans loud enough to wake the dead.

My heart pounds an erratic beat as I start fucking her. One hand grips her right ass cheek, the other curves over her left one, squeezing, kneading, spanking each time she begs for it. My hips piston, pushing my dick inside her. Deeper, faster, until we're both groaning in desperation as we hurtle toward the finish line.

She's still on all fours when the orgasm hits her, but by the time she's finished shuddering, she's flat on her stomach, moaning happily. I curve my body over her sweat-soaked back and angle my hips, driving into her with shallow thrusts. Fast, desperate strokes, while my heart threatens to give out and my balls tingle wildly.

"Coming," I grunt.

The pleasure slams into me, stealing the breath from my lungs. I collapse on top of her, only rolling over when she informs me she can't breathe.

I have no words as I yank her closer. She snuggles beside me, her chin on my shoulder. She doesn't speak either. There's nothing to say.

We both know how good that was.

We both know it's going to happen again.

And we're both perfectly okay with that.

30
DEMI

My parents betrayed me.

I'm talking Benedict-Arnold-screwing-over-America level of betrayal.

No—even worse. Brad Pitt cheating on Jennifer Aniston. *That's* how deep the well of betrayal runs.

I was under the impression that we would not be spending the holidays with Nico's family. My father never outright stated it, but the subject hadn't been brought up again after the night I told them in no uncertain words that having Nico around for Christmas would, and I'm quoting myself here, *hurt me*.

But I guess my feelings don't matter, because as we're driving away from the airport in our rental car, Dad informs me that the Delgados will be joining us tonight.

Yep, my parents waited until we arrived in Miami to drop this bomb, probably because they knew I'd never board the plane at Logan Airport otherwise.

With a family as large as mine, the holidays are always a huge production. Christmas Day is spent with my mom's enormous brood, but Christmas Eve is a quieter affair—just us, and Nico's family. It's been a tradition since I was eight years old.

This year, however, it'll be like the plot line of some awkward holiday comedy. *Christmas with the Delgados*, starring my cheating ex-boyfriend and my disloyal parents.

As I fume in the backseat, Dad explains that breaking our annual tradition is something he thinks I'd regret in the future. Awesome. Now even my life's regrets are being decided for me, and they haven't even fucking happened yet.

I find this absolutely egregious. I don't care that they're family friends. My parents could have compromised. They could've gone out for dinner with Nico's parents on their own, sparing me from having to spend any time with Nico. But *noooooo*, God forbid we break *tradition*. The world will end!

We arrive at Aunt Paula's house in the early afternoon. She's the only one of Mom's sisters who isn't married yet, and she owns a gorgeous beachfront property. Some people think there needs to be snow on the ground in order for it to be a real Christmas, but having grown up in Florida, for me the holiday season is sunshine and palm trees and the salty spray of the ocean on my face.

I'm still fuming by the time it's time to leave for Nico's house. As Dad searches for where he left the car keys, Mom notices my face and pulls me aside. "*Mami*, I know you don't like this—"

"You're right, I hate it," I growl.

"But your father made his decision, and you need to make the best of it. Dora and Joaquín are going to be in our lives regardless of whether you and Nico are dating. Dora is like a sister to me, and Papa views Joaquín as a brother." Mom's tone softens. "It's not easy for you, I know. But this is what happens when families are woven so tightly together. So, please, let this be your first test—a test to see if the two of you can be around each other without hostility. Nico is willing to try. He told Dora he was fine with this."

Of course he's fine with it. He probably thinks we're getting back together. That's what he's been saying to Darius since the second we broke up.

But Mom is right. The Delgados are their closest friends. They're family. I have no choice but to suck it up.

I'd debated looking extra hot tonight, but I didn't want Nico getting any ideas. So I did the opposite—I dressed down. A plain white dress, knee-length and with a modest neckline, paired with flat brown sandals, not even a hint of a heel. My hair is tied in a low ponytail with a red bow. I look like a child who's going to perform some cringe-worthy song for the adults after dinner.

Perfect.

Fifteen minutes later, we're entering the familiar house where I'd spent so much of my time. I honestly never envisioned Nico and me *not* being together for the holidays.

Or that I'd be sleeping with another guy.

On the regular.

My rebound with Hunter didn't stop after Conor's party. We slept together again the next day. And the day after that, and then the day after that. Yesterday we stayed up all night having sex, even though I had to get up early to meet my parents at the airport.

My body is already craving him again. I'm addicted to it. I never thought I'd be sleeping with a jock, but I kind of understand now why so many women love athletes. God. All those rock-hard muscles. The sheer strength of their bodies. Yesterday Hunter lifted me onto his dick and fucked me standing up against my bedroom wall. Apparently everyone in the house heard the wall banging, and my sorority sisters teased me mercilessly about it this morning. But they're happy for me. Hell, *I'm* happy for me. I deserve good sex with a man who isn't sexing up everybody else too. Every woman deserves that.

Nico's family greets me warmly. His little sister Alicia flings her arms around my neck and shrieks, "Oh my God, it's been *forever*!" She's thirteen and has always viewed me as a role model of sorts. I'm the one she called when she got her first period last year.

Dora greets me with smacking kisses and a bear hug, and then Joaquín steps forward to give me a hug.

"Damn fool," he mutters.

I frown slightly. "What?"

His expression turns wry. "My son's a damn fool." He says the words softly, so only I can hear him.

My frown dissolves into a faint smile. "Yep."

Nico still hasn't come downstairs, thank the Lord. I hope he's cowering in his bedroom. My family is ushered into the living room, where I'm fussed over by Dora and Alicia while Joaquín prepares drinks for my parents.

Then I hear his voice. "Demi."

I turn slowly. Unlike me, Nico did make an effort with his appearance. He chose black trousers and a white shirt with the top button undone. His hair is slicked back and he's fully clean-shaven. He looks really good, but the sight of him only evokes mild indifference. I haven't seen or spoken to him since the night we broke up. I thought it might be awful when we eventually came to face to face. That my heartbeat would accelerate, that I'd experience a pang of longing.

But I don't. If anything, I feel sorry for him. He almost looks like a little boy as he steps forward. He starts to open his arms, and I give a quick shake of my head.

"Let's not do that," I advise.

Disappointment clouds his eyes. "Come on, Demi."

The next thing I know there's a glass in my hand. Granted, it's just a soda, and not the full-to-the-brim glass of tequila I would've preferred. But still. Mom to the rescue!

"Let's help Dora with dinner," she chirps as she whisks me toward the kitchen.

I follow her without a backward glance at Nico.

———

Dinner is awkward, at least for me. If it is for our parents, they're not showing it.

Each time Nico speaks to me, I answer politely. But I don't engage or elaborate on anything he asks. He reveals that he quit the moving company, and I don't even blink because I don't care. Then he talks about his new job as a line cook at Della's Diner. I don't care about that either, except to make a mental note to not eat there anymore. He'll either spit in my food or mix a love potion into it.

After dinner, the men go outside on the bricked patio to

smoke their Cubans, and the women tidy up. Old-fashioned, maybe, but that's how it's always been. Alicia and I load the dishwasher and then wash the bigger dishes by hand. She chatters on about the eighth grade and her friends as I pass her pots and pans to dry.

"I can't believe you and Nico aren't together anymore," she whines. "I'm so sad."

"I know, hon, but things don't always work out the way you want them to," I answer ruefully. "Go grab that huge salad bowl from the table, will you? I think it's the last thing we need to wash."

As Alicia dashes off, Dora comes up beside me. "Nicolás told me what he did," she says softly. "I want you to know how disappointed in him I am, Demi. I raised him better than that."

I meet her unhappy eyes. "I'm surprised he actually told you the truth and didn't conjure up some story that painted him as the victim."

She snorts. "That boy is incapable of lying to his mama, you know that."

True. Nico is a total mama's boy. Besides, Cuban women are scarily perceptive—they can read minds. Even if he tried to lie, Dora would've known.

"It's his loss, Demi. I mean that, even though he's my son. And you know you'll always be a daughter to us, no matter what."

"I know." I give her a warm hug, and for the first time all evening I experience the rush of longing I hadn't felt with Nico earlier.

I do love his parents, and it elicits genuine sorrow, the

reminder that things will never be the same now that Nico and I are no longer together.

But things change. Relationships evolve. The same people could remain in your life, people you've known for years and years, only they play a different role now.

I blink back tears as I turn off the faucet and dry my hands on a dishrag.

Dessert is served in the living room, where Alicia demands we play a board game. "I got this new one called Zombies!" she exclaims, and I burst out laughing.

"Oh, I'm quite familiar with that one," I inform the thirteen-year-old. "I've played it numerous times at a friend's house. He killed me off the last time."

She gasps. "You got sacrificed!"

"Yep."

"What friend?" Nico asks suspiciously.

I want to tell him to mind his own damn business. But I can't be rude in front of his family. "Nobody," I say vaguely.

He raises an eyebrow. "Really? Nobody?"

For some reason, Dad decides this is a hill he wants to die on, too. "Which friend is this?" he asks.

I roll my eyes at his stern tone. "My friend Hunter."

"The hockey player?" Nico demands, eyes flashing.

"Yes, the hockey player. You know the one that you and your little buddies—"

"I know who you mean," he interrupts, a warning note in his voice.

Aw, he doesn't want me to rat him out to his parents. Of course not. Dora wouldn't like it one damn bit if she knew her baby boy was beating people up for no reason.

Our eyes lock for a beat. Nico looks worried I might tattle, and relaxes when I don't.

"Hunter and his roommates are hilarious," I say instead, glancing at Alicia. "They have a board game night a couple times a month, and this is their game of choice at the moment. But I don't think it's a good Christmas Eve game, hon. Maybe we should just play charades?"

Mom claps her hands. "Yessss! Let's do it!"

Dora smiles at her daughter. "Go find those charades cards we wrote up last year, *mami*. They should be in the game drawer in the family room."

Alicia hurries off excitedly.

I get up from my perch on the leather sofa. "I'm going to steal some candy from the bowl in the dining room. Anyone want some?"

"I'm surprised your teeth haven't rotted off by now," Nico's mother chides with a sigh.

"Good genes," I say, flashing my pearly whites. I'm a sugar fiend, yet I've never had a single cavity.

I pop into the other room and rummage through the bowl for something cherry-flavored. I'm barely gone five seconds before Nico's gruff voice comes from the doorway.

"Can we talk?"

I've been dreading this. "There's really nothing to say."

He steps into the room. "Look, I'm not going to try to win you back, if that's what you're worried about. I get it, we're done."

"Thank you. I appreciate that."

"But I did want to say I'm sorry. Not just for what happened with us, but for what I did to your hockey friend. I was drunk that night." He shifts his feet, looking sheepish.

"You can save your apologies for Hunter. As for me, no apology is going to make up for what you did to me." I suck in my cheeks as anger ripples through me. "We were together for so long and you played me like that?"

"I know. I'm sorry, D. I was an idiot, okay?"

"A horny idiot."

Nico shakes his head. "No. It was about more than just sex. I…"

"You what?"

He makes a frustrated sound. "I can't explain why I did it. It's just…it's hard to live up to your expectations sometimes, okay?"

My eyebrows fly out. "My expectations? Nico. The only expectation I ever had of you was to not stick your dick in anyone else. I hadn't realized that was an impossible standard to meet," I say sarcastically.

He scrapes one hand through his black hair. "You don't get it. You're so smart and you've always known exactly what you want to do with your life. And I'm just a fucked-up loser from Miami."

"That's not true."

"You're too perfect, Demi. Even back when we were just friends, I always felt this need to impress you. And then we started dating and the pressure got even worse. I felt like I was trying to live up to something. And those other chicks, they threw themselves at me, made me feel like a big man, and I just ate it up, okay?" He avoids my gaze. "Whatever, it's pathetic, but it's the truth."

"Yeah, it's pathetic," I agree, but my psychologist brain has already kicked in. Never in my wildest dreams had I thought that I was emasculating him. "I'm sorry if I made you feel that way, Nico. All I ever wanted was the best for you."

"I get it. And I tried to be that dude you wanted. I worked my ass off to get into an Ivy League—"

"I never asked you to do that," I protest.

"I felt like I had to. I knew I'd lose you if we went to different colleges. But…" He sounds frazzled. "But it's so goddamn hard, D. I study so fucking hard. And I work even fucking harder because my family's not as well-off as yours."

"I never asked you to do any of that," I maintain. But the guilt trip is having an effect on me. "You pushed *yourself*, Nico. Whatever urge was pushing you to do it, you still created that pressure within yourself. But if I gave off the impression that I needed you to be some perfect specimen, I'm sorry. I didn't mean to do that. I always liked you exactly the way you were."

"Liked?" he says sadly.

"Yeah. That's usually what happens when you sleep with someone who isn't me."

"I'm sorry, okay? I'm disgusting. There's no excuse."

"Nope. But here's a tip for next time, with the next girl— maybe you could talk to her about any insecurities you might be having, instead of needing to go out and get an ego boost from other women."

"You make me sound even more pathetic when you phrase it like that."

I sigh quietly. "The fact that you couldn't talk to me about how you were feeling only shows that our relationship was never going to work. We were kids when we started going out. We were naïve to think it was going to last forever."

"It would have, if I hadn't screwed up."

"But you did, and now we'll never know what would've happened." I brush past him, heading for the doorway. "It's Christmas, Nico. Let's go spend time with our families."

"Demi."

I glance over my shoulder and find remorse swimming in his dark eyes. "What is it?"

"There's really no chance, is there?"

"No. There isn't."

———

On the car ride home, I send Happy Holidays! texts to TJ, Pax, and the other Lost Boys, and then I finally get a chance to text Hunter, who's spending the holidays in Connecticut. Apparently his father's company held a holiday party tonight, which Hunter and his mother were expected to attend because, well, because they're nothing but props for his father.

> **ME**: How'd it go tonight?
> **HIM**: Not terrible. Open bar, good food. Danced with my mother to a live version of Baby It's Cold Outside, which was awkward.
> **ME**: Awkward? More like hot!
> **HIM**: FFS! We're talking about my mother here.
> **ME**: Was your dad on his best behavior?
> **HIM**: Of course. He's gotta put on a show for his adoring fans.

"Demi," Dad says from the driver's seat. "Could you please close your window? Your mother's cold."

"Mmm-hmmm." I absently hit the automatic button, but I press it the wrong way and end up opening the window fully rather than doing the opposite. "Oh shoot. Sorry, Mom." I drop my phone on the seat beside me and click the button again.

"Who are you texting with?" she asks curiously.

"Just a friend."

Dad pounces instantly. "This Hunter boy you mentioned earlier?"

I wrinkle my forehead. "Yes. Is that a problem?"

He doesn't answer for a moment. When he does, suspicion colors his tone. "Nico doesn't think much of him."

Interesting. Looks like Nico had more to say when the men went out for their second round of cigars.

"I see." I nod politely. "Because Nico's opinion is the mantle by which we measure all wisdom and purity."

"Demi," Mom chides from the passenger side.

"What? It's true? His moral compass isn't exactly in working order." I meet Dad's eyes in the rearview mirror. "When you were outside talking about my friend, did Nico also tell you how he beat Hunter up?"

Mom gasps. "He didn't! Did he?"

"Oh yeah. Hunter was the one who gave me the heads up about the cheating. Nico didn't like that, so he tracked Hunter down and roughed him up with four of his friends. Five against one, Dad. That's how mature adults deal with their problems, right?"

Dad's cheeks hollow as if he's grinding his teeth. "Well.

That aside, I wonder if perhaps you should keep your distance from this Hunter."

"Why? This is coming out of nowhere. You don't even know him, and I don't think you should be taking Nico's word for anything, please. He's a liar."

"He lied to you, yes. But that doesn't make him a liar."

"Daddy. If I murdered you, I'd be a murderer. He lied to me, therefore he's a liar."

"Semantics."

I heave a sigh. "Look, I like Hunter, all right? He's great."

"Are you dating him?" my father demands.

"Not really."

Mom twists around in her seat, her meddlesome instincts kicking in. "'Not really?' *Dios mío!* You *are* dating him! When did this happen?!"

"We're not dating." *Just having sex. Repeatedly.* "But if we were, I'd expect both of you to give him a fair shot. Nico isn't my boyfriend anymore, you guys. Eventually someone else is going to fill that role, and I need you to accept that and be open-minded about it." I shrug. "As for Hunter, he's a good guy and I like him a lot." I meet my father's eyes again. "And if you met him, you'd like him too."

31
DEMI

NEW YEAR'S EVE

HUNTER HAS ME ON THE BED BEFORE I CAN EVEN SAY HELLO. His greedy mouth latches onto mine, the kiss stealing the breath from my lungs.

"I missed this," I whimper, and I feel his answering groan vibrate through my body. I wrap my legs around his trim hips and shamelessly grind against his very prominent bulge.

"Missed you too," he mumbles. His lips are exploring my throat now. He sucks on the side of my neck, then rolls us over so that I'm straddling him.

His hands slide underneath my shirt to cup my boobs. I'm not wearing a bra, so his calloused palms are a delicious scrape over my sensitive flesh. My nipples instantly pucker and strain against his touch.

"Fuck," he groans. "Take this infuriating thing *off*." He peels the shirt off me and whips it across the room.

A laugh flies out. "Hey, now, my shirt didn't do anything wrong."

"It was covering these perfect tits. I'm furious at it." The hot whisper fans over my nipple and I moan when he draws it into his mouth and sucks deeply. *God*. I can't believe it's been two weeks since I've seen him. How have I gone without this for two weeks?

I roll my hips, grinding his covered erection. He cups and squeezes my breasts, then curls one hand behind my neck and tugs me down for a kiss. His tongue touches mine and it's like a bolt of lightning directly to my core.

In an unplanned synchronized frenzy, we fumble at each other's waistbands. He shoves my PJ pants down. I try to do the same with his jeans, but the denim snags on his thighs. He grins and lifts his ass to help me out. He's still wearing a shirt, but naked below the waist, and his cock springs up, long and thick. My mouth actually waters.

"Fuck," Hunter chokes out as his gaze roams my nude body.

Our gazes lock. A second ticks by, two, three.

And then we're mauling each other again. I find a condom and put it on him. He pulls me back onto his lap. I impale myself on him, and off to the races we go.

I don't know how long I ride him. It could be seconds, minutes or hours. All I know is that the knot of pleasure between my legs is almost painful, unbearable. My breathing is shaky. So are my hands. My fingertips tingle as I stroke them over his sculpted pecs. Lord, I know I'm close.

Pippa was right when she posited that maybe I've been having sex all wrong. Or maybe sex simply becomes predictable when you've been having it with the same person for years. With Hunter, it's completely unpredictable, and right now I'm relishing the newness of it, all these firsts with him.

First kiss.

First fuck.

First orgasm while I'm riding his dick.

I come first, collapsing onto him, and he thrusts his hips, digging his fingers into my ass. He bites my shoulder as he comes, and I laugh breathlessly against his damp chest. We lie there for a moment, his arms wrapped snugly around me, his dick still buried inside me.

"Oh my gosh," I say dreamily. "That was so good."

"So good," he mumbles.

We stay in that position for nearly a minute before he reluctantly withdraws. I sit up and help him remove the condom. "Here, let me get rid of this. I need to pee anyway."

I return to the bed a minute later and we snuggle up, still naked. Hunter reaches for the fleece throw at the foot of the bed, pinches the corner and drags it up to cover us.

"It's New Year's Eve," he remarks.

"Are you just realizing it now? Did you not see all the decorations the girls are setting up downstairs?" Theta Beta Nu is hosting one of the many parties on Greek Row tonight. Which means my presence is mandatory.

I'm touched that Hunter chose to come here tonight instead of chilling with his boys. His teammates are throwing a huge party in Hastings.

"Are you sure you don't want to go to Conor's?" I fret.

"No." He kisses the top of my head. "I'm never leaving this room."

"Well, we have to leave it at some point to make an appearance downstairs."

"Fine. We'll go down once every hour for twenty-minute intervals, then come back up here and fuck. After midnight, all bets are off and we stay in here forever." His hand slithers down to pinch my bare butt.

"You're insatiable."

"Babe. I'm literally coming off a nine-month sex drought. If it was possible, my dick would be permanently inside you for at least three weeks."

"Three *weeks*?" I yelp. That sounds exhausting. Fun, but exhausting.

"You're right. That's completely unreasonable. I'll need at least three months inside you before my balls return to normal. It takes a while for semen production to regulate."

I snicker loudly. "Gross."

Voices echo outside my door as several of my sorority sisters pass by.

"Well, if you do want to go and party with your friends, I wouldn't fault you for it," I say, carelessly stroking his ridged abdomen.

"Not going anywhere, Semi," he says stubbornly, his arm tightening around me.

"Can I ask you something?"

He snorts. "You'll ask regardless of my answer to that."

"True." My grin fades as I broach the subject I'd been avoiding since we first had sex. "Are you mad at me for pushing you to break your celibacy vow?"

"No." Nothing but sincerity there.

"Are you mad at yourself?"

"I was the morning after," he reveals.

"Really?" I say in surprise. This is the first time he's admitted to having any doubts or regrets about us.

"Yeah, for all of five minutes." His calloused fingertips tease my shoulder. "Then I saw you lying there naked in my bed, and I wanted to keep breaking the vow, over and over again."

"But it was important to you," I say guiltily.

"It was, but…" His hand continues roaming my bare skin. "This feels more important."

He doesn't elaborate, and I don't push him to. We lie there for a while, neither of us in a hurry to join the party, which has already started judging by the music that's rocking the house.

"Did you have a good time in New York?" After Christmas he spent a few days in Manhattan with Dean and his girlfriend.

"It was fun. The Bruins were playing the Islanders, so Garrett got us into the box. Fucking amazing game."

I reach up and run my fingers through his hair. "None of your hair seems to be missing," I tease.

"It's the gel, man. Stops me from pulling it out."

"What do you like better—watching live hockey, or playing it?"

"Playing, obviously." He doesn't even hesitate.

"Have you ever played in front of a crowd as large as the one in TD Garden?"

Hunter chuckles. "No college arena even rivals that. Now *that* would be a thrill, eh?"

I furrow my brow. "I still don't get why you can't do it.

From what Brenna's told me, someone would sign you in a heartbeat. She says if you announced your interest, half the teams in the league would be courting you after your graduate. But you keep saying you're not interested and it makes no sense to me. You said you don't want to be famous, but I don't believe that's the reason. I mean, maybe it's tied into it, but what's the real reason?"

"It's the lifestyle, Demi. I have a problem with debauchery."

"No, I think you *think* you have a problem with debauchery," I correct. "But from what I've gleaned, you don't drink to excess, you don't have any harmful sexual compulsions that interfere with your regular life, you don't do drugs. You're charming, so you could easily handle being interviewed or doing press." I inject a note of challenge into my voice. "So what are you really afraid of?"

Hunter is silent for a long time. He absently strokes my shoulder. When he finally speaks, his voice is rough. "If I tell you, do you promise not to make fun of me? Or judge me?"

I almost laugh until I realize he's serious. So I put on my best neutral tone. "I promise I won't make fun of you. And I'd never judge you, Hunter."

"Okay." His chest rises as he draws a breath. "I'm afraid I'll cheat," he confesses.

"Cheat? Like in the game?"

"No, the other kind of cheating." He exhales in a slow stream of air. "All those road games, all those hotel rooms and hotel bars, all those women throwing themselves at me. I know I don't have a sex addiction, but I've got my father's genes and they don't exactly have the greatest track record."

"Your father's a narcissist. You're not." I plant a reassuring kiss on his shoulder. "You're nothing like him, baby."

"He'd disagree with you on that. A few years ago he told me we're two of a kind."

My eyes narrow. "Why on earth would he say *that*?"

Hunter sighs sheepishly. "The summer before college, he caught me fucking a chick on our kitchen counter. Mom was visiting my grandparents that weekend, and Dad was supposed to be away on business, but he came home early." An edge hardens his tone. "You should've seen how proud he looked to find me buck-naked and going to town on a girl I wasn't even dating. I met her at a party the night before and she stayed over."

I try to imagine what my own father would do if he walked in on me having sex with someone in our kitchen. Commit a double homicide, obviously.

"He was genuinely *proud* to think his son was a depraved cad. But I guess that's not much of a surprise. I know Dad slept with at least three of his assistants—one I witnessed firsthand. And I just…I think about all the business trips he took over the years. I bet he had a woman in every city. I'm sure there were more affairs than Mom and I could even imagine."

"And you're worried you'll have a girlfriend or wife, and you'll be away a lot and cheat?"

"Pretty much."

"So you're punishing yourself for something you haven't even done."

His bare chest tenses. "That's not it."

"That's exactly it. You're preemptively punishing

yourself—depriving yourself of something you love, for fear you might do something you hate, some vague point down the line. That's not a healthy way to look at things."

"No. I mean, maybe? Maybe that's it, or maybe it isn't. All I know is that when I decided not to enter the draft after high school, I felt relieved."

"And yet every time I see you watching Garrett and Logan play, there's envy in your eyes."

Hunter's ragged breath tickles my head. His chest rises and falls again. "Let's put this on the shelf for now. It's hurting my brain. Tell me about your holidays."

"I already did—we texted every day," I remind him.

"I know, but I like your voice and I want to hear you talk."

I smile against his left pec, then offer a more detailed recap of my visit to Miami. I tell him about my new nephew, about my crazy aunts and my excitable cousins. Being a very Catholic community, Christmas is very much celebrated in Miami, and one of my family's favorite traditions is a visit to Santa's Enchanted Forest. I took my younger cousins there, and five-year-old Maria peed on one of the rides. While sitting in my lap. Fun times.

"Do you speak Spanish?" Hunter asks curiously. "I just realized I don't even know if you do."

"I understand it better than I speak it. Dad has a terrible ear for languages, so he only speaks English at home. Mom used to speak both to me because she didn't want me to lose the Spanish, but I kinda have," I say glumly. "Not entirely, though. I mean, I'd be fluent again in a week if I was around people who spoke it exclusively."

"I'd love to learn another language. You should teach me Spanish, and then we could practice together."

"Deal." I snuggle up closer to him. "Oh, and on the flight home, I tried bringing up the med school thing to my dad again. Mom is staying in Miami for another week, so it was just me and him. But he wasn't having it," I admit.

Hunter strokes my hair. "You still having doubts about that?"

"More than doubts." I inhale slowly. "I don't want to go."

It's the first time I've ever said that out loud.

"Then don't," Hunter says simply. "You shouldn't go to med school for your father—you should go for yourself. You need to walk your own path, and that means following your own dreams, not his. Your first priority should be pleasing yourself, not him."

A laugh tickles my throat. I try to hold it in, but it ripples out.

"What is it?"

"I just realized what a sad pair we are." I can't stop giggling. "Here I am sacrificing my aspirations to be like my father, and you're sacrificing your aspirations to *not* be like your father. That is fascinating."

"Jesus. You're *such* a psychologist. Is this what it's always going to be like? Lying in bed naked while you psychoanalyze us?"

I prop up on my elbow, biting my lip. "Does it actually bother you?"

"Nah." He flashes his dimpled smile, and I lean down and kiss one of those adorable dimples. "It's funny," he continues. "Most of the time, you analyze and rationalize and try to find solutions. And then other times, you're batshit crazy."

"I am not!"

"You have a violent streak, you maniac. You smash people's game consoles." He grins up at me. "Quite the dichotomy, Demi Davis."

"Both crazy and sane," I say somberly. "A rare condition, indeed."

"Anyway." He strokes his knuckles over my cheek. "You don't need to chase your father's approval—you already have it. I don't think he'll disown you if you choose grad school over med school."

"You don't know how he feels about PhDs, Hunter. For the rest of my life he'll be making wisecracks about how I'm not a real doctor." My buzzing phone captures my attention. "Shit, that's probably Josie ordering me to come downstairs and hang more decorations."

I stretch across his muscular chest to grab my phone from the nightstand. Hunter uses the opportunity to slide one palm between us to cup one of my boobs.

I shiver in pleasure, but my arousal dissolves when I see my father's name. Speak of the devil.

I click on his message, and my eyebrows soar. "Oh, this is interesting."

"What?" Hunter lazily caresses the swell of my breast.

"My father is inviting us to New Year's Day brunch tomorrow."

Hunter's hand freezes. "Us?"

"Yep." I sit up and grin at his panicky expression. "He wants to meet you."

32
DEMI

A FEW DAYS AFTER NEW YEAR'S, HUNTER AND I ARE BACK on campus walking toward the Psych building. It's the final lecture of the semester and we're supposed to be receiving our case studies back, but while I've got a spring to my step as we amble down the path, Hunter's long gait is stilted and his expression is sullen. He's been sulking non-stop since we had brunch with my father.

"God, could you try to smile?" I demand. "It's such a beautiful day."

"It's minus-fucking-twenty and your dad hates me. It's *not* a beautiful day."

I suppress a sigh. "He doesn't hate you. He liked you."

"If by liked, you mean loathed, then you're right."

"I see. Now he doesn't just hate you—he *loathes* you. Someone's been drinking the drama juice."

"And someone's refusing to face the truth," Hunter grumbles. "Your father did *not* like me."

I want to argue again, but it's getting harder to find a solid defense for my father's behavior.

I refuse to say it aloud, because I don't want to injure Hunter's pride any further, but brunch was…awful.

It did *not* go well.

I really wish Mom had been there to create a parental balance, but she's still in Florida, and it was me and Hunter versus my father from the get-go. After a whopping two questions about Hunter's background, Dad determined he was dealing with a spoiled rich boy from Greenwich, Connecticut. Which is absolutely not the case—Hunter is the most down-to-earth person I know, and his work ethic is stellar.

But my father is incredibly biased and impossible to please. He grew up poor and sacrificed so much to get to where he is now, so needless to say, anyone born with a silver spoon in their mouth already has one strike in my father's eyes.

And he wasn't even impressed by Hunter's athletic achievements. I thought for sure that would win him over. I not-so-subtly brought up how much work is required in order to excel in a sport, but I think by that point Dad was just *trying* to be difficult because he waved my comment off. Which is bullshit. He's a big football fan, and I've heard him say numerous times that football players possess an incredible work ethic.

Clearly, Dad is still on Team Nico. But I'm hoping he switches his loyalties, because I'm Team Hunter all the way.

"He'll warm up to you," I say, giving Hunter's hand a squeeze.

He slants his head. "Will he? Because that implies I'll be seeing him often."

I hesitate. We haven't formally declared ourselves as "dating," so I'm not entirely sure if he'll see my dad again. Also, until we define our relationship, I'm trying to avoid PDA, so I drop Hunter's hand as we reach the building, because Pax and TJ are waiting on the steps.

"Ah! New boots!" Pax shouts when he spots me. His envious gaze devours my footwear, which is indeed new—black leather boots with brown fur, to match the hood of my parka. "I *love*!" he announces.

"Thanks! I'd like to say I feel the same way about your hair, but…what the hell is going on there?"

Hunter snorts. "For real, Jax. I'm not into it."

I roll my eyes. He's well aware what Pax's real name is, but now it's just a running joke, and Pax plays along because he thinks Hunter is hot.

"When did you get that done?" I ask.

"And why?" TJ says, looking like he's trying not to laugh.

Sighing dramatically, Pax smooths a hand over the green streaks in his black hair. "This past weekend. And why? Because my little sister is in cosmetology school and her exams are coming up, so she was practicing her dye skills on me."

"I'm not going to lie," I inform him. "It looks terrible."

"Gee, thanks, bestie." He winks. "The guy I hooked up with last night didn't seem to mind."

"*Nice.*" Hunter holds his palm up for a high five.

Jax—dammit, now *I'm* doing it. *Pax* returns the high five, and then the four of us escape the January chill and enter the building. I notice TJ slide a curious look between me and Hunter, but he doesn't say anything.

We take our usual seats in the middle of the row, only this time Hunter usurps Pax's place beside me. Once again TJ's gaze takes note.

Anticipation ripples inside me when Professor Andrews arrives with her two TAs in tow. *Yes!* Either my eyes are projecting what they want to see, or the teaching assistants are carrying our graded assignments.

"Morning, ladies and gents. So... The previous times I taught this course, I used to return these at the end of the final lecture, with the simple goal of torturing everyone. I'm not certain what that reveals about my own psychological makeup—" Andrews grins at the class. "With that said, I'm in the mood to be nice today."

She's behaving atypically goofy, but perhaps that's because this is our last day. The TAs who ran our tutorials approach each aisle and begin calling out names. One by one, students get up to accept their assignments.

Although everyone worked together on the projects, each paper was handed in and graded separately. I practically dive out of my seat when my name is called. The moment the envelope that contains my submission is in my hand, I waste no time slicing it open. Beside me, Hunter does the same with his.

A cover page is stapled to the front of my submission, and I almost shriek out loud when I see my grade.

A-plus, baby.

Hell yeah.

Curious, I peer over at Hunter's sheet. "What'd you get?"

"B-plus." He looks pleased with that. I had proofed his research paper and thought it was excellent, but I probably would've gone more in-depth about certain things, so I think the grade is fair.

I flip through the pages of my case study to find that Andrews scribbled notes in the margins. The praise I find is ludicrously good for my ego. Things like:

Terrific insight!

Highly perceptive!

Provocative…

GREAT angle, she writes in the section where I discuss possible counseling tactics to try to help the narcissist reach the rare self-awareness. The slew of compliments has my ego swelling to monstrous proportions. This feels way more satisfying than the A-plus I got in Organic Chem. This one feels *right*.

Hunter leans closer to whisper in my ear. "You look so hot right now."

I wrinkle my forehead. "Really?"

"Oh yeah." His breath tickles my cheek. "It's that cocky look in your eyes. Never thought I'd get turned on by an academic, but *fuck*, I've got a semi, Semi."

I snicker softly. But I realize he's not kidding when he straightens up and I glimpse the hot lust swimming in his eyes.

I gulp through my suddenly parched throat, turning toward TJ as a distraction. "How'd you do?"

"An A," he replies, and Pax got a B, so all in all I'd say Abnormal Psych was a smashing success.

Since it's the last class, Andrews rewards us with a topic that I could probably spend a solid twenty-four hours listening to: serial killers. In fact, if you tally all the time I've spent watching crime shows, it probably adds up to a depressingly long portion of my life.

Andrews begins to discuss a case that's so macabre I'm on the edge of my seat. Ten minutes in, although she still hasn't named the killer, I grab Hunter's arms and hiss, "She's talking about Harold Howarth!"

"Who?"

"He was the subject of the episode *Brain Surgeons Who Kill*." I remember calling my dad immediately after watching that episode. I told him he's never, ever allowed to inject poison into a patient's frontal lobe, and he asked me if I was high.

As I resettle in my chair, I almost rest my hand on Hunter's knee, a habit I have when we're sitting together on his couch. This morning I forcibly have to stop myself. PDA isn't allowed until I know what this is. But my gaze keeps flitting toward him. I wish I could touch his leg. Or even better—slide my hand inside his pants and wrap it around his cock. I find myself wanting to touch this man all the time.

And I mean *all the time*. Sometimes I want him so badly I can't even wait for him to close the bedroom door before I'm mauling him. Today is one of those times, except we're not in a bedroom and my throbbing body is furious at this predicament.

By the time Andrews dismisses us, my core is one dull ache. I barely hear Andrews thanking us for being so attentive this semester, wishing us luck with our future. Any other day, I'd linger after class to express my own gratitude, but I think I'll need to settle for sending a lengthy email.

I'm so aroused, I'm practically leaping out of my own skin

as we exit the lecture hall. My impatient gaze darts around the wide corridor. We didn't drive, and there's no way I can last the long walk back to my house. So, as Pax and TJ walk on ahead of us, I grab Hunter's hand and drag him around the corner.

33
HUNTER

Demi shoves me through the nearest doorway. Luckily, it leads into an unlit room with tables and chairs arranged in a semicircle. The blinds are shut, but the room isn't pitch black. Just shadowy, with thin stripes of sunlight peeking in from the slats.

"What are you doing?" I ask in amusement.

She hurriedly shuts the door. "I was going crazy not being able to touch you in there. You have *no* idea how close I was to just taking off your pants and riding your dick, right there in front of everyone."

My groin clenches. Oh Jesus, that sounds hot. The two of us are all over each other, all the time. It's almost become an addiction. And I'm embarrassed to say it hasn't affected hockey whatsoever, which means my vow of celibacy was completely fucking pointless. If anything, I'm playing even *better* these days.

I've avoided talking about it with Demi, because I'm afraid she'll tease me, tell me I'd been acting out a scene from *Wizard of Oz* or some shit. Like, *you had the power to be a good captain and teammate all along, Hunter! It was your guilt, and your fear of being a selfish jackass like your father, that stopped you from seeing that.*

I can totally see Demi using a cheesy analogy like that.

But I guess it's a lesson I needed to learn. Last season's fuckery had scarred me. And I started this season wanting to put my team—and not my dick—first. I wanted to be a good captain. I wanted to prove to myself that I'm not a selfish narcissistic asshole whose needs are the only ones that matter. When our season went up in flames last year, it was a wake-up call for me. The first thing I thought after we lost that game was, *maybe we are two of a kind.* My father and I.

The first time he'd said that to me, I blanched inside. I felt dirty. Spooked by the notion that I could actually be anything like him. A dirt bag. An egomaniac.

But sex with Demi hasn't resulted in anything but me going to bed sated every night and killing it in practice every morning. Not to mention the playoffs—we're dominating the other teams.

Demi loops her arms around my neck and yanks my head down for a kiss. Christ. I love kissing her. I love fucking her. I love doing everything with and to her.

We both know this thing between us is more than a rebound. More than sex. But I don't know what that *more* is. And I'm enjoying it too much to rock the boat by asking.

I laugh when she pushes me against the door. She clicks the lock into place, and her hand is at my belt before I can blink. She undoes my jeans and tugs them and my boxers just low enough that she can reach inside and pull out my hot, heavy cock.

"Oh my God, I wanted this so badly the past two hours," Demi mumbles in anguish. "I want it all the time."

"Take it," I say huskily.

She sinks to her knees and my body tightens in anticipation. When her mouth engulfs my dick in one wet glide, I hiss in pleasure. So does she, and her brown eyes shine happily as she releases me to say, "I *love* having this in my mouth."

"You and your oral fixation," I mock, all the while trying to nudge my cockhead through her sexy lips again.

She laughs at my pathetic attempts. "So when I need my candy, it's, what did you call it the other day? A *serious problem*. But when I'm craving your dick, my oral fixation is just fine and dandy?"

I grin. "Now you're gettin' it."

Demi sticks out her tongue, and I take full advantage of that. Within seconds, I'm in her hot mouth again.

"Oh yeah." I hold the back of her head with both hands, guiding her along my shaft.

There's a murmur of voices out in the hall. I don't care. Demi makes me forget that other people inhabit the world with us. We're the only ones in this room, in this building, on this planet. When I'm inside her, nobody exists but us. When she's petting and rubbing and sucking on my dick, nobody exists but her.

She swallows me up, her eager tongue curling around the head of my dick. She gets it nice and wet, while her fist moves up and down the length of me. Squeezing the tip on each upstroke, sucking me to the root on the way down.

I rock my hips, restless, aroused, my balls beginning to tingle. When she pulled me in here, I assumed I'd fuck her against a wall. But this blowjob is so criminally good, I won't last long enough to get inside her.

"Baby," I groan, trying to still her.

She peers up at me with big eyes. Her lips are wrapped tight around my cockhead. It's the sexiest thing I've ever seen, and I trace that naughty O with my thumb, rubbing the corner of her mouth.

"I'm close," I warn. "If you came in here wanting to fuck, you'd better stop that."

Her wet mouth slides off me, and my cock emerges with a *pop*. "No, I want to make you come right now. I want to hear you moan my name when you shoot in my mouth."

Jesus. This girl will be the death of me.

She resumes her wicked task, and in less than thirty seconds I'm giving the woman what she wants.

"Demi," I groan when my climax breaks the surface. Her lips remain firmly around me as she swallows everything I have to give. I'm dead. She's killed me. She's perfect.

Demi plants soft kisses on my still-hard shaft as I float down from the high. Smiling, she tucks me into my cargo pants. Primly wipes her mouth with the back of her hand as she rises to her feet. She zips me up and stands on her tiptoes to brush her lips over mine.

I can't help but deepen the kiss, and when I taste myself on her tongue I'm damn near raring to go again. I shiver.

"You okay?" she teases.

"Peachy," I croak.

She snickers, then gives me a long appraisal before unlocking the door. We reenter the hall, and the bright fluorescent lighting blinds me for a moment.

"Are you coming over tonight?" she asks as we fall into step with each other.

"I can't. I'm having drinks with Hollis. But I can come over now and hang out with you till I need to meet him?"

"Booooo."

"Don't boo me."

"Why not? You boo me all the time."

"Because I'm a child, Semi. You're far too mature for that nonsense. Have some respect for yourself."

She bursts out laughing and I smile. I like making her laugh.

"I'd bail," I say, "but Hollis stressed that it was important."

Demi stops walking. "I'm sorry. Mike Hollis implied that something was *important*?"

"Implied? More like explicitly stated. He pulled me aside this morning and asked if we could talk tonight."

"Why was he even home? It's Monday."

A frown touches my lips. "He called in sick to work, but he didn't look sick to me."

"I hope everything's okay with him."

"I'm sure it is. Hollis is indestructible. I bet he just wants to talk about something random, like what to get Rupi for her birthday."

"Is it coming up?"

"Oh, you're going to love this. The girl was born on… wait for it…February fourteenth."

Demi gasps. "Valentine's Day! Oh my God. Poor Mike. He's going to have to go all out. Maybe even buy her a pony."

I snort.

When we enter the lobby, I notice TJ standing a few feet

away chatting with one of the TAs. A frown twists his mouth when he spots us. It seems like an extreme response for no reason, until I realize that his gaze is on my crotch.

I look down and swallow a curse. Demi must not have zipped me up all the way, because my fly slid right back down. I discreetly do it up, but that does nothing to erase the distrustful look on TJ's face.

———

Later that night I slide into the booth across from Hollis, signaling the waitress as I settle in. Hollis didn't order yet, despite the fact that he's already been here for ten minutes. I was late driving over because there was four feet of ice on my windshield when I left Demi's house. Nearly froze my balls off scraping it all away.

"Sorry, I was scraping ice," I grumble.

"Fuckin' ice. It should be banned."

"I'll be sure to let the climate know you feel that way, Michael."

I smile in gratitude when the waitress returns with my lager. Hollis ordered a can of Boom Sauce, which I think he likes just because of the name. We tap our drinks in cheers.

"So what's going on?" I ask my buddy. "Why did you drag me to Malone's in the dead of butt-fuck winter when we live in the same house and could easily have talked there?"

Hollis plays with the rim of his beer can. "Needed to get out." He shrugs. "How's it going with you? You still seeing Demi? Did Coach approve the pig yet?"

He's stalling, but I play along for the time being. Hollis is so dramatic that pushing him could potentially result in him storming out in a huff, and I'd really like to finish my beer.

"I'm fine. Did well in all my courses last semester. Still seeing Demi. And no, Coach hasn't green-lit the pig yet." I mull it over for a moment. "But I just realized—once he does, that means Pablo has to go." Shit. I don't know if I'm ready to say goodbye yet.

"Dude, it's about time. Do you know how much that little dude stinks? Eggs aren't meant to be out in the wild."

I chuckle. "I don't even notice the smell anymore, to be honest."

"We should get a pet for the house," Hollis says.

"Ha. Sure. Rupi would never let you have a pet. It'd mean less attention for her."

"True. It's hard enough only giving her attention on the weekends." Hollis rubs his eyes, and I notice that he looks deeply exhausted. I knew the two-hour commute to New Hampshire was taking its toll on him, but it appears it's gotten even worse. His eyes are actually puffy, as if he hasn't slept properly in years.

"You heading back to your folks' place tomorrow or calling in sick again?" I ask carefully.

"I'm heading back." He takes a quick sip. "Honestly, I don't want to sell insurance anymore, Davenport. I hate it up there. I hate living at home again, and I hate working with my dad. That dude's crazy."

"Mmm-hmmm, *he's* crazy."

"He is! And he tells the stupidest jokes all day long."

I stare at Hollis. "I truly cannot conceive of the kind of torture you must be going through."

"Right?"

Whoosh. Right over his head. "Why don't you try to find work in Hastings?" I suggest.

"I have, but nobody is hiring. Or at least hiring for positions I'd actually *want*. There's a job opening for a graveyard-shift clerk at the gas station, but what's the point of that? I'd just sleep all day and work all night, and the pay is shit."

"If I hear of anything, I'll let you know."

"Thanks."

"And I guess for now you just keep your full-time job of selling insurance during the week and your full-time job of Rupi on the weekends."

"Dude, she really is a full-time job." Yet he's grinning broadly as he says it.

"I don't understand your relationship at all."

"Of course you don't. It's transcendent."

"What does that even mean?"

"Exactly," he says smugly. But it isn't long before his blue eyes grow serious again. It's not an expression you often see on Mike Hollis's face. "She's only a sophomore, bro."

"Rupi? So?"

"So she won't graduate for two and a half more years. That means two and a half more years of me making this God-awful commute so I can sell insurance with my crazy father."

I put down my beer. "Are you considering...breaking up with her?"

He's utterly aghast. "What! What the fuck is wrong with you? Of course not. Did you not listen to the part where I said we're *transcendent*?"

"Right, sorry, I forgot." I study him again. "So what exactly are we talking about here? You hate your job. You hate living at home again. You hate commuting. You hate that Rupi has a couple more years of school left. But you love Rupi."

"Yes to all that."

I purse my lips. "Okay, answer me this. If none of those things you listed as hating were in the equation, what would you be doing?"

"I'm not following."

"Pretend you don't have to worry about jobs and commutes and all that crap—what would you want to be doing?"

"I would—" He stops. "Nothing. It's stupid."

"No, tell me," I order. "Let's figure this out, man."

Hollis gulps down some more Boom Sauce. "I'd travel," he finally confesses. "Like, dude, do you realize how many other countries there are in the world? Dozens!"

"Hundreds," I correct.

"Don't be crazy now. There's only seven continents, why would there be hundreds of countries? Your math is erroneous. But yeah, that's what I'd do. I'd travel all over the motherfucking world and meet new people and experience new cultures and eat weird food and—*oh*, Rupi and I could bang on trains and airplanes and camels if we go somewhere with camels—"

"Wait, Rupi's on this trip, too?"

He nods fervently. "Where else would she be?"

I nod back, but slow and thoughtful. "You want my advice? You should talk to Rupi about all this. Be honest about how exhausted you are, and tell her you'd love to go on a trip with her. Maybe you can plan something for the summer? It'd give you something to look forward to while you make that long commute to New Hampshire…" I trail off enticingly.

Hollis narrows his eyes at me.

"What?" I say.

"Have you always been this smart or have I just always been this stupid?"

I grin at him. "I choose not to answer that question."

34
DEMI

By the end of January, Hunter and I still haven't defined our relationship. We're just sort of floating along, having sex on a consistent basis, cuddling, texting, giving each other advice. I attend his hockey games even though I still don't care about hockey. He watches crime documentaries even though he finds them disturbing.

As Brenna likes to say, we're in a situationship. But according to Pippa, we're a married couple who won't even call themselves boyfriend and girlfriend.

Pippa's right. He's my boyfriend, and I'm his girlfriend. It's funny—for two people who communicate extremely well, neither of us has raised the subject. I know why *I* haven't, but I wonder what's holding Hunter back.

Me, I'm scared to make that commitment. What if things change the moment I call him my boyfriend? What if suddenly he decides I'm tying him down or cramping his style, and starts looking elsewhere? It's an irrational fear, and the bitter memory of Nico's cheating isn't helping matters.

The ambiguity of our relationship is a constant source of

anxiety for me. Human beings have a compulsion to define things. Definitions provide us with comfort. But I'm torn about what I want more—to label us, or to avoid possible rejection. For now, I simply don't bring it up, and neither does Hunter.

His team is in the midst of playoffs and he's been working hard this past week. Practices are grueling, and he's covered in bruises every time I see him. Tonight he was feeling particularly sore, so I decided to go out with my friends and give his body some time to recover. It's impossible for me to see Hunter without climbing all over that hard body and banging his brains out.

Hunter, however, is grumpy about being alone tonight. He keeps texting pictures of various parts of his body, some bruised and some not, begging me to come over and kiss them. Eventually, I interrupt Pippa midsentence and say, "Hold that thought. Let me just tell him to eff off."

ME: I'm with my friends, Monk. The world doesn't revolve around you.

HIM: Sure it does.

ME: I see. Are you channeling your father?

HIM: OMG you're right. I'm sorry. The world is not my oyster. I'm just one pearl floating in a sea of pearls.

ME: That analogy is nonsensical. Now go away. I'm with my friends.

HIM: Fine!

I put the phone down. "Sorry, that needed to be done," I tell my friends.

Pippa, TJ and I are in a cramped booth at one of the campus bars. Corinne is on her way to meet us, and this will be my third hangout with her since everything exploded back in November.

The first time was beyond awkward. We had a movie night at Pippa's and I couldn't bring myself to utter a single word to Corinne. Every time I looked at her I pictured her naked with my ex-boyfriend. The second time went better, because there was drinking involved. But then I had one too many tequila shots, which tipped me into Scorned Woman territory and I may have made a snide comment or two. I'm vowing not to do that tonight.

When my phone lights up again, I flip it over facedown. "This guy," I grumble.

"Hockey boy?" Pippa says with a laugh.

"Yes. He's all bruised up and sore, so he's taking it easy at home and he's bored. When he's bored, he gets annoying."

"Don't they all?"

"Hey, I don't annoy anyone when I'm bored," TJ protests. He casually swirls his straw in the strawberry daiquiri we forced him to order.

Originally this was supposed to be girls only, but TJ sounded glum when he realized he couldn't come, so I told him he could join us as long as he honored the rules of Girls' Night. AKA ordering lots of brightly colored drinks.

"What's going on with you guys, anyway?" he asks curiously. "It seems like it's evolved from just hanging out…"

"Um yeah," Pippa answers for me. "They're frickin' married."

TJ looks stunned. "For real?"

A snort slips out. "No, not for real. But we do spend a lot of time together." I pick up my obnoxiously pink drink with its gaudy purple umbrella. "I guess that means we're dating. I'm not entirely sure, though. We haven't even had the exclusivity talk."

"You haven't?" Pippa raises a brow. "It's been months, D. What if he's having sex with other women?"

"He's not."

"Of course he is," TJ says, rolling his eyes.

I scowl at them both.

Pippa objects. "Hey, don't look at *me* like that. I didn't say he was. That's all this one." She pokes TJ in the arm.

He raises both hands as if surrendering to enemy soldiers. "Hey, don't shoot the messenger. Of course he's sleeping with other people. I'm telling you this as a college dude who lives in the dorms surrounded by other college dudes. If you don't make it clear to a guy that you want to be exclusive, I guarantee he's seeing more than one woman."

"I mean…TJ has a point," Pippa says slowly.

"And he was out with all those girls, like, a week ago," TJ goes on. "He's definitely hooking up with other people."

A chill runs up my spine. "What girls? And how do you know what he was doing?"

"I saw something on Instagram."

"You saw something on Instagram," I echo uncertainly.

TJ nods. "I follow a shit ton of Briar people. Someone posted a picture of the hockey team at a party, not sure where it took place. Davenport was in the picture kissing some chick."

Bullshit, I want to retort.

But doubt creeps into me like strands of ivy and tightens around my throat. Hunter did go to an after party last week that I didn't attend, but that doesn't mean anything. Moreover, we're not even an official couple.

I bite the inside of my cheek. Hard. The pain triggered by my teeth doesn't even compare to the shooting pain in my heart. My stomach lurches. With shaky fingers, I flip over my phone. The last text from Hunter was a kissy face.

I ignore it. Suddenly wondering how many other kissy faces he's sending and to whom.

"I took a screenshot for you," TJ admits, "but I deleted it."

"What! *Why*?" Pippa thunders.

Misery clouds his eyes as he looks at me. "Because I didn't want you to think I was trying to cause trouble. I remember how much it annoyed you the last time we talked about Hunter behind his back."

"Thomas Joseph," Pippa snaps. "Get your phone out and recover the picture from the deleted folder. I bet it's probably still in there."

My heartbeat is erratic as TJ scrolls through his photo roll. I'm almost hoping he doesn't find the picture. I don't want it to exist. I want it to be a figment of TJ's imagination.

"Here it is!" he says, and my stomach plummets like a shot-down missile.

TJ slides the phone toward me. Pippa practically drapes herself over the sticky tabletop to get a good look.

The photo features half a dozen guys and a few girls. I recognize several faces: Matt Anderson, that Jesse guy, and I think that's Mike Hollis in the corner but it's hard to tell. Matt has his arm around a smiling redhead, and Jesse is posing next to a girl I think might be his girlfriend Katie. But I don't see Hunter—

Oh. There he is.

TJ's right. Hunter *is* in the photo.

And he is absolutely kissing someone else.

35
DEMI

My heart jumps to my throat in horror, tightening my windpipe and making it difficult to breathe. In the photo, the blonde's mouth is fused to Hunter's in a frozen kiss captured for all of eternity. Permanently documented for me, Demi Davis, to see.

Jealousy and anger form a pretzel in the pit of my stomach. I'm allowed to feel the former, but not the latter.

"D?" Pippa says.

I paste on a careless expression. "We never had the are-we-exclusive talk."

She sees right through me. "Oh, babe. We don't know when this was taken," she points out.

TJ speaks up. "It was posted like six days ago."

"That doesn't mean it was *taken* six days ago," argues Pippa.

"Why would someone post an old picture?"

"Are you serious? People do it all the time! Throwback Thursday? Flashback Friday? Way-back Wednesday?"

"The caption doesn't use any of those hashtags," TJ counters.

"Maybe they forgot. I don't know."

"You don't know what?" a third voice joins in.

I glance up at Corinne's arrival. She's wearing an oversized sweater and skinny jeans, her curly hair pulled back with a yellow scrunchie. She climbs into the booth beside me, and now it feels even more cramped.

"We're just arguing about this picture of the guy Demi is dating," Pippa explains.

"Hockey boy?" Corrine asks.

"Yeah." That awful cold sensation keeps fluttering through my body.

She picks up the phone. "Which one is he?"

I point at Hunter and the blonde. They're still kissing in the picture.

Dammit. I was kind of hoping I'd look at it again and they'd be standing on opposite sides of the frame.

Corinne studies the image. "This is the guy you're seeing?"

"Yep."

"Oh. I'm sorry." She seems genuinely upset on my behalf. Or maybe it's just pity. *Poor Demi, the girl who keeps getting shafted for other chicks.*

Pippa grabs the phone again and spends an inordinate amount of time examining the screen. "No, this is *definitely* an old picture," she finally announces. "I recognize this girl." She taps the face of the redhead beside Matt Anderson. "That's Jenny."

"Who's Jenny?" asks Corinne.

"She was in one of my acting classes freshman year." Pippa appears both relieved and triumphant. "It's an old picture, D. I promise."

"How can you be sure?" I'm almost embarrassed by the balloon of hope rising in my chest.

"Because she doesn't go here anymore. She transferred to the drama program at UCLA more than a year ago."

"Seriously?"

"How do you know it's her?" TJ asks. "It's not the clearest shot. Or maybe she's in town visiting friends, you don't know."

"Hold on. Let me find her Insta account so we can compare pics. Amuse yourselves for a minute, girls and boy." She bends over her phone, a woman on a mission.

I try to focus on Corinne as she chats about her new classes this semester, but when Pippa gives a shout of satisfaction, my focus ricochets back to her in an instant.

"See!" She lays down her phone, side by side with TJ's. "That's Jenny."

I compare the pictures. It's the same girl.

"And she's not visiting," Pippa adds. "According to her Insta, she's been in Hawaii with her family for the past few weeks."

Relief courses through me, so overpowering that I feel faint. And sick. And afraid.

Not defining a relationship is a terrible place to be in. But what's even more terrible is the current state of my mind and heart. I went from zero to infidelity in a nanosecond. Instantly succumbed to suspicion and assumed Hunter had made out with someone else at a party.

I force myself to drink my entire daiquiri. To listen to Pippa and Corinne, to express interest when TJ talks about how he's visiting his brother in England this summer. But I can't concentrate. I'm too riled up from that false alarm. I feel stupid and uncertain.

I need to talk to Hunter.

"Hey, I'm going to take off," I say when Pippa suggests ordering another round. "My head's not in this."

TJ looks disappointed. "It's only nine-thirty."

"I know. I'm sorry. But I'm emotionally exhausted."

"It's cool," Pippa says, waving a hand. "I'll see you tomorrow anyway. Dinner with Darius, remember?"

"Right." I say my goodbyes, then zip up my parka and exit the bar.

Greek Row is a three-minute walk from here, but I'm not headed home. I order an Uber, and fifteen minutes later I'm in Hastings, ringing Hunter's doorbell.

Summer lets me in. "Hey. I didn't know you were coming over." She greets me with a dazzling smile, because that's the default mode for her face. Dazzling.

"Last-minute thing," I answer vaguely.

Beyond her shoulder, I spot her boyfriend Fitz walking past the kitchen doorway in gray sweatpants and no shirt. He backs up when he catches sight of me, and lifts one tattooed arm in a quick wave. "Hey Demi. There's leftover pizza if you want."

"No thanks. I'm good. I'm just going to go up and see Hunter." My heart beats faster as I climb the stairs and approach his bedroom door.

When I knock, he responds with a loud growl. "Go away, Rupi. I don't want to watch *Riverdale*. It's fucking stupid."

"It's me," I answer with a laugh.

"Semi? Why did you even knock? Get your cute butt in here."

I enter the room to find him sprawled on his bed. A

hockey game flashes on the TV, but I can't tell who's playing. Hunter's head is propped up on a pillow, his dark hair rumpled, and stubble shadowing his jaw.

Those dimples appear as he smiles at me. "I thought you didn't want to come over."

"I wasn't going to, but then—"

"—but then you realized you wanted to get all up in my dick biz. Wise decision."

I crack a smile. "No. I just…" I trail off.

I suddenly feel ridiculous for showing up like this. What am I supposed to say? *I was out with friends and saw a picture of you kissing some girl and I thought it was recent and then I felt sick but it turned out to be old and yet I couldn't stop freaking out so I raced over here for no good reason.*

"What's going on?" he asks, his forehead creasing. "What's wrong?"

To my utter horror, hot tears fill my eyes.

"Demi." He sits up. "What's going on?"

"Nothing. Just…ah, I'm an idiot."

"No you're not. But I'll bite—why do you think you're an idiot?"

I exhale in a rush, and then the entire story spills out. Hunter listens without a single interjection, visibly bewildered.

"I'm sorry," I blabber on. "I'm not saying you did anything wrong, because you didn't—it was an old picture. But when I thought it *wasn't* old, my brain immediately jumped to you cheating on me. That's where my idiocy comes in, because how could you cheat on me if we're not even officially together?"

"Sure we are."

I falter. "We are?"

"Of course. Just because we haven't labeled this doesn't mean we're not together. When anyone asks, I refer to you as my girlfriend."

"You do?" I angrily swipe at my wet eyes. "Why the fuck don't you refer to me as your girlfriend when *I'm* there?"

He snorts with laughter. "I don't know, why don't you ever call me your man?"

"Because I didn't want to rush into things." I release a heavy sigh, trying to articulate the emotions swirling inside me. "I'm so embarrassed," I finally admit. "I like to think of myself as level-headed and mature, and yet I immediately jumped to conclusions and assumed you were sleeping around. And it made me realize that Nico really messed with my head. I thought I was over it, but apparently I'm not. Apparently now any time anything even the slightest bit sketchy happens, I'm going to assume the person I'm with is sleeping with someone else."

I finish with an anguished groan.

"C'mere," he says gruffly. He moves toward the foot of the bed where I'm lurking and pulls me into his lap.

I rest my chin on his shoulder, inhaling a weak breath.

"You didn't jump to conclusions, Demi. You saw a picture of me kissing another woman. Yes, it was taken last year, but you didn't know that at first. Believe me, if I saw a picture of you kissing another man, I'd lose my shit."

"You would?"

"Yes. Look, I know we kind of did this backwards. We didn't have any of those big relationship talks, or set any ground rules, but…" Hunter captures my chin with his hands and lifts my head so we're eye to eye. "I promise you, I'm not seeing anybody else. I'm not sleeping with anybody else. I'm with you, and I'm all in." His voice cracks. "I love you."

36
HUNTER

No one has a harder job than the man who comes after the cheater.

To be honest, I'm surprised Demi didn't experience a breakdown like this sooner. Yes, she had her violent breakdown, her fit of rage when she hurled Nico's stuff out the window and clocked him in the face. But I don't think she ever fully dealt with the emotional implications of what Nico did.

I know all about the aftermath of infidelity. I remember how my mom acted following the revelation of another one of Dad's affairs. She'd be jittery and suspicious for weeks and months afterward. Whenever he bent over his phone, her shoulders would stiffen. *Who is he texting?* she'd wonder. Whenever he had to go to the office, anxiety would flood her eyes. *Who is he going to fuck on his desk today?*

I used to have a lot of sympathy for her, but over the years it faded away. People are in control of their own lives and their own decisions. They're not powerless victims to some cruel overlord who keeps them trapped in a misery loop.

Mom made the decision to stay with him. I can't sympathize anymore, not when there are so many other solutions available to her. She doesn't have to be miserable, afraid, distrustful. She doesn't have to be a pushover. She chooses to be.

But Demi, unlike my mother, doesn't want to be stuck in this situation. She came directly to me to seek reassurance, and I'm going to give it to her.

"You love me," she echoes.

My pulse speeds up as I study her expression. It's impossible to decipher. I don't know how she feels about what I'd just said. Hell, I don't know how *I* feel about it.

I've only said those words to one other person, a high school girlfriend. And if I'm being honest, she said them first and I felt awkward not returning the sentiment. Teenage boys are stupid cowards sometimes. I wasn't actually in love with her, the girl from high school.

But *this* girl, the gorgeous woman in my lap—I'm definitely in love with her. I love everything about her. Her intelligence, her sassiness, her craziness. She has the most dynamic personality. There are so many different facets to Demi Davis, and the more I learn about her, the more I love her.

So yes, I'm going to take on this challenging task and face the brunt of the damage that Nico caused. I'm going to be patient and help Demi regain her trust in my foolish sex, which has been given a bad rap thanks to men like Nico and my father. I'm going to stick by her and shower her with assurances that I love her, until she realizes she doesn't ever need to worry about what I'm doing or who I'm doing it with—because she's the only one who matters to me.

A strange, unexpected sense of empowerment rushes through me. And I realize something. The same way my mother is in control of her own happiness, I'm in control of my own impulses. I'm not enslaved by my genetics, and I'm *not* my father.

"Fuck," I marvel.

"What?" She still looks a bit dazed by my admission that I love her.

I gape at her. "I would never cheat on you."

She snorts softly. "Don't sound so surprised."

"But I am. I'm thinking about the conversation we had a while ago, about my hockey career. About how I don't want to be like my dad, how I'm worried about being on the road, lonely and horny and giving in to temptation. But I can't even imagine being tempted by anyone else. Maybe that's damn naïve of me, but ten chicks could walk in here right now, buck naked, and I'd still only have eyes for you. Even with your face all puffy like that."

"Who are you calling *puffy*?" she objects.

"You. You're a terrible crier, Semi. You don't look good crying."

She punches me in the shoulder. "You're supposed to be acting romantic right now."

"I just told you I loved you! Trust me, I'm fucking romantic."

"True." She licks her lower lip. Then bites it. "I don't know if I'm ready to say it back," she confesses, and I chuckle because she looks so cute nervously nibbling on her lip like that.

"I didn't say it so you would say it back. I said it because I felt it. I'm in love with you. And I don't want to kiss anybody but you." I bring my lips to hers, and she wraps her arms around my neck and kisses me back.

We fall onto the mattress, kissing eagerly, and we're breathless by the time we come up for air. Now I'm propped up on my elbows, though, which puts strain on my sore body, sending a jolt of pain to my ribcage.

"I can't stay in this position," I groan. "My side is throbbing. I'm sorry, baby."

"Don't ever be sorry. About anything."

I grin. "About anything?"

"No, wait, I take that back. I'm sure you're going to be sorry for tons of things that deserve your sorryness, but this is not one of them. Lie back. Let me make you feel better."

"I'm supposed to be making *you* feel better."

"Then why have you been texting me pictures of your boo-boos all night?"

"Just to annoy you when you were out with your friends."

"Jackass. But, what, does that mean you're going to stop me if I start kissing all the boo-boos?" She lifts the hem of my shirt and plants a teasing kiss on my hip.

It sends a hot tremor up my spine. "Only a chump turns down free kisses."

"That's what I thought." Very methodically, she removes my shirt. She winces when she spots the bruises coloring my ribs. "Aw, those do look bad. Maybe I shouldn't be doing this." She runs a tentative palm over my abs, torturously close to my waistband.

"You should *always* be doing this," I disagree.

"Are you sure your body can handle it? Because I…really need this." Sheepish, she casts her eyes downward.

"We both do," I assure her.

Demi takes off her sweater and hops up to unbutton her jeans. She leaves me on the bed only to get a condom, and then she's back, tugging on the waistband of my sweatpants. I'm commando underneath and she moans happily. She grips my dick and gives it a slow stroke.

I'm hard, primed, ready to go. As she rolls the condom on, I reach between her legs and find her equally ready. Her wet pussy glides beneath my palm, and when I cup her, a dizzying rush of pleasure spirals through me. I can't get enough of this girl. She turns me on something fierce.

"Come here and fuck me already," I mumble.

Laughing at my impatience, she gingerly climbs onto my lap. She grips the base of me and guides my cockhead to where we both want it most.

"Fuck," I wheeze when she's fully seated. "Your pussy feels so good." Then she starts to move, and it feels even better.

She rides me, taking care not to jostle me. "Is this okay?" she murmurs.

As the pleasure rises, black dots flash in my vision. "More than okay."

Her hips roll seductively. My breathing quickens. I cup her ass, then skate my palms up her delicate spine, reaching around to squeeze her tits. I love touching her. Love the breathy sounds she makes as her body strains against mine, seeking her own pleasure.

I thrust my fingers through her dark hair and urge her head down. "Kiss me," I rasp.

And she does, whimpering when our tongues touch. We stay in that position forever, her mouth exploring mine, her body draped over me, slowly fucking me into oblivion. And when I come, white-hot pleasure engulfing my body, I know without a doubt that I truly am in love with this girl.

37
DEMI

TJ: You and hockey guy straighten everything out?

THE MESSAGE POPS UP WHEN I'M ON A BUS HEADED FOR Boston. I would've preferred taking the train, but none of the departure and arrival times lined up with my schedule for today. I wanted to visit Boston all week, but my dad's been in surgery nearly every day. Now it's Friday and he's available, but Hunter's team is playing tonight, so I'm squeezing in a quick trip to the city and then racing back to Hastings.

I can't miss this game. Apparently it's a crucial game in the playoffs. If they win, they go to the semi-finals? I think? I'm not entirely sure how it goes, but I know Hunter would appreciate it if I came to cheer him on.

I'm at the front of the bus, curled up in a window seat. Luckily, there's nobody with ferret pics sitting beside me. No seatmate at all, in fact, so my purse gets its own seat.

ME: Yep, it's all good. We talked at the beginning of the week.

HIM: Oh. You didn't mention it.

ME: You didn't ask :)

HIM: I'm sorry that pic upset you. Wish I never showed it to you.

ME: No, I'm glad I saw it. It was actually the catalyst we needed to have THE TALK. Anyway, how are you doing? Is your Lit prof still being an ass?

HIM: Sort of, but it's nbd. I'm more interested in your TALK. How'd that go?

ME: Well, we're officially together now, so I'm gonna say it went pretty well. Guess who has a boyfriend again lol I'm on my way to Boston right now to tell my parents.

HIM: Seriously? You're going all the way to Boston to tell your family you're dating some guy?

ME: Yep.

A wry smile tickles my lips. It's true, a phone call would have sufficed. A text, even. But my parents are a huge part of my life. It's always been just the three of us, and in my family we talk things out in person. Our little unit took a hit after Nico and I broke up, but Dad isn't pushing me to get back with Nico anymore. Granted, now he's regularly dropping hints about how I should stop seeing Hunter.

I honestly don't know what his problem with Hunter is, other than Hunter's wealthy background, which is a non-issue. Dad is just being extra protective, and I'd like to get to the heart of that.

And because I'm feeling so emboldened, I'm also going to tell him I'm not applying for med school.

Which means I'll either be at Hunter's game tonight, or I'll be dead.

> **TJ**: Well, good luck with that. Doesn't your dad hate him?
> **ME**: Don't know if he hates him, per se. But he does disapprove.
> **HIM**: Same thing.
> **ME**: No it's not. But it doesn't matter. Hunter is my bf, and Dad will just have to deal. Anyway, gotta go! Just got to the station xo

I tuck my phone away and slip on my parka in preparation of leaving the warmth of the bus. The air is frigid as I walk through the bus station toward the taxi and ride share lines outside. There's a taxi right there and it's too cold to wait for an Uber, so I hop into the back of the cab and provide my address.

Mom told me that Dad had pulled an all-nighter at the hospital and only got home at ten-thirty this morning. That means I'll most likely be dealing with Grumpy Papa today. It's not ideal, but I can't schedule my life around my dad's various moods.

When the taxi reaches my brownstone, I take a deep breath before getting out of the car. I need to gather every ounce of courage I possess, because my father won't be happy to hear what I have to say today. But Hunter was right—Dad's not going to disown me. I know in my heart he won't. He might huff and puff, but he's not blowing any houses down.

I just need to stick to my guns, and not let him bulldoze me, especially about medical school. It's time for me to stop being Daddy's Little Girl and be my own woman.

As usual, numerous aromas greet my nostrils when I stride into the house. "Mom?" I call.

"In here." She's in the kitchen, where else?

I pop through the doorway and almost collapse in a puddle of ravenous drool. She's pan-frying chicken with peppers and peas, and the spicy smell draws me toward the stove.

"Oh my God, Mom. Please move into the Theta house with me," I plead. "You could cook for us every single day. Breakfasts, lunches, dinners." I shiver in pure joy. "I'd be living the dream."

Mom snorts.

I wrap my arms around her from behind, giving her a kiss on the cheek. Then I try to steal a piece of chicken and she smacks my hand with her spatula.

"Go away! Shoo!" She flaps her arm around like she's trying to get rid of a pesky fly.

"You're mean," I gripe.

She rolls her eyes and continues cooking.

Because the food looks and smells so delicious, I make an executive decision to wait until after dinner to start dropping truth bombs. Dad looks exhausted when he joins us in the dining room. His dark eyes are lined with fatigue, and he keeps rubbing them throughout dinner.

"Tough surgery?" I sympathize.

"Surgeries, plural. I performed back-to-back craniotomies—one biopsy and one tumor removal. And just when I thought I was done, a third patient was airlifted in with a subdural hematoma." He goes on about each case in depth, which includes a shit ton of technical details. I don't understand half of what he's saying, but he seems content to just chat with me about it.

"I can't imagine being in an operating room for so long," I confess. "I'd probably fall asleep on the patient."

"It requires great discipline." He chuckles. "It's funny— this was indeed a long night, but I'm nowhere near as wiped as when I was completing my residency or going through medical school."

It's the perfect opening.

Take it, Demi, take it!

But I'm a wimp. So I don't.

Instead, I bring up the other reason I'm home. Better to start small, right? Revealing that I have a new boyfriend isn't as extreme as telling them I'm switching career paths.

I clear my throat. "I wanted to talk to you guys about something."

Mom scrapes back her chair and starts to rise. "Let me put everything away first."

"No, Mom. Come on, sit down. We can do that after."

"After?" She sounds horrified. Because in our house, you eat a big meal and then you clean it all up. But then she sees my grave expression and sinks back down, concern flickering in her honey-brown eyes. "Is everything all right?"

"Everything is more than all right," I confess.

At the head of the table, Dad's expression clouds over. Dammit. I think he knows what I'm about to say.

"I wanted to let you know…" I blow out a hasty breath. "I'm officially dating Hunter."

Silence.

"Um. This is good news…?" I prompt, looking from one parent to the other.

Mom is the first to speak. "Okay. Marcus. What are your thoughts on this?"

"You already know my thoughts. I don't think he's good for her."

She nods deliberately before turning back to me.

"And that's it?" I exclaim in disbelief. "He says that and you just nod along like a little puppet?"

Mom frowns. "Demi."

"It's true. You haven't even met Hunter!"

"If your father says he's not good for you, then I agree with him."

"You. Haven't. Even. Met. Him." I spit out each word through clenched teeth. Then I suck in several breaths, trying to calm myself. "Seriously, Mom. I'm so disappointed in you right now."

Indignation darkens my mother's face. She opens her mouth and I know the Latina temper is about to be unleashed. But mine beats her to it.

"You're constantly letting Dad dictate how you think! You yell and scream and throw temper tantrums when it's about your stuff. *Your* kitchen, *your* wardrobe, *your* interests. But when it comes to important things, he has the run of the house—and the run of your brain, apparently."

"Demi," my father rumbles.

"It's true," I insist, angrily shaking my head at her. "You haven't even given Hunter a chance. I expected better from you. And you," I turn toward Dad, "you did meet him, and he was nothing but nice to you. He wasn't rude, he listened when you spoke, tried to pay for lunch—"

"Because he's a rich boy," Dad says snidely.

"No, because he's a nice person. And I'm really, *really* into him." Anguish rises in my throat. "You guys don't have to like him if you don't want to—that's fine. But he's going to be in my life either way. We're dating now, and it's serious between us. We've talked about going away for spring break, and maybe Europe this summer. Hunter will be in my life whether you like it or not."

Dad is frowning. "You're supposed to take Molecular Biology in the summer," he reminds me.

Frustration seizes up all my muscles. For a moment I find myself too tense to move, let alone speak. I inhale again, willing myself to relax. I know from experience that temper tantrums don't work on my father. He's impenetrable to yelling. If you want to get through to my father, you need to use logic.

"I'm not taking that class," I tell him. "I'm not interested in taking any more sciences."

His brow furrows. "What are you saying?"

"I'm saying my brain is going to explode. I don't care about bio or chem or any of the pre-med courses I've been taking these past couple years." I lick my suddenly bone-dry lips. "I won't be going to med school after I graduate."

The ensuing silence is deafening. Nobody says a word, and yet my head is a cacophony of noise thanks to my shrieking pulse. Dad's shock is unmistakable, but I can't tell if he's angry.

"I'm not going to med school," I repeat. "This is something

I've been thinking about since…well, pretty much since I started at Briar. I want to go to grad school, get my master's, get my doctorate. And while I do that, I can get a counseling degree and actually see patients—"

"Clients," he corrects stiffly. "There's a difference."

"Fine, whatever, it won't be patients. It's still *people*—people I'll be able to help. That's what I want to do," I finish, and when I realize my shoulders have sagged in defeat, I force myself to straighten up. Because fuck that, why should I be defeated? I'm proud of this decision.

Dad flicks up one bushy eyebrow. "What does your new boyfriend think about this?"

"He supports me one hundred percent."

"Of course he does," Dad sneers.

"Marcus," Mom says sharply, and I look over in gratitude. Maybe what I said got through to her a little.

"Is he the one who talked you out of going to med school?" my father demands.

"No. I told you, I've been struggling with this forever. I make my own decisions—Hunter just supports them. Unlike you." My chest clenches with disappointment. "Anyway. This is why I came home today. I wanted to tell you guys, in person, about the two very important life changes happening for me right now. I'm with somebody new and I'm pivoting career-wise. I'm sure there are lots of interesting specialties within psychiatry, but that's not the path I want to take." I pause. "Oh, and since I'm being extra honest right now—I don't like hoop earrings and I gave Pippa your birthday present because I'm never going to wear those earrings."

The dining room falls silent.

Mom rises and starts gathering up the dishes. Without a word, I help her. As we trudge silently into the kitchen, I notice that her eyes look moist.

"Are you crying?" I ask in concern.

She blinks hard, and her long eyelashes shimmer with tears. "I'm sorry, *mami*. I didn't realize… I…" She pauses, then tries again. "You know your father, Demi. He's an alpha male. And you're right, I defer to him a lot and I'm sorry for that. I should be forming my own opinion of your new boyfriend."

"Yes," I agree.

She rubs her knuckles beneath her wet eyes. "The next time you're in the city, why don't you bring him and we can go out for lunch or dinner?" she suggests, her voice soft. "How does that sound?"

"It sounds wonderful. Thank you," I say gratefully.

"As for the rest of it, you know I'll support you no matter what career you choose." She winks at me. "You could be a stripper and I'd be in the front row cheering you on—but please don't choose that path because I think your father might actually kill you."

I let out a shaky laugh. "Do you think he'll kill me for the med school thing?"

"He'll come around."

"You really believe that?"

"Absolutely." She sighs. "But I don't know if he'll ever forgive you for giving away your birthday gift. He picked those earrings out himself, Demi."

———

The journey home is timed perfectly. Hunter's game starts at eight, and the bus pulls into Hastings just before seven. That gives me plenty of time to go home, shower, and make my way to the hockey rink to meet Pippa, and Hunter's roommates. Well, except for Hollis and Rupi. They're away on a weekend trip, which is a relief because the arena is already loud enough without adding Rupi Miller's voice to it.

I do have one more task to complete, though. I've been thinking about it for days now, ever since Hunter told me he loved me.

I feel like a jerk for not saying it back, but I didn't want him to think the only reason I was saying it was because I was upset, or simply grateful that he wasn't cheating. When I do say it, I want to be calm and centered. I want him to look into my eyes and see the sincerity shining there when I tell him I love him. Because I do love him.

And when I love someone, my first instincts are to protect them, support them, encourage them to embrace their strengths and combat their weaknesses. I heard the confidence in Hunter's voice when he announced that he would never cheat on me, and it told me something important.

It told me he's starting to trust himself.

Sure, it helps that his season didn't fall apart after we started sleeping together, as he feared it might. But even if it had, I still think he would've learned these same lessons. That he's capable of staying faithful. He's capable of playing hockey and having a girlfriend, a sex life.

I truly believe he can succeed in the NHL without letting the lifestyle corrupt him. Don't get me wrong—I can see how it would freak him out. Garrett Graham can't leave his house without a disguise, for God's sake. And Garrett's girlfriend told me at the nightclub that there's a woman who lurks outside their city brownstone hoping to catch glimpses of him.

So yes, it's a daunting life. It's long stints away from your loved ones. It's sex on a platter. But I have faith in Hunter. And although he's finally starting to have faith in himself, he still needs one last push.

I pull up Brenna's number and gaze out the window as I wait for her to answer. The bus is about ten minutes from the station in Hastings.

"Hey," Brenna greets me. "Are we still good for tonight?"

"Of course. I'm going to take an Uber to campus and stop off at home first to shower and change, though. But I just had a quick question for you."

"What's up?"

"Do you have any way of contacting Garrett Graham?"

A beat. "Um. Yeah, I should be able to do that. Why?"

"I'm planning a surprise thing for Hunter," I answer vaguely. "I could use Garrett's help."

"Sure. I don't know if I have his cell saved in my phone, but Fitzy would definitely have it, or Summer's brother. I'll ask them."

"Thanks, chica. I'll see you in a bit."

The moment I get home, I strip off my clothes and take a hot shower, hoping to inject some warmth back into my bones. We've reached that hideous part of the winter where you can never, ever feel warm. February in New England is a glacial hellscape, the time of year when my mother and I are in wholehearted agreement. She hates the winter from start to finish, I hate it in February. It's like a Venn diagram and we're finally in the same circle, clinging to each other for body heat.

I bundle up in my terrycloth robe and approach my closet, debating what to wear. I'd like to look cute for Hunter if we're hanging out afterward, but the arena is so damn cold. Sure, there are heaters and enough bodies in the place to generate some heat, but it doesn't completely eliminate the chill.

I finally settle on thick leggings, thick socks, and a thick red sweater. Key word: thick. I look like a marshmallow, but oh well. Warmth trumps cuteness.

I'm about to start doing my makeup when my phone lights up. I hope it's not Hunter calling to ask how it went in Boston. He needs to focus on the game tonight, and hearing that my father and I aren't speaking right now probably won't pump him up for the playoffs. I'll tell him later.

But it's not Hunter; it's TJ. "Hey," I greet him. "Are you coming to the game? You never gave me an answer."

"No. I'm not."

"Ah. Okay. That sucks." I open my makeup case. "It would have been nice to see you."

"Really? Would it have?" His mocking voice ripples into my ear.

I furrow my brow. "Are you all right? You sound a bit drunk."

He just laughs.

My frown deepens. "Okay, then. Well. I'm getting ready right now, so tell me what's up, otherwise I'll call you tomorrow."

"Mmm-hmmm." He's still laughing, but it's tinged with hysteria.

"TJ." A queasy feeling tickles my stomach. "What the hell is going on?"

Silence. It lasts about three seconds, and just when I'm about to check if the call dropped, TJ starts babbling. He talks so fast I can barely keep up, and my constant interruptions—*"wait, what?" "What are you saying?" "What does that mean?"*—only agitate him further. By the time he winds down, I'm on the verge of throwing up.

I draw in a fearful breath. "Stay where you are. I'm on my way."

38
HUNTER

Excitement sizzles in the air as my teammates and I gear up. Whoever wins tonight will progress to the conference finals, so we're all feeling the pressure. Last season we made it to those finals, and I suffered a broken wrist thanks to a scorned boyfriend. This season my wrist is perfectly fine and my dick hasn't gotten me into an iota of trouble.

Beside me, Bucky is shoving his pants up to his hips, while babbling to Matt and Alec about some new radical therapies being used on athletes these days.

"Swear to God, this chamber looks like something they'd torture James Bond with. They blast you with liquid nitrogen to like minus-a-hundred-and-fifty degrees."

"And then what?" Alec sounds fascinated.

"Well, in theory it stimulates healing. In reality I think it just gives you frostbite?"

I glance over in amusement. "What's this you're talking about?"

"Cryotherapy," Bucky replies.

"Sounds intense," remarks Conor, who's sitting on the

bench beside me. He lifts a hand and tucks his blond hair behind his ears.

"Dude," I tell him. "Not sure if anyone's told you this, but… you're treading pretty damn close to mullet territory."

From his locker, Matt hoots. "Bizness in front, party in the back, yo."

Conor just gives that easygoing shrug of his. Even being informed he's rocking a mullet doesn't faze this guy. I wish I could bottle up his confidence and sell it to pimply-faced teenage boys. We'd make a killing.

"You should cut it," Jesse advises. "It's a lady-boner killer."

Con rolls his eyes. "First off, there's nothing I could *ever* do that would kill a lady's boner."

He's probably right about that.

"And secondly, I can't cut it. Otherwise we'll lose the game."

"Shit," Jesse says, paling. "You're right."

Hockey players and their superstitions. Looks like Con ain't getting a haircut till April.

"Jesus *Christ*, what is that stench?" Coach demands from the doorway. He strides into the locker room, his nose wrinkled in repulsion.

I exchange a look with the guys. I don't smell anything, and everyone's blank expressions say they're equally stumped.

"It smells like a sulfur factory exploded," Coach growls.

"Oh," Bucky realizes. "Yeah, that's Pablo."

"The egg?"

I can't help but snicker. "Yup yup—"

"Don't fucking say yup yup, Davenport."

I ignore him. "—because that's what happens when you

ask someone to take care of an egg for like five months. It goes rotten. We're all used to the smell now." I glance at Bucky, who's pulling Pablo Eggscobar out of his locker. "I thought you were keeping him in that zippered pouch to try to contain the stink."

At the current moment, Pablo is wrapped in numerous layers of cellophane, his pink drink-cozy stretched tightly around the plastic bundle. You can't even see his little pig face anymore because the odor-suppressing plastic wrap is an inch thick.

"I took him out because I felt bad for the guy, always being locked up like that. He's not a criminal."

Snorts and chuckles ring out in the locker room. Coach, however, is not amused.

"Give it to me," he orders, sticking out a meaty paw.

Bucky looks alarmed. He checks with me as if to ask, *should I?*

I shrug. "He's the boss."

The second Coach has our team mascot in hand, he marches over to the wastebasket by the door and unceremoniously dumps Pablo in the trash.

A strangled cry bursts out, courtesy of Bucky, followed by a widespread hush that lends a spooky air to the room.

I feel like the wind was just knocked out of me. Pablo's been a part of us for so long that I don't even know what to say. My teammates' stunned faces confirm they feel the same way.

Coach Jensen crosses his arms. "Congratulations, you passed the absurd task I didn't want to assign or think you'd remember to carry out. But—" His voice becomes gruff.

"—you all showed some real teamwork and responsibility passing that egg around. And I'm a man of my word—I spoke to the dean and he said we might be able to make something happen with the pig."

Bucky looks ecstatic. "Seriously? We get the pig? Guys, we did it."

"Pablo the Pig," Jesse says slowly. "Doesn't have the same ring to it. We need a new name."

"Pablo Pigscobar," Conor and I blurt out in unison, then turn to each other, grinning.

"Oh Jesus," Matt says with a wail of laughter. "That's it, everybody stop talking. Nothing you say could ever top that."

The rest of the team is cackling their asses off. Even Coach's lips are twitching. But then he claps his hands to signal that Happy Time is over, and everyone resumes getting ready.

I'm about to slide my chest protector over my head when my phone buzzes. I peer into my locker to see an incoming call from Garrett.

"Hey Coach," I call out. "Your favorite child Garrett Graham is on the line. Mind if I take this?"

He glances at the clock. We have thirty minutes before the puck drops. "Yes, but make it fast, Davenport. And tell him that was a brilliant play at the end of the third during yesterday's game against Nashville."

"Will do." The locker room's too damn loud, so I step out into the hallway, where I nod at the security guard standing there. Briar takes the protection of its athletes seriously.

"G," I answer, raising the phone to my ear. "What's up?"

"Hey, glad I caught you. I was worried you'd already shut your phone off."

"Aw. Calling to wish me good luck?"

There's a snort in my ear. "Nah, you don't need it. BU doesn't stand a chance."

Damn right they don't. They've been our toughest competitor this year, but I'm confident we can beat them. Granted, I would've preferred playing a softer opponent. Like Eastwood College, who, just as I suspected, couldn't pull their shit together despite their amazing goalie. Kriska can stop a thousand goals, but it won't help if his forwards aren't scoring any on the other net.

"Anyway, I'm with Landon in his office right now. He's headed for LA tonight and will be gone for two weeks, but he wanted to touch base with you before he leaves."

"Landon?" I have no clue who G is talking about.

"Landon McEllis? My agent—but that word isn't allowed to be spoken right now, so pretend I never said it. In fact, we're not having this conversation at all, okay?"

"Okay? Why are you calling exactly?"

"Because I was just talking to Demi and she said you were hoping to sign with a franchise after graduation."

I almost drop the phone. "What?" When the hell did he speak to Demi?

"Yeah, she and I spoke at length about it. She was wondering if you'd need an agent in order to do that, and I explained that technically you can't have an agent while you're in an NCAA program. But I was with Landon when she called, and he wanted to have a quick chat with you. Just remember—this conversation ain't happening."

I understand his need for secrecy. NCAA athletes aren't allowed any contact with sports agents. Even guys who've already been drafted are required to officially end their player-agent relationship for the duration of their college careers.

That's the official party line, anyway. In every sport, there's a fair bit of shadiness behind the scenes. But it's important to be careful.

"I'm putting you on speaker now," Garrett says. "Cool?"

"Sure." I'm still a tad dazed.

"Hunter, hey. This is Landon McEllis."

"Hello, sir."

"Can it with the sir stuff—call me Landon." He chuckles. "Listen, when G mentioned you might be in the market for an agent next year, I just about jumped out of my chair and dove for the phone."

Damned if that doesn't puff up my chest a little.

"I wanted to introduce myself," he goes on. "Unofficially, of course."

I try not to laugh. "Of course."

"And I won't beat around the bush—you're one of the top college players in the country. If you're interested in going pro, I can put together a deal for you without even lifting a pinky."

"Really?" I know it's far easier for the eighteen-and nineteen-year-old guys to land somewhere big. But I'll be twenty-two when I graduate. Yup, I'm getting up there in my years, an old man at the current age of twenty-one. But athletic careers have short life spans.

"Absolutely. And look, I can't sign you right now, and we can't speak again after tonight. But I just wanted to gauge your interest, find out which other agents you might be considering."

"I'm not considering other agents," I admit. Hell, I didn't expect to hear from *this* agent. I don't know whether to be pissed at Demi's interference, or eternally grateful for it. I could get in trouble with the university if anyone found out Landon and I were even having this conversation.

"Then you're interested," he says.

"Definitely." Even if I had a dozen agents knocking on my door, Landon McEllis would still be at the top of the list. His client roster is staggering, and Garrett's said nothing but good things about him.

"Perfect, then we're on the same page." He chuckles again. "I'll touch base with you next year."

"Sounds great. Thank you, sir—Landon."

"Kick ass tonight," Garrett's voice chirps in my ear. "I'll talk to you later."

"Later, G." I hang up. Once again I feel winded, as I stand there staring at my phone. Fuckin' Demi. That woman is literally the best thing that's ever happened to me.

"Davenport," booms a deep voice.

The universe has a real sense of humor, because the moment I think about Demi, her father appears like a scary apparition.

I stare in confusion, because either I'm hallucinating it, or that's actually Marcus Davis at the other end of the hall.

A second security guard is preventing him from entering. The university started taking more precautions after one too many troublemakers snuck into the team locker rooms. It never happened in my day, but Dean said that when he was a freshman, a rival team smuggled in a duffel full of chocolate syrup containers and sprayed the brown sauce all over our locker room. When the Briar players showed up before the game, they thought there was actually diarrhea dripping down the walls.

"Hey, it's okay," I call to the guard. "I know him."

The guard steps aside, and Dr. Davis comes stalking toward me in all his terrifying glory. Jeez, he is a *big* man. Ironically, he's only two, maybe three inches taller than me, but he's built like Dwayne the Rock Johnson, and looks twice my size. It boggles the mind that this enormous man spends his days performing delicate surgeries in an operating room. But never judge a book by its cover, right?

"Hello, sir." I brace myself for his response—I suspect it won't be pleasant. I haven't seen him since our very short, very awkward brunch back in January, when he made his dislike for me crystal clear.

"It's time we have a talk," Dr. Davis retorts. "Man to man."

I swallow a sigh. "I would love to do that, sir, but I've got a game starting in about twenty minutes. Maybe we could postpone this until tomorrow?"

"No. We can't. I take matters regarding my daughter very seriously."

"So do I," I say simply. "She means a lot to me."

"Does she? Is that why you're encouraging her to throw her future away?" Ice hardens his tone, and his harsh features are even more forbidding when he's pissed.

Evidently Demi's trip to Boston didn't go as well as she'd hoped.

"She's not throwing her future away," I reply in a careful tone. "She's staying in the same field, just taking a different direction to get there."

"Do you know how much a psychiatrist makes on average? Over two hundred K annually. Two seventy-five, on the top end. Want to compare that to a clinical psychologist? Or better yet, a run-of-the-mill therapist? There's one of those on every street corner."

"Demi doesn't care about money. And she doesn't want an MD. She wants to get a doctorate."

"Look, son, where do you get off dictating my daughter's life choices?"

"I'm not dictating her life choices. If anything, *she's* the dictator in our relationship." I can't help but snort. "Have you met your daughter? She's the bossiest person on the planet."

For one fleeting second a flicker of humor lights his eyes, and I think maybe, just *maybe*, he's softening. But it's gone in a flash, and his face turns to stone again.

"I don't trust you," he says tightly.

I let out a tired breath. "With all due respect, sir, you don't even know me."

"You and my daughter are too different. She's—"

The door behind me flies open without warning. I expect Coach's furious face to appear, so I'm already uttering, "I'm sorry, I—" when I realize I'm looking at Matt.

Matty is startled to find a beefy bald man looming over me, but then he shakes himself out of it. "Dude, you need to get in here right *now*." He waves his phone under my nose. "It's fucking chaos."

I knit my brows. "What is?"

"Shit's going down at Bristol House. There's two people up on the roof, and it looks like they're going to jump.

Someone's live-tweeting it, and a chick on the top floor of Hartford House managed to snap a picture." Matt thrusts the phone in my hand. "One of them is your girl."

39
DEMI

NONE OF THE DORMITORIES ON CAMPUS OFFER ROOF ACCESS to their residents. In fact, it's explicitly disallowed, which is understandable. The administration doesn't want raucous parties up there. Drunken kids accidentally falling to their deaths.

Or, in rare cases, *not* accidentally.

Most schools have safeguards against this shit. Locks that only the maintenance staff has keys for. Some of the newer dorms require keycards to access the roofs. But Bristol House is known for its lax security. The door to the roof is old, and the lock is easy to pick. If you live in the dorms, as I did in freshman year, it's common knowledge how easy it is to sneak up to Bristol's roof. Most residents stay under the radar, usually going up there to smoke weed or have sex. It's widely understood that if you use Bristol's roof, you don't make a big production out of it.

TJ, however, apparently never got the memo.

And I've never been more afraid in my life as I stare at my friend standing up on the ledge, his thin body silhouetted in the dark night.

"TJ, please." My voice cracks. It's been difficult to speak since I got here. No, even before that. Since he called twenty minutes ago and informed me he was going to kill himself.

How the *fuck* did I not see the signs?

I'm planning on becoming a psychologist and I couldn't fucking tell that one of my close friends was *suicidal*?

I want to cry. I truly hadn't realized TJ was suffering. Yes, he gets moody every now and then, but not once since I've known him, not even *once*, has he expressed feelings of hopelessness or talked about suicide. He might've displayed anxious tendencies, but not suicidal ones.

So far, all of my attempts to talk him off the ledge have failed. I don't know how to get through to him.

"TJ," I plead. "Come down from there."

"Why do you care?" he spits out. "You don't care about anyone but yourself."

His harsh words sting, but I banish my own emotions from this equation. This isn't about me. TJ is clearly going through something.

Going through something? a voice in my head shrieks. *Understatement of the fucking year!*

My heart is jammed in my throat, liable to choke me. The rooftop is covered in ice, because nobody ever comes up here to lay down salt. To make matters exponentially worse, it's starting to snow, and the wind is picking up. One misstep and he'll—

Do NOT even go there!

"TJ, please get off of there and come back," I beg. "Come talk to me."

"No. I don't want to talk. I fucking hate *talking*, Demi."

"I know you do," I whisper.

I edge closer to him. The synapses in my brain are firing in total panic mode, trying to catalogue the red flags I'd missed.

TJ's always been antisocial, but he also made an effort to go out with me, to socialize with my friends. He didn't isolate himself from everyone, so I didn't consider it a red flag. He barely drinks, doesn't abuse drugs, so no red flag there. He has trouble opening up to people, expressing his emotions—but that's not unique. Corinne is equally guarded, and I didn't peg her as suicidal either.

God. I don't know what to do.

I truly don't.

This isn't a class project, or a fucking true crime show. This is real life, and I'm utterly helpless.

I try again. "Listen, it's obvious you've been drinking—"

"No, I haven't." His voice is unnervingly composed.

I bite my lip. Shit. He's sober? He's literally standing on a ledge, four stories off the ground, and he's stone-cold sober?

I suddenly hear the wail of sirens in the distance. My heart jumps. Is this about us? Did someone spot us up here and call the police? God, I want the police to come. I want them to bring one of those negotiators who talks to potential jumpers and convinces them not to commit suicide.

I'm not equipped to handle this.

The wind snakes under my hair and makes it flap around me like a panicky bird. I didn't even grab a coat when I ran out of my house. I'm in my red sweater and leggings and boots, and it's so cold outside I feel the chill in my lungs. I can't even imagine how cold TJ must be—he's in a thin T-shirt.

His slight build could get knocked over by a strong gust. And judging by the snowflakes falling and swirling wildly in the air, that gust could come any second.

"Okay," I say weakly. "Okay. If you're not going to come down, then I'm coming up."

"Stay away, Demi." TJ's shoulders set in a tense line. "Seriously. I'll do it."

I clench my teeth, in fear, not anger, and inch closer to the ledge. "I don't want you to," I tell him, as my heart drums a terrified rhythm on my ribcage. "First I want to talk to you. After that, we can discuss your next move."

"There's nothing to talk about. Go back to your new boyfriend."

I reach the ledge. And almost throw up when I glimpse the thin layer of white frost spanning the cement. At least I hope it's just frost, and not a solid stretch of ice.

"Is that what this is about, then?" I ask quietly. "Me and Hunter?"

"Yes, I'm standing here about to jump to my death because of you and Hunter. Christ, Demi! You are *so* fucking self-absorbed."

I flinch. Then I suck in a gulp of frigid air and lift one foot onto the ledge. It slips on my first attempt. Fuck, that *is* ice. Oh Lord. What am I fucking doing right now?

Saving your friend. He needs help.

Yes. TJ needs help.

I take another breath.

The second time, I manage to climb up. And then I'm standing beside him, and I make the mistake of looking down and oh my fuck, looking down was a *terrible* idea.

I inhale through the rush of dizziness that hits me. Inhale. Then exhale. I force myself to keep breathing. I don't look down again. But the image has already been branded in my brain. That huge drop. No grass or bushes down there, either. Nothing but pavement.

My breath escapes in frantic white puffs. That was legit the scariest sight I'd ever seen.

But what's even scarier is the thought of losing TJ. I may not have heard his cries for help before, but I sure as hell am hearing them now.

"Get *down*," he snaps at me, but the anger has left his voice. It's been replaced by worry. Desperation. "You could get hurt."

"So could you. And I'm not getting down until you do."

"Really? Suddenly you care so much about me?"

"I've always cared about you, TJ. You're one of my best friends." *Do not look down again, Demi. Do not—*

I glance down again and almost puke. Four stories is, what, fifty feet? Why does it seem so much higher from where we are? I never thought fifty feet was so fucking high.

"Best friends," TJ scoffs. "Do you know how patronizing that is?"

"What, calling you my friend? I've known you since freshman year, TJ."

"Exactly! Freshman year! That means I waited almost three years for you to wake up and see what a douchebag Nico was."

The wind ruffles our hair. This time I refuse to take another peek over the edge.

"And then you broke up with that asshole, and I gave

you space and time to heal. I thought, just be patient, man. We have this connection and I thought, she's finally going to see what was in front of her fucking eyes for *three years*." Anguish clouds his face. "I thought you would come to *me* after you dumped Nico and instead you go for that fucking hockey asshole?"

I don't defend Hunter. I'm scared it will trigger TJ to take drastic measures. But I do hedge in with a soft observation. "I thought you said this wasn't about me."

"Fine, I guess it is. Not entirely, but part of it. I'm just tired of being fucking invisible. Invisible to you, invisible to my family. My parents are obsessed with my brother and his big fancy job in London and I'm just an afterthought to everybody, if I even cross their fucking minds. Which I highly doubt."

"That's not true." I met his parents once and they seemed to really love their son. Appearances can be deceiving, I know that. But my gut says that TJ's parents would fly into a panic if they knew what their son was considering doing right now.

"I don't think you're giving yourself enough credit," I tell him.

The sirens get louder.

TJ stiffens. He shifts his feet and I instinctively brace myself for the worst. But then he rights himself, and I'm so dizzyingly relieved that I nearly lose bladder function and pee my pants.

I have literally not moved an inch since I climbed up here. I'm a statue on this ledge. It's two feet wide, so it's not like my toes are dangling over the edge, but I feel like I'm balancing on a paper clip.

"Why didn't you ever talk to me about any of this? Feeling ignored by your parents, feeling inferior to your brother, feeling like you wanted to…" *Die*. I don't say it out loud. I bite hard on the inside of my cheek. "You know I would've been there for you. Why didn't you ask for help?"

"Why did you pick him?" he says instead of addressing my question.

"It wasn't a matter of picking." I sigh wearily. "It's not like you and Hunter were both there in front of me and I needed to choose between you. He and I were friends, and it just developed into something more—"

"You and I are friends—why didn't *we* develop into something more?" Hurt and betrayal darken his eyes.

Fuck, that was the wrong thing to say. "I don't know," I say simply. "Chalk it up to chemistry, I guess. I have chemistry with him."

"And not with me?"

What do I do now? Lie? Get his hopes up just to get him off this ledge?

But that feels disingenuous and cruel. Also, I think he'll be able to see through me. I don't have romantic feelings for TJ. I never have.

I decide to be honest, because that's who I am. "I don't feel any sexual chemistry with you," I admit. "I think you're attractive—"

"Bullshit," he spits.

"I do," I insist. " You have the kindest eyes, and a great butt."

He hesitates, as if trying to assess whether I'm lying.

"But I also objectively think Liam Hemsworth is

gorgeous and I have no desire to sleep with him. I can't explain chemistry. Some people have it, and some don't."

"Chemistry," he echoes. Pain twists his features. "Why don't I have it with anybody?"

"Can I hazard a guess?"

He gives me a sharp look.

"You just said that for the past three years you've been waiting for me to break up with Nico. Stands to reason, then, that you haven't been putting yourself out there. In almost three years, you've only gone on one date, as far as I know—the sorority sister I set you up with. If you're closed off to the potential of dating anyone, you're not going to find anyone."

"I'm not closed off." But he sounds unconvinced.

The wind rustles my hair again, and shivers break out at the nape of my neck and scurry down my spine like rats fleeing a sinking ship. I wish I could flee, too. It's so cold up here. But I'm not leaving this roof without TJ. I'll stand up here all night if I have to.

"Yes, you were," I tell him. "And I get it, okay? Pining over a girl with a boyfriend sucks. Even worse, it means you're not giving out the vibes you should be transmitting. You wasted almost three years, TJ. But, and here's the good part, you still have a year and a half left of college. You've got plenty of time to put yourself out there."

"I'm done putting myself out there," he argues. "Not after you."

I swallow my frustration. It doesn't seem to occur to him that he never actually put himself on the line for me, never once expressed his emotions to me—he just stood there passively waiting for me to notice that he had a crush on me.

I guess that was easier for him than putting his feelings out there.

But why didn't I notice, dammit? Misery crawls up my throat as I think back to all the times Nico, and even Hunter, told me that TJ liked me. I didn't see it.

Or maybe I didn't *want* to see it.

Maybe, like TJ, like everyone else in this world, I chose to take the easy way out. Subconsciously, anyway. Maybe it was easier to remain blind to TJ's true feelings, categorize him as a needy friend, instead of processing what those feelings might mean for our friendship.

"TJ," I say softly, and for the first time in five minutes—I move. I hold my hand out to him. My fingers are shaking harder than they've ever shaken. I'm so afraid I feel like it's inevitable I'm going to pee my pants.

He stares at my visibly trembling hand, unhappiness in his eyes as he brushes snowflakes off his face. "You're scared," he mutters. "I don't want you to be scared."

"Then come down from this ledge with me," I plead.

He doesn't answer.

I let my hand drop, pressing it tight to my side once again.

The faint murmur of voices drifts up toward us. A crowd has gathered below. I can make out uniformed officers, and I wonder if the one who arrested me and Hunter is down there. Officer Jenk. That jerk. An ambulance and several police cruisers have pulled up to the small parking lot in front of the dormitory.

"There's nothing for me here," TJ mumbles. "I'd rather just be dead than deal with this stupid shitty life anymore."

"You might not die," I point out.

"We're four stories up. That's like a fifty-foot drop."

"A fall from four or five stories has about a fifty-percent chance of survival. A hundred feet, sure, you'd probably die." I arch a brow. "But most falls from this height aren't fatal."

His eyes flash. "I'm not in the mood to listen to your bullshit statistics, Demi."

"It's not bullshit. I was literally just talking about this with my father tonight."

"Why the hell would you be talking about that?"

"Because Dad operated on a man who fell about sixty feet from an apartment window. He was trying to sneak a cigarette without his wife finding out, so he was leaning out the window and lost his balance. Fell headfirst to the pavement." I swallow. "Do you want me to tell you what happened to him?"

"He survived his big adventure and even though his wife divorced him for smoking behind her back, he's now living happily ever after with the hot nurse who gave him sponge baths," TJ says sarcastically. "Moral of the story: life is always worth living. Nice try, Demi."

I give a humourless laugh. "No. He survived the fall, but suffered a skull fracture, which led to a subdural hematoma. My father operated but the damage was too severe. He's still alive, but he's badly brain damaged. He'll never live a regular life again. Oh, and he's blind in one eye because the fall severed his ocular nerve. It's still too early to tell the extent of cognitive damage, but Dad isn't hopeful."

TJ looks stunned. He goes scarily silent, his gaze glued to the ground below us.

The flashing red and blue lights slice through the

darkness. Thick clouds obscure the moon, and the falling snow is a blinding array of white against the backdrop of the inky sky. Despite the crowd gathered in front of Bristol House, it feels like TJ and I are the only two people in the world right now.

My stomach is in knots as I rack my brain wondering what else to say. How to help him. "So," I say softly. "Here we are."

Pain flickers across his face. "Here we are."

40
HUNTER

I have no fucking idea what's going on as I charge into the locker room. The guys are all suited up. I'm the only one half-dressed and I don't give two shits right now. Demi's father is on my heels, startling every single one of my teammates by his appearance.

Coach's eyebrows fly up. "Who's this?" he demands.

"This is Demi's father," I explain. "Dr. Marcus Davis."

"Wow," Bucky blurts out, gaping at the newcomer. "You got here fast! This news literally just broke."

"What exactly is going on?" Dr. Davis demands, ignoring everyone but the other adult in the room.

Jensen sticks out a hand. "Chad Jensen, and I'm afraid I can't answer that for you. All we have is a grainy picture on a phone."

"It's Demi," I say through gritted teeth.

Dr. Davis nods grimly. "That's my daughter. Where is this place exactly? Bristol House?"

"It's a dorm on the west side of campus," Matt supplies. "Ten-minute walk, two minute drive."

Dr. Davis is already back at the door. "Davenport," he barks. "I need you to show me where it is."

My feet stay rooted to the floor. Because...the team's about to hit the ice. This game determines who goes to our conference finals, and from there it's on to the national tournament. The Frozen Four.

But I can't play hockey right now. My girlfriend is up on a goddamn roof in the middle of February, trying to talk down a *suicide jumper*. I skimmed several tweets in the stream Matt showed me, and it doesn't sound like it's just two people simply hanging out up there. TJ is clearly threatening to jump.

I rake both hands through my hair. My fingers are shaking wildly. I'm geared up in my lower pads, hockey pants, and socks. But up top I'm in a wife-beater. My shoulder and elbow pads spill haphazardly out of my locker. My chest protector is on the bench.

Swallowing hard, I sweep my gaze around the room. I'm about to break every rule in the captain's handbook.

I wanted to be a good captain. I wanted to put the team first, support my guys, be patient with them, follow all the rules I've been compiling since the season started. I promised myself I wouldn't let girls interfere with hockey, and now I'm about to throw the rulebook out the window...for a girl.

But there is literally no other choice here for me. Guys like Garrett, Dean, Logan—I think they'd understand. I think they'd never put sports ahead of their women. So if my team hates me, so be it. All I know is, if Demi's in trouble, then she comes first.

"Guys." My voice is rough. "I'm sorry. I can't play tonight."

Nobody utters a word.

Guilt spirals through me and forms a tight pretzel in the pit of my stomach. "Trust me," I continue desperately, "I don't want to miss this game, but even if I went out there right now and played, I would only be a detriment to you. My head isn't here, it's with Demi. I won't be able to concentrate until I know she's safe and—"

"She just climbed onto the ledge," Matt blurts out, his eyes glued to his phone screen.

Dr. Davis freezes in the doorway. I'm sure the sheer terror in his eyes reflects my own.

"She did what?" I demand. "What's happening now?"

"I dunno. This tweet just says there's now two people up on the ledge. No other deets."

My heart pounds so fast I feel faint. I suck in an unsteady breath, then scrub my hand through my hair again. I want to tear it out. "I'm sorry," I tell my team. "I need to go."

"Dude, why the fuck are you sorry?" Matt demands.

"And why the fuck are you still here?" drawls Conor. The lazy tone is belied by the serious glint in his eyes.

I wearily glance at Coach, who offers a brisk nod. Then I snatch my sneakers off the floor and race out of the locker room.

———

"This is it," I announce five minutes later, concern and impatience warring inside me. "The lot entrance is up there on the right."

But when we try to turn into the parking lot, we find the Hastings police sectioned it off. Across the lot, I spot an ambulance and three police cruisers, along with two campus security cars.

I curse in frustration. "Just stop here on the side of the road. If you get towed, I'll just give you my car, okay?"

He's as impatient as I am as we dive out of his BMW. The winter chill slaps me in the face, same way it did when we'd barrelled out of the arena. It's freezing out. Yet it's not the temperature that's making my bones ache. It's fear. Pure, paralyzing terror.

When I gaze up at the roof of Bristol House, a hiss of horror flies out. "Jesus."

"Oh my God," Dr. Davis says at the same time. He lets out a tortured moan, and when I look over he's covering his eyes with the back of his hand, as if he can't bear to look again. Then his arm drops limply and he gives a determined nod. "Let's go."

We hurry forward, but the police roped off the scene. The *scene*. Christ, I'm already viewing this as the scene of a crime. Or rather, a potentially devastating accident.

I stare up again, my throat tightening to the point of asphyxiation. Although Demi's dark hair is blowing in the wind, she stands as motionless as a statue. She's in a red sweater and black leggings, and she looks so small and vulnerable up there. I wish I could hear her voice or see her eyes.

Beside her, TJ is in a T-shirt and sweats, his skinny arms planted firmly at his sides.

They're talking. I don't know what they're saying. I don't *care* what they're saying. I want to go up there and pull that little asshole off the ledge—and then throw him the fuck over it for endangering Demi's life.

I force myself to take a breath. Then I notice that Demi's father is about to hurl himself over the blockade, despite the protests of the young officer who's attempting to stop him.

"You can't go beyond this point, sir!"

My gaze flies toward the cop's face. I *know* that guy. What was his name again? Alberts? Albertson!

"That's his daughter," I explain, stepping between the two males. Albertson's eyes widen when he recognizes me. "And she's my girlfriend. You know her, Albertson—she was the one in the holding cell with me."

Dr. Davis turns to glower at me. "What holding cell?"

I wave off the question. "Please. Albertson." Somehow my voice sounds calm.

The uniformed man throws a discreet glance over his shoulder, then dips his head in a tiny nod and allows us to rush past him.

We skid to a stop about twenty yards from the entrance of the dormitory. Near the front doors, several officers are engaged in intent conversation with a man in a suit. The dean, I realize. Other faculty members are also present, along with a small crowd of observers that the cops are trying to corral to one area.

Dr. Davis grabs my arm suddenly. I flinch, because his steel grip is definitely going to leave a bruise. "Do you know how to get up there?" he demands.

I hesitate. Because I *do* know. It's not a well-kept secret that Bristol is the place to go if you want to hang out on the roof and smoke J's. But the wild look in his eyes tells me it's not a wise idea for him to be anywhere near Demi right now. Hell, I can barely keep my own cool, and she's my girlfriend.

I can't imagine how I'd feel if I was looking up there at my *daughter*.

Fear and desperation form a lethal cocktail in my bloodstream. My hands won't quit shaking. I can barely stay upright without stumbling, and my bare arms are covered with goose pimples.

"Even if I did, there's no way the cops are letting us enter that building. I think we're gonna have to stay out here."

Rage burns hot in his dark eyes. "And you claim to give a shit about my daughter?"

"I do give a shit." I exhale weakly. "Dr. Davis. Marcus. Look at her—look at them."

His anger dissolves into agony as he tilts his head back. His scalp is shiny under the glow of the streetlamp at the foot of the path.

"Trust her," I urge.

He blinks. "What?"

"Just trust her. I know you want to run up there and storm the roof, but all you're going to do is scare the shit out of TJ. Trust me, if I was up on that ledge and *you* came out...?" I shake my head in warning. "You'll make things worse, I promise you that. I know how much you love your daughter—I mean, you drove all the way from Boston to order me to stay away from her. Which I still don't understand, by the way, because I've done nothing but love that girl with all my heart. And because I love her, I have faith in her."

He visibly gulps. His massive Adam's apple bobs like there's a whole other entity in his throat.

"She's so smart," I tell him. "And she knows what she's doing—she and I spent the entire semester working on a project that required her to pretend to be my therapist. If anyone can get through to TJ, it's her. Trust her."

All the fight seems to drain out of him. His massive shoulders sag.

After a second of hesitation, I reach over and touch his arm reassuringly.

His eyes narrow at first, but then his expression softens. "You do love her," he says brusquely.

"Yes."

We both turn our attention back to Demi. Time ceases to exist. It's frozen like the air. Frozen like the ground beneath my feet. Frozen like the fear in my heart. Minutes pass, or maybe it's hours. Days. I don't know.

What I do know is that I don't breathe easy until Demi finally takes TJ's hand and safely helps him off the ledge.

41
DEMI

I'M IN SHOCK. MY ENTIRE BODY IS ICE-COLD AND TREMBLING like a leaf in a windstorm. My eyes are blinking and in focus, but I don't see anything. My ears are working but no sounds register. When I exit the front doors of Bristol House and spot Hunter and my father standing off to the side, I assume they're not real. A figment of my imagination, a product of my shock. So I keep walking with my arm around TJ.

"Demi."

I stop. Because that *did* sound real. That sounded like my father.

But the cops are now closing in on us, distracting me from my dad. TJ looks as shocked as I feel, panic swamping his eyes when one of the officers tries to lead him toward the ambulance.

"I don't need to go to the hospital," he protests. "*Demi.*"

"Yes, you do," I say quietly, giving him a tight squeeze. "You need to talk to somebody about what happened tonight."

"I talked to you."

He did, but I've done as much as I can. The fact that

he seriously contemplated suicide and took action to try to implement it, is beyond my capabilities. Plus, he has no choice but to go to the hospital. They'll probably admit him into the psych ward and keep him under observation for seventy-two hours to ensure he doesn't harm himself or others.

"I'll come and see you the moment I can," I assure him. "I promise."

That gets me a weak nod. He's in a total daze as he follows the cop toward the waiting ambulance.

I turn around, and the next thing I know, my father's huge arms envelop me whole. I was already having trouble breathing. Now I'm choking.

"Dad, please," I wheeze desperately. "I can't breathe."

It's with great reluctance that he releases me and sets me on my feet. I blink and then I'm being hugged again, not as violently as before but with an equal amount of emotion.

"You have no idea how worried we were," Hunter says hoarsely.

Dad makes a guttural noise as he nods in grim agreement.

"I don't understand," I say slowly. "Why are you here?"

"Someone snapped a picture of you on the roof and a bunch of people are tweeting about it," Hunter explains.

"No, not you." I stare at my father. "Why are *you* here? Why aren't you in Boston?"

"I came to…" He stops for a beat, and Hunter smoothly finishes his sentence.

"To see you."

My dad smiles wryly. "No, kid, I don't need you to cover my ass." He shrugs. "I came here to tell him to stop seeing you."

"*Dad*." My jaw drops.

"I know, sweetheart. I'm sorry. I just…" He drags a hand over his bald skull. "You're my baby girl. You'd just had your heart broken and I didn't want it to happen again. Nico hurt you, and then I saw who you went out and picked right afterward?" He tips his head at Hunter. "Rich boy, hotshot athlete? In my experience those two qualities indicate a player. Seemed like a recipe for another broken heart," he growls protectively, "and I wasn't gonna let that happen to you."

"I'm sure you had the best intentions, but Hunter's not a player. And like I told you earlier, we're together now, and you're just going to have to deal with it. You could either make this hard on everyone, or you could accept that this is my new boyfriend. And yes he's a rich hockey player, but—*oh my fucking God*!" I suddenly burst out.

"Demi, language."

My upset gaze swings toward Hunter, and for the first time in five minutes I realize he's wearing the lower half of his hockey uniform. "What are you doing here? What time is it?" I scramble to get my phone out of my pocket. "It's eight-thirty! Your game started at eight!"

"Yeah, I know."

His careless shrug triggers another rush of panic. "Then why aren't you playing? What the *fuck* are you doing here?"

"Language."

"Dad, I swear to God!"

Hunter's lips twitch as he reaches for my hand. "Babe. Do you honestly think I would just suit up and play hockey while you're standing on a ledge a hundred feet off the ground—"

"Fifty feet—"

"—A *thousand* feet off the ground, with a dude threatening to jump? One, that speaks volumes about how little you think of me. And two…well, I don't have a two, okay? One is bad enough. Fuck's sake, Demi."

"Language," my dad chides.

Hunter dons a sheepish smile. "Sorry, sir."

"You need to get to the arena," I order. "We need to get him to the arena." And then I'm hurrying past them. "Where's your car, Dad?"

He leads the way to his silver BMW, and I'm amazed to discover that the engine is still running, both driver and passenger door are thrown open, and the vehicle's back bumper is sticking out toward the road. Wow. They must've *really* been worried.

Dad slides behind the wheel, with Hunter next to him, and me in the middle of the backseat.

"I can't believe you're not on the ice right now," I say in dismay.

"You mean more to me than hockey," he says simply, and damned if that doesn't make my heart expand. "Get it through your stubborn head."

I lean toward him and reach for his hand. He grips mine tightly, and I know he must feel how icy my fingers are.

"You have no idea how scared I was," he says roughly.

"Not as scared as I was," I admit.

Dad peers sharply at me. "Are you sure you don't want to go to the hospital and get checked out?"

"I'm fine. Just in shock." I bite hard on my lower lip. "I was so afraid he was going to do it. You have no idea."

Briar's hockey facility comes into view. Dad bypasses

the parking lot and stops directly out front. To my dismay, Hunter doesn't immediately dive out of the car.

Instead, he twists to meet my eyes. "I knew you'd be able to help him."

"Help him?" Anguish clogs my throat. "I didn't even see that he needed help, Hunter. How did I miss all the signs? And what kind of shrink am I going to be if I can't even see the warning signs in my own friends?"

"A brilliant shrink," Dad replies, his tone stern. "Human beings aren't infallible, sweetheart. Sometimes we make mistakes. Sometimes we fail. I've lost more patients on that table than my conscience can handle, but you? You didn't lose your friend tonight. You saved him." Dad gestures toward Hunter. "And he's right—he knew you'd be okay. I was seconds away from scaling the building like Spider-Man to rescue you, but your boyfriend here convinced me to have faith."

"In what?"

"In you," Hunter answers, and he and Dad exchange an awkward smile.

I'm touched to see it. "Mom says she wants to take me and Hunter out the next time we're in the city," I say after a beat of hesitation. "Maybe you could join us and we'll have a redo of the brunch?"

My father nods. "I'll be there."

"Thank you." I turn to Hunter. "And thank you for coming to save me. With that said—get out of this car, Monk. Now. If you hurry, you could probably get ready in time to play in the second period." My teeth dig into my lip again. "Would you be horribly upset if I didn't go in and watch the game?

I need some time to process what happened tonight. Just… decompress, you know? And I want to call my mom."

Hunter cups my cheek. "It's absolutely fine. Maybe you and your dad can grab a coffee and get you warmed up? Your hands are freezing." He glances at my father expectantly.

Dad replies with a firm nod. "I'll take care of her. Go play your game, kid."

"I'll come find you afterward," I promise Hunter.

He leans in to plant a chaste kiss on my lips, then hops out of the car. Tears fill my eyes as I watch him dart toward the entrance of the arena.

"It's fine," Dad says gruffly. "I'm sure his absence didn't hurt his team too ba—"

"I'm not crying because of that," I interrupt between sniffles. "I don't even know why I'm crying. The tears just started pouring for no reason."

"Not for no reason. The shock is wearing off, and it's finally hitting you—the gravity of what happened tonight." My father's smile is tinged with sadness. "Come up here in the front, sweetheart, and we'll go somewhere and talk. Okay?"

I rub my tear-streaked cheeks, then nod and reach for the door handle. "Thanks for being here, Daddy."

"Always."

42
DEMI

I FEEL LIKE I'VE RUN TWO MARATHONS AND GONE TO WAR all in one night by the time Hunter and I walk through his front door later.

His team won the game, so everybody is out celebrating tonight. But we decided to bail on the after party, along with Summer and Fitz. And Brenna, who said she'd rather Skype with her boyfriend than "deal with a bunch of horny drunk boys slobbering all over her."

The house is pitch black and dead silent as the entire group files inside.

"Okay, this is fucking creepy," Brenna remarks.

"It doesn't feel right when they're not here," Summer agrees.

"Who?" I ask. "Hollis and Rupi?"

"Yeah." Summer vaguely waves a hand over the shadowy hallway. "Listen to it."

I wrinkle my nose. "To what?"

"Exactly!"

As we enter the living room, the haunting, albeit tinny

notes of a familiar song waft out of Brenna's phone. It's Simon and Garfunkel's "The Sound of Silence." I burst out laughing as she solemnly holds it up for all to hear.

She has a point, though. This is the quietest I've ever heard this house. "Where did they go, anyway?" I ask.

"No idea," Hunter replies. "Hollis said it was a surprise."

"A surprise for who?"

"For Rupi."

"So then why couldn't he tell the rest of you?" I counter.

"Because it was a surprise."

I let out a sigh. "I don't understand that guy."

"Nobody does," Brenna says frankly. "Don't waste any more brain cells trying to."

"Anyway, if you'll excuse us," Hunter announces, "Semi and I are heading up to bed. She's had a tough night."

"I'm so sorry you had to go through that," Summer says sympathetically. She and I aren't super close, but she surprises me with a hug tight enough to steal the breath from my lungs.

"Thank you. It was terrifying, not gonna lie."

"I hope your friend is going to be okay," Fitz says gruffly.

"Me too." I wonder what the shrinks at the hospital will make of TJ's mental state. I think he's suffering from depression, and he definitely has dangerously low feelings of self-worth. I hope whoever he talks to will provide him with the help and guidance he needs.

I'm sure the school or the police already contacted his family, and I'm planning on seeing him the moment he's allowed visitors. TJ was always there for me when I needed to talk, when I needed someone to listen, and I plan on doing the same for him.

But tonight I don't want to spend another second reliving what happened on that roof. Dad and I discussed it at length over a cup of coffee in my kitchen, and the pride shining in his eyes when I described talking TJ off the ledge made my heart clench with emotion. I hope he eventually accepts my decision to forgo medical school. Maybe one day he'll be proud of that too.

I check my phone as we enter Hunter's room. A million messages await me. Pippa, Corinne, Darius, Pax, my mom, and even one from Nico, who I unblocked after Christmas. It says he heard about TJ, he's glad we're both all right, and that I'm a very good friend. It's a sweet message, and I make a mental note to reply to him, and everyone else, tomorrow.

"Congratulations on your win," I tell Hunter.

"Congratulations on saving someone's life."

"I feel so awful for him," I admit. "He's always been shy, reserved. But I didn't think he was suicidal, Hunter. I truly didn't."

"I know, baby."

"I wish he'd spoken to me about it and shared his feelings, instead of letting things get so bad that he felt like his only option was to kill himself." I swallow the lump of sorrow in my throat. "I just...you know what, I can't talk about this anymore tonight. Just distract me. Please."

"Sure." He flicks up an eyebrow. "Want me to tell you about the call I got from Garrett's agent today?"

Panic flies through me. "Oh my God! No!"

"What do you mean, no?"

"Garrett says you're not allowed to have an agent. It's against NCAA rules—"

"Don't worry, it's okay," Hunter interrupts with a smile. "He just called to say hello. A very unofficial hello. And, well, perhaps there was also an unofficial expression of interest on both our ends."

"*Both*? You're interested?" I try valiantly not to break out in a satisfied smile. I knew calling Garrett would be the push that Hunter needed.

He nods. "I mean, we don't even know if any teams will want me after I graduate—"

"They will."

"—but if one does, and it's a good deal…" He trails off.

"You'll sign?" I prompt.

"I'll sign. But…" He curls his arm around my waist and pulls me toward him. "That means you need to apply to grad schools in whatever city I land in. Or," he mulls it over, "I suppose we can see where *you* land and then I'll tell G's agent to get me in with that team."

"We'll figure something out." I love how we're already making plans for the future. And why not? I'm excited for it. I want nothing more than to work toward my master's and open up a counselling practice, while the man I love plays—

"Oh fuck," I blurt out. "I forgot to tell you I love you!"

Hunter's startled gaze snaps to mine. Then he starts to laugh. "I'm sorry, what?"

"I forgot to tell you I love you. I wanted to say it the night you said it, but—"

"You weren't ready, I get it." His voice comes out husky.

"It wasn't the right moment, given the circumstances. But I do love you." I feel my cheeks heating up. I never thought I'd fall for Mr. Hockey, with his cocky dimpled smiles and strange sense of humor. But life is full of strange surprises. "I love you, Hunter Davenport."

"I love you, Demi Davis." He leans down to kiss me. Meanwhile, his warm palms slide underneath the back of my shirt to stroke my back—and then he squawks in horror. "Holy shit, you're like a block of ice, baby. C'mere."

I grin as he begins to expertly tug off my clothes. "If you're trying to warm me up, you should be putting *more* clothes on me."

"Nah, I should be putting *me* on you." He wiggles his eyebrows playfully and nudges me toward his bed. Then he lifts the corner of the comforter and we crawl underneath it, our naked bodies tangled together.

He slips one hand between my legs, probing, stroking gently. "How are you already so fucking wet?"

"That's what happens when you're around," I mumble, and then my fingers find his dick. Big, thick, so warm.

Except he robs me of enjoyment, shoving my hand away with an outraged shout. "Oh my fucking God, Demi! Never touch my dick again."

I let out a howl of laughter. "Hands are too cold?"

"*Too cold* is an understatement. Nope. Nope nope nope nope. You're not allowed to touch me tonight." Hunter pushes me onto my back, locks both my wrists with his left hand, and thrusts my arms over my head. "Don't move," he warns.

"Or what?"

"Or I won't fuck you."

I pout. "That's mean."

"No, what's mean was that war crime you just committed against my penis."

Gales of laughter shake my body. I love this guy. We have so much fun together, no matter the circumstances. We could be studying or sitting in a jail cell or lying naked in bed, and he'd never fail to crack me up.

His grip tightens on my wrists. "I'm warning you…"

"Oh fine. Go ahead and do your thing."

Grinning, he lowers his head to kiss me, and I let him seduce me with his mouth, his tongue, his calloused fingertips. Eventually he releases me, but I keep my hands over my head, letting him have his way with me. His mouth is warm, wet, as it closes around my nipple. He sucks gently, swirls his tongue around that aching tip, and my hips move restlessly, seeking relief.

Hunter reaches between us, his knuckles grazing my clit before one long finger slides inside me. "Aw, fuck," he groans. His hot mouth stays latched onto my breast as he starts fingering me. "Jesus motherfucking Christ, babe, I need to be inside you." He's grinding shamelessly against my bare leg, his dick leaving stripes of precome on my flesh.

I grumble impatiently when he leaves the bed to get a condom. "You should have done that first!" I scold.

He responds cheerfully. "Please don't lecture me when I'm about to give you an orgasm."

"Who says you're going to give me an orgasm?"

He grips his dick and wags it at me. "This guy."

Another laugh shudders through me, but it transforms into a throaty moan when Hunter climbs on top of me and enters my pussy in one smooth glide. He fills me completely, my body stretching to accommodate him, and I stroke the sinewy muscles of his back as he fucks me in slow, sweet strokes.

"I love you so much," I whisper.

"Love you too." His hips retreat, then flex forward in a deep thrust that makes me see stars.

Pleasure forms a tight knot in my core and then slowly unravels, ribbons of heat traveling through my body. I'm not cold anymore. I'm on fire. Hunter's body is a furnace. His tongue is hot and eager. His dick elicits the most incredible sensations inside, stoking my arousal.

When the orgasm reaches the surface, I cry out and cling to him. He swallows my moans with greedy, desperate kisses, and then grunts huskily as he gives in to his own release.

"I'm never gonna get tired of this," he croaks. He rolls us over so that I'm lying on his warm chest.

"Good thing you never have to," I tease, still shivering from the aftershocks of release.

His strong arms wrap securely around me. "Oh really. So what are you saying? We're going to be together forever?"

Smiling, I peer down at his gorgeous face. Then I brush a light kiss over his lips. "That's exactly what I'm saying."

EPILOGUE
DEMI

IT'S ELEVEN P.M. ON SUNDAY AND WE'RE ON HUNTER'S COUCH watching my favorite show. Tonight's episode: *Magicians Who Kill*. Summer is fast asleep on the other end of the couch from us. Brenna's curled up in one armchair, watching the screen in fascination, while Fitz takes up residence in the other armchair, still on the fence about the episode. We're only ten minutes in and he's already said the words "this is fucked up" half a dozen times.

"Swear to God, if her severed head appears in his magician's hat, I'm getting up and leaving," Fitz warns.

Hunter leans forward when his phone buzzes on the coffee table. "Hey, it's Hollis."

"Answer it," Brenna orders. "Find out when they're coming home."

"But it's a FaceTime call," Hunter complains.

"So? What, you need to touch up your makeup?" she mocks.

I giggle.

"Whatever." He presses a button, and a moment later an explosion of noise rocks the living room.

"AHHHHHHHH! YOU GUYS!"

Summer shoots up into a sitting position, wide awake in a heartbeat. "What the fuck? What's wrong?" she demands, rubbing her eyes in alarm.

"Guys! Can you hear us?!" It's Rupi, shrill and worried. "Mike! I don't know if they can hear us!"

"They can hear us, babe!"

"We can hear you!" Hunter says in exasperation. "What the hell? Where *are* you? Why is it so bright?"

I peer at his phone, but I can't figure out where they are either. It's daylight, that's for sure. What time zone are they in?

Brenna hops up and settles on the arm of the sofa to get a better look, while Summer peeks over my shoulder. Fitz doesn't leave his chair, although I can tell his interest is focused solidly on the conversation.

"We're in Nepal," Hollis reveals.

We all freeze.

"What do you mean, you're in Nepal?" Brenna demands.

"I mean we're in Nepal. Dude, we're staying in the coolest place ever! It's like on top of a mountain and there's a Buddhist monastery right *there*, and, oh, Davenport! There's actual monks here, and these dudes don't have sex at all! A lot of them took a vow of silence, so I can't really get any deets for you, but—"

"Hollis," Summer interrupts. "Why are you guys in Nepal?"

Rupi re-enters the frame, her perfect white teeth sparkling in the sunshine of the Nepalese mountains, or wherever the heck they are.

"We're on our honeymoon!" she shrieks.

Summer gasps. The rest of us gawk at the phone.

"Is this a joke?" Brenna asks, her dark eyes narrowing.

"Nope!" Hollis replies. His and Rupi's faces fill up the whole screen, and I can't deny I've never seen two people look happier. "We got married on Friday! I'm sorry, I know you guys would've wanted to come. And Fitz—I know, I know, you've always dreamed of being my best man—"

"Always," Fitz says dryly.

"I'm sorry, man, I'll make it up to you. We're having a real wedding this summer. It's in India, and you're all invited."

"What is happening?" Summer sounds utterly baffled.

"You seriously got married?" Hunter asks incredulously.

"Yeah, we did it in a courthouse in Boston. Our witness was a dude trying to get out of a traffic ticket."

I tamp down a laugh.

"And now you're on your honeymoon in Nepal," Brenna says, each word coming out slowly and lined with bewilderment. "But you're having an official wedding this summer. In India."

"Yes!" Rupi say proudly. "Isn't this *amazing*?"

Nobody answers.

The brief silence summons a shriek from her throat. "Are none of you going to say congratulations?" she demands, her eyes on fire.

That snaps us into action, and soon we're all blurting out our congratulations.

"We're so happy for you! I promise!" Summer assures them, and there's nothing insincere about it. "We're just stunned. We didn't expect you to elope."

"That's why people elope, because nobody expects it!" Rupi chirps happily.

"So how long are you in Nepal?" Fitz calls toward the phone. "When are you home?"

"We'll be back in a year," Hollis says.

"A year?" Summer echoes in amazement. "But…"

"What about your job?" Hunter asks Hollis.

"Rupi, what about school?" I pipe up.

"I quit." Hollis.

"I dropped out." Rupi.

I gape at both of them.

"I haven't even picked a major," Rupi says, waving an indifferent hand. "I don't care about college."

"And I don't care about my job," Hollis chimes in. "Davenport said we should travel, so that's what we're doing."

I glance at Hunter as if to say *what the fuck?*

"I advised him to take Rupi on a weekend getaway or a summer trip," Hunter retorts. "Not to elope and run off to India!"

"Nepal," Hollis corrects. "Jeez, pay attention, dude."

"Well." Summer clears her throat. "We're all thrilled for you. I can't believe you're married."

I can't either, but Rupi and Hollis seem over the moon about it, and who am I to judge?

"Okay, you guys, it's like eight in the morning here and we have a big day planned," Rupi announces in her shrill, bossy *voice*.

"We'll call back in a few days," Hollis assures us. "Or a month. Whatever. Love you guys! Be back in a year!"

The call disconnects.

And we all exchange mystified looks.

"She dropped out of college," Brenna says, sounding impressed.

"They got married," Fitz says, sounding horrified.

"She's only nineteen," I realize.

"Yeah, but in Rupi's defense, she knew she was going to marry Michael Hollis the second she met him," Summer points out.

"True," Brenna agrees.

"They'll either be divorced in a week, or they'll be together forever," Hunter predicts with a sigh. "There's no in between with those two."

Summer tucks her golden hair behind her ears. "I'm happy for them, I really am. But holy shit, that came out of left field."

Hunter shakes his head a few times, as if trying to come out of a daze. "Okay, then. That was…fascinating." He picks up the remote control. "Should we keep watching? We were about to find out if the dismembered head winds up in the magic guy's hat."

"I'm going upstairs to play Fortnite," Fitz grumbles.

"I'm going to sleep," Summer says.

Brenna stands up. "I'm going to see if Jake's still awake so I can tell him about this latest development."

"Party poopers," I accuse.

As Hunter's roommates scatter and disappear, he tugs me closer to his warm, muscular body. "What do you say, babe? Shall we?"

I slant my head and grin up at him. "Yup yup."

The End

Read on for a sneak peek into *The Dare*, the next book in the bestselling Briar U series

1
TAYLOR

It's Friday night, and I'm watching the greatest minds of my generation get destroyed by Jell-O shots and blue concoctions served from ten-gallon paint buckets. Sweat-beaded bodies writhing half-naked, frenzied, hypnotized with subliminal waves of electronic arousal. The house is wall-to-wall psych majors acting out their parental resentment on unsuspecting future MBAs. Poli-sci students planting the seeds of the blackmail checks they'll be writing in ten years.

AKA your typical Greek Row party.

"Have you ever noticed how dance music kind of sounds like listening to drunk people having sex?" Sasha Lennox remarks. She's standing beside me in the corner, where we've wedged ourselves between the grandfather clock and a standing lamp to best blend in with the furniture.

She gets it.

It's the first weekend back from spring break, and that means the annual Spring Break Hangover party at our Kappa Chi sorority house. One of the many events Sasha and I refer to as mandatory fun. As Kappas, we're required to attend, even if that means our presence is more decorative than functional.

"Like it wouldn't be so offensive if there was a melody, at least. This…" Sasha crinkles her nose, and her head twitches to a siren wail that blares through the surround sound system before another shattering bass line thunders in. "This is some shit the CIA used on doped-out MKUltra test subjects."

I cough out a strangled laugh, almost choking on the cup of whatever YouTube party punch recipe I've been nursing for the last hour. Sasha, a music major, has an almost religious aversion to anything not performed by live instruments. She'd rather be front row at a concert in some dive bar, the reverb of a Gibson Les Paul ringing in her ears, than be caught dead under the flashing techno kaleidoscope of a dance club.

Don't get me wrong, Sasha and I certainly aren't fun-averse. We hang out at the campus bars, we do karaoke in town (well, she does, while I cheer her on from the safety of the shadows). Hell, we once got lost in Boston Common at three in the morning while stone-cold sober. It was so dark that Sasha accidentally fell into the pond and almost got molested by a swan. Trust me, we know how to hang.

But the ritualistic practice of college kids plying each other with mind-altering substances until they mistake inebriation for attraction and inhibition for personality isn't our fondest idea of a good time.

"Look out." Sasha nudges me with her elbow at the sound of shouts and whistles from the foyer. "Here comes trouble."

A wall of unabashed maleness crashes through the front door to chants of *"Briar! Briar!"*

Like Wildlings storming Castle Black, the towering

goliaths of the Briar University hockey team trample through the house, all thick shoulders and broad chests.

"All hail the conquering heroes," I say sarcastically, while Sasha smothers a snide smirk with the side of her thumb.

The hockey team won their game tonight, putting them into the first round of the national championship. I know this because our Kappa sister Linley is dating a benchwarmer, so she was at the game snapchatting rather than here with us cleaning toilets, vacuuming, and mixing drinks for the party. The privileges of dating royalty. Although a fourth-stringer ain't exactly Prince Harry, but maybe somewhere closer to the coke-addict son of someone prince-adjacent.

Sasha pulls her phone from the waistband of her skin-tight faux leather leggings and checks the time.

I peer at the screen and groan. Oh man, it's only eleven p.m.? I already feel a migraine coming on.

"No, this is good," she says. "Twenty minutes flat and those goons will have the keg killed. Then they'll blow through whatever's left of the liquor. I'd say that's quitting time for me. Half hour, tops."

Charlotte Cagney, our sorority president, didn't explicitly mandate how long we had to stay to fulfill our attendance requirement. Usually, once the drinks run dry, people go looking for the afterparty, at which point it's easy to sneak out unnoticed. With any luck, I'll be back in my apartment in Hastings and in my pajamas by midnight. Knowing Sasha, she'll drive into Boston and find a live show.

Together, she and I are the outcast stepsisters of Kappa Chi. We each came to be among their ranks for our own ill-conceived reasons. For Sasha, it was family. Her mother, and her mother's mother, and her mother's mother's mother, and so on, were all Kappas, so it was never a question that Sasha's academic career would include carrying on the legacy. It was either that or kiss something as "frivolous and self-indulgent" as a music major goodbye. She comes from a family of doctors, so her decisions are already heavily contested.

For me, well, I suppose I had grand designs of a college glow up. From high school loser to college It Crowd. A reinvention. Total life makeover. Thing is, joining their clubs and wearing their letters and enduring their weeks of sacramental indoctrination didn't have the desired effects. I didn't come out the other side all shiny and new. It's like everyone else drank the Kool-Aid and saw the pretty colors, but I was just left standing there in the dark with a cup of water and red food coloring.

"Hey!" a bleary-eyed guy greets us, staggering to sidle up next to Sasha while openly talking to my tits. We tend to make one perfectly desirable female when standing side-by-side. Her exquisite facial symmetry and slender figure, and my enormous rack. "You wanna drink?"

"We're good," Sasha shouts back over the pounding music. We both hold up our mostly full cups. A strategic device to keep the horny frat bros at bay.

"Wanna dance?" he then asks, leaning toward my chest like he's speaking into the box at a fast food drive-thru.

"Sorry," I retort, "they don't dance."

I don't know if he hears me or understands my contempt, but he nods and strolls away just the same.

"Your boobs have a gravitational force that only attracts douchebags," Sasha says with a snort.

"You have no idea."

One day I woke up and it was like two massive tumors just erupted on my chest. Ever since middle school I've had to walk around with these things that arrive everywhere ten minutes before I do. I'm not sure which of us is the greater hazard to each other, me or Sasha. My boobs or her face. She causes a stir just walking into the library. Dudes stumbling over themselves to stand in her presence and forget their own names.

A loud *pop* bursts through the house, causing everyone to cringe and cover their ears. Silence ensues in the confusion while our eardrums drown in the lingering echoes of tinnitus.

"Speaker's blown!" one of our sisters yells from the next room.

Boos fill the house.

A mad scramble ensues as Kappas scurry to find a quick fix to save the party before our restless guests revolt. Sasha doesn't even try to hide her excitement. She eyes me with a look that says we may get to escape this party early after all.

Then Abigail Hobbes happens.

We see her sashay through the tightly packed crowd in a skimpy little black dress, platinum hair curled into perfect tendrils. She claps her hands, and in a voice that could cut glass, demands all attention fall on her bright red lips.

"Listen up, everybody! It's time to play Dare or Dare."

Cheers erupt in response as the living room swells with more bodies. The game is a popular Kappa tradition, and it's exactly what it sounds like. Someone dares you to do something and you do it—no truth option. Occasionally amusing and often brutal, it's resulted in more than a few arrests, at least one expulsion, and rumor has it, even a couple babies.

"Now let's see…" Our house vice president puts one manicured finger to her chin and turns in a slow circle to survey the room, deciding on her first victim. "Who shall it be?"

Of course her evil green eyes land squarely on where Sasha and I are plastered against the wall. Abigail strides up to us with pure sugary malice.

"Oh, sweetie," she says to me, with the glassy stare of a girl who's had a few too many. "Loosen up, it's a party. You look like you just found another stretch mark."

Abigail's a mean drunk, and I'm her favorite target. I'm used to it from her, but the laughs she elicits every time she uses my body as a punchline never fail to leave a scar. My curves have been the bane of my existence since I was twelve years old.

"Oh, sweetie," Sasha mimics, making a show of flashing her the bird. "How about you eff right off?"

"Aww, come on," Abigail whimpers in a mocking baby voice. "Tay-Tay knows I'm just kidding." She punctuates her statement by poking my stomach like I'm a goddamn Pillsbury Doughgirl.

"We're keeping your thinning hairline in our thoughts, Abs."

I have to chomp down on my bottom lip to stop from laughing at Sasha's retort. She knows I disintegrate amid conflict and never shies away from a chance to trade barbs in my defense.

Abigail answers with a sarcastic laugh.

"Are we playing or not?" demands Jules Munn, Abigail's sidekick. The tall brunette saunters over to us, donning a bored look. "What's the matter? Sasha trying to back out from doing a dare again like she did at the Harvest Bash?"

"Fuck off," Sasha shoots back. "You dared me to throw a brick through the dean's window. I wasn't about to get expelled over some juvenile sorority game."

Jules arches a brow. "Did she just insult an age-old tradition, Abs? Because I think she did."

"Oh, she did. But no worries, here's your chance for redemption, Sasha," Abigail offers sweetly, then pauses. "Hmm. I dare you to..." She turns toward her spectators while contemplating the dare. She's nothing if not in it for the attention. Then she snaps back around to face Sasha. "Do the Double Double then sing the chapter symphony."

My best friend snorts and shrugs, as if to say, *Is that all?*

"Upside down and backwards," Abigail adds.

Sasha curls her lips and sort of snarls at her, which gets the guys in the room hooting in amusement. Dudes love catfights.

"Whatever." Rolling her eyes, Sasha steps forward and shakes out her arms like a boxer warming up for a fight.

The Double Double is another Kappa party tradition, which entails downing two double shots of whatever's lying around, then a ten-second beer bong followed by a ten-second keg stand. Even the sturdiest drinkers among us rarely make it through the gauntlet. Throwing a handstand on top of it while singing the house song backwards is just Abigail being a spiteful bitch.

But as long as it won't get her expelled, Sasha is never one to back down from a challenge. She ties her thick black hair in a ponytail and accepts the shot glass that materializes out of nowhere, dutifully tossing back one shot, then the next. She powers through the beer bong while a couple Theta guys hold up the funnel for her, the crowd around her screaming their encouragement. To a cacophony of cheers, she muscles her way past the keg stand with a six-three hockey player keeping her legs in the air. When she's right-side up again, everyone's impressed to see her even able to stand, much less looking mean and holding steady. That girl's a warrior.

"Stand back!" Sasha declares, clearing people from the far wall.

With a gymnast's flourish, she thrusts her arms in the air and then sort of half-cartwheels so that her backside is flush against the wall in a handstand. Loud and confident, she belts out the words to our house song in reverse while the rest of us stupidly try to keep up in our heads to make sure she's getting it right.

Then, when she's done, Sasha completes an elegant dismount back to her feet and gives the crowd a bow to resounding applause.

"You're a fucking robot," I say, laughing when she prances over to resume her spot slouching in our losers' corner. "Beautiful dismount."

"Never met a landing I couldn't stick." Freshman year Sasha was on her way to Olympic qualifiers as one of the best vaulters in the world before she busted her knee slipping on some ice, and that was it for her gymnastics career.

Not to be outshined, Abigail sets her gaze on me. "Your turn, Taylor."

I take a deep breath. My heart races. Already I feel my cheeks burning red. Abigail smiles at my discomfort like a shark alerting to the vibrations of a wriggling seal in distress. I brace myself for whatever evil endeavor she's concocting for me.

"I dare you to…" She drags her teeth across her bottom lip. I see my impending humiliation in her eyes before she even opens her mouth. "Get a guy of my choice to take you upstairs."

Bitch.

Debauched hoots and catcalls burst from the men still watching this display of female aggression play out.

"Come on, Abs. Getting date-raped isn't a party game." Sasha steps forward, shielding me with her body.

Abigail rolls her eyes. "Oh, don't be so dramatic. I'll pick someone good. Someone anybody would want to get sweaty with. Even Taylor."

God, please don't make me have to do this.

To my sheer relief, help comes in the form of Taylor Swift. "Fixed it!" a sorority sister yells, just as music once again fills the house.

T-Swift's "Blank Space" elicits a wave of excited cheers, drawing attention away from Abigail's stupid game. The crowd promptly disperses to refill their drinks and get back to the rhythmic foreplay of dancing.

Thank you, hotter and skinnier Taylor.

To my dismay, Abigail is undeterred. "Hmm, who will the lucky boy be…"

I swallow a groan. I was naïve to think she'd drop it. Once a dare has been issued, any sister who fails to complete the task to the best of her ability is punished mercilessly until some poor sap is unlucky enough to take her place. And if Abigail were to get her way, that'd be three weeks after forever. I already have a hard time fitting in with the rest of the sisters. This would make me a pariah.

She scans the room, standing on her tiptoes to peer over people's heads and get a thorough look at available options. A wide grin spreads out across her face when she turns to me again.

"I dare you to seduce Conor Edwards."

Fuck.

Fucking fuck.

Yeah, I know who Conor is. Everyone does. He's on the hockey team and a regular face at the parties on Greek Row. A regular face in the sorority beds on Greek Row, too. But his real claim to fame is being arguably the hottest new guy in the junior class. Which puts him way out of my league. A perfect choice if the goal of this dare is my utter humiliation at being resoundingly rejected by a guy laughing in my face.

"Rachel is still in Daytona," Abigail adds. "You can use her bedroom."

"Abigail, please," I say, begging she let this go. But my plea only emboldens her.

"What's wrong, Tay-Tay? I don't recall you having a problem kissing other guys on a dare. Or is your kink just hooking up with girls' boyfriends?"

Because that's what it always comes back to with Abigail: revenge, and the mistake she's been making me pay for every single day since sophomore year. No matter how many times I apologize, or how sincerely I regret hurting her, my life is but to amuse Abigail with my suffering.

"You should see a doctor about your raging bitchitis," Sasha snaps back.

"Oh, poor Taylor, such a prude. Don't turn your back or she'll steal your dude," Abigail sings. Her mockery becomes a chorus when Jules jumps in to sing along.

Their taunting stabs at the nerves behind my eyes and makes my fingers go numb. I want to shrink into the floor. Disappear into the wall. Burst in spontaneous flames and become ash that settles in the party bowl. Anything but me, here, now. I *hate* unwanted attention, and their mocking has recaptured the eyes of several drunken faces around us. A few more seconds and the whole house will bust out in song about how I'm a prude, like a horrible scene out of my worst nightmare.

"Fine!" I burst out. Just to make it stop. Anything to shut them up. "Whatever. I'll do the dare."

Abigail smiles in triumph. She couldn't be more obvious if she were drooling. "Go get your man, then," she says, extending a gracious hand behind her.

I bite my lip and follow the line of her thin arm, finally spotting Conor by the beer pong table in the dining room.

Fuck, he's tall. And his shoulders are impossibly broad. I can't see his eyes, but I do have a clear view of his chiseled profile and longish blond hair slicked away from his forehead. It should be illegal for someone to be that good-looking.

Big-girl pants, Taylor.

On a deep breath, I steel my nerves and make my way toward an unsuspecting Conor Edwards.

ACKNOWLEDGMENTS

This book was a joy to write! Hunter and Demi's friendship, banter, and sparks kept me on my toes during the entire writing process, and I couldn't be happier with how their story played out. With that said, please note that I took some liberties with the college semester/hockey season schedule, extending them for plot purposes.

I've said it before and I'll say it again, but this book (and life in general) would be a real bummer without the love and support of some amazing people:

My editor Lindsey Faber—reunited and it feels so good! And my agent Kimberly Brower for making sure I stay on top of things, and serving as my occasional relationship therapist.

The beta reading skills of Nikki Sloane ("suck his $#&! why don't ya!"), K.A. Tucker (winery champ and all-around hottie), Robin Covington (THANK YOU!) and Sarah J. Maas (Garrett Graham's #1 fan, and—finally!—someone as dorky as I am!).

Sarina Bowen, just because I love her. She's so sa-weet!

Vi Keeland, my frenemy, who lives vicariously through my love life. You're welcome.

Monica James, my Australian soulmate. You are so genuine and wonderful, and I know your dad was so very proud of the woman you are. I'm lucky to know you.

Nina, my publicist and wifey, who loves me so much she wouldn't even divorce me after finding out I've never read Harry Potter.

Aquila Editing, for proofing this book (Sorry for all the typos!)

Nicole, lifesaver extraordinaire.

Heyyyyy, Natasha. Set it free!

Damonza.com, for bringing Demi to life with this stunning cover!

All my author friends who shared this release and offered their love and support—it's truly remarkable how supportive this community can be. So many big hearts and talented writers!

And as always, the bloggers, reviewers and readers who continue to spread the word about my books. I am so thankful for your love and kindness. You're the reason I keep writing these crazy stories!

Love,
Elle

Don't miss the rest of the bestselling BRIAR U series from ELLE KENNEDY

THE CHASE

She's the one girl he shouldn't want . . .

Everyone says opposites attract. And they must be right, because there's no logical reason why I'm so drawn to Colin Fitzgerald. I don't usually go for tattoo-covered, video-gaming, hockey-playing nerd-jocks who think I'm flighty and superficial. His narrow view of me is the first strike against him. It doesn't help that he's buddy-buddy with my brother.

And that his best friend has a crush on me.

And that I just moved in with them.

Oh, did I not mention we're roommates?

I suppose it doesn't matter. Fitzy has made it clear he's not interested in me, even though the sparks between us are liable to burn our house down, I'm not the kind of girl who chases after a man, though, and I'm not about to start. I've got my hands full dealing with a new school, a sleazy professor, and an uncertain future. So if my sexy brooding roomie wises up and realises what he's missing.

He knows where to find me.

THE RISK

Everyone says I'm a bad girl.

They're only partly right – I don't let fear rule me, and I certainly don't care what people think. But I draw the line at sleeping with the enemy. As the daughter of Briar's head hockey coach, I'd be vilified if I hooked up with a player from a rival team.

And that's who Jake Connelly is. Harvard's star forward is arrogant, annoying and too attractive for his own good. But fate is cruel – I require his help to secure a much-coveted internship, and the sexy jerk isn't making it easy for me.

I need Connelly to be my fake boyfriend. For every fake date … he wants a real one.

Which means this bad girl is in big trouble. Nothing good can come from sneaking around with Jake Connelly. My father would kill me, my friends will revolt, and my post-college career is on the line. But while it's getting harder and harder to resist Jake's oozing sex appeal and cocky grin, I refuse to fall for him.

That's the one risk I'm not willing to take.

THE PLAY

She's about to put this player in his place . . .

What I learned after last year's distractions cost my hockey team our entire season? No more screwing up. No more screwing, period. As the new team captain, I need a new philosophy: hockey and school now, women later. Which means that I, Hunter Davenport, am officially going celibate . . . no matter how hard that makes things.

But there's nothing in the rulebook that says I can't be *friends* with a woman. And I won't lie – my new classmate Demi Davis is one cool chick. Her smart mouth is hot as hell, and so is the rest of her, but the fact that she's got a boyfriend eliminates the temptation to touch her.

Except three months into our friendship, Demi is single and looking for a rebound. And she's making a play for me.

Avoiding her is impossible. We're paired up on a yearlong school project, but I'm confident I can resist her. We'd never work, anyway. Our backgrounds are too different, our goals aren't aligned, and her parents hate my guts.

Hooking up is a very bad idea. Now I just have to convince my body – and my heart.

THE DARE

Some risks are meant to be taken ...

College was supposed to be my chance to get over my ugly-duckling complex and spread my wings. Instead, I wound up in a sorority full of mean girls. I already have a hard time fitting in, so when my Kappa Chi sisters issue the challenge, I can't say no.

The dare: seduce the hottest new hockey player in the junior class.

Conor Edwards is a regular at Greek Row parties ... and in Greek Row sorority beds. He's the one you fall for before you learn that guys like him don't give girls like me a second glance. Except Mr. Popular throws me for a loop – rather than laughing in my face, he does me a solid by letting me take him upstairs to pretend we're getting busy.

Even crazier, now he wants to keep pretending. Turns out Conor loves games, and he thinks it's fun to pull the wool over my frenemies' eyes. But resisting his easy charm and surfer-boy hotness is darn near impossible. Though I'm realising there's much more to Conor's story than his fan club can see.

And the longer this silly ruse goes on, the greater the danger of it all blowing up in my face.